S̲ ̲

The author was born in ... ph
Robb and now lives in O̲... ur
children.

His early life in Wolve... ...y described in his much-praised aut... ...graphy, *Memoirs of a Karate Fighter*: 'An exciting and informative read which presents a type of karate that is now practically obsolete in modern society. It is a page-turning told-from-the-heart which is written with passion and precision.' *Combat Magazine*

'Well written and sweating with authenticity, Ralph Robb has produced a powerful book. Not only is it informative about karate but with its themes of prejudice, violence and friendship, its relevance is international.' Robert Twigger – Award-winning author of *Angry White Pyjamas*

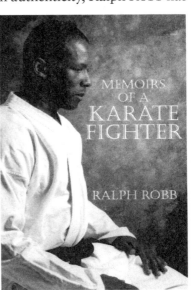

'*Memoirs of a Karate Fighter* is a highly inspirational and thought-provoking exploration of a life shaped by discipline, hard work and the quest for perfection. It is a life worth reading about and Ralph Robb's writing is as compelling as it is impeccable.' *Irish Fighter Magazine*

Also by Sylvester Young
More than a Game
What Goes Around

First published in 2007
By Raldon Books
Co. Cork
Ireland

A CIP catalogue record for this book is available from the
British Library

ISNB: 978-0-9552169-3-0

Typeset by Dominic Carroll, Ardfield Co. Cork
Cover design by Artwerk Ltd., Dublin
Printed and bound in the Republic of Ireland by BetaPrint Ltd, Dublin

Sleeping Dogs Lie

Sylvester Young

Raldon Books

With thanks to . . .
Janet Commock, for all the time and kind support she
has given me. Helen Simpson for her assistance with that
first draft of *Sleeping Dogs Lie*, many years ago.
Joan Deitch and Rosemarie Hudson for their interest
and advice with my very first novel, which has continued
to help me with all my subsequent work.
Siobhan Blaney for reading the many rewrites
and remaining enthusiastic!
And last but not least, my wife Hilda and our four kids –
just for putting up with me.

Prologue

ABOVE ME, CORRUGATED METAL clanked rhythmically as wind whistled through rusting girders. In the darkest hours before daybreak, a sulphurous stench rose from the water and swirled around the New Jersey waterfront. I looked across the Hudson River, to the lights where the Twin Towers had once stood and I shivered. Laughter, sharp enough to hack its way through all the noise of the storm, turned my gaze away. My head squeezed its way down into my shoulders, as I again fixed my eyes on the shapes of the three Belfast men. For almost an hour I had watched them from the shadows and I was beginning to feel a little nauseous. What put that sickly feeling in my gut was not the water's foul odour, nor my broken sleep, but a growing sense of foreboding. The tallest of the three was my friend Danny Maguire, the self-appointed chief executioner. While the other two swapped banter between the pulls on their cigarettes, Danny remained silent. I could tell that he was preparing himself for what lay ahead.

I had been in bed asleep when he arrived at my apartment in East Harlem and roused me with an urgent rapping at my door. "Go you and put all your gear together, Robbie," he'd said, "we're having to leave this town."

In Manhattan the smoke had cleared and the dust had long since settled on a piece of land now called Ground Zero but the air remained thick with fear and suspicion. It was not a good time to be an illegal immigrant in New York – however, it was much worse to be a fugitive from the law, or, as in our case, on the run from the British security services.

Shaking my still sleepy head, I'd gritted my teeth and tried to make light of my disappointment, as I sensed we were not about to leave America for either England or Ireland. "You know, Danny, after all this time, I was actually just startin to turn around when people called me Pete Foster. So where are we headin?"

"I don't know. Just away and that'll do me, so it will. Hurry on, mate, the INS could be here any minute."

It wasn't hard for me to leave a city of bad memories and growing paranoia. In the years we had stayed in New York, I had always

1

been aware that neither of us could allow our guard to drop for a second. Keeping who we really were secret from everyone we came into contact with was like being locked in solitary confinement in a prison of our minds. Danny had also warned me not to take up any activity that might lead to trouble. "So keep away from door work and that sort of job, eh?" he had told me during our first days in New York. "And I'm not telling you how to run your personal life, but it would be better if we kept away from women for a while. If you can't, buy what you need. Nothing good can come from either of us getting involved with a woman, Robbie, it can only lead to complications."

Consequently, I had never been able to talk to him about my relationship with Natasha, and how it had ended. "This won't take long," I'd said, while throwing an empty bag onto my bed. For the first two years I'd led a makeshift life out of a single holdall because I'd thought we might be heading back across the Atlantic at a day's notice. But as time passed my expectations dimmed and I bought myself another bag.

After putting on some clothes, I crammed my few belongings into my pair of long canvas holdalls and followed Danny downstairs to a waiting car and the other two Belfast men. "'Bout ye," they said to me in turn as I sat into the back. The one in the front passenger seat extended his hand. "We've heard a lot about you, Robbie," he said. I looked at Danny as he too clambered onto the backseat: there was something important he had yet to tell me.

Ignoring the questioning look I gave him, he told the driver to get a move on. To the one who had given me his hand he said, "Has your man been told where to meet us, Cian?"

"Sure. He was grumbling about leaving his bed in the middle of the night, but he'll be there all right."

Danny pushed back into the seat and sneered, "He won't be grumbling for much longer."

I was wondering how much longer we'd have to wait for the truck that would get us out of New Jersey when I heard the sound of an engine, distant at first but rapidly growing louder. The three men shielded their eyes from the glare of the headlights, which turned out to belong to a car, and not a truck. The car drew up and a hefty but stooped silver-haired figure got out and approached them. He had the scarred eyes and bent nose of a fighter. The wind had dropped, quite suddenly, and now there was an atmosphere of deceptive calm.

Danny said, "'Bout ye, Paulie."

I recognized the man as Paulie O'Sullivan. I had met him only once, when we had arrived in New York, and his greeting then had been less than cordial. Word had been sent to O'Sullivan from Ireland to expect two men. Danny Maguire was more or less what he had expected, but I, a black man born in England, had been something of a surprise.

I watched O'Sullivan thrust his hands into the pockets of his overcoat and I could tell, even from a distance, that he had not mellowed with time. "Fuck you," he snarled at Danny, the vapour of his breath giving shape to the venom in his words. "Tell me what this is all about, so I can get back to my bed."

The two men either side of Danny laughed gruffly and blew smoke through their tightened lips. Danny rolled his shoulders and said, "What this is all about is my friend over there." He pointed at me. "Robbie, step you out and let Paulie get a good look. You remember him, Paulie? The 'bloody nigger,' as you yourself called him."

When I went closer I saw a change in O'Sullivan. His façade was crumbling. To the men in front of him, his reputation, the man he had once been, meant nothing. Aware of his vulnerability, he pulled his hands out from his pockets and raised them close to his head. "W-Water under the bridge," he said, faltering. "I said at the time that all I had for you fellas was work in a few bars, the sort of bars where that fella would stick out like a fucking black sore thumb, that's all. It was nothing personal. I meant nothing by it, I was telling you how it is in this country."

"Problem is," continued Danny, in his most even and threatening tone, "me and him are having to leave this town . . . because someone's touted, because some snivelling bastard has been talking to the INS about my friend over there."

Paulie began to shuffle backwards, his hands still aloft: he knew that where Danny came from informing carried only one penalty. More nervously, he said, "Hold on, just hold on. I'd never tell anyone anything about you fellas. I swear on the lives of my grandchildren . . ."

A blow to his body from the man I knew as Cian cut him short.

My stomach lurched as the old fighter collapsed, retching and coughing, into a puddle of oil-streaked water. I had seen Danny Maguire kill the men who had murdered his father and recognized what was in his eyes as he looked at the man writhing at his feet. Without shifting his gaze, to the other two he said, "Take this miserable piece of shite to where my comrade was standing and we'll do it in there."

Watching them drag O'Sullivan over the concrete, I felt responsible for him. After what I had done to Natasha, I had been barely able to tolerate living in New York and increasingly watched out for signs of being tailed. Anyone I had glimpsed walking behind me, or hanging about on a street corner, preyed on my mind, and I reported to Danny my suspicion that the authorities were on to me. I had no proof of being followed, and neither had Danny, but suspicion fell on Paulie O'Sullivan and started a train of events which, for him, would end in a disused warehouse in New Jersey.

Paulie sat precariously on the remains of a wooden packing case. Even in the half-light I could see that his eyes were glistening with fear. "I don't want any more unpleasantness than necessary," Danny said to him, "so how about if we have a wee drink, a wee chat, and then we might part as friends. Brian, give this man a taste of the half-bottle of Irish in your pocket."

O'Sullivan pawed at his cheek before taking the bottle that was thrust at him. He took a tentative sip, then, urged on by the three pairs of hard eyes, he tilted his head and let the whiskey pour until it dribbled down his chin. Hesitantly, he offered the bottle to Danny.

"That's all right, Paulie," Danny said, "I'm off the drink. Go ahead, you finish it off. You're known as a man who can handle his liquor. A half-bottle isn't a problem to a man like you, sure it's not."

From near where we'd entered the ramshackle building I watched with growing anxiety as O'Sullivan swallowed the rest of the whiskey. An informer could have called his handler before leaving his house and cops, or government agents, might be on their way – none of which seemed to concern the others. Paulie smiled sadly and looked longingly at the empty bottle, as if wishing it had anaesthetized him, or at least made him a little drunk. He said, "I'm no informer, lads, but I know ye're going to kill me anyway. Go easy on me, lads, eh, make it quick and clean." To me he called, "And you, my black friend, forgive me for calling you a bloody nigger. I

4

tried to explain that I meant nothing by it, but they never told me to expect a coloured man, and I didn't know what to do about you, that's all. But I swear that I have not said a word to no one about you or your friend here."

I did not respond, partly because of my nagging doubts about whether I had actually been followed, or whether it was my own actions, rather than those of an informer, that had alerted the authorities to my whereabouts. I had wanted to raise these points with Danny – after all, it would only be human to slip up once or twice – but this was not the time to tell him some the things I had done. Watching him stand over O'Sullivan, I remembered how Danny had reacted to his remark during that first meeting. He had grabbed Paulie, slapped him and swore he'd kill him if he ever called me a nigger again in his presence. Danny Maguire was always one to hold a grudge but I also knew he had reacted in that way because he felt responsible for me, too, becoming a fugitive after he had killed his father's murderers. O'Sullivan was about to die and there was nothing I could say that would make it easier for either of us.

The man called Brian produced another bottle and told O'Sullivan to take a swig. In an instant he spat it out. "Christ," he spluttered, "are ye trying to poison me?"

"Drink," said Brian. "It's only water, the Hudson's finest."

O'Sullivan blinked slowly, as if rousing himself from some terrible dream. "What shite is this? What fucking shite is this?" he roared at Cian and Brian. "This has fuck all to do with any informing - which, for the record, I'm not guilty of. Give me a few more hours, just a couple of hours, and then we'll see if the INS is raiding that man's, or anyone else's, apartment." To Danny he said, "I never got to know your real name but, by Jesus, I curse your lying black heart, you hear me? I curse ye and all who belong to ye!"

"Brian, put some water down him," Danny said, "Cian, you make sure he keeps that big mouth open." It was a signal for the execution to begin. The wind gusted again and the metal sheet began to clash against the girders like a slow and harrowing drumbeat. O'Sullivan struggled and turned his head as the bottle touched his lips. He lashed out with his feet but overbalanced and fell to the floor. He squirmed violently as Cian descended upon him to pin his shoulders; Brian carried on pouring water indiscriminately. "Pinch his fucking nose!" barked Danny, over the growing noise from up amongst the girders. O'Sullivan's strength ebbed; he gurgled and spat weakly. From his pocket, Danny then produced a towel he used while tending bar.

"A prayer," coughed Paulie O'Sullivan. "Have pity and allow me one prayer."

Danny said, "Make it quick."

In a faltering voice O'Sullivan whispered, "Oh my God, because Thou art so good, I am very sorry that I have sinned against Thee, and by the help of Thy grace I will not sin again."

It was not a prayer I knew but it became inedibly etched on my mind. "You're definitely not sinning again, you treacherous bastard," Danny hissed, as he crouched and began to force the towel between O'Sullivan's teeth. First came the coughing, then muffled screams, then a dull choking sound while leather-soled shoes frantically scraped the concrete floor. I turned my head away and willed the dreadful noise to stop, while silently cursing the absence of a gun. Killing another human being can sometimes be surprisingly easy: flying at thirty thousand feet in a bomber, or through telescopic sights; when the victim is either unseen or remote, death can be a simple and impersonal affair. But I knew from experience what it was to get close, to touch and smell, to look into the wide eyes of someone about to die. I wondered if Danny would cope with the memories any easier than I had done, if he would react any differently to the images which would return to haunt him.

Paulie O'Sullivan did not go quietly; his death seemed to take minutes, long and torturous minutes. The last sound he made was a barely audible high-pitched howl, which was almost lost in the wind that was shrieking at the horror of it all. Finally, the wind waned and the clanking ceased and it was only in the silence that I could bring myself to look back again.

The three men remained completely still, as if they had lapsed into some deep contemplation – until Danny got to his feet. He rolled up the towel, using only one trembling hand, and put it back into his pocket. Panting, he said to the other two, "Put him into the car, and off he goes into the water. Make sure to fasten his seat belt."

They dragged the body past me but my gaze was fixed on Danny. Even if he could not show the others what he was feeling, I wanted him to somehow communicate to me that he felt the same nauseous pulse that was at the base of my throat: it was important for me to

6

know that killing had not become a simple task for him. His eyes were squeezed tightly shut. His lips were drawn against his teeth. With the slamming of the car door his mouth fell open, and when the engine fired up he, at last, looked at me. I was strangely relieved to see his pained expression.

"Are you sure, Danny?" I asked. "Are you sure he was an informer?" I willed him to tell me what I wanted to hear.

A roar from the motor preceded the splash before he said to me, "Away from killing the slime who murdered my da, killing a man – even a touting bastard – doesn't come easy to me, Robbie, I swear to God, especially like that. But I did it exactly how I was ordered to, and I know if that man had lived another twelve hours, you and me mightn't have. That's the truth. Come on, we have get ourselves out of this town."

1

THE SUN WAS SETTING ON the town of Petra. Instead of follow-ing my instincts and escaping, I went to a rundown bar in the Creektown district. Its window shutters had been closed to provide some protection from the strength-sapping heat and I blinked the sweat from my eyes as they adjusted to the shadows. On the ceiling a fan throbbed and barely managed to circulate the sweltering air, while the TV high up in a far corner sent out a flickering haze, which allowed me to make out a black-haired woman with a jowly, weather-beaten face. She was sitting at a table and began fidgeting with her blouse but she quickly returned to nursing her near-empty glass when she saw that I was not interested. Three old black men, who were playing cards at a table, gradually came into view, as did a couple of Latinos who had propped themselves against the far end of the bar. Overheated and surly, Duke asked, "Are you buyin or just lookin fer someone?" Anyone who stepped over Duke's threshold was expected to buy a drink if they were to remain on his premises for longer than ten seconds – he did not want a trail of men ogling the women and then wandering out again. After all, he wasn't "runnin no damned whore-house" but merely renting out a few rooms above the bar to those of his patrons who needed to "relax" for a while. A towel dabbed at the glistening dark face as he began his silent countdown. I continued to scan the bar until I caught a glimpse of a familiar figure I needed to talk with, before I returned to my place. To Duke I said, "Two cold beers."

He took two bottles from the cooler and slid my money into the till with one fluid movement. "Yeah, well," he grumbled, "you sure as hell don't want no warm beer in this weather."

The lights over the pool table made a silhouette of Calvin's tall and lean figure. He was hunched over a cue, with his chin resting on hands that were gripped around its tip. Like a bunch of young guys hanging around on the corner outside, Calvin dressed like the ubiquitous 'pimp-rapper' but he was not one of the gang and it was not unusual to find my neighbour alone. Like me, he was a newcomer, something of an outsider, even though he had a lot more in common with the local townspeople than I did. For the most part,

Petra's population was a transient one and made up of seasonal agricultural workers, or people like Calvin and me who had stopped off for a while to work in the lumber yard, or the turkey factory. He was staring at the TV until I nudged him gently and offered him a beer. "Hey, Robbie, what's up," he said, "an' where you get to since Friday?"

"I headed up to Atlanta."

"Yeah? What part? I used to live in Atlanta."

I cursed myself and my lack of sleep for not remembering that – but thankfully, distracted by the TV, Calvin turned and sipped at his beer. "My sister will be on any minute now," he said.

Changing the subject, I asked, "Did you see anyone callin to my place while I was away?"

"Anyone? Anyone like who?"

"Just anyone."

He took another sip and cast me a sideways glance. "Nope, can't say I did." He smacked his lips and then said, "Now hold on a while, Robbie, Vonette will be on any second."

The black guys threw in their hands and swapped a joke at the lone woman's expense as we watched the bulletin in silence. Most of it was taken up with the results of the local Democratic primary. It had attracted more media attention than normal because the incumbent, Jerome Moses, had unexpectedly lost the contest to stand in the midterm elections. I had taken an interest in Moses' campaign mostly because Calvin's sister Vonette worked for him. Known locally as "Little J", despite standing six-foot-four, he'd followed his father, "Big J" into politics and had attained national prominence when, in the House of Representatives, he'd become one of the first Democrats to back the plans to invade Iraq. It may have seemed a good idea at the time but now it was more like a shortcut to political oblivion. As his father had been, Little J was also a part-time preacher and he had continued to back the war from the pulpit as a "crusade against evildoers" while seemingly indifferent to the changing moods within his either his congregation or the electorate. Maybe he'd had a conviction that his well-oiled campaign machine and preaching, would always bring out the African-American vote, no matter what. The voters had turned out all right – but for his 'anti-war' opponent for the Democratic nomination rather than for him. As his ratings had dropped, Little J had tried to campaign on

'Southern' values of 'God' and 'family' but the contest had rapidly turned dirty. When affairs were rumoured he had brought his wife and family to a church service in Atlanta and vehemently denied the allegations before going inside to pray to a *Christian* God. "These attempts to destroy my political career, my credibility, my family," he had said in a voice shaking with emotion, "are something every African-American recognizes. It is nothing more than a modern-day lynching by the media. But I know that *my* people will come to my aid. They will not allow my political and personal life to be torn to pieces. And for the record, it is the right-thinking people residing in the great state of Georgia who are my people!"

Bill Clinton could not have delivered it any better, even down to the biting of a quivering lip. However, if Little J Moses had thought accusations of racism would get the media to back off, he had again miscalculated. He could protest all he wanted but it seemed that everyone who had an axe to grind with him for jumping on the 9/11 bandwagon was now pouring money into the coffers of his opponent, a self-assured black attorney named Marjorie Pointer. To me, neither of them had any policy of substance. Both campaigns had been dominated by made-for-television slogans and she had a range of them revolving around being "sharp" and "getting straight to the point." She had poured scorn on his lynching jibe by calling it the last refuge of a scoundrel. Moses responded by calling her a "Tomette" but he knew all along what I had gradually learned about politics in this country: the voters follow the trails laid out by the almighty dollar.

Calvin snorted disdainfully as Moses emotionally conceded defeat after two recounts. I caught sight of Vonette Norbury at the edge of the screen. Small, shapely and attractive, she, along with several other solemn-faced members of his staff, gave well-rehearsed nods as Moses spoke of the possibility of standing as an independent in the midterm elections. I'd been surprised when Calvin told me of her line of work. When I'd spoken with her during her occasional visits to her brother's home, she had not mentioned the congressman but only said that she worked in an office in Atlanta.

"Did you see her?" asked Calvin. His question roused me from my thoughts of the imminent dangers I faced. I had been asking myself – yet again – why it had been decided that Danny and I should have come to a town like Petra, where it was not so easy for a black man with a "strange" accent like mine to avoid drawing attention to himself. I was beginning to conclude that a lot of what Danny had told me all those years ago, before we left my apartment in New York, had not been the whole truth. Not that I had been completely truthful, either. That was our way: rather than lie to each other, there had been times when we deceived by omission. I never did find out if the INS had ever raided my apartment. I finally drew my blank eyes from the TV and said, "Sure, an' she was lookin good, which is more than I can say about her boss. Look, Calvin, I have to get home. Do you want a lift?"

Calvin titled back his head and drained the bottle. "Yeah," he said, "I'm all done here."

I turned east and drove for home in my old Ford. Calvin and I lived in a cluster of ten wooden houses which were sited in a clearing amongst tall pine trees a few miles off Interstate 16, on the road to Cobbtown. The house I was renting, which backed onto the Canoochee River, was the furthest from Petra. The closest of the ten was inhabited by a large black woman called Miss Boo; she was the mother of eight children and also the local drug dealer. Mostly she sold marijuana, as people in this part of rural Georgia did not have the money to develop a cocaine habit. Outwardly, her dealing had provided little more than a wide-screen TV and a satellite dish. Leroy, her husband, a scrawny man with several teeth missing, supplemented the household's income by collecting scrap metal and old drink cans.

In between us lived three "Mexican" families who worked on the local farms. The locals called them Mexicans but in truth most people did not know – nor give a damn about – where they actually came from. They had clambered aboard the tops of trains, crossed deserts and risked death from thirst, or at the hands of robbers and vigilantes, to get to the USA from Central America and further south. It was only through a crude sign language that I'd got to know my younger neighbours who turned up to box in my back yard, as their parents and older siblings were often at their jobs before I woke. In the house opposite mine was Calvin Norbury; he lived alone but for his dog Hercules, or when his sister Vonette travelled down from Atlanta and stayed the occasional weekend. On his side of the road there were another three families who had smuggled themselves across the Mexican border and the Fentons, the only white family in the locality. Wayne Fenton was an enthusiastic supporter of the constitutional right to bear arms and so was his wife Darlene – so much so that when arriving home at night he would call her on his cell phone for fear that she would put a few heavy-calibre rounds through the door as he approached. Wayne found it difficult to hide his bemusement brought about my accent but because I came from a country which was an ally in a so-called 'war on terror', he had always been polite, almost deferential. But I had remained wary of Wayne – especially after hearing that he was part of some local 'citizens' militia' that had been formed to repel 'Islamic hordes' in the weeks following the 9/11 attacks. After a couple of fruitless years of waiting for another strike, the militia had disbanded. But Wayne remained at the ready and after church he would spend his Sunday afternoons hunting in the surrounding woods with his two young sons, while I gave the other local youngsters some boxing lessons in my yard. The Fentons had hit hard times but his faith in God and the 'American way' had led Wayne to believe his family's troubles – unlike those of the rest of us – were only temporary and it would not be long before they were moving on to something better.

Close to home, Calvin said, "So whereabouts in Atlanta did you get to?"

I was still distracted by what I should do next to put much effort into my response. "Just here an' there. I was just drivin around an' tryin to get my head together. Stopped off at some motel, for a change of scenery so I could think."

He let out a short, sardonic laugh. "So, did you think the thoughts, you thought you would?"

"More or less."

"Must be 'bout that woman in that fancy 'mobile, or you're thinkin of movin on, right?"

"Could be both."

"I'll be sorry to see you go, man. We gots to be good neighbours these last few months."

I pulled up outside his gate. "I've not made up my mind quite yet."

"You mean you ain't axed her yet if she wants to come too."

"Somethin like that."

Calvin opened the door and gave me a smile that signalled his regret that I would not be more forthcoming with him. "Hey," he said, tapping my wrist, "a new watch. Looks like you did a little shoppin therapy too, huh?"

"Kind of," I said. His smile remained regretful. Calvin was a needy young guy who had tried to adopt me as an older brother figure. He had told me stuff about a troubled childhood in an orphanage with Vonette, stuff I really did not want to know. I sensed that he, in return, wanted to be taken into my confidence but I could never allow that to happen. "I'm beat, Calvin," I said to take the edge off his disappointment, "but how about if we meet up after work some time next week an' shoot some pool?"

"Sho thing, Robbie, sho thing. We'll meet up after work one evenin, okay?"

I watched him go into his house before I pulled across the road and parked at the rear of mine. Convinced I'd had unwelcome visitors while I was away, I went from room to room checking out all my rudimentary warning devices: coins balanced on the edges of drawers; fragments of tissue paper on the tops of doors; and sprinkles of talc on the floor. They were items I put in place almost every time I left my house for more than a couple of hours but nothing had been disturbed. I checked every room – and double-checked – before I looked at the wristwatch and thought about how I could reach Danny to tell him that we were in grave danger. I had tried to call him from a payphone, without success, and I guessed using my cell phone was no longer a safe means of communication. While I thought about my next move, I anxiously paced the house and checked the watch until I realized that I might find a way out for the two of us if I could only get my mind to slow down. For two days I had been swept up in a storm and pounded until very near my breaking point and now I needed a period of calm. There was only one thing for it – and I headed for Miss Boo's.

Children were chasing chickens around her back yard in the fading light. Miss Boo asked if I had come for my "usual" and I nodded and pressed the folded bill into her plump hand. She said, "Give me a few minutes. Go on home an' I'll send Stella aroun with it in a short while."

Walking back to my house, I imagined someone was amongst the tall pine trees, watching me.

2

THUNDERCLOUDS, BLACK AND red-rimmed, were darkening the sky when Stella appeared at my kitchen door. She said, "Momma say to give you this."

I took the small package and went and put it on my bedside locker alongside my cigarette papers. By the time I returned she was at my sink, pouring herself a glass of water. The young woman plucked her cotton dress from her damp skin and said, "It's been one hot day, Robbie."

"Sure has."

"I was watchin you boxin in yo yard the other day, you boxed real good."

"Not really, Stella. I'm too old to box good."

"You don't look old. All your muscles sho look real fine. You sho boxed Calvin good."

I smiled but I wasn't anxious to continue the conversation; all I wanted was to roll myself a joint with what she had brought and relax in bed. Stella seemed in no hurry to leave. She put the glass to her mouth and I could not help but smile as she fluttered her eyes flirtatiously. I was thinking she should really practise on a guy of Calvin's age when the rim of the glass slipped from her lips. The water cascaded over the front of her dress, which almost immediately became transparent. She smoothed her hand over it and it became obvious that she was wearing nothing underneath. Pulling back her shoulders, said, "Would it be all right if I took this off an' dried myself?"

My smile vanished and I gently pushed her toward the door. "Dry off at home," I said, guiding her outside. I closed the door on her pretty, if frowning, face before going to my bedroom to smoke my joint. I lay down as rain began to clear the sticky air and patter my upon roof. I hoped that my mind would also start to clear and that somehow I would figure out what I should do next. But as my lids grew heavy, all that stayed in my mind was the hope that I would not dream of all that had happened to me during the previous forty-eight hours. With a last blow of blue smoke I watched the edges of the yellowed ceiling grow darker

14

until it finally disappeared into the blackness and I knew all my hopes would count for nothing.

* * *

I had just finished another week at the turkey factory and as I got close to my car I saw a piece of paper under its windshield wiper. It was a note written in block capitals. It read: '*ROBBIE, COME TO OLD GLORY MOTEL IN SWAINBORO. ROOM 41. 7 O'CLOCK.*'

It had to be from Danny; I hadn't seen him for a while and it would be just like him not to put his name to it just in case someone else read it. I turned the ignition and headed north for Swainsboro, unsure if I should be cussing or fretting about him.

I got to the motel six minutes late. It was on the outskirts of town on the road to Twin City, hemmed in by cotton fields and a tree-covered hill to its rear. Business wasn't too brisk, judging by the number of cars in the parking lot. I scanned every window as I walked across the tarmac, hoping to see Danny looking out for me but the only sign of life was an arguing couple leaving a room, while dragging their suitcases behind them. Number 41 was at the end of a row of identical doorways. I had misgivings when I found the door ajar but, as I heard the sound of Danny taking a shower, I figured that he must have left it open for me. "Hey," I called as I stepped inside, "people takin a shower should be more careful." Nothing came back but the sizzle of water. I closed the door behind me and went toward the bathroom. "Hey, I said . . ."

The words caught in my throat as a man, heavy and fully clothed, appeared. He pointed a gun at my face and said, "Nice of you to come, Robbie. Please, take a seat and make yourself comfortable."

The strength in my legs leaked away into my shoes but somehow they carried me to a chair and lowered me onto it. The man then disappeared from view as someone came up behind me and put a hood over my head. Before I could even cry out my arms were behind my back and my wrists tied together. I was still trying to make sense of what was going on as I was pulled to my feet and led out of the motel and pushed onto the backseat of a car.

The journey seemed a long one but I couldn't be sure: I was too preoccupied with the thought that this might finally be my day of reckoning. They'd hooded me and I wondered if I was being prepared for something worse than arrest. But, as I'd found out before, when in a dangerous predicament a strange calm came over me. When boxing as a much younger man, I had trained myself to leave fear behind in the dressing room so by the time I ducked between the ropes my mind was clear of everything except what I had to do to win. Now I managed to convince myself that I could get out of this situation if I kept a cool head. The car turned onto a bumpy surface and after a couple more minutes we came to a halt. The driver got out and I was left alone for a time, wondering what sort of place this was. I could hear voices in the distance but otherwise all was quiet. With strong hands suddenly gripping me, I was hauled out and made to start walking. I could tell at once that the place was rural: the path was grass and dirt, rather than concrete, and although I couldn't detect any scents through the hood, I did hear the breeze in the trees.

After negotiating a short flight of wooden steps I was made to pause as a door creaked open. The floor of the room I entered was timber and had no carpet, the chair I was thrust onto felt like one of those plastic ones with metal legs. I guessed I'd been brought to something like a hunting lodge in the middle of a wood and immediately felt even more vulnerable: it might well be so isolated that no one would hear my screams.

There were more footfalls on the wooden boards and the sound of someone leaving, but I knew I wasn't alone. I let my chin drop to my chest and concentrated on my breathing, all the time sensing eyes were on me, watching my reaction. I tried to recall everything that Danny had told me about interrogation: the first two hours were critical and the time in which the interrogated was at his most vulnerable. A hand gripped my wrists and, with a jerk which produced stabs of pain, my bonds were cut. While the blood coursed back into my hands, I heard him move to my front. Another chair scraped over the floor and what sounded like an ample backside flopped down onto it. An instant later I was squinting in bright light.

The man sitting astride the chair with his elbows on the backrest was the one who had exited the motel bathroom with a gun. We stared at each other. He had a bulbous nose and a blue scar on his hairline. The hood dangled limply from the thick fingers of one hand. In his other hand was a leather-bound badge. My eyes were still adjusting to the brightness but I was able to make out the letters "FBI." He tossed the hood behind him and put the badge in the inside pocket of his jacket. He shifted on his seat and scratched his neck. He said, "You're up shit creek without a paddle but I'm prepared to help you, Robbie. But first I need to judge if you're a player or not. If you're not, well, I might be able to save you from something very unpleasant. How you react to me in the next few minutes will affect the rest of your life. Now, I'm going to ask you for your *real* name." I opened my mouth but before I could utter a sound he went on, "And I warn you to listen carefully and think before you answer. Your whole future depends on it. Since 9/11 I've been working on a Homeland Security operation code-named 'Sleeping Dogs'. Its purpose is to track down possible terrorists, of all political persuasions, currently residing in the United States. I'm going to put this as clearly as I can: my colleagues call me a human lie detector and I'm not prepared to have any sleeping dog lie to me, mister. I know your name isn't Barrett and I know you used the alias Peter Foster in New York. I also know that you were there with an IRA terrorist named Danny Maguire. Now, if you tell me your real name we might come to some sort of deal. But if you don't, well, who can say what might happen? We might just let you go, without our protection, I'd say, given what I know already, you'd live less than twenty-four hours."

It was clear that he knew my real identity but he wanted me to admit to it, and if I did I was certain I'd be asked to admit to other things. Danny had warned me to not to let the interrogator set the agenda by answering any question but I decided that I was in no position to follow that particular piece of advice. "If I told you my real name," I said, "I'd be at a disadvantage. Can I have a look at that badge again an' see your name?"

The thick pink lips made a pout. "You'll get my name once I hear yours."

I sucked in a breath around my teeth. "Walker, Robbie Walker."

"Robert Alphonsus Walker?"

"Yeah, but I don't like anybody knowin about the Alphonsus. So what's yours?"

"Later." He stood up and retrieved the hood. "Now we've made that first step, tell me why you left New York and came to Georgia."

"Man, believe me, I've often asked myself that question."

17

He picked up a jug of iced water which clinked as he filled two glasses. He passed one to me and retook his seat. "You must be thirsty," he said. He saw me hesitate before taking a drink and he made a show of letting the water swill around his mouth. He swallowed and smacked his lips. "It's only water," he said. Because my mouth was stale and dry I drank deeply, too deeply, and pain struck me between the eyes. I smoothed my brow with the heel of one hand and remembered the times as a child when I had eaten ice cream too quickly. "So, what answer did you come up with about why you left New York?" he asked.

"It was a long time ago, I got spooked, I suppose. There were lots of rumours about the INS pickin up undocumented immigrants an' knockin the shit outta them in the MDC in Brooklyn. I thought it best to leave town before they found me."

"And why were you living under a false name?"

"Because I was undocumented."

"And you were undocumented because . . . ?"

My mind raced: how should I reply? If he knew about Pete Foster, he must have already known the answer to his question. Betrayed by my hesitation, I said, "I entered the USA on a false passport."

"Where did you come from?"

"Shannon, Ireland."

"When and why did you leave New York?"

"Early 2002. Not sure exactly, an' because I got spooked by the INS."

"And you chose Georgia for what reason?"

"It happened to be at the end of the road I was travellin."

"That you and Maguire were travelling. One more time: why did you really leave New York, Walker?"

"After 9/11 it wasn't an easy place for someone undocumented."

"Try it one more time. Why did you leave New York? And this time forget the bullshit about the INS, or 9/11. Talk to me about Maguire. Tell me what happened to Paulie O'Sullivan."

I pinched the flesh between my eyes and tried to massage away the pain. "You'll have to excuse me," I said stalling for time, "I got a headache from drinkin that water too fast."

He got up, stretched, cracked a few bones. "Take your time. Think well before you answer. Think about O'Sullivan and about what Maguire and the other two did to him. Before you answer, think about what sort of man could do that. And think again about why you ended up in Georgia."

Silently, I cursed him. He knew a lot about Danny and me but he couldn't know everything, because I was the only person who had witnessed the killing of Paulie O'Sullivan. Or could it be that Cian or Brian had been arrested and confessed? Plea bargain, or something. Now regretting my decision to answer questions, I decided to continue to talk – but without any mention of Paulie O'Sullivan. I looked up and said, "Yeah, I did come to Georgia with Danny Maguire, an' about six months ago we came to Petra but I lost contact with him recently. That's the truth."

"When, exactly, did you lose contact?"

"A few days back, perhaps ten or twelve."

"So you saw him fairly regularly, then. How's that?"

"He drives a truck that delivers turkeys an' I work at a place that processes them."

The Fed ran a hand over his fleshy throat and nodded as if I had only confirmed what he already knew. "And you don't know where Maguire is now?"

"Not a clue."

"What about O'Sullivan?"

"What about him?"

Sauntering over to a table in a corner of the room he said, "Maguire and two other men killed him in a disused warehouse in New Jersey, dumped his body in his car and put it into the river after forcing a towel down his throat. Supposed to look like an accident." When he turned back to face me, he had a file in his hands. He hummed for a moment as he turned the papers. "Hm, seems you were right about the INS: they were onto you. Looks like they received a tip off from GCHQ in England – they intercept communications for the security services over there – they picked up on some calls made to a Mrs M. Walker. They got numbers and could pinpoint where the calls came from, and they faxed an interesting story to both the FBI and the INS. My, my, they must want you pretty badly . . . Maybe you were spooked, after all . . . You know what, Walker, I figure you told Maguire you suspected that you were being watched, and he got the notion that O'Sullivan was passing information. Don't suppose you mentioned the phone calls to your mom, huh? No, didn't think so. Shit, that must make you feel bad. A man

19

dies because you didn't tell Maguire that the reason the INS was onto you was because you couldn't help but ring mommy. No criticism from me, Walker, I think it shows you've remained a human being, unlike Maguire."

I didn't respond but tried instead to figure out his strategy. He had hinted about some sort of deal while getting me to talk about matters of which he already knew, then he'd surprised me with information he'd got from elsewhere. But I had yet to detect the divide between what he actually knew and his educated guessing. He was keeping my mind off balance and I was becoming disorientated. My thoughts were racing and I wondered if I had been given some sort of drug. I thought about the water and how he had smacked his lips after tasting it – could there have been something in the ice cubes he had put into my glass? Or was it that my mind was already weakening in the face of his psychological assault? Again, he sat in the chair in front of me, checked his watch and smiled. I ground my teeth and did my best to recover my bearings. He put the file on the floor by his feet and offered me an open packet of cigarettes.

"Don't smoke," I said, "an' anyway why would I take a cigarette from a man who won't tell me his name?"

"Didn't I say?" he said, lighting up.

"No, you didn't."

He inhaled deeply and, tilting back his head, he blew smoke toward the ceiling. "Mitch," he said, "you can call me Mitch."

3

A SHAFT OF LIGHT CREPT across my room as I lay in bed. I checked my watch. A new day. Instinct told me to get far away from this place as quickly as I could but reason countered that I had nowhere to go. I had been instructed to continue with my usual routine and that Danny Maguire would make contact with me. "Why should he?" I had asked Mitch.

"Because he can't afford not to."

If he were around, I knew Danny would somehow reach me. The

20

last time I saw him was at my kitchen table after we had each done a few rounds of punching the heavy bag in my yard. He was caressing a cold can of beer with both hands. "And when are you going to fix that lock on the back door, Robbie? You have to keep things secure."

The frame was rotten and, if you knew how, it was simple enough to ease it back and open the door when it was locked. When I'd collected the keys months before from a ramshackle supply store on the outskirts of Cobbtown, a grizzled and small man named Cuthbert, had told me that the rent was low and that he expected me to do any minor repairs. "If anyone makes their mind up to come in here," I'd said to Danny, "they're gonna do it no matter what lock is on that door. For me, security is about the things I put in place to let me know if anyone has been snoopin about in here. That's the important thing, I mean, there's nothin much worth stealin an' nothin about identity."

Danny swatted the insects flying around his head. "Yeah," he said. "Well, there's no point making it too fecking easy, now is there?"

I did not like his hectoring tone, nor the feeling of sweat running down my back and I pulled off my vest and went to the sink to wash. It was another sign that our relationship was getting fractious. Our first major quarrel had come about not long after our arrival in Petra when he had warned me about my occasional trips to Creektown, a place where every vice was catered for. I snarled back a question about why we had come here and then told him that I'd done all my abstaining in New York. He could see that I had not reacted well to our fourth enforced relocation in less than five years and muttered something about "security." Saying it was for the sake of our friendship, a day later Danny moved out and found another place to stay.

In the months since then we had spoken at length only half a dozen times, always at my place, and usually out in the yard as we took turns with the punch bag before we shared a beer or two. The topics rarely changed. Occasionally we talked boxing, or took turns to berate the godforsaken place we'd come to, but mostly it was Danny, who seemed to be growing more anxious as time went by, checking that I was not slipping up in any way. At the factory we occasionally bumped into each other and exchanged a few words but when we did talk at length, long pauses and awkward silences gradually punctuated our conversations, mostly because of the things we had mutually decided to leave unspoken. In America we never talked about Ireland, in Ireland we'd never discussed what happened in England, and here in Georgia we never brought up why we had left New York.

It was a strange bond that Danny and I shared. It was more than the friendship that had ebbed and flowed since we were teenagers, it was that our fates had become entwined and stuck fast to one another like conjoined twins. Perhaps now there could be no separation without dire consequences for one, or maybe both, of us. I turned to face Danny as I dried myself off and saw him staring vaguely out of the window. It dawned on me then how much he had changed. The thick black hair he'd had as a young man was now mostly silver bristle. The tight stomach muscles had softened, the swagger in his step had long disappeared. I had seen his best years, as he had seen mine, and now we watched each other's decline. He looked troubled and my anger evaporated instantly. "What's on your mind, man?" I asked. For a while he said nothing and only sipped his beer, barely wetting his lips. Then, pinching the bridge of his nose, he sighed deeply. "Robbie," he said, "I'm after thinking about this life you're leading because of me. Ach, when I see you in this place, miles away from your son and your ma, the people you love, I feel real bad, so I do . . . And when we talk I'm always telling you to watch out for this or that. You must think I'm trying to send the both of us crazy, and I wonder why you don't hate my guts."

I sat down across the table from him, surprised, and a little concerned, he was talking this way. "Look, I can't pretend that you don't piss me off sometimes, or that I've never thought about how things might have turned out if I hadn't helped you. But I was still a grown man back then an' I've always been prepared to take the consequences of my actions. Sure, there are times when I wish life was more comfortable, but put it this way, if I had ended up in a maximum-security prison, maybe seein Nathan every few months, my mom gettin searched before every visit, I don't think I could've seen them anymore – I just couldn't have put them through that. So, in a way, maybe we're all better off like this. What's done is done, Danny, an' you never know, one day you might hear that we can go home. I mean, it's all over now in Ireland, there's peace there now."

"But that's just it, Robbie. I'm after getting word from home,

22

about how the negotiations about fellas on the run are getting on and . . ."

"And?"

". . . And it seems that me and you are serious embarrassments."

"We weren't the only ones involved. What about Martin, Eamonn an' Kevin?"

"Christ, those three are even bigger embarrassments, so they are. They're after getting themselves lost in some jungle in Central America. There's big bother 'bout those fellas at the minute, and the last thing the movement needs is our case being raised. See, Rob, there's a couple of problems with us getting amnesty. One, for a start, we not only killed an MI5 agent but also a big-shot who had contacts in the British Establishment . . . And two, our operation took place long after the cease-fire was declared. The British government is telling the negotiators there can be no amnesty for the likes of us."

"Without the bullshit, Danny, what are you tellin me, exactly?"

He took another sip of beer and rolled his lips. "I'm saying that people are still fighting our cause, but I suppose I'm also saying that people, particularly the Brits – who reckon we've gone unpunished – want us to stay disappeared. Gone, as in forever and ever, amen. We've got to be careful, Robbie, and I know I'm sounding like a stuck record saying that. British Intelligence is still trying to track us down, and I don't think they'd be interested in extradition if they found us." He looked at me to check that I'd understood the implications, then went on, "But I'm talking with a man who says there might be a way out for us, a compromise of some sort."

Right then, I felt like a prisoner who was being told that there was never going to be a chance of parole. No matter how much I had denied it, it was the pinprick of light in the far off distance, that tiny prospect of seeing my son and mother again, that had just about kept me sane. That tiny light, which I'd imagined as brightening just a little bit with every passing day, had dimmed abruptly and I felt stripped of hope. I fought to stop the painful images and memories returning and with what little strength remained I pushed myself up from the table. "Compromise," I muttered sourly. "I remember a time when that was a dirty word to the likes of us . . .an' now you tell me it's our only hope."

Discomfited by my scorn, he gazed down at his beer again.

Eventually, he raised his head and let out a bitter breath. "I'm not saying that *we* compromise," he said. "We still live by a code only few share, and no matter what, that will never change." When he saw my disappointment, he added, "There might be developments. I'll let you know as soon as I hear something."

It took all my self-control to stop me ranting at him and demanding that he tell me what was this code he was talking about and who else shared this delusion. After he had driven away in his battered pick-up I went back to drinking my beer while I engaged in a cruel and masochistic mind-game that I played periodically, called 'What if?' What if Danny hadn't joined my boxing club all those years ago and I hadn't travelled with him to Belfast and drunk that heady cocktail of revolutionary slogans? What if I hadn't punched the son of a local drug-dealer who then kidnapped my son? What if I hadn't asked Danny and his comrades to help me get Nathan back? Perhaps so many people would not have died and the twelve-year-old son of a good friend would not have been cut down in the crossfire. . . What if, while in New York, I had not allowed Natasha to fall so in love with me? Perhaps then she would never have shared her deepest secret . . . and I would not have told her mine . . . What if, what if, what if? I had lost count of the times I had tormented myself in this way.

When I finally crawled out of bed I made up my mind to break my routine and rather than call to 'Harry's Bar and Grill' for breakfast, I would go to where Danny lived before I headed to the factory. The chance of him being there was somewhere between zero and remote but I figured that there just might be a clue about what had led us here – and what had led Mitch to me.

Danny lived in what he called an "immobile home" in a trailer park mostly inhabited by seasonal migrant workers. It was a few miles downstream from my place on a piece of ground between the Canoochee River and Sam Creek. I'd never been there before. He had written down his address and given instructions on how to find it before he told me to memorize them and then destroy the piece of paper. I was to go to his place only if he could not be contacted in any other way and only in an emergency. I decided that what had happened to me over the weekend qualified. By the time I drove into the trailer park it was around seven, and I was surprised to see Danny's pick-up truck there and the door of his trailer open.

The park was nothing like how I had pictured it: there was none of the trash supposed to be associated with a place like this and the dirt road was clear of litter. A few of the cars did look ready for the scrapheap but the homes looked mostly in good repair and many owners had taken the trouble to make the patches of ground outside the doors into miniature gardens. As well as the absence of trash, I noted the lack of the American flags which seemed to be festooned everywhere else since 9/11. Danny had told me that these people had no medical insurance nor pension, that they eked out a living on less than the statuary minimum wage. He said they were victims, not beneficiaries, of 'The American Dream'. I guessed that around here there hadn't been the hysteria I had witnessed in New York, that these people hadn't seen vapour trails from planes, nor traces of any white powder, as evidence of a biochemical attack. Whatever the 'terror alerts' issued by the government, their humdrum lives had not altered for one moment, their children had not woken screaming in the night as visions of Armageddon faded. There was too much grief in their everyday lives to mourn over strangers. Manhattan was another country.

I entered Danny's trailer and almost bumped into a tiny and startled Mexican girl. "Is this Danny McNulty's place?" I asked. She looked blankly at me. "Señor McNulty," I said slowly, "I am his am-i-go."

"Can I help you?" called a voice from behind me.

Outside stood an older girl, she was perhaps fourteen or fifteen. She had large brown eyes and very long black hair, and in her slender hands she carried a mop and bucket.

I stepped out and said, "I'm sorry. I thought at first I had the wrong address, but that's Danny McNulty's pick-up, isn't it?"

She frowned suspiciously. "What is your name?" she asked.

"Robbie, Robbie Barrett."

The frown lifted and the brown eyes shone again. "You must forgive my little sister but Danny told us never talk to anyone about him, unless it was his" – she tittered shyly – "his *amigo* Robbie Barrett. Do you want to come inside?"

Confused about the girls' relationship with my friend, and not wanting to seem impolite, I went back into the trailer as the girl told me her name was Conchita. Everything looked spotlessly clean – even his copies of *National Geographic* were on a shelf in chronological order. This was not how I envisaged any home of his could be, if Danny were living on his own.

"He pays me and my sister to clean his trailer every morning," Conchita explained, "and my little brother to wash his truck and keep his garden tidy." She spoke so rapidly that she had to pause for breath. "Danny is a very good person," she continued at the same pace. "When my father was sick, he took him to the hospital and paid his medical bill. Now he is home again, because of Danny. Every day he brings my mother a turkey and between the three of us we earn almost as much money as our father did. Everyone around here loves Danny very much. He is a hero like Major John Riley, the Irish soldier who fought for Mexico against the Yankees."

Again she drew breath and smiled up at me. I had heard the tale about Major Riley and could imagine Danny regaling his neighbours with tales of the Saint Patrick's Brigade and impressing them with his knowledge of nineteenth-century Mexican history. She had obviously been bursting with admiration for some time, and I felt embarrassed at the prospect of becoming a recipient of some reflected glory.

What she had told me summed up the compassionate side of Danny Maguire. Over the years there had been many times when he'd been generous to people in less fortunate circumstance than his own, although he always played down such acts and said they were brought about by a guilt-ridden Catholic upbringing. He was a principled man and unflinching in the face of all sorts of temptations I could not resist. He had all the characteristics which I thought made up a good person – and yet I had witnessed him mercilessly kill several men. Years ago he had told me how his father and four other bystanders had been cut down by a squad of British agents posing as loyalist paramilitaries in a Belfast bar during a mission to take out a top IRA operative. I understood why Danny had needed to avenge his father's death; it had been his personal war on state-sponsored terrorism. Although he and I were still living with the consequences, I had thought that war was over – until he killed Paulie O'Sullivan. Perhaps Danny's war would never be truly over.

"So," I said to Conchita, "where is he?"

"We don't know, señor. He went out last Thursday night with someone and did not come back." She saw my immediate concern and added, "It will be all right. He went with a beautiful woman. Sometimes when she calls he does not come home for a day or two."

"Danny went with a woman?" I said, unable to disguise my surprise. "What, she comes an' picks him up?"

The young girl blushed, aware that she had, perhaps, been indiscreet. "Sí, señor. But do not worry, Danny will be back – he always comes back."

4

DANNY'S WARNING ABOUT THE first, critical two hours of an interrogation had become an irrelevance. Time had stopped having much meaning for me, as Mitch paced the room without saying a word. The air around him seemed to crackle with menace, as if he were doing his upmost to refrain from physically attacking me. His footfalls were like the slow ticking of a clock which regulated my breathing; on the occasions he paused I held my breath and readied myself for an assault that never came. When he had finally halted, and I had to inhale again, I looked up to see him gazing through a window, out at the darkness. I saw his shoulders loosen and I imagined that he was travelling to somewhere else in his mind. "Funny how life works out," he said laconically, without looking at me. "Funny how you and I have ended up here. Personally, I don't care what you did with Maguire back in England, that's beyond my brief, Walker. Except for breaking immigration laws, as far as I know, you've committed no other crime in the United States. I've got no beef with you." He allowed another minute to pass before he looked over his shoulder to me. "What happened in New York, Walker, where did it all start to go wrong for you?"

* * *

It started to go wrong the day I plucked up courage to talk with her. It all started with a lie. There had been a couple of months of exchanging glances in Beanie's Caribbean restaurant in Brooklyn, then smiles – and then brief hellos as we passed each other's table, but it was not until one hot summer's evening did we strike up a conversation. She was a tall, good-looking woman in her late-twenties, who wore her hair in plaits bunched at the rear of her head and except for a subtle lipstick her beauty looked completely natural. Standing at the other side of her table, I said, "Hi. I thought it was about time I introduced myself." After a moment's hesitation, she took my hand and I noticed that she had long manicured but unvarnished nails. "Pete Foster," I said.

She said, "Natasha Taylor. Please excuse me. I was just leavin."

For the next few weeks we bumped into each other sporadically, whenever I called in for something to eat on my way from work. There had never seemed time to exchange more than brief and awkward pleasantries, and I guessed she wasn't interested in anything more than that.

I'd had a particularly hard day painting a new apartment when she unexpectedly turned up at my table. "Hm, well, Pete, if you don't mind me sayin, over the last few weeks, of all the things about you, I couldn't help but notice that you're not wearin any jewellery."

I did not have it in me to be polite in the face of such brazen materialism. With a fork laden with food hovering below my mouth, I silently rebuked myself for judging her more positively just because of her good looks. I replied, "Yeah, well I have a problem with this bling-bling culture, Ms Taylor. Every piece of gold around a neck, every diamond on a finger, I see drippin with the blood of the poor people who dug it outta the ground. Now if you don't mind. . ."

"Ah, so you're concerned with the blood of the poor African."

"Wherever it comes from, the blood's still red. Now, Ms Taylor, if . . ."

"It's Natasha, remember?" she laughed. "Can I join you?"

I was trying to swallow a mouthful of goat and rice and could only give her my most baleful stare as she seated herself opposite me. Again she laughed in the face of my irritation, while holding up her unadorned fingers at me. She pulled down the neck of her tee-shirt and showed me her bare neck. "You know," she said, still laughing, "you're just like how I thought you'd be."

* * *

The air was thick with bugs and the temperature was already close to oppressive as I headed to the factory from Danny's trailer. Grain silos glistened in distant fields and the road in front of me shimmered as I reached the highway. The Stars and Stripes still dotted the countryside but what had changed most about the landscape over recent times was the appearance of yellow ribbons tied around trees and gateposts. Some were now wind-torn symbols of desperation and fear for loved ones far away in Afghanistan and Iraq. They were the most vivid reminders that I was a stranger in a foreign land and made me think of days at home with Nathan and my mother. Mom had raised me all by herself, after my father died when I was a small child. Into my adulthood I continued to draw on her indomitable spirit and all the principles she had lived by and imparted. I'm sure I'd had a happy childhood, but the memories of good times with her, or with any of my friends, vanished the day I had to leave Nathan, who was then barely eight years old. Even when the nightmares of violence and sadness faded away, recollections of my previous life were not sweet, not even bittersweet; they were just bitter. Bitter like the struggle I'd had with his mother to keep Nathan – only to lose him because of some strange adherence to my own ill-defined principles and, perhaps, my friendship with Danny Maguire. In the darkest times the only thing I could cling to was my conviction that there had been no other way – that it had been necessary for me to help see the men who had murdered Danny's father put to death. As the years passed I didn't think of them very much. It was more the fate of the living, that of my mother and son, that so often returned to grieve me.

I was perplexed to see the words 'Praise be to GOD!' appear in the midst of the yellow-green smears on my windshield. It was only the sight of a large billboard extolling the Christian version of the Supreme Being that ensured I slowed down in time to take the turn for the factory. I had been so immersed in my memories and thoughts about Danny Maguire that I had driven along Interstate 16 without conscious thought. It unsettled me that, during our last meeting, Danny had finally been so openly regretful about what had happened in England all those years ago. He had not expressed regret for any of the men he'd killed, nor for the death of a twelve-year-old boy named Tim, only that he had involved me. What was going on in his head to make him regret my involvement after so long?

Once, when I was having a bad time in New York, Danny told me that reflection was something that happened when the mind had nothing better to do; so why had he brought up what had happened in the past?

At the factory gates, the black and overweight security guard waved me through. He was too busy scrutinizing the lunch box of a member of the night crew to give my identity card more than a cursory glance. As I walked past, I heard him say to the tired-looking man, "I'm just havin me a look-see in this here box 'cause I know what you fuckin spics are up to."

Stuff like that had me grinding my teeth. Darren had been doling out similar treatment to a Hispanic worker a week before, and I'd felt moved to say that he, of all people, should know better.

A plump finger ran along the inside of his navy blue collar, before it jabbed at me. "Are you talkin to me?" he had yelled. "Two pieces of advice. Get the fuck outta my face, man, an' save that kinda shit for someone who gives a damn."

"Yeah?" I'd countered, "Well it's that sorta disrespectful shit goin on in Iraq that is helpin to fill all those body-bags."

His face had curdled with rage and as I moved on he'd yelled at my back, "I got your number, you goddamn sick bastard!"

This time Darren only glanced disdainfully my way before emptying the lunch box onto the ground. "Hey, fat-boy," I sneered at him, "remember what I told you about those body-bags." I continued my way past the new office buildings which looked out from behind a grid of scaffolding. Metal rings clicked rhythmically on two tall aluminum poles; as flags of the Union and the Georgian state (an old version complete with the Confederate 'Stars and Bars') did their best to raise a flutter in the faint breeze. With a derisive suck of my teeth, I decided to take a shortcut through the refreshingly chilled air of the production area. Hygiene regulations prohibited anyone entering this section unless wearing the mandatory protective clothing but I didn't have time to skirt around the exterior of the factory to get to the laundry department. However, I should have taken more notice of the clouds of steam created by the pressure washers that were hovering high up above the stainless steel machinery as the sanitation crew prepared for an US Department of Agriculture inspection. I had barely got into the place before I was challenged by one of the factory's hygiene inspectors and made to go back the way I'd entered. Before long there would be government inspectors, followed by a small, grovelling, group, going from section to section, machine to machine, to take swabs for bacteria and check for oil leaks in areas that had been missed by the sanitation crew's pressure washers. The reviled USDA inspection teams had halted the process of transforming shit-smeared turkeys into sanitized, vacuum-packed supermarket products almost a dozen times in the six months I had worked at the factory.

My enforced alternative route took me to the back of the plant, where convoys of flatbed trucks brought cages of turkeys to waiting areas before they advanced to their inevitable fate. Huge fans blew air over the stacked birds to calm them before the slaughter, so as to prevent the taste of fear permeating the meat. When I had first arrived at the factory, the stench of the killing line had turned my stomach – it was like something that greets you when opening a refrigerator that's been switched off for days – but after a few weeks of exposure the smell registered for only a few moments. Once sufficiently calmed, the turkeys were loaded into the kill tunnel where dead-eyed immigrant workers placed the flapping masses of feathers onto shackles dangling from the conveyor system which then took them to be stunned and have their throats cut. A little further on, a machine plucked, declawed and decapitated them. I'd been told that only a few years ago it had been blood-splattered brown-skinned girls who'd chopped off the heads and feet and plucked the feathers. I could easily imagine what a truly awful job that must have been, and it set me thinking that the way to cure America of its obesity problem was to have everyone kill their own food.

The frantic flutter of wings which signalled a clumsy attempt at escape turned my head but the bird only managed to put itself under the wheel of a reversing truck. Well, if it hadn't avoided death, it had at least escaped becoming a TV dinner.

I was collecting my overalls when a voice from behind me called, "Barrett, you're late . . . I said, Barrett, you're late again."

The guy behind the laundry counter tilted his head for me to look over my shoulder and it was only then I realized that someone had been calling to me. After all this time, being called Barrett – the identity Danny Maguire had given me upon arriving in Georgia – still took some getting used to, even though I was thankfully back to using my actual first name. I turned to the pointed features of

Billy Joe Watson, the factory's manager. He looked more sombre than usual as he said, "There's been some bad news and Mr Lavette is in and wants to see you right away."

Henry Lavette's family owned the factory and just about everything else of worth for miles around. He didn't visit too often and I was immediately suspicious about his reasons for seeing me. "What has he got to tell me that you couldn't?" I asked Billy Joe.

Obviously irritated that be had been temporarily dethroned, the manager replied, "Barrett, I'm busy with the USDA right now. Mr Lavette says he wants to talk to you, so he talks to you. Get your overalls on and my PA will come and fetch you once you've punched your card."

In the office block, I waited for Billy Joe's PA behind plastic curtains that were supposed to keep out the dust from the construction work. Henry Lavette had a good reason for wanting to see me, and I just hoped that he hadn't found out about it just yet. But the anxiety I might have felt about meeting Lavette had been curbed by my experience during the weekend with the government agent called Mitch – most things after that did not seem all that serious. One way or another I would be out of this factory, and this town, very soon. If I were about to be fired I reckoned that Mitch's plans for me might start to unravel and that Lavette was unknowingly doing me a big favour.

Finally, the PA arrived. She was so dowdy that she'd obviously been selected by Billy Joe's new and younger wife to save him from temptation. While his new office was being finished, his temporary one was a portable cabin situated across a paved yard. One of my first jobs at the factory had been to plumb the cabin's small washroom. I saw it as some sort of test – of attitude and not just of my expertise. It didn't help my humour when the unappreciative manager instructed me not be tramping in and out his office so often but instead I was to use the small trapdoor in the floor that provided access for the waste pipes. A day of crawling over the dirt had me scheming and a week later I got my own back when, using the trapdoor, I crawled into the washroom and put a dead rat into the toilet bowl. Apparently, Billy Joe's roar of horror was heard all the way to the canteen.

I climbed the concrete blocks, which acted as steps, to see Henry Lavette sitting in Billy Joe's swivel chair behind his large desk. He pushed a sheet of paper back into an envelope and fixed me with a stare. He bared his teeth at me and tried, unsuccessfully, to make a welcoming smile before inviting me to take a seat. Lavette was a big man with a thick mop of brown hair that had just started to grey at the temples. His green eyes were naturally narrow and cold, his square jaw was trained to be set contemptuously. I knew a lot about him, and what I knew I did not like. We had first met some months before when I had driven out with Colin the electrician to fix the airconditioning in Lavette's imposing mansion. I had asked Colin why it was that we were going out to repair it, rather than aircon-ditioning engineers, and he answered that using factory employees to work on their houses and gardens was something the Lavette family had always done. "This is the third time I've been out to Henry's house," Colin explained. "His great -great-granddaddy ran a plantation and I'm sure Henry and his old man still have the notion that we are overpaid slaves. That's why the mean sons-of-guns are billionaires." It was during that one and only visit to his home that I met Cristina. The attraction was mutual, immediate and intense. It had been during the early morning when we'd met and yet she looked as if she had just stepped from the pages of a glossy magazine. It was a big house with many rooms but, wherever I was working, she always seemed to have a reason to be alone with me. Before I left, she had slipped me her cell phone number and a week later we were lovers. I wondered if Lavette had found out as, for a moment, he sniffed the air as if I carried something of her scent.

"Barrett," he said sharply, "I expected you in some time ago. We have got a USDA team in and Billy Joe has to follow them around . . . and I've got more bad news." He looked into my eyes and I prepared myself to be confronted with how he had found out about Cristina and me. I feared for her well-being rather than my own. He went on, "We've lost a damn fine worker. During the weekend the sheriff's office informed us that they pulled a body from the river. It turns out it was José Ruiz. And because he had no kin here it was left to Billy Joe to do the identification. Looks like his car went off the road and straight into the water. It's a damn shame and that's the second maintenance man we've lost in less than a year. What are the odds of that happening, huh? We need a new maintenance foreman. You do a good job and I was impressed with how you got my airconditioning working, but you'll have to buck up your ideas

33

about your timekeeping. It's worth another fifty dollars a week."

The shock of José's death prevented me from responding immediately. What were the odds of two men of a similar background, from the same department in the same factory, meeting a premature end within a few months? In an instant I was back in a derelict warehouse in New Jersey watching a man's body being dragged to his car before it was driven into the Hudson River. And then I recalled a time in the factory, near the killing tunnel, when I had spotted Danny Maguire and José Ruiz deep in conversation. I couldn't hear what was said, but I could tell by their grim expressions that they weren't exchanging idle chitchat. Yet Danny had never once mentioned to me that he knew my foreman, and not once had José's name cropped up in conversations about the plant. Now I wondered if he'd had anything to do with José's death.

"Well?" asked Henry Lavette.

Still distracted, I took a moment to figure out what he was asking. "Why me? I mean, I'm the newest recruit to the maintenance crew. There might be a few guys who figure they're more entitled to the job. What does Billy Joe reckon?"

He exhaled sharply. "It may have escaped your notice, Barrett, but I'm the man who owns this plant. But, as it happens, it was Billy Joe who suggested that you're the best man for the job."

"Can I think about it?" I said. "It's a kinda big step to fill the shoes of a man like José Ruiz."

The heavy eyebrows arched and then descended into a frown as he said, "Well, I have to admit that's not quite the answer I expected. Sleep on it and come back to Billy Joe tomorrow."

With that he swivelled his chair and picked up a pile of papers. I rose to my feet feeling that something about my meeting with Lavette was not quite right. He had said that the decision to promote me was Billy Joe's but, rather than being told by him as I collected my overalls, I had been made to go through the rigamarole of seeing Henry Lavette. It had not made any sense but I left Billy Joe's office with a lot more serious matters playing on my mind: as well as the probability of being watched by persons as yet unknown, there was now the possibility that my friend Danny Maguire had killed José Ruiz.

By midmorning the inspectors had gone and most of the factory production lines were running at full capacity. The mufflers that protected the workers from the deafening noise sealed them in so that they were alone with their thoughts. I wondered how many of the migrant workers took their minds off the monotony by reliving times back home and fantasizing about the day they would return. I imagined that we had a lot in common during the times we shielded our ears from the din. The ear protectors were one of the few consolations of my job: they were a barrier against intrusion and gave me an excuse not to speak to anyone if I didn't want to. But, unfortunately, it was getting close to break time and my fellow maintenance workers would want to talk about José Ruiz and quiz me about my visit to Billy Joe's office. And at least two of them would not be pleased about me being offered promotion. This would be the second time that Chuck Woodlow had been overlooked for the foreman's job and I could not imagine him reacting graciously.

Shortly after starting work at the plant I had been warned several times, mostly in broken English, about Chuck Woodlow. He was around my age, tanned with straw-coloured hair – and he was also a sexual predator who regularly boasted about his 'conquests'. He habitually looked disdainfully down upon the migrant workers, but whatever he felt about the men from south of the border, it was well known that he often attempted to seduce their female compatriots. Every occasion he could, he would brush his hand against their breasts, knowing full well that they would not dare to object. But his actions were also a challenge to José Ruiz's authority. José had taken some of the women's complaints to Billy Joe Watson only to be told that the factory was a 'happy boat' and management didn't want anyone rocking it. Much to my surprise, and his evident shame, José backed down. "I don't understand it," he had said to me. "It's obvious that he doesn't like the men he calls 'spics' but he can't leave their women alone." I replied that I'd already met men like Woodlow and I knew that their urges were about power and possession, that their instinct was to dominate. Normally I wouldn't have given him any more thought than I gave all those dead turkeys but I could guess his reaction to Lavette's offer and I knew that there might be problems as far as he was concerned.

But Chuck Woodlow was not the only potential source of trouble. John Hunter was a broad and self-assured African-American who, I reckoned, would find it difficult to take orders from me. We had got off on the wrong foot when, during our very first meeting, he had not taken kindly to me pointing out that he was making a simple error when attempting to repair a machine. He was a decorated war hero who had served in Grenada, Panama and the first Gulf War but his grasp of mechanics was little more than rudimentary. He had been a mechanic before enlisting and was only taken on because a number of the original maintenance crew were part-time soldiers with the National Guard who now found themselves in Iraq. Whatever the rank he had attained in the military, I felt he was now out of his depth and had only got the job because of a skewed sense of patriotism on Billy Joe's part. I did little for my chances of establishing any kind of congenial working relationship with Hunter when I later told him of my Jamaican parentage. He sneered that he had never met a Jamaican who he'd liked. His eyes had then flashed angrily when, in my retaliation, I mentioned the mess the American military had made of Iraq. "Talk about snatchin defeat from the jaws of victory," I snorted.

At lunch break I was relieved to find only the young Panamanian named Ricardo in the washroom. Mostly because of his wispy moustache, he looked barely out of his teens. His cockiness and smart mouth did not make him popular with his co-workers but news of our foreman's death had stripped at least one layer of machismo from him. As we scrubbed our hands, he struck up a conversation about José Ruiz and he asked me about who would take the foreman's job now.

"Henry Lavette has already offered it to me but I . . . "

At that moment Chuck Woodlow came in and immediately halted my reply. He said, "Did I just hear right, Barrett? Lavette really offered the foreman's job?"

"Nothin wrong with your hearin, Woodlow."

"That's bullshit! There ain't no way he should be giving that job to a man here less than six months, and over the heads of guys who've put in a lot more time. No way, man, no way am I accepting this without some answers." He stood back with the type of smirk on his face I had come to know so well. "I see the way you operate, Barrett, you know what I'm saying? Something about you ain't quite right. Shit, I'm outta here before I lose my appetite."

The two black women who worked behind the canteen counter were like a double act. Lilli, in her fifties and much larger of the two, was the comedian who was always quick with her sexual innuendos. Since her recent holiday in Jamaica, Lilli's jokes had become even more risque whenever she saw me. It was nothing unusual for her to put an extra portion on my plate while telling me I reminded her of the big, strong men she had met in Montego Bay. Myrtle, older and slightly stooped, was constantly scowling at Lilli and putting even more lines on her leathery skin. A quote from the Bible was never far from Myrtle's lips and she was always seemingly taking offence at Lilli's double entendres but I figured that she secretly enjoyed the banter. And yet there was sorrow in those eyes now sunken with age. Thirty-five years ago, her son had met a violent end. She was the one who had found him hanging from a tree and it was that tragic event which was at the root of her religious fervour. "Are you ever gonna come to my church, Robbie?" she asked.

"Myrtle," interrupted Lilli, "hush now 'bout church. That man ain't done enough sinnin yet." She put another piece of fried chicken onto my plate and then frowned as she caught sight of Chuck Woodlow. "He ain't a happy man since he heard Mr Lavette offered you the foreman's job. Watch out fo him, Robbie," Lilli whispered. "He's as slippery as a bag-a snakes, so you jus watch out fo him, you hear? There's sumpin I don't like 'bout that man, sumpin that ain't right."

"Yeah, Lilli? Well, he's the one man around here who doesn't have a good word for me right now."

"You take no notice, sugar. There ain't nuthin wrong 'bout you a good woman couldn't fix."

5

MITCH HAD CONTINUED SMOKING. Perhaps he was thinking of his family and what he'd normally be doing on a Friday night, or maybe this was just another part of his strategy and he was only mulling over his next line of questioning. At last, he drawled, "9/11, wacky conspiracies about our government killing its own citizens aside, how the hell did that come about?"

By now I was increasingly wary about offering my true opinions as I realized that I was in the presence of a sharp and cunning intelligence. "I'd say you're the expert on that – or are you gonna tell me it was the CIA's, an' not the FBI's fault?"

"Fault?" he huffed. "The only ones at fault were the sons-of-bitches who hijacked those planes. Hindsight is twenty-twenty vision, Walker. It's too damn easy to reckon now about how they could've been stopped and then figure out, because they weren't, it was all a scheme cooked up by the Pentagon so we could go to war. No, what I'm asking is what you think, on a personal level, was the reason a bunch of people would want to attack the United States of America like that."

"I'm not a mind reader, on a personal, or any other level, Mitch, an' I don't think you brought me here to talk about US foreign policy an' stuff."

"Well, we've got plenty of time and I'm kind of interested in an outside view, the view of a terrorist. I'm writing a sort of thesis on the subject."

"I'm not a terrorist."

"The British want you for something, but I guess that's because they think you know where Maguire is. And believe me, he *is* a terrorist and they want him badly."

"Like how badly?"

"Badly as in dead-or-alive badly, preferably dead badly. Killing a blue-collar joe is something he might've got away with but he made the mistake of murdering Sir Philip Parkinson, friend to members of the British royal family, and a former prime minister, as well as a donator to several organizations which have had the ear of the UK Government." Mitch bent down, picked up the file and thumbed through its pages again. "You know what, Walker, maybe you're not a terrorist. If you cooperate, I might be open to the idea that you're more of a guy who's found himself in a mess of somebody else's making. May surprise you, but I think I do have some understanding of why those folks in the planes attacked this country. May surprise you even more, but I think if I was from their country, their faith, shit, I just might hate America, too."

"Bang goes your promotion, Mitch."

"Well, you have to understand your enemies before you can defeat them. You said something interesting a minute ago: when I asked you about the 9/11 attacks, you mentioned US foreign policy. What do you think that policy is?"

I sat back into the chair and stretched out my legs. Part of me figured that to play along with his mental game of chess might just put off the time when things could become more unpleasant. But I was still cautious in case whatever I said led me into a trap. "You know," I said, staring into his eyes, "it's not a subject I've given much thought to."

"My antennae tells me that's not true," Mitch sneered. "Bet you think the United States is sucking the rest of the world dry to maintain its decadent lifestyle. Bet you think that we want the rest of the world to conform to our views, to our values, bet you think our so-called freedom of speech only goes as far as to be free to agree with all things American. Bet you think that this country's policies are driven by vested interests who care as much about democracy and the principles this great country was built upon, as much as Osama bin Laden does. Bet you think those vested interests have subverted democracy in a bloodless coup and installed a former drunk and a moron of a president who'll do their bidding, despite all the advice to the contrary from the real experts in the fields. Pinko liberal bullshit, of course, but it stokes the fires of anti-Americanism throughout the world. Like I said, you have to know how your enemies think if you're ever going to defeat them."

Some of those words could have come straight from my own mouth. Was it that he had summed me up extremely well, or was it that I had been closely monitored?

He went on flicking his way through the file and then he looked up and gave his first hint of a smile. "They call you Robbie," he read. "According to this date of birth you're thirty-six. You look younger, I'm only five years older but I look more like fifty. This fugitive life must have something going for it, eh, Walker? . . . Says here you are an only child brought up by a widowed Jamaican mother. Ah, a child of your own, a boy, Nathan, a teenager himself now. You never married his mother, Sharon Thompson, but you lived together for a time . . . Interesting, says here that she married a Jamaican national named Rodney Dixon a couple of years ago and moved to the States. But I guess your mom told you that." He paused and looked up at me again. "Maybe she didn't, huh? Small world. You and the boy might have walked the same streets and never have known it." My gut twisted as he went on, "Unsavoury character, Mr Dixon, wouldn't want any boy of mine in the same

39

house, but I guess Sharon will keep Nathan on the straight and narrow, huh?"

I tried not to show it but he had found my weak point. So this was his deal: my son – my son, for whom I'd begun to give up hope of ever seeing again. I waited for Mitch to tell me what kind of deal he had in mind but he closed the file and put a hand over his mouth to cover a yawn.

He said, "Well, Walker, that's enough talk for tonight. I'm tuckered out." He produced his gun again. "By the way, I suppose you've already guessed, but this place is surrounded by people who'll shoot you if you so much as put your nose outdoors without my say-so. I'm going to take you to a bed now, and one of your hands will be handcuffed to it. I apologize for that, but you might just succumb to temptation and try and get out of the window, which would be a fatal mistake. We'll talk some more in the morning."

With my fastened arm acting as a pillow, and despite all the questions and images playing in my head, it wasn't long before my confused mind shut down for a while. When Mitch woke me, I felt sick with tiredness. It was barely first light and I looked to my watch to check the time – but it was missing. Mitch led me by my cuffed wrist to a small kitchen and fastened me to a pipe which ran down a wall. "Doesn't do to give a man a knife and fork in this kind of situation unless you stop him moving around," he said. Moments later he put the fried food onto two plates and pushed one of them in front of me. "No grits," he said. "I remembered your usual breakfast order at Harry's."

There was another hint of a smile on his lips as he chewed a piece of bacon. It was obvious that I been watched, even at Harry's Bar and Grill, and that I had been ensnared in a well-planned operation.

* * *

I wasn't in the mood but ever conscious that I had been ordered by Mitch to do nothing out of the ordinary, I kept to my usual Monday evening routine and headed for town to see Cristina.

The fan in the corner whirred as I lay on a bed watching the local TV news. In her slender bare feet, she tiptoed along the polished wooden floor, her jeans unbuttoned and her shirt undone. She ran her hands through her long, silky black hair until they met somewhere at the back of her head. She held the pose, hoping for a response. Normally, I would have been tantalized by her but now I merely smiled and turned my gaze back to the screen. Cristina Méndez was a very beautiful woman and maybe I should have remained flattered that she wanted me – but desire was not the reason I had come to the apartment.

"Robbie," she said, in a voice that had been moulded by Spanish long before she had travelled north from Colombia, "I know how you feel about seeing him today but Henry knows nothing about us, there is no way he could know. Are you okay?"

"Sure, I'm okay," I replied, "I just wanna watch TV for a while."

"So what are you watching that is so much more interesting than I am?"

"The local news. I'm lookin out for a report about a guy I worked with at the factory. His car was pulled outta the river some time over the weekend. Henry offered me his job this mornin. His name was José Ruiz." Cristina stood quite still until I said, "From your reaction, I take it that you knew him."

Her hands went to her face and she muttered something in Spanish before easing herself onto the bed next to me. "M-Most Hispanic people around here would know him. He was a good man."

"He seemed that way to me."

"What else have you heard about how he died?"

Danny, and my suspicions about any part he may have played in his death, came to mind but I reached over and put an arm around her. "Nothin, that's why I'm watchin the news," I said.

Cristina put her head on my shoulder and we watched the bulletin in silence. It began with Marjorie Pointer's victory over Little J Moses and then the deaths of four marines in Baghdad got a brief mention before the news turned to the recovery of a car from the Canoochee River. I felt Cristina tensing; like me, she was impatient for news of José Ruiz. When the footage finally came, the lack of drama made it strangely poignant. Like footsteps leading to a cliff's edge, there were rubber marks on the road where the car had swerved before coming to a bridge. More evocative were the deep furrows in the earth where it had crashed through a fence before heading down a steep bank and into the river, which was swollen by the torrential rain of the previous week. Cops from the sheriff's office stood around and one of them told the reporter that the body had been washed away but had been found downstream, caught in the branches of a fallen tree.

The rest of the report became a blur as the television pictures of the car being dragged from the water again roused memories of how Danny had killed, and then disposed of, Paulie O'Sullivan.

The shrill ringing of Cristina's phone broke my thoughts. She quickly left the room and I heard her talking in Spanish. It was always in English to me. In many ways Cristina Méndez was two different people: Spanish-speaker, English-speaker; hard, soft; open, closed. Well, maybe not entirely open, perhaps only as open as I had been with her. I had not asked about her past and she had not volunteered much more than she had travelled with her young daughter Goretti from Colombia to join Henry Lavette three years ago. I guessed that, intuitively, she knew I'd kept parts of my life from her. My life had become shrouded in various shades of dishonesty and yet there was some kind of honesty between us, if only in the recognition that our relationship was little more than the servicing of each other's needs.

I had originally figured she was just looking for a one-night stand – and that suited me fine. But when she suggested that we should meet again, I allowed desire to overpower my initial intention to cut and run. Perhaps what drew me in was not just her beauty but the element of risk because she also happened to be the mistress of one of the richest and most powerful men in the state.

"Robbie," she called from the doorway, "I'm sorry but I have to go out for a while."

"Is it to do with José?"

She took a long breath. "Yes . . . Yes, it is to do with José," she said, buttoning her shirt. "Some other people I know have just heard the news and want to meet up. I think they just want to talk."

"What's so urgent that you have to see them now, I mean, can't it wait until the mornin?"

"He was a stranger here with no family," she smiled sadly. "They want to find out if we can get his body home. Will you stay tonight? You know how I love waking up beside you."

"I've told you already, not when I've got work in the mornin. Look, I'll watch TV for a while an' maybe you'll be back before I'm ready to go."

She pushed her feet into a pair of sandals. "You are the only man to ever refuse me, Robbie. Maybe that's why I like you. I have yet to tame you properly."

"Keep tryin, baby, keep tryin. That's where all the fun is."

She bared her teeth at me playfully before disappearing from view. I heard her car start up and the engine's roar fade into the distance. Not for the first time, I questioned myself about my real motives for being with her and felt a twinge of regret about the lack of openness between us. I countered this rare pang of conscience with the thought that if my feelings for her had been really that strong I would have already considered asking her to come away with me. With hindsight, love, in its truest form, was something I had only ever shared with Natasha while in New York and the price demanded for it had been so high that I doubted if I could ever afford to pay it again.

The images from the news bulletin came back to me as I lay waiting for Cristina to return. I thought about Danny and – as it would be from now on – I also immediately thought of Mitch and the diabolic bargain he had offered me. It had come after the break-fast he'd served. I had eaten it as best I as I could but it wasn't easy with one wrist chained to a pipe. When I finished, he took away the cutlery, removed the handcuffs and gave me a fruit juice. He sat down across the table from me, brought his pistol from inside his jacket and held it up for a moment before tucking it under his leg. "I'm sure you don't need reminding," he said.

"It's quite a coincidence," I said, "that my son an' Sharon are in this country right now."

"Obviously you've given it some thought. Let me guess, you're about to tell me that you don't believe in coincidence." He pulled out a cell phone and pushed a few numbers. "Mrs Walker? Hold the line please, I have a call for you." He covered the phone with his hand and whispered, "Go ahead, check with Mommy. And don't worry, the Brits won't trace this phone."

It had been so long since I'd talked with my mother that my heart began to pound when I heard her tinny voice asking who was on the line. I took the phone from him. "Hello, Mom."

"Robert? Robert, is that you?"

I wanted to end the call right then. "Yes, Mom, it's me."

"Robert? Praise the Lord, me get to hear your voice. I prayed last night for Him to let me speak to you one more time before me pass."

Her voice sounded so fragile that her words barely registered "Are you all right, Mom?"

"You woke me up. I was havin a lie-in. Are you still in America?"

The lump in my throat made it hard for me to answer. "Yeah, Mom, I'm still in America. You never told me Nathan was here. I just found out from somebody, an' I could hardly believe it."

"But last time you called you told me that you never wanted to hear another word about Sharon. I could tell that you're still upset, an' then you're always so quick on the phone. I kept tellin myself that next time you'd call I'd tell you, but you never gave me a chance. Anyway, it has been so long since Nathan called that I'm not sure where he is right now. Robert, are you comin home soon?"

"I need a little more time, I'm gonna try to find Nathan first." The lie came easily. "Anyway, how are you? Last time we spoke you were havin trouble with your knees, I remember you . . ."

"Stop it, Robert, please don't torture me this way. All this carry-on for all these years. You go away an' never say why, an' you want me to talk about my knees? My heart can't take this loneliness much more. I only wanted to see you an' Nathan one last time before me die."

I didn't think I could take much more, but there was one question I had to ask. "Is it right she's married to a Jamaican guy?"

"Yes, I met him once an' I can't pretend I liked him. Robert, as God is mi judge, I'm not comfortable with him bringin up mi grandson."

I looked across the table and saw a satisfied look on Mitch's face. "I've got to go now, Mom. I'll ring again soon. You take care, yeah?"

"Come an' see me soon, Robert, promise you'll come an' see me soon."

I thought about trying to answer but I pushed the disconnection button and handed the phone back to Mitch. He allowed me a few moments of silence and then said, "Can't be easy for her."

"Why don't you fuck off!" I snarled.

He shrugged and said, "I can play hard-ball with you, Walker, if that's what you want. But what for? You get me Maguire and I'll set you up with a place and money, so you can have your son and get your mom over here. I hear that she's not in the best of health, and you would have enough money to get the finest doctors here to look after her."

"An' what would you do with Danny?" Even as I asked, I already felt as if I were betraying him.

44

"Put it this way, he'd live, which is more than he'd do if some other people caught him."

"Would you hand him over to the British?"

"Hell, Walker," he snorted, "they're the ones who've hired a group of ex-special forces to 'liquidate' him – and you. Luckily for you both, I want him alive."

6

THE NOISE FROM THE TV woke me. Bleary-eyed, I switched it off. Once my vision had sharpened enough to make out the clock, I could see it was almost one-thirty and that Cristina had not returned. Part of me wanted to succumb to sleep but the chance that Danny might somehow turn up at my place made me get up and go to my car.

Despite the hour, the air was pleasantly warm. The few people who walked the streets of Petra at this time of night were mostly male and black or Hispanic; they were guys who forgot about families and drank away their earnings in order to face another day of gruelling work. The centre of town had grown up around a junction where six roads converged. An old disused gas pump stood at the crossroads and acted as a reminder of a time when farmers had gathered there in their tractors and trailers to sell their hogs, cotton and grain so they could return home laden with provisions. Petra's buildings were mostly old three-storey brick affairs that housed a sheriff's substation, a variety of stores and bars, a couple of barber shops, a garage and body-repair shop and quite a few places to eat. There were also three brightly painted timber-framed churches, where the poor went for hand-outs and something to eat. The churches had been built during the Great Depression of the 1930s, and they helped keep an old-fashioned feel about the place.

To find modernity you had to go out into the suburbs. When the good people of Petra weren't at prayer, they could be mostly found at the shopping mall on the outskirts, or the plethora of drive-thru eateries. More cerebral stimulation – Internet cafes, theatres, multiscreen cinemas and a university – could be found a little further away in the direction of Statesboro but stimulation of a more carnal kind could be found locally. East of the railroad tracks which bisected Petra was the area called Creektown, where all manner of darker urges were catered for. I was a frequent visitor and had met there the sorts of people who neither had the will nor the ambition to cross the line from the other direction. There was a barrier in Petra that was much more than two rails of iron and a bunch of wooden sleepers. Most of the inhabitants of Creektown were poor, black, or brown, and I figured the white people I saw there were just passing through.

A police car carrying two white cops moved slowly down the street ahead of me as I pulled out. Jennifer Lopez's voice was wafting from my car radio and thoughts about her cute ass brought my mind back to Cristina, who I thought was a way better-looking woman with a straighter nose – and cuter ass. So why had she ended up in small-town Georgia? Like my own reasons for being in Petra, hers were starting to make less and less sense to me.

Once out of the suburbs the road became pitch black. It was the lack of electric light that made me aware that there was a car behind me. I was sure that the headlights in my rearview mirror were the same ones I'd caught sight of shortly after leaving the apartment which belonged to a friend of Cristina's. But I was only certain it was following me as I joined the Interstate. After a short distance, and though my tank was three-quarters full, I abruptly pulled into a gas station without giving a signal. The car sped past as I drew up to the pumps. By the light from the forecourt I saw it was a Chevrolet, new-looking and possibly dark blue or green.

An old black man with a face like a weathered prune stared at me suspiciously through the perspex of his booth. His expression didn't change as I sat for a couple of minutes with the engine idling. When I waved to him before pulling out again, his yellowed eyes narrowed and he lifted a notepad to show me he'd taken my number in case I planned to return with bad intentions.

There was no sign of another vehicle, not even the Chevrolet's tail lights. Except for a startled racoon, I saw nothing on the road as it cleaved its way through the dense pine woods. Years of being a fugitive had taught me to err on the side of caution: everything and everyone, posed a potential risk to my liberty unless it was proved otherwise. I was aware that a similar state of mind had tipped me over into paranoia in New York, but Mitch had confirmed that my instincts had been correct about the authorities being onto me back then and I trusted my intuition now.

Close to home, a set of distant headlights reappeared in my review mirror and I felt certain that they belonged to a Chevrolet. I pushed the gas pedal to the floor. It did occur to me to drive straight past my place and head for Twin City but as the road straightened I turned off my lights and eased off the gas, as I thought it would be safer to stay around where I knew best. It was so dark that it was almost like driving blindfold but, luckily for me, Miss Boo had kept a light on in her porch which helped me to keep my bearings.

Once past her house, I slowed the car by crashing into a low gear but it was still going far too fast for it to make the tight right turn into my driveway – so I spun the wheel to the left, and swept in towards Calvin's. The tyres screeched and I had to hit the brakes to regain control. I could almost feel heat on the back of my neck as the brake lights lit up the road behind me – and in doing so they gave away my position. The car was still swaying as I drove around the side of Calvin's house and into his backyard. It had barely stopped before I was out and running to the gap between the propane gas tank and an old wooden outhouse which had once been a chicken coop.

It was a good vantage point: not only could I see out to the road but I also had a view of the front of my house. But nothing came. No lights, no sound, no vehicle. It would take thirty seconds for a car to travel half a mile if it were doing sixty miles an hour and I wondered if the Chevrolet had stopped somewhere. It was too dark to check my watch but I guessed it had been fifteen seconds since I'd left my car. I counted another fifty seconds – and if a car had been following me, I should have seen it passing. I was about to start cursing my irrational behaviour and step out, but at that very moment the Chevrolet glided to a halt right outside Calvin's gateway.

Two men got out. One black, one white; the black guy carried a lot of good living around his waist. The pair were straight-backed and fairly large and wore dark, wrinkled suits. They looked to me like cops, or worse. I pushed my back into the wooden shed and a sprinkling of termite dirt fell onto my face from the eaves. I covered my mouth to prevent a cough and held my breath as they walked over to my car.

The black guy said, "The hood's still warm – this is the one all

47

right." He straightened up and scanned the yard.

The white guy said, "Let's take a look around."

They had moved a couple of paces toward me and I'd taken another step back – into something that felt unpleasant underfoot – when light suddenly filled the yard.

"Hold it right there!" yelled Calvin. He was looking along a hunting rifle and his dog Hercules stood growling beside him. "Either of you mothers makes a move an' I'm gonna have me some target practise. Now git yo hands up!"

"There's no need for that, bro'," said the black guy. "Are you the owner of this car?"

"Are you crazy, nigger?" Calvin snarled. "You come trespassin on my property an' then you start to ax me questions? Another word outta your dumb mouth an' you's gonna see this here gun workin, fo sho!"

"Let's calm down here," said the white guy. "We're not trying to harm you in any way. A car hit our vehicle in Petra and drove off. We followed it awhile but lost it. We thought it might be this one."

"Then you thought wrong, cracker. That car has been parked here all night."

"Okay, we take your word for it. Hey, we're sorry if we startled you . . ."

"You got me outta my damn bed, that's what you did. Now you guys can git or my girlfriend rings fo the damn police. What'll it be?"

The black guy said, "Since there's no harm done . . ."

"Except to my love-makin."

" . . . we'll be on our way, if you accept our apologies."

"I ain't interested in fuckin apologies, man. Jus get the hell off my property!"

I stayed where I was, grimly trying to control my ragged breathing. I heard the car make a turn and drive off toward town with Hercules scampering after it, barking wildly. After extracting my foot from whatever it was, I stepped out into the yard, only to find myself looking down the barrel of Calvin's rifle.

"It's all right, man, they're gone," Calvin said with a wide smile. "I got outta bed as soon as I heard yo car pullin in, an' when I saw you hidin by the chicken house I guessed sumpin was wrong. What the hell was that all about? Did you really hit their car an' drive off?"

"Did you see any damage while they were turnin?"

"Now you come to mention it, no, I didn't. But then agin, I wasn't lookin too hard."

"Well, if their car was really hit, it wasn't by me."

"So what then?"

I shook my head. "I don't know. I suppose it could've been a genuine mistake."

"It's a long way to drive from town if you don't know who you lookin fo. Those men were lucky they came to my house 'cause I know the Fentons would-a shot their sorry asses. Uh-huh, then there's any of those crazy Mexicans around here who would-a snuck up an' cut their fuckin throats fo sho. They were lucky, Robbie, damn lucky."

"You never said you owned a gun," I said.

He pushed out his lower lip, while tracing the smooth curves of the stock with one hand. "I never mentioned it," he said bitterly, "an' I know this is gonna sound strange to you an' all, but it don't do fo a black man to show off he got a gun, not around these parts, anyways. White trash like Wayne Fenton can have as much artillery as he can lay his hands on, he can go into the woods with his kids an' shoot anythin that moves, an' he'll tell you that it's his constitutional right. But for some white folks a black man with a gun ain't got no same rights. Shit, a black man with a gun is a *threat* to the American way of life."

Knowing to where this conversation was heading, I smiled sympathetically and asked if I could leave my car in his yard in case the two guys doubled back. Calvin said I could and then his eyes widened and betrayed his excitement and a little fear, as if the consequences of his actions had just occurred to him. "Say, uh, how's about if you stay in my place, jus in case those guys come back? At least I've got this gun to scare them off with."

I would have preferred to go to my own place but Calvin had put himself at some risk by leaving his bed and I felt obliged to take up his offer, mostly because I could see it would put him at some ease. The dog returned, panting heavily, from his part in putting the men to flight. "An' we got ol' Hercules," I said, giving him a pat of gratitude.

After a quick check over at my place to see if Danny was, or had been, around, Calvin led me to the room Vonette used during her short stays. The lack of a feminine touch struck me. Like the rest

49

of the house it was very clean, yet sparsely decorated: the floorboards were bare, the walls were painted but unadorned by pictures of family or friends.

I checked my watch and set the alarm clock on the bedside locker. It wasn't until I'd pulled my shirt over my head that I was aware that Calvin was seated on a wooden chair near the door. I took off my pants and got under the covers before I asked if he intended to stay there all night.

"Jus fo a while," he replied. "I suddenly feel wide awake."

"Then shouldn't you go back to your girlfriend – an' your love-makin?" I joked.

"Hey, man, you know there ain't no girl, but I thought I'd better let those two think that there was someone else in here."

"That was some good thinkin."

"Yeah, well it's you that got me thinkin good, Robbie. I was chillin with some guys at work today an' I ax them the question you put to me one time, 'bout how come we's at war with Iraq when there was no Iraqi man in any-a those planes on 9/11. I ax them if they know when Osama bin Laden transformed himself into Saddam – like, when *exactly* did that change take place? An' you know, not one-a them had an answer. I sure wish you'd come an' talk to those guys like you talk to me."

It was if that last charge of adrenalin, which went through me as I hid by the old chicken coop, had cleared my body of any ability to resist sleep for a moment longer. With some effort, I propped a hand under my head so he could see my displeasure. Mitch had quoted back to me some of my own views and now I immediately figured how he had got to know of some of them. "That ain't gonna happen. But Calvin, you didn't . . ."

"Naw, man, before you say it, I didn't say nuthin 'bout you. Anyways, wha about those two guys, Robbie? They was no cops, man, 'cause the second they saw my rifle they would-a reached for their badges an' my black ass would be in jail right now. An' if it was bullshit 'bout someone hittin their car, wha were they doin comin all the way out here?"

My tired mind had already turned over a number of possibili-ties and I thought that the most likely was that they worked with the FBI. Mitch had told me to keep to my routine and I had already ignored that order by visiting Danny's place. I guessed that the visit was both a warning and a reminder that I was being watched. The actions of the two men gave me some comfort: they had been clumsy and were indicators that Mitch's team was not totally made up of super-efficient operators. What had just happened offered a glimmer of hope that Danny and I could get out of this. But I could not share any of this with Calvin and so I gestured with a nod toward the rifle. "Can you use that?"

"Man, good enough to have nailed those two guys."

"You a marksman?" I asked, more drowsy.

"Hell, no. But there was a time I had thought 'bout enlistin. It happened befo I wised up, man. Befo Katrina showed where black people are still at in this country. Naw, man, this is one guy who knows there's a thief in the White House," he said with all the zeal of a convert. "I was tellin the brothers that I ain't gonna die fo the rich who bought the presidency an' took us to war so they could get their greedy hands on Iraqi oil. I tol' them, plain an' clear, not to join up either."

My lids were drooping and I couldn't even pretend that I was listening. As I drifted off into a deep sleep, I heard Calvin say, "Robbie, you know you can trust me, man, tell me anythin, if you in trouble, y'know wha I'm sayin? I trust you, Robbie. I feel as though I could tell you any damn thing an' it would be safe with you." As Calvin talked on his voice became fuzzy and perhaps I was already dreaming but the last few words I thought I heard properly were: "I got secrets, Robbie, secrets I wanna share with you."

Months of early rising had set my body clock and I woke three minutes before the alarm was due to go off. I managed to get out of bed and dress without waking Calvin, who was slumped open-mouthed in the chair, his head propped against a wardrobe. After gently easing the rifle from his grasp and laying it on the bed, I went into the kitchen to make coffee when my cell phone rang.

"It's me," said Cristina.

Her tone, and the fact that she was ringing me so early in the morning, immediately made me think something was wrong. I said, "Are you okay?"

I heard her take a breath. "I'm okay but I need you to do something for me."

"Sure, what do you want me to do?"

"Come back and see me straight after work. I really missed you last night when I had found out you had gone."

It would be another change to my usual routine but I did not have it in me to refuse her. "Sure, baby, I'll come see you after work but you know I can't stay all night."

"I know," she said, "but I really want to see you later." With that she disconnected and I slipped my phone back into my pocket while mulling over why she had rung me so early in the morning. Something about her voice said it would not be good. My thoughts were interrupted by Calvin appearing in the doorway, contorting his caked lips and showing off a horribly coated tongue. "Man," he said to me, "*you* look like shit."

His attempt at macho bluster brought a thin smile to my lips. It occurred to me that leaving Petra would be a lot harder than I had originally thought. Partly it was because of Calvin, but mostly it was because of Cristina: it suddenly struck me what leaving her behind would mean to me. She would be another loss, another person to join the small line of those who sometimes wandered through my mind at night and set a tear straying from the corner of my eye. Until that moment, until faced with the prospect of leaving her, I had not recognized how my feelings for her had grown.

"You off to work?" Calvin asked.

"Yeah, got business to attend to. It's supposed to be my first day as foreman."

"So you wanna use my car, jus in case . . . y'know, those two guys, or whatever?"

His car, a decrepit Oldsmobile, was even older than my Ford. Under a hood not much shorter than a football pitch were eight cylinders which moved it along at the rate of about ten miles to the gallon – but it did have air conditioning. I took a deep breath to try and clear my head: the possibility that the two guys might come back and follow me again was something I should have considered. "Okay, thanks, Calvin," I said, "I'm not going too far. I appreciate the offer. Good thinkin, man."

He compressed his lips into a smile. "An' maybe when you come back, if you have time . . . we might have a talk 'bout sumpin."

"'Bout what?"

"Um, sumpin personal I need yo advice on."

I looked at him over the rim of my cup for a hint of what he wanted to talk about but he refused to look my way. Maybe it was fatigue, or the little drama on the way back from Petra, but more likely it was because of Natasha that I had no desire to hear or share another secret. And even before her, while growing up, I had learned a hard lesson from my friendship with Errol Morgan. We had been like brothers while growing up but whatever the benefits we'd both derived from it, I discovered after his untimely death that it had been the sort of relationship which came with a heavy price. I made exceptions for Cristina and Danny Maguire but I was starting to tire of Calvin's admiration and his treatment of my every observation like they were profound revelations. I tried to be sympathetic when he projected of all manner of virtues onto me and I realized that he had grown up without many of the reference points and experiences I had taken for granted, but I sensed that the burden he was looking to transfer onto me was a weighty one that I was not willing, nor able, to share.

"Right," I said, feeling awkward, "I had better get movin." Before I left, we swapped car keys and he went to his bedroom to get ready for work at the timber yard. After a quick check of my own place I headed for breakfast at Harry's. I had a routine to keep.

7

'HARRY'S BAR AND GRILL' was the centre of many of the factory workers' social lives: during the mornings and evenings they ate their meals there, and at night some of them gathered in the bar on the other side of the double doors. It was owned and run by a Greek called Harry Aledis. In his thirties and balding, what hair was left on his head was jet black and I had been told that he had once sported a thick moustache until someone commented that it made him look like Saddam Hussein. Harry was telling a man at the counter what was on the menu before he abruptly turned to me and asked if I wanted anything.

"The usual breakfast, Harry," I replied, "without the grits."

He looked at me quizzically and said, "Hey, Robbie, what happened to you yesterday?"

"I was runnin late. Don't forget now, no grits."

Harry laughed briefly before his voice turned sombre. "I was just talking about that drowning in the river, you knew him, didn't you, Robbie?"

"Yeah, José Ruiz. He was my foreman, a decent kinda guy, too."

Swivelling away to flip some eggs, he said, "Hm, he seemed that sort of man. Always polite, you know, always polite."

I hovered for a moment. My ever-suspicious mind immediately conjured a thought that Harry was about to turn around again and whisper that, as was his habit, José had been here the night he'd died and that he was seen leaving with a shady-looking type, whose description fitted that of Danny Maguire. But Harry only called over his shoulder to tell me to take a seat and a waitress would bring my order over.

"Hi there," said the man who was also standing at the counter. "So you knew Mr Ruiz? I'm a reporter and I was just asking Harry about him." The man in the tan suit was thickset, bespectacled and bearded. "Perhaps, while you're waiting for your order, you could give me a few minutes of your time."

I was about to politely refuse when I saw the blue scar on his hairline. Mitch gave me a thin, satisfied grin and gestured at a table for two. When I sat opposite him, I appraised him for a few moments. His appearance at Harry's was a sign of his confidence and it signalled to me that I was in the presence of a man who was not averse to risk-taking. He had control of me, over my destiny, but maybe the trait I now saw within him was a chink in his armour that I could find a way to exploit. "Nice disguise," I said, "an' I take it that you didn't do anythin with that scar on your forehead so I would instantly recognize you."

"My lie detector is working again, Walker," he huffed, "it tells me that you didn't know it was me until I brought myself to your attention. I take it that, as I have received no communication from you, that Maguire has not been in contact, despite you taking the trouble to go and visit his place." He looked down to the watch fastened around my wrist before he continued, "He will, Walker, he will, and when he does, don't you hesitate for one second, you do exactly as I've instructed. And keep to your routine. Routine, is breakfast here, Walker, and not driving out to a trailer park. Do I make myself clear? I'd better be, because I'm giving you the chance to be saving his life, as well as helping your sick mother and that son of yours. What were you doing going out there, planning to warn him off? Didn't it cross your mind that we had staked the place out?"

"Yeah, I figured you'd be watchin, Mitch, you're always watchin, right? I went out there 'cause I want this thing finished as quickly as possible. I didn't think Danny would be there, otherwise you wouldn't have gone to all this trouble with me, but I kinda hoped to pick up a clue about where he might've got to."

"And obviously you didn't find out anything."

"Obviously, or we wouldn't be sittin here now."

"Just remember this, Walker, I'm your new best friend, without me it's Maguire dead, your sick mom dying alone, your boy involved with a drug dealer and the rest of your life in prison." Mitch buried one of his thick hands into a jacket pocket and then slid something across the table to me. "Here, you keep it," he said, his voice dropping to a harsh whisper, "It was taken a day ago. That's your boy, Nathan, still a fine young man by all accounts. No slip ups now. He's counting on you. . . By the way, congratulations on your promotion."

I murmured that I had yet to accept the foreman's job but I was staring so intently at the photograph that it barely registered Mitch had left the table. During the time he had held me captive he had used his phone twice to break down my defences: the first was a call to my mother, the second was to my son.

After I had spoken with my mother, I'd asked Mitch what was his deal. "It works like this," he'd said. "You help me get Maguire and I guarantee you at least a quarter of a million dollars to start a new life with all the usual benefits of an FBI witness protection programme. I'll see to it that your mom is able to come and stay with you and that you will able to contact your son."

"I want Nathan's address an' a way of verifyin he really lives over here . . . "

"You got it."

" . . . before I give you Danny."

"Understood."

"So what . . ." the words lingered in my mouth, ". . . do you want me to do?"

"First, you go back to work and go about your business as normal.

I'm quite certain that Maguire will contact you before long." Mitch held up a wristwatch. "I want you to wear this. See this button on the side? Don't touch it until he makes contact. When he does, press it twice quickly if he's arranged to meet and is on his way – try and give us as much notice as you can – and then press it once for three seconds when you're actually in his presence. We'll arrest you with Maguire, let you go because of a technicality, and he'll be none the wiser. I guarantee that you won't have to stand witness against him." As I reached out to take the watch he grabbed my wrist and yanked me toward him. "And, Walker, foul up in any way and you'll find yourself in serious shit alongside him. Just think about that, think about seeing your mom again, and think about seeing your son."

I examined the watch, and he frowned as I pushed it back across the table to him. I was not in much of a position to negotiate, but if I were to strike any kind of bargain this was the time to do it. "You'll see me wearin this watch as soon as you give me Nathan's address. Once I'm satisfied he's where you say he is you've got a deal. Two quick pushes for when Danny's on his way, one for three seconds when he arrives. Now, if you don't mind, I need to go to the bathroom to be sick."

The moment the bathroom door closed, I had to spew up my breakfast, grits or no grits. I felt as though I had just stepped off the edge of a cliff and, the instant I began to fall, I regretted jumping. But there was no going back. The best I could hope for was a ledge a little way down, because I knew that if I hit the very bottom there was nothing but hell waiting for me.

"Are you okay, Walker?" Mitch called from the other side of the bathroom door.

"Yeah," I called back, "just cleanin up."

His gun was pointing at me when I opened the door. "You're going back to bed for a while before we return you to your car," he said.

I was crushed by the notion that I had joined the ranks of some of the most reviled characters in history: there was no one as despised as a traitor. No doubt, like me, they had justified their treacherous acts by making out it was for the sake of others – including the ones they were to betray. I offered Mitch my wrist and, once cuffed, trudged ahead of him back to the bedroom. I lay down thinking about what I had done and how easily I had been broken. Previously,

I had imagined that I could withstand any pain, resist any temptation. In my younger days I had believed that I was invincible, and that crazy notion had been maintained until I met Natasha. Our relationship had changed me irrevocably; she had tested me to a point just short of destruction. She had found me out, and drawn from me the truth about who I was: not only had I told her my real name, and the reasons why I was in America, but also, she had torn away all my layers of pretense. After I had left her for that final time, I knew I would never be the same again.

I had believed that I would be strong enough not be broken during any interrogation because I thought I had nothing to lose. For so many years I had functioned rather than lived as I placed myself into some sort of prison of the mind. But Mitch had done his research thoroughly. He was offering me much more the chance of a life – it was a life, possibly, with Nathan and Mom. He had given me something to lose again. The price was my friend Danny Maguire, and he'd sugar-coated that bitter pill by telling me that I would also be saving Danny's life. There should not have been any dilemma but I could not shake off the sense that I was betraying the one person who had always stuck by me.

These thoughts played and replayed in my mind, until Mitch came into the room. "We'll be going soon," he said, "but I have another call for you." While he tapped out the numbers on his phone, he told me that I would be speaking to Nathan. I could ask which city he was living in but I was not to ask for an address.

"How do you know it'll be Nathan who answers?" I asked.

"Because I'm ringing his cell phone. It was a birthday present from his stepfather."

"Stepfather" – that hurt. The number was still ringing out as he passed me the phone. It was all I could do to stop my hands shaking.

"Hi, who's this?" The voice was young and confident, with a hint of an American inflection.

For a moment my mind went blank. "Look, if this is Latisha messin around I'm gonna hang up. Latisha, is that you?" Girls, he had girls ringing him? Last time I had seen Nathan he'd been a small child and it came home to me then how much I had missed. "Right, I'm hangin up."

"No," I gasped, "no, Nathan, don't do that."

"Who's this?"

57

I bit my lip and tried to stop it trembling. "Your dad. . . It's your dad, Nathan."

"Dad? Is that you? Is it *really* you?"

"Yeah." Searching for words, I asked, "When did you last ring your grandmother?"

"Mom ain't keen on me ringin her, and Rodney doesn't want me usin my cell phone to call, 'cause he's payin the bill. . . I can't believe it's you, Dad. This is like a dream. Dad, is it really you?"

Stern-faced, Mitch held up his ten fingers.

Hastily, I asked, "What city are you livin in, Nathan?"

"In Chicago, right now. Can't say for how long. Rodney was talkin about takin us to Toronto the other night. Are you comin to see me?"

"I'll be comin soon. Look, Nathan, I gotta go now. Don't tell anyone we were talkin, okay?"

"Sure, Dad." He began to giggle. "I can't believe it's you. How did you get my number?"

Mitch's hand gripped the phone.

"Gotta go, Nathan. I'll see you soon, yeah?"

The line went dead.

Mitch pocketed the phone and took off the handcuffs. "The watch," he said. "You put it on now and you make sure it stays on if you want to keep your word to Nathan. There's a device that lets us know the moment you take it off and instantly gives us your location. Once it's on, Walker, it stays on until we have Maguire, is that clear? "

The watchstrap was made of chunky black plastic, with a type of fastening I had never seen before. Once it was on my wrist I was told stand and face the wall with my hands behind me so I could be cuffed again. The hood went over my head and I heard other people come into the room. "Put him in the car," said Mitch.

"Walker," he said, as we drove back to the Old Glory motel, "there's going to be all kinds of doubts and crazy ideas filling your head once you leave this car. You might think you can take off the watch and leave it on a bus or a train while you skedaddle in the opposite direction, but we'll know the second you take it off, so don't even think of trying anything foolish. Don't try and warn Maguire. You're saving his life by bringing him to us. Put all crazy thoughts about not going through with this outta your head."

I did not reply, mostly because I had thought of ditching the watch once I was out of Mitch's car – and on my way out of Georgia. I was almost glad of the hood: at least he couldn't see my expression. Except for the rumbling of the tyres on the road, it was silent for the rest of the journey. When we stopped, I heard the driver get out and another car drive away a few moments later. Mitch lifted my shoulders, so that I was sitting up, before removing the hood. I blinked hard as I brought my surroundings into focus.

Mitch said, "Look, Walker, this isn't going to be easy for any of us. But this man Rodney Dixon, your boy's stepfather, from the reports I've read, he's involved in getting Jamaican women to act as drug mules – some fly here and others to go to England. Those poor dumb bitches risk their lives for a thousand bucks, while guys like Dixon makes a hundred times that amount for every load they stuff down their throats or up their pussies. Outwardly, the guy's very respectable but inside he's one rotten son-of-a-bitch. It will be my pleasure to tell you where he is so you can get your boy away from him."

He didn't wait for me to respond, but he helped me out and then took off the cuffs. I said nothing, and I didn't look back as I walked to my car. "Don't forget, Walker," he called, "twenty-four-seven we'll be waiting for that signal."

I was still staring at a plate of food and trying to figure out how Mitch had got to know about Henry Lavette's offer of the foreman's job before I caught sight of a slightly dishevelled waitress. "Is there anything else I can get you?" she asked. I mumbled at her that there wasn't but ideas about being under surveillance while in the factory prevented me from giving her a coherent answer. She flounced off, muttering to herself. Harry had put grits on my order again but I had already lost my appetite. I put the photo of Nathan into a pocket and on the way out I threw some bills onto the counter before I headed for the factory.

Mitch's appearance at Harry's diner and his mention of the offer of the foreman's job had been designed to unsettle me but by the time I got to the manager's office I was gradually becoming aware of some of the mind games he was using against me. If I were watched all the time, he would have had no good reason to remind me of the fact, or, more importantly, had the tracking device fitted around my wrist in the guise of a watch. "I'll take that job," I said to Billy Joe Watson.

He looked up from the papers on his desk and crinkled his lips. "Barrett, I know you're good at your job and, uh, though you have a tough act to follow in José Ruiz, I don't expect you to fail. You know the score, you've worked here long enough, so, uh, get on with it. . . Besides, thanks," he said to fill the uncomfortable silence, "have you anything else to say to me, Barrett?"

"Er, no," I said, "I guess not."

"Then, please," he said with a sarcastic grin, "don't let me detain you any further. Hanging by the door you'll see bunches of keys. Yours has a blue tag. Make sure it's back, with a worksheet for the night shift, before you clock out."

After looking through the list left by the night crew, I put the maintenance team to work. Woodlow and Hunter gave a few derisory grunts but otherwise my first stint as foreman went smoothly. I spent most of the morning alone and preoccupied by thoughts of how easily I had been trapped and then manipulated by the FBI agent I knew only as Mitch. By midday my head felt wrecked. I stripped off my overalls and went to the canteen. "What's up with Myrtle today?" I asked Lilli.

She gave me a plate of fried chicken, okra, and corn on the cob, with a large glass of something cold and pale green. "Her son's anniversary's comin up soon," she said. "After all these years it still don't get no easier fo her."

I didn't know what to say, but nodded as though I understood. And perhaps I did: Myrtle probably saw men maturing and having children of their own, and thought about the times she'd missed with her own son, just as I looked at young boys and wondered about Nathan.

The green fruit juice was cooling my throat and I was looking at Nathan's photograph again, when a uniformed man loomed over me. "Hi," he said. The wannabe-cop was the sort of guy who had stubble on his chin an hour after he'd shaved. His broad face broke into an uneven grin and he pushed a hand through his receding, wavy hair. I guessed by the way he stood that he wanted to come across as threatening. I put the photo back into the breast pocket of my shirt and took another drink while trying to think if I knew him at all.

"Jack Kirby," he said, by way of introduction. When I merely carried on drinking, he went on, "Head of security. I've come to have a word with you about your behaviour at the gate." I drained the glass and wiped my lips with the back of my hand. "I'm talking about your inappropriate language to Darren Clayton and the unacceptable references to Iraq and what our boys are doing out there."

I was still edgy after my unexpected encounter with Mitch and I really wanted to punch somebody. I asked myself if the language Clayton directed at the Hispanic workers was "appropriate" before imagining telling Billy Joe that I had driven my fist into Kirby's face because he had addressed me in a way I thought was far from "appropriate". My readiness for violence was reaching critical mass when something touched me lightly on the shoulder. I turned and saw a gnarled old hand and then a mostly toothless smile. "I got sumpin fo you to try. Some of my favourite pie," Myrtle said, laying a restraining hand on my arm.

"I hope you've taken on board what I've said, Mr Barrett," said Kirby, as I got to my feet. "And perhaps you might be man enough to apologize to Darren Clayton tomorrow."

I told Myrtle to lead me to the pie. When we got to the counter she said, "How many times have you talked to that white man since you worked here?"

"I'm glad to say that was the first."

"Exactly wha I thought. Usually, that man says nuthin to nobody, but when he do it means trouble. Rumour has it he used to work on Border Patrol an' he got away with killin a lotta people."

"Yeah, well, Myrtle, rumours are like mushrooms an' they have a way of growin from a pile of manure, puttin it politely."

"Robbie," the old woman snapped impatiently, "I've a lotta time fo you – there's sumpin 'bout that look in yo eyes that reminds me of my Michael. But that don't necessarily make me feel good. Jus by the way he was, Michael used to upset people, especially white people. His attitude, they called it uppity. Now, it still don't do to upset white people aroun here. You might think I'm talkin 'bout a long time ago but everyone here, the coloured an' the white, is still cut from the same cloth. We walk on history aroun here, son. It's in the bones that are in the earth that makes the cotton that makes the clothes. We's all still the same cloth."

"I've often thought the same kinda thing, an' I appreciate . . ."

"Naw, you don't. That other white man who works with you,

wasshisname, Woodlow. Him an' Kirby been in here talkin lately, an' I hear your name mentioned more than once or twice. That ain't good. In fact, it could be dangerous."

"Myrtle, don't worry about me, Chuck's just sore over me gettin the foreman's job."

"Maybe it's more than that, maybe not, but I still see an' hear things 'bout those two that make me think the devil hisself is alive an' well in this here town of Petra."

"I'm sure you do."

Not liking my tone, she raised a weathered finger and put it under my nose. "I see those two men sittin in a corner an' see how they cut the coloured folks an' the Mexicans with their eyes. I know sin like I know the Lord, Robbie, an' I see sin in the eyes of those two men. So you be careful, you hear?"

To humour her I said, "I'll be very careful."

"I've said wha I've said," she grumbled, "an' I ain't sayin no more 'cept fo one mo thing."

"An' what's that?"

"I lied about the pie."

The hooter sounded and I joined the rest of the workers as they returned to their mind-numbing labours. While I was collecting my overalls, Ricardo yelled mockingly, "Mister Foreman!"

"What is it, Ric?"

"Meat grinder in bay six again, the breakers keep popping. So who are you going to line up for that shit job, Mister Foreman?"

"You an' me, Mister Smart-mouth. I never ask a man to do somethin I wouldn't do myself."

Truth was, I was not sure enough in my new role to delegate such a gut-wrenching task: asking someone else to do it could have led to either mutiny or confrontation. As Ricardo muttered curses to himself, the two of us went around to the back of the factory. I hated this section even more than the killing tunnel. The strict sanitation procedures did not apply in the area where all the waste was ground down, conveyed into huge boilers and then dried to make feed for livestock. Some of the largest flies I had ever seen lazed in the baking sun and feasted on the rotting flesh, which at times seemed to be moving because of the millions of writhing maggots within it.

After isolating the electrical supply by locking it out with two sets of padlocks, Ricardo and I clambered up the steel ladder to the platform that skirted the grinder. The grinder's design and function were similar to that of tabletop grinders in kitchens all over the world. It was the scale that made it different: it was large enough for a grown man to fit inside. One of the steel corkscrews did not rotate and the first thing I had to do was to make sure no steel had found its way into the mechanism and wedged it. It was not unknown for foreign objects to find their way into delicate machinery inside the factory. The culprits were usually the stressed-out workers on the production lines, who would do anything for a break.

We began the repulsive chore of stripping down the machine in order to find the problem and, taking turns, used our gloved hands to scrape away dollops of putrid meat. In such high temperatures to put on a mask was to come close to suffocation so, consequently, the stench had my stomach heaving my last meal back into my mouth and some of the bloated black flies were so brazen that they landed expectantly on the edges of my lips.

The plates and the knife of the grinder came out easily. The auger was a different matter because the problem turned out to be a stainless-steel shackle wedged between it and the throat of the grinder. We took turns to hammer and prize the shackle for a few minutes until the urge to vomit became too strong. Ricardo had been in the bowels of the grinder while I stood above on the platform until he could no longer suppress the pulse at the back of his throat. He clambered up and looked at me through watering eyes. Neither of us dared to open our mouths to speak. I lowered myself down to the narrow base at the side of the corkscrew, determined to free it this time. Desperately trying not to draw deep breaths, I brought the hammer down with as much weight and accuracy as I could muster. There was a crash of metal against metal, the sound of the shackle ricocheting, and then another noise, a loud humming. I knew as soon as I heard it that I was in danger. I started to straighten up. The machine roared into action. The corkscrew began to spin at a frightening speed. The hammer was pulled from my hand and disappeared with a metallic screech as it was devoured. I checked that my arm was still attached to my body and then I heard Ricardo yelling above the deafening whirr. I took his outstretched hand and scrambled up.

He looked at me in bewilderment. "How the fuck that happen, man?"

I shrugged and shook my head. We went down the ladder to the switchgear and found the padlocks still in place. I told Ricardo to go inside the factory and knock off the breakers. "Looks as though we got ourselves some faulty switchgear," I said.

"Hey, Robbie, you could've been eaten up in there," he gasped, his mask of bravado slipping momentarily. "Look at your fucking sleeve, man, that thing nearly chewed your arm right off."

I looked and saw that the cuff of my overalls was frayed before I patted him on the shoulder. "Yeah, but we got the grinder fixed, Ric."

"Fixed my ass, man. It was me or you nearly fixed in there." Ricardo's eyes were ablaze with anger and I told him to freshen up and to take a break in the canteen while I tried to find out how the grinder's control switches had malfunctioned.

"Accidents happen, Colin," I agreed.

I had stayed over to find out what had gone wrong with the grinder's switchgear. It was no hardship for me as Cristina would not get to the apartment in town until the evening. The electrician, a man with a big paunch, pawed nervously at his fleshy throat as he explained to me how the short circuit, which had almost made me into animal feed, had come about. He could not explain why the circuit breakers had been switched on again, but thought they had probably been flipped on again by accident. "Thank God no one was hurt," he said.

"Yeah, an' let's make sure we got some procedure in place so nothin like this happens again."

"Are you filling out a report?"

"Not unless you want me to."

"Thanks, I appreciate that. You know, there's only two of us doing the electrical maintenance, and it's so damn hard to keep on top of everything."

"No need to explain, Colin, it was just one of those things."

"Can I buy you a beer?"

"Thanks but it's a bit late. Another time, okay?"

I knew that my calmness about my close shave had baffled him and that later on, maybe while at home reflecting on the day, Colin might think my composure was down to shock. But he did not know how many times I had smelled and touched death, how often it had brushed my lips with an exquisite tenderness. I feared the process of dying as much as anyone else, but figured once I was dead I wouldn't feel a thing. My first thought was that I had survived – and that was all I had to dwell upon, rather than anything that had almost happened.

I drove from the factory with something else on my mind. When I was young, I had scoffed at the idea of a man becoming besotted with a woman to the point that he did not know his own mind. But Cristina had me confused: she was desirable, captivating, she was the sort of woman who could make a man forget the oaths he had taken and all the promises he had once made to himself. Somehow, the idea had come to me that if I were to escape, it should be with her and not Danny. My previous experiences should have informed me that the chances of sharing any sort of future with her were slim. And yet . . . and yet, I still wanted her. It was though I'd become infected with a virus which had started to eat away at the logical part of my brain and now I ached when I simply thought of being without her.

I turned off Petra's main street and drove into a parking lot. The apartment block in which Cristina waited for me was a square three-storey building with a bad paint job. Someone had tried to spruce up its exterior but had stopped halfway, as if they had run out of either paint or enthusiasm. Cristina had told me it belonged to a friend who had given her a key before heading off for a while. Not that I cared too much, but I did not think that was the whole truth and neither did I think that I was the first and only man she had brought there.

During the journey from the factory my thoughts kept changing about asking Cristina to come with me and memories of New York and Natasha resurfaced. In many ways the two women, and the nature of my relationships with them, were complete opposites. Perhaps, deep down, that was why I found myself wanting to be with Cristina.

After that first time we had spoken, I didn't see Natasha outside the confines of Beanie's Caribbean restaurant for several weeks. When we did start seeing each other, her caution was obvious and I figured that she must have been badly hurt by a past relationship. I could relate to that and, because of my nagging thoughts about my own dishonesty with her, I was happy to go along at her pace. We met regularly after I finished work and before Natasha started her shift at a health centre for women.

I found her easy to be with, perhaps easy to fall in love with, if I allowed it to happen. But I reckoned I never would: after all, if she responded in kind who would she be falling in love with, Pete Foster or Robbie Walker? For the most part, I thought I was the only one who was thinking about that kind of relationship as she hadn't signalled that she was interested in me in that way. If my hand strayed across the table and touched hers, she would withdraw and look deeply into me as if searching out my true motive. Her expression was enough for me to suppress all manner of carnal thoughts. Maybe it was maturity on my part, or simply a drop in testosterone levels, but her attitude did not make me want to see her any less. It wasn't until after our trip to Coney Island that she talked of her feelings for me. In the time that had passed since then, the good times we'd shared had become increasingly difficult to recall. Most of what I remembered about her was the pain that we both endured following that crisp dark night when I found out that we could never be lovers.

In contrast, Cristina oozed sexuality, and my attitude toward her right from the start was wanton. She knew me only as Robbie Barrett, and, at first, I was more comfortable with my deception. Many times I had told myself that what Cristina and I felt for each other was simple lust, but as I sat in Calvin's car staring at her apartment window it was hard to dispel the memory of how often she'd clung to me on the nights I'd stayed over. Sometimes, when she thought I was asleep, she had got out of bed and peeked through the window blinds. On getting back into bed she often whispered words I did not understand, and her tears fell onto my shoulders. I'd told myself to harden my heart: I figured she was talking to someone from her past, and her tears were for him. But gradually those tears had seeped through my skin and softened my heart, I was no longer so untroubled with Cristina giving so much of herself to a man who was living a lie.

Eyes fixed intently on her window, I got out of the car and strode toward the apartment block, still uncertain about what to do or say when I saw her. If she gave me a glimmer of hope, if she said she would come with me, then I would take her and her daughter and make a new life somewhere else. I wanted an end to the type of life Danny Maguire had led me into. I knew what I was thinking was not rational, but with every step all I could think of was how much I wanted her, now strangely more than ever.

As I neared the door I heard footsteps behind me. Before I could react, I was belted between my shoulder blades and yanked aside. My head turned instinctively and the side of my face was smashed into a wall. My shoulders and forearms were gripped so fiercely that I cried out in pain. From the corner of a wet eye I saw the blurry shape of a face come into focus. It was the white man I had seen in Calvin's yard. I guessed the man at my other side, and almost breaking my arm, was the black guy.

"We've got a message for you," the white guy hissed.

I never got to hear it. Blood pounded through my ears as the pain increased until vomit rose in my throat. They were yelling and snarling but nothing they said registered. They slammed me against the wall again, winding me, and one of them punched me expertly in the kidneys. I'd taken many blows as a boxer but few as vicious as this one. Like a charge of a thousand volts, the hurt shot through me and stiffened my every sinew. I groaned through teeth that pain had welded together and I hit the ground before feet began thudding into my curled-up body. The concrete began to spin, and the vomit spewed from my mouth. The pounding in my ears ceased and I knew I was losing consciousness. The last thing I heard was a woman's voice screaming that they were killing me.

8

LIQUID RAN DOWN MY FACE. I heard the noise of dripping water and felt something soft against my brow. I caught Cristina's scent and decided it was safe to look. My eyes refused to focus at first, and when they did I was confused by my surroundings and then her absence.

My heavy lids closed again and I was still trying to make sense of it all when she appeared beside me. "Thank God," she breathed, gently raising my head. She put two tablets against my lips and I let them fall onto my tongue. A glass touched my mouth, and she said, "Take a little water." I drank and swallowed, with some difficulty, then she lowered my head back onto the pillow. "I got them from the drug store, they will take away some of the pain," she continued. "I have to go. Sleep a while and I will come back shortly." I wanted to catch hold of her and prevent her leaving but I was too groggy. The last thing I remember was the faint click of the door catch and a spinning sensation, as if I had been caught in a whirlpool which was pulling me down, which was pulling me back.

* * *

We spent our day in Coney Island acting like two big kids until I felt sick on the Wonder Wheel. I blamed it on the hot dogs and Natasha said that I might feel better if we walked along the boulevard and took in some fresh sea air.

"Makes you feel kinda small, don't it?" she said, as we gazed out at the ocean. "I mean, like an insignificant dot." When I continued silently looking out at the distant horizon and thinking of the people beyond it, she said, "You got somethin on your mind that you wanna share?"

What was on my mind were the reminders all around me of my son: boys of all ages with their dads and even the hot dog delis had his name emblazoned over their front doors. "'Nathan's'," I said half-truthfully, "their chilli dogs taste too damn good. I shouldn't have eaten that fourth one." She smiled as if she didn't altogether believe me, and I added, "Anyway, there's no way you're insignificant. You're a special person, Natasha."

"Smooth-talkin dog, you. Or should that be smooth-talkin chilli dog?"

"No, I mean it – woof, woof."

She laughed and then looked at me seriously. "I suppose we're all insignificant compared to the vastness of creation. I mean, you can be the president of the United States, or a pope, but you're still gonna die an' the world will continue to turn, it won't stop spinnin, even for a split-second. It won't stop for me, it won't stop for you. Do you believe in God, Mister Smooth-talk?"

"Only when I'm in serious trouble. As in, what are a few prayers as insurance just in case some of it turns out to be true? My mom believes, so I let her do most of the prayin for the two of us."

"Yeah, well, my family are believers but I'm sorta the white sheep of the family. I was a bit of a wild child an' decided to commit all the sins for my sisters, too." She paused so I could ask what sort of sins they might have been but I didn't and so she went on, "I don't criticize their faith but I was thinkin that if it's true that all matter existed at the Big Bang, then all those atoms, that make us an' everythin else, could've been there in the presence of God. Maybe that's how this religion thing came about, some kinda shared memory in our atoms. Or does that sound like more of my weird stuff?"

"Well, it ain't no weirder than the stuff I had to listen to in church when I was a kid. Say, what about if we set up our own cult? There's big money in it."

There was a momentary sadness about her but then she smiled. "Right," she said brightly, "you don't wanna talk theology an' we have a lot more things to do. I'm goin to walk those chilli dogs off you 'cause I know a nice Caribbean restaurant I want you to try before we go home. Let's head for the aquarium."

After the fireworks display on the beach we took the train home. As we neared our station, she took my hand. "Pete," she said, "I've had a wonderful time."

"So did I."

"An' I really think you're a great guy."

I forced a laugh and mumbled that I thought she was great, too. Deep down I wondered if she was going to ask me back to her place and how I would respond if she did. Part of me was comfortable with how our relationship had – and had not – developed. We shared points of view about American society and the world at large, and had discovered we had a lot in common. I had grown to look forward to our chats, and some of her more unusual topics of conversation while we ate, as the highlight of my day. But another part, the deep-seated, innate instinct within me, couldn't help but notice the roundness of her breasts and hips as her coat slipped from her shoulders. I always averted my eyes, but in my unthinking moments I found myself staring at her shapely body as she walked to and from the washroom. Because she had given no sign that her mind wandered in that way, I always felt even more of a fraud when my eyes strayed.

"You might think I'm a bit of a weirdo," she continued. "But I kinda get excited about meetin up with you in Beanie's. It's like . . ."

"Your highlight of the day?"

"Yeah," she laughed, "and yours too, huh?" She bit her lip and the happiness in her eyes faded. As at Coney Island, sadness drifted fleetingly across her beautiful face and I could tell that she was about to say something that neither of us would enjoy. In a quiet voice she went on, "Don't you think it's strange that I've never invited you over to my place?"

"No," I said. "I mean, I've never invited you to mine."

"You don't wonder why I took so long to talk to you after you came over to my table an' introduced yourself?"

"I guessed you thought I was weird, or too forward."

"Or why, after we did start to talk, it took me so long to go out with you?"

"Look, Natasha, I reckon you had good reason, an' if you think it's important for me to know what it is then you'll get around to tellin me. But everythin is cool with me, Natasha, honestly."

She tried to smile, but what she was about to say overpowered it. "Pete, Pete, I really . . . really appreciate your easy-goin attitude. It's so different from the other men I've met. Y'know, they buy me a meal or two an' suddenly they think they have a ticket to my bed. But you, you've never made a move, even though I've caught that look in your eye from time to time."

"Really? I thought I was doin a fair impression of a eunuch."

"Even eunuchs look, don't they? But I do appreciate how you've never tried to rush me into somethin we might end up regrettin. It's not that I don't find you attractive – in fact, I find you very attractive, physically and in other ways. But I've gotta tell you somethin, Pete, somethin that might mean you won't want to see me ever again."

She squeezed my fingers so tightly that she almost stopped the circulation and I wished the train would stop and give me an excuse not to hear the painful description of a previous, or maybe ongoing, relationship.

I said, "Hey, I kinda guessed that you've been hurt. I'm sorry for that, Natasha, but you don't have to talk about it if you don't want to."

The train halted. Her voice breaking, she whispered, "Pete, oh, Pete . . . there's no easy way to say this."

I didn't think this was the right time or place for this sort of conversation and I got to my feet. "Then it's cool. . . Save it for another day."

We stepped out onto the platform. Natasha was still clutching my hand, and she pulled me back as I tried to walk on.

"No," she said desperately, "I have to tell you now. It can't wait any longer. I was more than hurt . . . I'm HIV positive."

* * *

When I woke again, the air was full of electricity. Even before I called Cristina's name, I somehow knew that I was alone. Although I vaguely remembered that she'd said she would return, I knew that I had to get back to my house. It was as I eased myself out of bed that I discovered that my sinews had turned into stiff and painful cords which grated with one another. When I was young, I had sat in a church with my mother and listened to a preacher say that even pain was a gift from God. Though I was only twelve, it was obvious to me that the good reverend had never taken a hook to the liver or a shot to the kidneys, otherwise he would have thought it wicked rather than divine. A bolt of lightening ran across the sky and I wondered if the Almighty had been listening in on my thoughts. Maybe to punish me for my insolence, the next flash of lightning suddenly brought back memories of my son and how he used to climb into my bed during storms. He was six going on seven then; now he was not far off seventeen. I'd left him with my mother, but before long Sharon returned to claim him. I knew that much because, despite giving my word to Danny Maguire, I'd telephoned my mother from time to time to find out about Nathan. I'd heard her fight back the tears as she told me that Sharon, as was her right, had taken her only grandchild away.

With another flash of lightning Natasha's face came and went. There was more lightning and Paulie O'Sullivan's face replaced hers. It was the way he had looked at me, resigned to his fate, that stayed with me. Sometimes I remembered his expression as more accusing, as if he'd been condemned because of my actions rather than his own. Since that night in New Jersey, every time I had thought about telephoning my mother the recollection of his death returned to prevent me from doing so. But Mitch had skillfully exhumed all the memories that I had tried to leave buried so they could visit me at any given moment.

My mother had often warned me that every action is followed by

71

consequences, some of which cannot be foreseen. She had got that much right. With Danny I'd continued the violent journey I'd begun as a much younger man and now, as a consequence, I was separated from the people I loved most. So many nights I'd sat up watching the night sky, visions of the past chipping away at the composure of my mind. I may not have seen the inside of a prison for what I had done, but I had not gone unpunished. I had paid a very high price for my actions.

More thunder rumbled and with the flash of lightening that followed came the realization that the FBI agent was waging a war on my mind so successfully that I had yet to think about who had attacked me and why. I thought there could only be one answer: Henry had found out about Cristina and me. I prayed that she was all right as I limped to my car. Floating in a puddle was the sopping remains of the photograph of Nathan. I picked it up but let it fall to the ground again when I saw that all traces of my son had been washed away.

9

DARREN CLAYTON, THE SECURITY guard on the gate, snorted gleefully as I limped past his kiosk. From over the heads of the night-shift workers milling around him, he called out, "You stick your nose in somebody else's business again, Jamaican man?"

I was stiff and sore but I could not resist the opportunity he had given me. I called back, "Not nose, Clayton, my prick. Ask your wife when you get home." There was a delay, while the English-speakers translated for their colleagues, before an eruption of laughter drowned out the torrent of curses coming my way. I could tell by Darren Clayton's face that some lunch boxes were about to be violently emptied onto the ground.

Once I was in my overalls, I collected the keys and worksheet from Billy Joe's office. I had anticipated that he would tell me that Henry Lavette had sent word for me to be fired, as I now figured that he had sought a meeting with me either to satisfy his curiosity, or to provide a description for the two heavies who had jumped me. But Billy Joe neither commented on my less than perfect state of health, nor mentioned Lavette, rather he merely noted that I was on time "for once" before I headed for the payphone in the canteen to ring Cristina's number. There was no answer. Her cell phone was switched off – and mine had been broken as I was attacked. I ground my teeth in frustration but sought some comfort in that the two guys had left her physically unharmed. I guessed that she had returned to Henry Lavette. There was nowhere else for her to go.

Back in the factory I put the guys to work. We were a man down as young Ricardo had not shown. I guessed he was still recovering from our experience in the grinder. A motor on a conveyor had burnt out and I went looking for John Hunter to replace it, as it was a job within the bounds of his limited capabilities. He wasn't where he was supposed to be and I walked around the plant searching for him until I eventually found him out by the cold storage area talking to a man named Miguel. I was surprised that straight-laced, play-by-the-rules Hunter was talking to a lowlife like him. The word around the factory was that Miguel somehow smuggled condemned and contaminated meat out of the plant and sold it to his compatriots. "Hey, Hunter!" I called out. He stiffened slightly and Miguel pivoted and furtively made off in the opposite direction. Hunter could not disguise his feeling of indignation about my new position. When he came over to me he barked, "What the hell do you want, Barrett?"

"A bit of cooperation, Hunter. We're two men down an' you seem to think we've got time to stand around an' chat. There's a motor out on conveyor number three an' I need a hand with it. Anyway, what are you doin talkin to a guy like that? Miguel must be the biggest crook in the place. The only one who doesn't know that is Billy Joe Watson."

John Hunter rolled his lips contemptuously. Threatening, he said, "Barrett, a word of advice, you've made a mistake, you never saw me talkin to anyone. . . Conveyor three . . . Let's go."

It was some time after lunch when Cristina finally answered her phone. In response to her question I told her I was okay, before I asked her how she was. I heard her inhale deeply. "I am all right. I was not harmed. I am at my home but it is difficult to talk right now," she whispered.

"Then can we meet up later?"

There was a silence and then, "Where? When?"

"Duke's in Creektown. In one of the rooms above the bar."

"I cannot give you a time . . . but yes, I will see you later."

There was a noise coming from the other side of the door but it was only a drunk making a hollow promise to give some woman the time of her life. I returned to the window and looked for a sign of Cristina, or of one of Mitch's men hanging about and checking on me. It was getting late and I wondered if she would turn up. Duke's bar may not have been a good choice for Cristina but it was the one place that I could think of which might make anyone tailing either of us stand out in the crowd. I had been in the fusty room for almost three hours and had only left it twice to get myself a beer from Duke. I had originally given him the hourly rate and on my second trip downstairs he advised me to pay for the night – it might just turn out to be cheaper for me that way. I gave him enough for another hour, figuring that if Cristina had not arrived by then, she would not be coming at all.

Looking out at the figures moving along the street below, doubts returned about my decision not to start running the moment Mitch had dropped me off at the Old Glory motel. I was the bait in his trap but what would happen if Danny did not come back, what would Mitch have in store for me then? But both Mitch and I knew that, if he were alive, Danny would make contact. He had saved me in New York, when I had tottered on the very brink of destruction – and though I had given him good reason – he did not abandon me then and I knew he would not abandon me now. And yet the reward for such loyalty would be betrayal. I massaged my temples, looking for some relief from the pain such thoughts were causing me.

There were only ten minutes of my time remaining when one of Duke's bartenders led Cristina to me. When the door had closed behind her, she kissed me tenderly. "You do not look too bad," she said.

"I've taken worse in my time," I replied. "What has he said?"

"Henry? He said nothing. He has gone to Atlanta on business this evening but before he went he mentioned nothing. That is his way. Henry rarely gives away what he is really thinking."

"Then were these guys anythin to do with him? I mean, could it be someone else?"

She compressed her lips and a ripple went through her cheeks. "Are you serious?" she hissed.

"Look, Cristina, don't come all vestal virgin on me. You've been with Henry a while now an' I don't expect to be the first lover you've had in all that time. I'm only askin because I expected to be fired this morning but it was business as usual."

Eyes alight with barely suppressed anger, she said, "Henry does not mix his personal life with business. If you are of use to him, he will keep you. When you are no longer of any use he will get rid of you, it is called capitalism . . . And no, you are not my first. But what business is it of yours, Robbie? I have never asked any questions of you. For all I know, you could be anyone, a man with a wife and children somewhere, or a man with a criminal past. A woman knows when a man is keeping secrets but I asked no questions, I took whatever part of you that you were willing to give. Well, sure, Robbie, ask about my past, my life – but then be ready with answers to *my* questions."

I was not ready to give her any answers. I had made that mistake before and it had led to terrible consequences. "I'm sorry, Cristina," I said. "I didn't mean it the way it came out. But do you have any doubt it was Henry who sent those guys?"

"If you mean, as far as I am concerned, could anyone else have sent them, then no. It has to have been Henry."

"So where does that put you?"

"In some danger but not for a while. Henry is a man who plans his moves extremely well and only executes them when it is to his advantage. When that time comes he will make me pay for what I have done with you."

As soon as I heard Cristina's words there was a moment of clarity which cleared every scintilla of confusion from my mind. She had pointed the way out of this mess and I almost felt elated. Deep down I had wanted to run but had not found the justification to do so: if I escaped it meant that I would probably never see my mother or son again; if I stayed I would end up betraying my closest friend. But if I took Cristina and Goretti with me, I would be vindicated in getting out of Petra before Mitch could spring his trap. By leaving with them I would be ending any hope of reuniting with my family and I would be consigning Danny to his fate – but I could absolve myself from a lot of the resulting guilt with the thought that I would be saving two people from the clutches of Henry Lavette.

"Then let's leave now!" I gasped. "Let me, you an' Goretti go tonight. Come on, Cristina, we'll go back to your place, pack, get Goretti an' go before Henry gets back."

Incredulous, she frowned at me. "Are you serious? Where do you think we could go?"

"Outta Georgia. Say, head north, west, south. Come on, let's hit the road an' see where it takes us." I took hold of her hand. "You say you could be in danger but we can go now."

Cristina stood her ground and then pulled away. "I can't. Henry has taken Goretti with him. She's his insurance that I will go nowhere while he's gone."

I searched her face and thought I saw regret. Or maybe it was just wishful thinking. "When are they back?"

"Not until next week. But, Robbie, even then, even then . . . Henry would not stand by and let us go."

"I'm a determined man, Cristina. Neither him nor those guys he hires could stand in my way to get you two out."

"If we were to go with you, it would have to be carefully planned. And I don't want you even thinking about confronting Henry, that would put us all in danger. Like all rich men, he sees the world merely as what he possesses and what he wishes to possess. He is not a man to give up any of his possessions easily." She rested a hand on my shoulder as Duke's bartender knocked the door and called that we either gave him more money or had two minutes to get out. "Look, Robbie, we're going to need as much money as we can get. I'd love for us to go with you right now but we can't. And if you are serious . . ."

"I'm serious, Cristina, deadly serious."

". . . Then you'll go back to the factory for another week, earn as much as you can while I get my business sorted out and then the three of us can go. Well, are we agreed?"

There was another impatient call from the landing before I told her that we were. Cristina pulled my head down and kissed me hard and passionately. I rolled my stinging lips and then she led the way out.

I drove for home. Previously, I had been wishing that Danny would come to me and there would be some sort of resolution – for good or ill. Now I prayed that he would not turn up before I had worked out and then executed an escape plan. I was now sure that life with

Cristina and her daughter was what fate had decided for me and from now on I was not going to consider any other outcome. I was already imagining what I would do with Mitch's wristwatch: I would get on a train with a pair of cutters and as it was leaving the station I would remove the watch and then jump before running to Cristina who would be waiting for me in her car. The light in Miss Boo's porch signalled an end to my dream for the future and drew me to a stop. I figured I owed it to myself to get a good night's sleep with the aid of a little 'something' from her.

I went around the back and knocked twice on the kitchen window. Miss Boo came to the door with a comb stuck in her hair and a slightly glazed look in her eyes. At about five-eight and two hundred and fifty pounds she filled a lot of the doorway. She rubbed her damp hands over her printed cotton dress before there was the first hint of recognition in her eyes. "You come fo a little medicine, Rob?"

"Yeah, just a little bit."

"Herbal?"

I told her it was always going to be herbal and she waddled around and disappeared for a couple of minutes. When she returned, Miss Boo deftly took my folded bill and simultaneously put a small package into my hand. "Befo you go," she said, pushing the money into her ample cleavage, "I was thinkin you must get awful lonely all on yo own."

I thought she was about to offer me a stomach-turning proposition I could easily refuse, but she shifted to one side and said, "You know my daughter Stella? She a good girl who could come an' keep you company some nights. Y'know, fo a little conversation an' such."

My attention turned to the dark-skinned girl in a short dress who stood awkwardly in the kitchen. Her straightened hair was combed over one eye. I hoped that I had misunderstood what her mother was offering me. "Yeah," I said, "she looks a good girl, an' I hope she stays that way, but I'm okay for company. Thanks anyway."

Miss Boo puckered her lips sourly. "Okay," she sneered, "but don't you be gettin the wrong idea now. I love my Stella." I turned and walked away, not wanting to hear any more, as she called after me, "Maybe you's mo happy with a faggot."

I parked Calvin's car in his yard, crossed the road to my house, and went in through the back door. Distracted by whatever avaricious demon had taken hold of Miss Boo, I went to my bedroom for the cigarette papers without giving a thought about checking my warning devices. As soon as I opened the bedroom door, I sensed something was wrong: there was a strange, yet familiar smell that I could not immediately identify. Instinct told me to keep the light off. My finger froze on the switch while my eyes slowly adjusted to the dim light. The cool blue glow of the moon came through the window and cast strange shadows onto my bed, but I could make out the shape of an arm dangling from under the covers and my mind was immediately flooded with ideas about whose arm it could be.

I was about to flick on the light switch when I heard a faint sound, a creak of the step outside my back door. I pushed my back against the wall and slid sideways along it toward the kitchen. I heard someone try the handle and I wondered if I had locked the door behind me. The answer came with the next sound and my heart raced even faster. The door opened. If I were to survive, I would have to strike first. I moved quickly and was almost upon the intruder before I recognized him.

Calvin's eyes were wide and fearful. "Robbie," he said, "I've been waitin fo you to come home. . . I'm in big trouble, man."

It was then that I saw he was holding a large knife in his hand.

10

THERE WAS REAL TERROR IN Calvin's eyes and I could tell that he was temporarily uncoupled from reality. We stood in silence for what seemed an agonizing time, until I said quietly, "Listen to me, Calvin. Take a seat, an' put the knife down."

He did not respond at first. "Put down the knife, man," I said, "an' tell me what happened." As I spoke, I was trying to figure out what had taken place. At once, all my senses were heightened and as he blinked I noticed a bead of sweat that trickled down from the edge of his eyebrow. The body in my bed must be one of the guys who had jumped me; I figured that Calvin must have seen them back at my place and killed one of them. I urged him, "Come on, sit down, Calvin, an' tell me what's gone on."

The knife fell to the floor from a hand suddenly gone limp. He tottered over to the kitchen table and collapsed onto a wooden chair. It was dark, but I thought better of switching on the light and so I drew up another chair and joined him at the table. For a while I did nothing but listen to his laboured breathing. When eventually it got softer I put a hand on his shoulder and said to him, "C'mon, man, you got to tell me what happened an' who's that guy in my bed."

"Little J Moses," said a crisp feminine voice. I pivoted on my chair and saw Vonette Norbury picking up the knife and closing the back door behind her. "Let's put a little light on the subject, shall we?" she said.

She was a cool one. When the light came on I saw that her pretty eyes were clear and calculating. She was wearing a black suit with padded shoulders over a black shirt which was unbuttoned enough to show a silver cross. Her high heels still didn't make her very tall but, for a moment, she towered over the two of us.

"Some light on the subject would be good," I said. "Like how come I've got a dead congressman in my bed. Can I take it that *he is dead* an' not just a heavy sleeper?"

"I killed him, Robbie," groaned Calvin, as a tear dripped from his chin. "I butchered him like a fuckin hog, man."

More fearful of the consequences for me, I turned back to Vonette and asked her the question which was uppermost in my mind. "Have the cops been called?"

In the moment before she answered I saw something in her expression that meant trouble for me – but I had a feeling that cops arriving here was not going to be an issue. "No, Mister . . . Barrett," she said, her eyes searching my face. The pause before "Barrett" communicated a threat but I did my best to pretend I hadn't noticed it. "For the police to get involved," she continued, "would not be advantageous for any of us."

"Any of us?" I growled. "Shit, woman, all *I've* done is stumble in on a murder scene."

"It wasn't murder!" she snarled back.

"Then," I said, "put your backside down next to Calvin an' start tellin me what happened."

She edged past me, her eyes defiantly holding mine. She was doing what I asked but in no way was she acquiescing. It was little more than a manoeuvre, to give the impression that she was not calling the shots, but I knew that, even before she started to speak, there would be something unpleasant for me at the end of her story. Vonette sat down beside Calvin, who buried his face in his hands, as she began to tell of how her boss had become more and more depressed since losing the Democratic nomination. Within hours he had lost sponsors, money and a lot of the stuff he had thought was friendship; the media were still on his case, pressing him about contributions, and questions were again raised about his infidelities. As she spoke, Vonette fondled the silver cross that glinted against her flawless mahogany skin. "Things were getting warm for Little J in Atlanta," she said, in a flat, detached tone. "He and his wife had just had one mother of an argument and he wanted me to get him out of the city for a while."

"So you brought him to my place? That don't sound right, Vonette."

"Of course not," she answered, her tone changing to one of condescension. "Me and Little J went to Calvin's place. He had been drinking while I was driving and he was pretty drunk by the time we got here. At about seven Calvin said he'd come over and see if you were back. Apparently, some white man had been here earlier in the day."

"Who was it, Calvin?" I asked, in a tone which betrayed my anxiety.

"One-a those guys who followed you into my place, the other night. He was talkin 'bout you hittin his 'mobile again," he replied through his fingers.

I'd anticipated that he was about to say it was Danny and for a few seconds my head was spinning with consequences for my new plans if it had been him. "If I can continue," Vonette said to bring me back to her. "So when Calvin came across here, Little J started to get more than a little frisky once we were alone. I had never seen that look on his face before. He started grabbing me but I got away and ran across the road to here. I came around the back, I didn't see Calvin, but the door was open so I came inside. Little J had followed me. He picked me up and before I knew it I was in a bedroom, and he went crazy and ripped off my clothes and threw me onto the bed. I was screaming for help when Calvin came in and saved me."

There were several things that immediately made me doubt the truthfulness of Vonette's story. The first part seemed plausible, and I doubted if it had been the first time that she and Little J Moses had gone for a drive somewhere. It was the second part, the bit about the attack, that didn't ring true to me. I wanted to ask Calvin what he was doing going inside my place when he saw I hadn't returned from work, but he didn't look able to give a coherent answer. Vonette's shirt was partly unbuttoned, yes, but her clothes were not torn, though I supposed she could have changed them since Moses had assaulted her. But I couldn't see a mark on that flawless skin of hers, and Moses had been a big man who could have done a lot of damage to a petite woman like Vonette. But most of all it was not what she had said but the way she had said it. Vonette's words had sounded rehearsed and lacked emotion. Something else had gone on, something she was not about to tell me, but I knew that she had already planned her next move.

To draw out her intentions, I said to Calvin, "Man, you did right. You had to save your sister an' I don't believe a court in this country will convict you because of that. You gotta ring the cops, Calvin, there ain't no other way."

Vonette stood up. "Are you outta your fuckin mind?" she yelled, momentarily reverting to the way I imagined she had spoken before she headed for the big city. "This is Georgia and there's not a court around these parts that wouldn't have a needle pushed into Calvin's arm!"

"He killed a guy attemptin rape, right? Nothin was premeditated. He saw you about to be raped an' took on a much bigger man, a big drunk man, the only way he could. All you gotta do is tell them what you've just told me. An' hey, Moses wasn't the most popular man around here after the primaries."

She came close to me. "You don't really understand this country, do you, what it is for a black man like Calvin? You don't have to look no further than New Orleans to understand that the powers-that-be still look at African-Americans like they're the dirt. Oh sure, you're black, Robbie, but not in the same way. As soon as you open your mouth and give us a sample of your English education, the red-necks give you honorary white-man status. But it's different for people like my brother. For them there is no chance of justice 'cause no one will listen."

"Then tell me, what the hell are you thinkin of doin, Vonette!" I snarled. "I mean, people will know you left Atlanta with Moses,

81

so you can't just go back an' make out that you don't know where he is!"

"You're wrong, Robbie, plain wrong," she said. She sauntered over to the sink, turned and propped herself against it. "Moses was always careful, and he made sure no one knew he was going with me."

Calvin was still sitting with his head in his hands, as if trying to shut out the dreadful reality that lay only a few feet away from us. He reminded me of my friend Errol and his reaction after we had killed a Jamaican gangster who had been terrorizing our community. Errol had become all emotional and fearful of the consequences of our actions, but for me killing bad people was never a problem: it was simply a means of making more room for the good. As with a soldier in wartime, once I had set my mind on what had to be done, fear and doubt were pushed to one side as I focused on my objective. Over the years, I gradually convinced myself that the things I had done in the past were regrettable but necessary and now all I asked myself was what I would have to do to remain free. Looking at Calvin, I could see that an emotional storm, like the one Errol had experienced, was gathering inside his head, and I could only hope that his mind would survive the pounding.

Vonette moved away from the sink. For a moment she took in her brother's hunched figure, and then her jaw set determinedly. "Like I said," she said to me, "no one knows Little J's even outta Atlanta right now, and I can see no good reason for taking him back there, though it did briefly cross my mind. I mean, a lot of people heard him and his wife having that argument."

Her callousness astounded me and had me groping for words. "Am I hearin you right? You were thinkin of goin back to Atlanta an' maybe framin his wife?" I spluttered.

If my question affected her in any way, she did not show it. One hand was still playing with her cross while the other rested on her hip, as she studied me with a gaze that never wavered. "I'm prepared to do anything to protect Calvin," she hissed between her teeth, "anything."

I said, "Then do what you have to, but get that body outta my house!"

"In a few minutes," she said, licking her lips, "we're all going for a drive and I'll show you where you and Calvin will put him."

I shook my head. "You must be in shock, woman. I'm not gonna let you involve me in this any more than you have already. Put him where you want, as long as it's nowhere near here, an' I'll do my bit by not sayin a word to anyone about what I've seen here tonight. I will swear on that."

When her scornful laughter faded, Vonette frowned and said, "I'm not interested in you swearing or any damn thing, Robbie . . . Barrett, because you haven't fooled me since the moment I laid eyes on you. You really think you can come to a place like this, this part of Georgia, and not draw attention to yourself? No, sir, you got 'looking for a place to hide' written all over you."

"Please, Vonette, don't," said Calvin, at last raising his face from his hands. "He's my friend an' I don't want him involved."

"He's involved whether he likes it or not!" she spat. "How come he's not axin what he ain't fooled me about, or what I think he's hiding from? Because he knows I must know something, don't you, Mister Barrett? And you know what, Calvin, if the police did get involved, Mister so-called-Barrett here would vanish, disappear, gone without a trace in a minute, because Mister Barrett ain't really Mister Barrett."

Like Paulie O'Sullivan had said about me working in an Irish bar in New York, every time I opened my mouth around here I stuck out like a black sore thumb and it had always puzzled me that Danny had brought us from a string of big cities to a place like this. It was out of the way, as in it was distant from New York, but in reality capture was only the distance between a local cop's hand and a phone. Coming to a town like Petra had never made sense to me.

I was about to deny her accusations but seeing the way Vonette looked at me, I knew it would be futile. I had to buy myself some time. I asked, "What do you want me to do that will help Calvin?"

"Help us get rid of the body."

"Not around here."

"No. Little J has gotta go to a special place. We'll put him in Calvin's car and I'll show you where."

Calvin grimaced apologetically. She had left me no choice but to do exactly what she asked

Vonette drove ahead of us and went east along Interstate 16, far enough for me to begin to taste the salt coming off the ocean. I continued to follow with Calvin sitting beside me as she turned and headed south toward Jacksonville. We passed signs for the coast towns of Sunbury, Eulonia and Darien, before she took a turn and headed inland again. For most of the journey he had stared blankly at the road ahead and mumbled barely coherent apologies for getting me involved. I responded by saying, truthfully, that I did not blame him. I told him that there was no point wasting time in wishing it had never happened; we now had to concentrate on getting rid of the body without being detected. "It's like steppin into the ring, Calvin, do you understand?" I'd said to him. "You fix your mind on the fight plan, an' nothin else but what you have to do to come out the winner."

He nodded and managed a strained smile. "Yeah, you're right. It's jus that I feel a bit . . . numb, like it's all a dream an' none-a this is really happenin. I guess I ain't cut out fo no killin. But don't worry, man, I won't let you down. We'll put that bastard in the ground an' I swear I'll make sho there's never no comeback on you."

It was not long before we were driving along roads hemmed in by more giant pines. It was dark and threatening and I thought that anywhere around here would do, but Vonette had been insistent about where Little J's body had to go. Back in my kitchen she had said, "I reckon he might as well go to a place that will cause his enemies most harm if he ever gets found. Maybe in death he can do something he could never do in life."

Once the body had been loaded into the trunk of Calvin's car, I asked her, "But why bring me into this? The less people who know about this, the better it is for you two."

"There's no way me and Calvin can handle a man as big and as heavy as Little J and somehow I don't see you as in a position to blackmail anyone, Mister Barrett."

The memory of Vonette's steely glare faded when I saw her car come to a halt. She wound down her window before she leaned out and gestured to me. When I got to her she nodded in the direction of a long brick wall; it stretched into the distance and was about ten feet high. "He's to go in there," she said.

"That won't be easy. I mean, humpin a man as big as Moses over somethin that high . . ."

"Don't act stupid with me, Robbie. I mean I want Moses on that estate. You'll find a way in."

"So, who owns this place?"

Her hands tightened on the wheel. "Mister so-called Barrett, you're in no position to ax me questions. Do as I say and your little secrets are safe." I knew that she could not know why I had become a fugitive and part of me wanted to call her bluff but I resisted the temptation and she went on, "I'm heading back to Atlanta to cover things at that end. I'll call Calvin an' let him know how things are going down." Her window glided shut and she took off after casting a final warning glance at me. Calvin got out of the car and stretched his legs. The sky was clear and star-filled, and the moonlight was bright enough for us to see our surroundings without much difficulty.

"Vonette reckons this is the place," I said, "but there ain't no way we're gettin Little J over that wall."

"Damn right," said Calvin.

We went back to the car and drove on for half a mile, cursing the length of the wall, until we saw a single metal gate. I stopped and got out, only to find the gate was locked and that my approach had switched on a powerful halogen light. I hurried back to the car and drove on. After turning into a much narrower road we eventually came to a likely spot. Bricks had tumbled from a small section of the wall and it looked as though either it was being rebuilt or that another gate was in the process of being installed. "I think this will do us, Robbie," Calvin said. "Let's drag that mother out an' go bury him."

"No," I said, "first thing we do is dig a hole. We don't want him where he just might get seen any longer than absolutely necessary."

We each took a shovel from the back seat. Once through the gap and about ten paces in, we started to dig but the ground was iron-hard. I told Calvin to stop and went in a little further before quickly finding a place where my shovel easily cut through the layers of needles and sandy earth. It went in so deep that I had trouble pulling it out again.

I beckoned Calvin over. "Right," I said quietly, "this will do here. Before we start diggin a hole, we clear the area of needles so when we cover him up we can spread them again an' it won't be so easy to see that the ground's been disturbed."

For the first time that night, I saw the gleam of Calvin's usual wide smile. He said, "You gots me thinkin you've done this type-a thing befo, Robbie."

I got on with clearing the pine needles and didn't tell him that I had, although it was IRA guns, rather than bodies, that I'd buried, what seemed a lifetime ago in England. The hole we dug was no deeper than two feet and circular, rather than rectangular like a grave. We'd had to bend Little J's tall frame to get it into the trunk, and even before we lifted him out I had been thinking about the difficulty we might have in ever straightening him again.

11

LITTLE J MOSES DID NOT go easily into what, I hoped, was his final resting place; he must have weighed close to three hundred pounds. The last I saw of him, he was lying in the ground under the bright moon, curled up like a baby and suckling the earth. The tang of the sandy soil and pine needles wafted around my nose and put a bitter taste upon my tongue as I shovelled the earth over him. Calvin's mouth moved in a silent prayer – but I didn't think it was said for Moses – while I remembered all those I had seen buried over the years. Once the needles were scattered over the disturbed earth, I took Calvin's arm and tugged him back toward the gap in the wall.

When we got back to his house we didn't talk much before we hit the sack. I'd decided to stay at Calvin's place, partly because I didn't want to leave him on his own but mostly because I was uncomfortable going back to the scene of Moses's death. Like Calvin, I'd suddenly got very tired as the rush of adrenaline dissipated.

He followed me to Vonette's bedroom. At the door, he drew a breath but I simply closed the door on him. I was in no mood to listen to whatever he had to say to me.

Calvin was still asleep when I left his house to stiffly cross to mine the next morning. I had been woken some time earlier by the sun's rays on my face. I lay there thinking about how a dead congressman had ended up in my bed and how Vonette had manipulated me into becoming an accessory to his murder. To make a run for it now might only end in bigger trouble for me – Vonette framing me for murder, for instance – and I made up my mind to go and see if there was much evidence of what had gone on in my bedroom.

There was plenty: bloodstains were splattered on the mattress and over floorboards. While surveying them all, I cursed both Vonette and her brother. To get rid of the evidence was going to take a bonfire and a couple of large bottles of bleach. My mood did not improve when I went to the toilet: my piss still had the consistency and colour of tomato ketchup because of the beating I'd taken. Blood seemed to be everywhere I looked. I didn't feel like it, but I knew if I did not make it into the factory it would draw Mitch's suspicion. The last thing I needed right now was him having something else to use against me, if it ever came to light that I'd been involved with the disappearance of Little J Moses.

Those sparring partners 'panic' and 'reason' were fighting it out inside my head again, but my old boxing coach used to warn me that panic only ever made a bad situation worse. I told myself that I had kept up a pretense for years in New York, and I only had to maintain this current masquerade for another few days, or so I hoped.I put on my working clothes and went back to Calvin's. I poured myself a coffee, took one sip but let the rest go cold as I repeated to myself what had to be done. The first thing was to get Calvin out of bed and tell him what he had to do but a sharp rap on the front door halted me mid-stride as I went toward his bedroom. It was still too early for a social call and, hesitantly, I stepped to take a look through a window in the front room. My first glimpse of a sheriff's car set my pulse racing. I hadn't expected my resolve to be tested so quickly. Another rap on the door made me take a deep breath before I went back into the hallway and opened up. "Yes, can I help you, officer?" I said.

The deputy was a well-built man with shades and a large moustache. He said nothing for one long, drawn-out moment. He shifted uneasily on his feet and I guessed he was surprised by my accent. Finally he replied, "I was wondering if you could tell me anything about the incident that took place around these here parts last night."

Every vein in my body began to throb. I instantly figured that Little J must have been seen running across the road to my place in pursuit of Vonette – and until then I had not given that possibility any thought. I searched the deputy's face for a clue as I asked, "What incident would that be, officer?"

"Around 12.30 . . ." I managed to hide my relief: Vonette, Calvin and I had already been heading east around that time. ". . . there was an incident involving a firearm over at the Fentons' place. I was wondering if you could tell me anything about it."

"Sorry, officer, I was in Statesboro last night with my friend who lives here. I'd say we couldn't have got back here until three or later."

He flipped open his notebook. "For the record, you are?"

"Robbie Barrett. I live across the road," I said, keeping it short and slow so he could write it all down. "I just came across a few minutes ago to make a cup of coffee an' see if I can raise my buddy so he can get to work. His name is Calvin Norbury, an' this is his place. He's the one I was with in Statesboro. We didn't see anythin, officer. If you look around, you'll see that you can't even see the Fentons' place from here because of the trees."

I waited for an anxious few moments while he went on scribbling, and prayed he would bid me good morning and be on his way as soon as he had finished. After glancing over his shoulder and checking that I was correct about the view, he turned down the corners of his mouth and said, "But you could see where the Fentons live from your place, Mr Barrett."

"As I said, we didn't get back until long after the incident. It was so late that I decided that I might as well put my head down in here. When I got up, I went across home to get ready for work an' I've just come across again to wake Calvin."

He stuck out his lip and made a note. "Mr Norbury," he said, still writing, "did you get him out of bed yet?"

"I was just on my way to his room when you knocked. Can I get you a cup of coffee, officer?"

"No, thank you, sir," the deputy replied with well-practised courtesy. "I'd prefer if you got Mr Norbury. It could save me a trip."

My lips did their best to smile, rather than twitch nervously, and I went to Calvin's room. I entered without knocking and placing a hand over his mouth, I gently rocked him. He immediately tried to sit bolt upright and yell out. My hand tightened and stifled his noise, and his eyes swivelled frantically in their sockets.

"Calvin," I whispered, "there's nothin to worry about but there's a deputy at the door. There was a shootin at the Fentons' place last night, with a bit of luck Darlene will have shot Wayne. Understand? There is nothin to be worried about. I told him we were in Statesboro last night, so you say we were shootin pool until about three, so we didn't hear or see nothin. Have you got that?"

His eyes gradually stopped moving and fixed on me. He nodded slowly. I took my hand away and whispered, "Right, so let's go see him. . . An' keep it simple."

Not knowing how Calvin would react made my stomach churn as I followed him out to the front door. I knew that he liked cops even less than the Fentons and I was afraid that, as he shook the sleep from his head, he would say something that would lead to conflict.

"Don't let me delay you, Mr Barrett," the cop said to me, as he looked over Calvin's shoulder. "I'm done with you, and thank you for your help."

"It's all right, officer, I have to, um, take Calvin to work this mornin. He's got trouble with his car."

The deputy did not react but merely turned his eyes on Calvin. "Right, Calvin," he said, "Mr Barrett says you were with him in Statesboro last night. So, uh, where were you and what were you doing?"

"Shit, I don't know. I remember shootin some pool an' drinkin beer. Wha I do in my social life gots nuthin to do with the Fenton bitch shootin her ol' man, right?"

Part of me wanted to punch Calvin in the back of his head – as this was building into exactly the sort of needless confrontation I had feared. Not that Calvin was entirely to blame. The cop's body language had changed the moment he saw Calvin: his head had dropped to one side and his lips wrinkled contemptuously as a thumb found its way under his belt. By his tone and manner he addressed Calvin as if he were a boy and not a man.

"If you were in Statesboro last night, how is it you know about the shooting?"

Calvin snorted scornfully. "Robbie jus told me, man, as he was gettin me outta bed. Now I'm gonna step back inside an' git myself ready fo work. Yeah, work, you heard me right. This nigger ain't on welfare, can you believe that?"

I pulled his arm roughly and told him get dressed. To the deputy I said, "That's if you have no more questions for him, officer."

He shook his head. "I guess there's still alcohol in his system. It's a good thing that you're driving him to work this morning. Be a shame if he got himself pulled over DUI." He flipped his notebook shut and put it into a breast pocket. "I take it by your accent that you're not American."

Over the years I had imagined being questioned by a cop and had on many occasions rehearsed a response that I hoped would extricate me from a difficult situation. Luckily for me, lying had become easy with practise. "My father was American, officer," I said in a clear voice, "an American who proudly served his country in the US Marine Corps. He met my mother in England and settled there. When he died, I followed his wishes and brought him home. I've stayed in this great country ever since."

I could hardly believe his reaction, it was if I had just given a rendition of the 'Star-Spangled Banner'. "Goddamn it, sir," the cop said, removing his shades, "my daddy was a marine. Damn fine body of men, sir, a damn fine body of men. The type of men our country needs more of right now." He put his sunglasses back on again. "Pleasure meeting you, Mr Barrett."

"Oh, before you go, officer, how is Wayne Fenton?"

"Wayne Fenton is fine, sir, it wasn't him his wife was shooting at. From what we can tell, she blasted a pump-action shotgun through her door. It looks like a stranger was looking for directions, he saw a light on over the door, and when she heard a foreign accent she opened up. If he pulls through they'll be picking buckshot outta him for the next twenty years."

"What type of foreign accent would that be, officer?" I asked.

"Not sure, sir. Darlene Fenton was wrong to shoot through the door, but she was a woman on her own who was only looking to protect her children." I nodded, as I though I could see some sort of justification for her action, and the deputy went back to his car.

As I watched him drive away, I imagined that her attorney was already constructing a similar defence: she was a patriotic citizen who had been terrified by the foreign accent. Given the present climate, I doubted if any jury around these parts would convict her. I closed the door and turned back into the house. The first thing I saw was Calvin peering out of his bedroom doorway. He stepped out with a relieved smile on his face – and the rifle in his hand. I gestured at the gun and said, "What were you thinkin of doin with that?"

"I thought if he started axin awkward questions an' rilin you, I'd step out an' plug him."

With one hand I seized the rifle while the other struck Calvin across his cheek. His whole body turned with the blow, and I threw the rifle into the bedroom. He rubbed his face and looked at me in bemused pain. "Shit, Robbie, that hurt, man, hurt more than any punch you ever hit me with when we's boxin!" His eyes flashed with the kind of foolish angry pride I had once possessed. I grabbed him by the throat and stopped matters getting out of hand by pinning him against a wall. I did not want to hurt him but I was doing what was necessary. I said, "Look into my eyes, Calvin, 'cause I'm deadly serious. I want you to remember the pain, I want you to remember everythin I tell you."

The eyes looking back at me were no longer angry, they were uncomprehending. I relaxed my grip. "Calvin, if you want to get outta this you have to be disciplined, do you understand? When a cop talks to you, even talks down to you, asks you anythin, you eat crow. You talk to him sweet: 'Yes, officer, no, officer.' You're careful with words an' you're careful with what you do. Walk softly, Calvin, an' all three of us, me, you an' Vonette, are safe."

His head dropped. "Guess I wasn't thinkin right, man. Sorry. It won't happen agin."

I lifted his chin and gave him a tight smile. "I didn't want to slap you, you know that."

"Naw, you did right, man. I needed sumpin to get my brain workin agin. I don't know why, but I feel there's a reason why you know 'bout wha to do. An' I'm listenin. I don't want any of us in trouble because of that bad sumbitch, who only got wha was comin to him. Is there stuff I gotta do, Robbie?"

I told him there was and turned him toward the kitchen. Once fresh coffee was made, I told him I wanted my mattress destroyed and my bedroom floor and walls bleached and scrubbed. He nodded and said he had plenty of bleach, a scrubbing brush and gas, too, to make sure the mattress made a good fire.

"Don't set it alight in my yard," I warned him. "Put it in your trunk an' take it some place where the smoke won't get seen too easy. But bleach an' scrub that room first."

Frowning with concentration, he nodded again. "Don't worry, Robbie, my head's clear now. I'm gonna do exactly wha you say."

I told I would have stayed to help but I did have to go and report in at the factory. "That's all right," he said. "But, Robbie, befo you go . . . I had to tell you some lies last night." I had already figured that Vonette's version had been less than the whole truth and I immediately expected him to come clean about how Moses had ended up being killed in my bedroom. "You know when I said that I saw a white man aroun your house," he went on, "an' I said he was one of the guys who followed you into my yard?"

"Yeah."

"Well, that wasn't right. I only said that 'cause Vonette was there an' I promised him I wouldn't tell no one but you. He said fo you to ditch yo cell phone, take out the batteries an' that he would meet up with you the day after tomorra, if he could. Y'know, Robbie, if you's in trouble you can tell me, if you want. Look, I didn't say nuthin in front of Vonette, so y'know anythin you ever tell me will be safe with me."

"Sorry, Calvin, but you've lost me. Who told you all this?"

"It was yo white truck-drivin friend, Danny. It was Danny who called."

With so many conflicting thoughts, for the second morning in a row I failed to finish my breakfast at Harry's. I parked in my usual place and traipsed toward the factory gate. Two killings within hours of each other, so close by, and the unexplained death of José Ruiz reinforced my feeling that coming to Petra had been a big, big mistake. And now I had been blown off course again by the news that Danny had come to my house and that he would return, perhaps the day after tomorrow. Mitch had been right: although Danny could have got far away, by now, he would not leave without me. Calvin had also said that Danny had looked as though he had been sleeping rough and that he had as good as emptied my refrigerator before he left, only minutes before Moses arrived on the scene. While I was glad that he was alive, part of me just wished that I had heard the news sooner – or maybe it would have been even better if I had got word from him after I had left town with Cristina. My fate was now in the hands of others: if Henry Lavette returned with Goretti in time, then maybe I would be spared from an awesome dilemma when finally making contact with Danny.

One thing I had definitely decided upon was avoiding any confrontation with Darren Clayton. As I neared his booth he saw me coming and moved out into the early sunshine with another man close behind him.

"Mr Barrett," said Jack Kirby, stepping right in front of me, "I thought we'd straightened things out."

I stopped and said, "Besides your guy's behaviour, what was there to straighten?"

"See wha I'm talkin about?" whined Darren.

Kirby spat a ball of phlegm onto the tarmac close to my feet and said, "Obviously there has been a breakdown in communication, Barrett. You made an unacceptable comment to one of my men, of a personal nature about his wife, in front of the wet-backs, and in doing so you have undermined his credibility and his authority. I think I've already said that an apology is in order."

I took my time in replying and spat out what saliva I could summon near Kirby's shoes. Licking my lips, I looked at him and then said to Darren, "The only one I see underminin your so-called credibility is this guy who's goin on like he's your masser."

Kirby adjusted his stance and made like he was about to make a move on me. He could have been bluffing, another piece of macho bluster from a 'good old Southern boy', but I was not about to stand there and take the chance. I caught him unprepared and pulled him towards me, before pivoting on my right foot and pushing him against the booth. The booth shook and Kirby's sunglasses fell to the ground. Darren stood gawping and motionless.

"Another word, Kirby," I snarled, "another fuckin word an' I might take Darren's head an' push it up your ass. You want an apology? Then get fat boy to apologize to all those men you call wet-backs, get him to say sorry for all those times he's emptied their lunch boxes onto the ground. Then, just then, he might get back some credibility."

It turned out that Jack Kirby was not a man for whom words were enough. I had caught him off guard because he was not used to having his authority challenged but now he was ready to retaliate. He grasped my wrists in an attempt to free himself but I was ready for him and rammed my knee up into his balls. His grip loosened and he collapsed to the floor, retching and gasping for breath. Darren made to come at me but stopped as soon as I looked at him. "An', fat boy," I said, "I don't wanna hear another damn word outta your mouth either."

I walked away and collected my overalls while thinking that when I was younger I would have been proud of my physical prowess and my reactions when threatened by a man like Kirby. Now I was merely resigned.

It had taken until the afternoon before I got word to report to Billy Joe Watson's office. The only thing that surprised me was that he had left it so late in the day. The call came to go to the manager's temporary office after lunch, when Lilli was piling even more food onto my plate while Myrtle voiced her disapproval and concern. "I'm gonna pray fo yo safety," she had said. "I heard wha you did to Kirby this mornin an' I know where that white man is comin from. Robbie, Kirby's people all used to be in the Klan, includin his uncle who was once the sheriff, an' don't think there ain't nuthin else but badness runnin through that man's veins." Myrtle's warning had not done much for my appetite, but it was more my inability to make contact with Cristina that had taken the edge off my hunger. In my anxiety to get away from this town, I had rung her more than a dozen times during the morning without success. Every time I dialled, I hoped that she would tell me that Henry had returned with Goretti and that she was free to leave with me.

It was a sign of all the other, far more serious, matters going on in my life that I had not given my spat with Jack Kirby much thought until I entered the office to see him standing in front of Billy Joe's desk. There was a foul odour in the makeshift office that came from a Doberman which sat in one corner, growling and baring its teeth. I thought it was safe to assume that if it were to attack anybody, it would go for the black guy first. Billy Joe sighed, "Okay, Jack, I'll take care of this."

Jack Kirby limped out of the office, cutting me with an ominous sideways glance as he went The dog was still growling. Impatient for a response, Billy Joe said, "Well?"

I shrugged. "It seems to me that Kirby an' Clayton have had their sense-a humour surgically removed."

Billy Joe leaned back into his chair. "A knee in the balls, uh, kinda takes away a man's sense of humour, Barrett. I, uh, took a gamble making you up to foreman. Looks now as though there's no way you can keep that job."

"That's cool with me. Just pay me what you owe me an' I'll go."

The freckled hands interlocked on his chest as he snickered, "I can't allow that. We're short in the maintenance department already, and Kirby is ringing the sheriff's office and a charge of serious assault is coming your way if you quit before I find someone to replace you. I've told him you're fired as soon as it suits the company and not before. I'm busting you back to private, Barrett, but there's no way am I letting you quit right now." His grin turned malevolent and the dog squirmed restlessly. "From tomorrow you're back to where you were. Do I, uh, make myself clear?"

I concentrated on not giving away any sign that I would be leaving this factory, and Georgia, very soon. "Okay," I said, "but Kirby doesn't seem like a man who would be happy with that."

Billy Joe scratched the side of his nose and quietly ordered the dog to stop barking. "Don't worry about Jack," he said to me, "he's like the dog – he only attacks if I tell him to. Carry on and do your job like I ask you to and you have nothing to worry about as far as Jack is concerned."

Before I left the office I told Billy Joe Watson that Jack Kirby was the least of my worries.

12

MY FINAL AFTERNOON AS foreman proved to be a long and tedious one. Machines seemed to break down every five minutes; the fans that calmed the turkeys failed; and at one point the conveyer which took them to be decapitated and plucked got stuck and made a terrible mess of the birds still in the device. I wanted something to ease the knots of tension within me before I headed for home to face whatever awaited me there. Although I had regained some confidence in Calvin, I did not know what his sister was up to and my suspicion grew every time I thought about her. Hoping for some relief, I rang Cristina yet again but all I got was her messaging service. Dented, if not crushed by the disappointment, I went for my second choice and accepted the offer of a beer from Colin the electrician.

Colin had heard of my demotion and, as well as sympathizing, offered a guess about who would be taking my place. "Chuck Woodlow is favourite," he said. "No offence, but it was a bit of a surprise that you had got in ahead of him, if only because he's been at the plant for so long." I had followed Colin in my car to Petra and then into a bar that was a little more gentrified than Duke's place in Creektown. John Hunter was there and saluted us with a bottle in his hand. My last chat with Hunter had been a fractious one over his 'non-conversation' with Miguel the condemned meat thief, so when he came over and offered to buy us drinks, I made an excuse and left.

On the way home I caught sight of a road sign for Cobbtown, which reminded me that I was also overdue paying my rent to Cuthbert. Concern about how Calvin was coping almost made me change my mind, but I reckoned it was better to go to my landlord and pay what I owed rather than risk having him coming around looking for his money.

Old Cuthbert was a curmudgeonly man with sharp blue eyes and false teeth that were constantly loose in a mouth made ragged in one corner by shrapnel. As a young man he had proudly served in Custer's old regiment during the Korean war and had been caught in a blast from a hand grenade, or so he told me. The house I rented from him was hardly palatial, but it looked a lot more comfortable than the two rooms at the rear of his general store from where he sold gas, hardware, some haberdashery, and provisions. It was the sort of business that belonged to another age and, as he had no family of his own, I imagined that when he died his business would go with him.

"You're late," he said, teeth clacking. "But I figured you'd get here before the end of the week."

"Sorry, Cuthbert. My foreman was the one who died in that car that went into the river, so we've had a busy time at the factory."

"I told you, rent is due first Monday of every month, and not any other day. I'll let it go this once, but if it happens agin I'll be looking to git myself another tenant."

I apologized again and, remembering that Danny had emptied my refrigerator, I collected milk, bread and a few other items which I figured would tide me over for a few days. The sharp blue eyes greedily followed the dollar bills as I put them on the counter in front of him. As usual, he counted them again before putting them into the till. He pushed a small amount of change my way and stared for a moment, before beckoning me closer with a waft of his leathery hand. His voice dropping to a whisper, he said, "A fella was in here last night, looking fer someone. Heard the same fella got shot, heard that Darlene Fenton put a big hole in him."

"Yeah," I said, while gathering up the change. "I heard he was foreign or somethin an' his accent spooked her."

"I've always said women and guns don't mix, like women and cars, they don't have the mind to handle them. But the man was a damn fool to stay in front of her door like he did, and I almost sent him to your place . . ."

"My place? Why were you sendin him to my place?"

"I said 'almost'. He said he was over from England looking for an old friend of his, some fella named Pete Foster." He paused and I tried not to give any sign that my heart had started to thump the moment he mentioned the alias I had used in New York. "I says to him that I never heard of no one by that name," Cuthbert continued. "He says this Foster's a black man who served in the British Army with him and I told him that the only black man from England that I know of is you and there's a chance that you might know his friend, birds of a feather and all that. I started to tell him you lived back the road a ways, back towards Petra, when something made me stop. Can't say what exactly, maybe it was 'cause he was kinda big and mean-looking. So I thinks better of it and I tells him to leave a telephone number and that I'll be seeing you any day now with the rent and I'll ask you if you know this Pete Foster. He thanked me for my help but he didn't leave a number. Got me figuring that the man wasn't talking the whole truth."

Those old, sharp, blue eyes searched my face as I said, "I don't know any Pete Foster. In fact, besides me, I never heard of another black man from England around these parts."

Cuthbert juggled his teeth with his tongue and sucked noisily to bring them back to their proper place. "No," he chuckled, "neither have I."

I gathered up my provisions from the counter with a tingle of foreboding coursing through my chest. Just when I thought things could not get any worse, the day of reckoning Danny Maguire had longed warned me about had come. The mention of the British Army convinced me that Cuthbert's visitor had been one of the hit squad that Mitch had cautioned me about. I had thought he was lying but it seemed they were now in Georgia to kill Danny and perhaps the only way to save him was for me to make sure that the FBI got to him first. It was about all I could do to stop myself running out of old Cuthbert's place – and probably confirm his suspicions as I did so. "Okay, so I'll see you next month," I said, heading for the door.

"Sure, Robbie, but one more thing," he called.

"What's that?"

"'Bout the fella who was shot by Darlene. I don't suppose they found his car parked outside the Fenton place, did they?"

"I couldn't tell you."

"See, I had a feeling that there was someone else outside in the car with him. Now, if I'm right, what sort of man would drive off and leave his buddy lying in a pool of blood? That's what got me thinking that this fella who got shot wasn't totally straight, if you understand me, and that Darlene Fenton might've done this Peter Foster a favour."

"You never know," I said.

Mosquitos were looking for a meal from me as I parked behind my rented house. I checked that Calvin had cleaned up as I had told him before I headed over to his place. Calvin looked relieved to see me when I entered his kitchen. "Hungry, Robbie?"

The smell put my stomach rumbling. "I could only manage half a horse."

"You'll have to do with cow, man, 'cause it's oxtail I'm cookin tonight." He saved me asking the question that was on my lips when he went on, "An' no need to worry, I fixed up everythin good. The only thing I didn't do was get you another mattress. Robbie, I know this ain't my business an' all, but I'm worried fo you. First, these guys follow you an' now there's another one shot an' it got me wonderin if they was linked up somehow."

"Did you hear anythin about how that man arrived at the Fentons' place?"

"Funny you should ax that. Word is that the man was with another guy who jus drove off when Darlene opened up with the shotgun. I heard on the radio that the police is axin for the man to come forward, that he must've panicked, or some such, an' that he ain't gots nuthin to be worried about. I thought to myself, shit, that man ain't steppin forward 'cause they was up to no good. That's wha I think. Man, you don't have to say, 'cause I'm only lookin out fo you, but is there any reason why a group of guys might be tryna find you?"

I thought then it was best to keep Calvin on side somehow, if only so he remained vigilant. "That woman, the one with the fancy car, I was seein," I replied, "it turns out she's already with someone, some rich guy who is pretty pissed about it."

". . . Hey, yo private life ain't none-a my business. I was jus worried, that's all."

"Don't worry about me, Calvin, just keep your mind on what you have to do. Thanks for takin care of my place."

"Man, you ain't the one who should be thankin anybody. Robbie, as I was scrubbin that floor I kept thinkin that if I hadn't gone over to yo place then . . . y'know."

"I know," I said, "but, as a friend once said to me, if your auntie had balls she'd be your uncle. You can keep sayin 'if' for the rest of your life but it won't change one damn thing. All we can do is make the best of *what is*, right?"

I felt a hypocrite over the advice I offered him – but did not follow myself. Calvin merely compressed his lips into something like a smile. "I guess you're right," he said. "Anyways, you had better clean up 'cause dinner's 'bout ready."

I sucked the bones and mopped the plate with a piece of bread, before sighing contentedly. "Calvin, next to my mother's, that was the best oxtail I've ever eaten. Hey, I even feel moved to do the washin up – it must be somethin to do with the hormones an' the rest of the shit they put into those animals."

"No need," he laughed. "One extra plate ain't gonna make no difference to me." He looked out to the screen door and saw his dog's tail wagging furiously. "Ol' Hercules will do his level best to see if you left anythin on those bones," he said. "Say, why don't you go sit yoself down in the front room an' I'll bring in some coffee an' cookies."

I looked anxiously from his front window for a sign of anyone snooping around my place and took in a deep breath to ease the tension in my chest. It occurred to me how anxiety had taken its toll over the years but I had perfected disguising any outward signs of what it was doing to me. Mostly, I coped by imagining a day, then a week, then a month, then a year into the future and how I would look back and see any trouble in its true perspective: it was all only temporary. My house looked perfectly tranquil; a bit like me, it betrayed nothing of what had gone on inside.

Thoughts of the man shot by Darlene Fenton had me turning

on the TV for news of his condition and to find out anything that might give me a clue about his identity, although I remained quite certain that he had been working for the British secret services. Such was my shifting priorities, that it was only while I waited for the bulletin to begin did I also think about the possibility of any report of Little J Moses going missing. I sat in an old armchair and looked around the sparsely furnished room. A sadness went through me as I saw how little Calvin had. It wasn't just the lack of furniture: where were all his friends; and where was his family? Calvin cut a solitary figure. Vonette's statement that I did not appreciate his predicament as a black man in this part of the world returned to me. He hardly ever talked of friends or family, or, indeed, of anyone except for the guys he worked with. He had once briefly talked about his life before the orphanage: the death of his mother; his father's abandonment of the family home; and that he had been raised by his grandmother until she died when he was nine. He had never mentioned aunts, uncles, or cousins. Later on, Calvin referred to poor schooling, which was only enough to get him a dead-end job in a lumber yard.

I could relate to his loss and a poor education. Despite already being able to read at the age of five, I had left my mother at the school gates to face a world of preconceptions and prejudice. And yet it took racism, in all its forms, another twenty years to reduce my ambitions into something that revolved merely around survival. By that time I had a son and, hoping that the world would become a more tolerant place as he grew into a young man, I invested my ambitions in him.

My hopes seemed misplaced now. Maybe John Hunter had been right when, during one of our many disagreements, he had said to me that as black men living in a white world we had much more in common than I would admit to him, that our patterns of thought, our aspirations, the way we judged others as well as ourselves, had been moulded by a dominant, white culture. But whatever the true causes, many of my own ambitions were destined to remain unfulfilled the day I chose to walk the path of violence. "Here's yo coffee," said Calvin.

My thoughts broken, I took the mug and smiled at him as he sat in the other torn armchair. I was thinking about what it would be like to be Calvin's age again and about all the things I would do differently.

"Sumpin wrong, Robbie?"

"Nah," I chucked softly. "I was just thinkin 'bout some stuff." I took a taste of the coffee and tried not to grimace as its bitterness coated my tongue. He looked at me expectantly but I did not want to elaborate. For a while he kept his lips busy on the rim of his mug and I could tell that he was trying to choose his moment to speak.

"Robbie," he said at last, "I'm worried . . ."

"About Moses?"

"Well, sorta. But I'm worried 'cause I don't give a damn 'bout wha happened to him. I was brought up religious, if y'know wha I'm sayin, an' part of me is thinkin that I should be remorseful or sumpin. But I don't, I don't feel nuthin like that an' I'm gettin kinda worried, like some kinda guilt will wash over me an' drown me later on. . . Have you ever killed anyone, Robbie? I know it's a strange question to ax someone but fo some reason I have a feelin you might know wha I'm goin through right now."

The last person to ask me a similar question was Natasha. I sucked in a breath. "No," I lied, "no, I've never killed anyone. But my friend Errol, the one I told you about, he once killed a man."

Despondency overtook a certain expectation in Calvin's face and brought back the memories of Errol's trauma after we had left the Jamaican gangster lying dead in a stinking bathroom. Although he had only put bullets into the dead body I had dragged out from a bath of cold water, Errol's mind had been almost paralyzed by the enormity of what we had done. On the other hand, I had been clear about what we had to do next and I reminded him of another of our boxing coach's adages. "Discipline is everythin," I had told Errol, gripping his shoulder and shaking him. "Stay disciplined, guy, an' we're safe." Truth was, we were never safe from that day.

"How did Errol react?" Calvin asked.

I looked him in the eyes and decided this was no time to respond completely honestly. "Mostly the same as you. Like you, he didn't kill the man for any gain for himself. The guy he killed was a dog turd on the sole of society, a no-good bastard who was messin up a whole community. All Errol did was to give nature a helpin hand an' make a bit more room for the good people. Calvin, this guy Moses was about to commit rape, an' you said it yourself, he got what was comin to him. Don't worry 'bout him no more, concentrate on you an' Vonette stayin safe."

101

He nodded and said, "She called earlier. She couldn't say much over the phone but she told me people in his office have decided to tell the cops but say nuthin to the media in case he turns up. Folks are sayin that he was depressed an' shit 'bout not gettin the nomination. They say they's gonna start draggin the river if he don't show soon."

I drank the coffee, mostly because enough had been said about Moses and I had a feeling that if the conversation continued in the same vein it might degenerate into speculation about whether the cops might track back to here. I figured if that happened it would be down to Vonette, and not Calvin, and hopefully I would be long gone by then. The news finally came on and we both turned our attention to the television. The bulletin started with Darlene Fenton. I was curious to see what she looked like, for we had never met – and such was her reputation that I did not feel as if I could knock on her door and introduce myself. As she was led to the court I saw that she was slim, with short dark hair and nothing like the stereotypical frumpy peroxide blonde I had imagined. "She looks a cool character," I said.

"Could be that she's numb," Calvin suggested. "I know all 'bout that."

"I don't see any sign of Wayne."

"Man, he's probably gone off into the woods with his kids an' enough artillery for a small army. I ain't jokin with you, Robbie. I'd bet my week's pay that he thinks that the man at his door was a government agent who came spyin on his activities with the militia. Him an' Darlene have got a conspiracy theory for every damn thing an' they reckon it's the government that's behind most of them, includin using cruise missiles made to look like planes on 9/11. The crazy red-neck sumbitch. "

I sucked at my teeth and turned back to the TV. Using the media throng on the steps of the court as a backdrop, a newscaster with lacquered blonde hair and a face made expressionless by botox, reported that the man Darlene Fenton had shot had died an hour before the hearing commenced and now the charge was one of murder. His identity had not been released but a spokesman for the sheriff's office confirmed that he was a foreign national. The bulletin concluded with the news that, despite her attorney's best efforts, Darlene was not going to be sleeping in her own bed for quite a while.

Calvin came with me over to my house once the bulletin had finished so he could be there as I inspected the job he had made of cleaning up. To the naked eye it was impossible to see any suggestion of what had taken place in my bedroom less than twenty-four hours before. I grunted my approval but I figured it was the least either he or his sister should have done in the circumstances. "Thanks, Calvin. It looks as if you did a thorough job. Right, I'm turnin in for the night," I said as a prompt for him to leave.

"Well, it shouldn't have happened here in the first place. I'm sorry it did . . ."

"I said before, what's done is done. Just keep your eyes on what you have to do now, okay?"

"Sho thing," he said, as he turned for the kitchen. I walked out to the yard with him. "An' remember yo friend Danny is turnin up tomorra," he said. "Man, he looked so dirty it could be that he's joined Wayne Fenton's militia an' is hidin out with him in the woods."

"I don't he's the type Wayne would want," I replied.

Walking back to his house, he called back, "I'll have to take yo word fo that. I don't see wha you two have in common, I really don't."

That last remark was down to a mutual antagonism between the two. They had not met very often but Danny had no patience with Calvin and thought of him as too inquisitive and anxious for approval. Danny had the ability to unsettle anyone who was unsure of themselves and Calvin had summed him up as arrogant. Arrogant and white was about as bad a mixture as Calvin could imagine.

It was not only the memory of Little J's body in my bed but also the stench of bleach which had me heading for the second bedroom, with little expectation of a good night's sleep.

13

DANNY HAD TOLD CALVIN that he would call some time during tomorrow and as I lay down to sleep I asked myself, when the time came, if I would really trade his life for the chance of a future with my mother and son, or would I, if fate allowed, take a gamble for a new type of life with Cristina and Goretti? But my chances of disappearing again, without Danny's expertise, were slim. America was a place with millions of people called 'illegal aliens' but if I were to work and drive about the country with any degree of safety I would need Danny's knowhow and the type of false documentation which he could get his hands on. I closed my eyes while cursing my constant changes of mind and my confused feelings for Cristina. As I tried to imagine a future with her, my mind went back to New York, to when Danny had warned me that a man with secrets who got involved with a woman would eventually find himself in trouble. My relationship with Natasha should have been enough for me now to pay heed to his advice.

Mitch had questioned me about Danny's life in New York. He seemed to know a lot and referred to places where he had worked and the names of people he had mixed with. "Maguire," he said, "seems to have cut himself off from the decent side of humanity."

"Not really."

"No? Walker, your friend is a cold-blooded killer, who is Georgia to kill a lot more people."

Mitch lit himself another cigarette and began to pace the room again. "I don't see a mention of any woman in his life," he said. "Is it that he doesn't feel like me and you, or have needs like we do, Walker?"

Danny's own relationships with women was the one topic he had steered clear of until our third Christmas in New York. I'd guessed that he'd had a few but, over the last few years, it was mostly hiding from law enforcement agencies that had preoccupied his mind, rather than any affairs of the heart. So it was something of a shock when he told me that he had once loved and lost – and it had been too painful an experience for him ever to want to try again. Thinking I had found out all there was to know about him, I was astonished when Danny told me that he had been engaged to be married before I had even met him in Bubby's boxing gym when we were both young men. He told me that he been engaged at nineteen to a girl who was two years younger – he never mentioned her name – and that they were parents four months later. Not long after the birth of their daughter he left Belfast for England. "That's why I admire how you stuck in there and kept your wee Nathan," he'd said, after a fourth belt of whiskey. "But I knew I wasn't cut out for fatherhood – or marriage, for that matter. After a couple of years I went over home to see her and the baby only to find out that they were shacked up with some fella." He took another sip and let the whiskey run around his teeth before going on, "Ach, he seemed a decent type; he's been a good father to the girl, the only father she's ever known, and I suppose he's done a way better job than I would have managed."

There was hurt in his eyes but I had to ask why he'd never before mentioned that he had a daughter. He pulled at his lower lip. "I was never one for the Bible, Robbie," he said in a soft voice, "but I always liked that Samson and Delilah story. I never read it though, you understand, but I did see the film with that Victor Mature fella. What it boils down to is that a woman can respect and resent a man's strength all at the same time, but once she sees you weak she just resents you. I was young, messed up in the head because of all this new responsibility, and I told her something that should've been kept a secret. I tell you, mate, the look she gave me made me feel two inches tall, so it did. Once they give you that look it's all over because they'll never see you in the same way ever again. The following morning I caught the boat for England. It's stuff that's hard to talk about and I tell you now that I won't be mentioning it again."

Danny was true to his word and firmly closed the door to that period of his life. I had never known a person who was as disciplined as Danny. Even amongst a crowd he would remain a solitary figure. He led a simple life and followed simple rules and, as he himself had said, followed a code only very few shared.

Perhaps, like me, he did look back with regret but, except for that last time as he sat at my kitchen table, he had never shown any sign of it. He was determined and once his mind was set, he doggedly kept to whatever choice he'd made. When he had decided to avenge his father, he did not deviate from the courses of actions which had led to the deaths of several people. His single-mindedness was in contrast to my indecision and made me feel as small and inade-quate as when I walked the sidewalks of New York.

* * *

We left the station still holding hands, with Natasha doing most of the talking. Only a little of it registered. There were mentions of initials and numbers I did not understand: CD4 count, AZT, words like 'viral load', 'antiretroviral' and 'undetectable'. Maybe it was because I hadn't yelled out in revulsion, nor ran away in fear, that she continued to talk to me as if I understood.

"All it means is that we have to be careful."

I stopped walking. "Careful?"

"I mean, it isn't as though we'd be doing anything differently from what we should be doin in the first place. It's just that you know my status now."

The eyes that looked up into mine communicated that what she had just shared with me had taken an unquantifiable amount of trust. Yet, she had given it all to a man who did not exist. She had conjured up and then projected onto me virtues I had probably never possessed. I was an imposter. Awkwardly, I said, "I've an early start tomorrow. Will I see you at Beanie's after work?"

Her thin smile conveyed confusion and then disappointment, but within a moment she had rallied and seemed to convince herself that everything she felt for me was reciprocated. She reached up and put a hand on the back of my neck. "Pete," she said, "I think I've fallen head over heels in love with you."

She pulled my head down and planted her pretty mouth onto mine. My lips instantly became tight and unyielding as I felt them coated by her saliva – a bodily fluid swimming with a deadly virus, or so I thought right then. Were my lips cracked? Had my mouth ulcer fully healed? Jesus, was this woman trying to infect me? I angrily pulled her hands away and wiped my mouth on my sleeve. If I had driven a knife into Natasha's heart right then, I doubted if I could have hurt her any more. She staggered back, "I – I'm sorry," she said. "I pushed you too soon. I should have waited. I'm sorry, Pete, I'm so sorry."

I watched her turn and hurry away until she was enveloped by the bustle of a busy sidewalk. I didn't try to catch her. Instead, I ran back to my apartment and spent several minutes in front of the mirror inspecting and washing my mouth. What had I been doing all these months, inveigling my way into Natasha's life, living out a lie and allowing her to invest in me such a special trust? What the hell had I been playing at? My next thought was to get myself tested as soon as possible. I dabbed my face with a towel and caught sight of my reflection. It was a moment of intense detestation. I hated what I saw. I hated the person I had pretended to be. Even more, I began to hate the person I really was.

The tests came back negative but my relief soon turned to bitter regret as I thought about how I had reacted to Natasha's kiss. For two months I spent my evenings in Beanie's restaurant, with the insane hope that she would turn up again. It was another example of my messed-up thinking: how could I have expected that she would want to lay eyes on me ever again, after the way I had treated her? I was haunted by what I had done and agonized about whether I should try and find her.

We did meet again, after I sent her a bunch of flowers with a note in which I begged to see her one more time. For five weeks there was no response but then one day the guy behind the counter at Beanie's handed me a note. It simply said that she would see me the following night and if it wasn't convenient I was to leave a message at the centre.

All the words I had rehearsed over many nights left me as soon as she sat down at the table for two. She saw how I was struggling and in another show of kindness she told me that no apologies, nor explanations, were necessary. I reached over and held her hand. She looked down at our interlocked fingers and I waited for a smart comment about whether I needed go to the washroom to scrub my hands. But Natasha said, "I'm not hungry. So how about if we find a club an' do some dancin?"

I knew a place that played Jamaican-style lovers' rock. It was in a basement of an old brownstone in the Bronx and I was reminded of the 'blues parties' I had attended as a young guy in England. In the dim light we held each other and danced until the early hours. Natasha rested her head on my chest and draped her arms around my shoulders as we moved in slow, rhythmic gyrations. I sensed how much she wanted to be held, how much she needed a tender touch. And as we moved to the music maybe we both fantasized about how things might have been. But when the music stopped and reality returned, the guilt gripped my heart once more.

The apartment I was renting was only two blocks away, so we walked to it, picking up some food and a bottle of wine on the way. When we had finished eating, Natasha smiled at me and said, "That was the most enjoyable night I've had for a long, long time. Thank you, Pete."

I took her by the hand and she questioned me with a look before I led her to my bed, where we lay down and held each other. For an age we just looked out of the apartment's window. There was not much to see except for an identical window across the street and in my mind I turned over excuses for why I was not trying to undress either of us.

"Natasha," I said, "I don't have any . . .you know, an' that means that, um, nothin can go on, if you understand me."

She laughed quietly. "I *understand*, Pete. It's okay, really. Wrong time of the month, if you understand me."

I kissed her, thinking she was only making it easier for me. As a jumble words began to gather in my mind, I wished that she did not have to call me Pete and, most of all, that she was not HIV positive. To relieve some of the tension I let out a heavy sigh, and she asked what was on my mind. Half truthfully I told her I was thinking of, and regretting, her HIV status. "How the hell did it happen, Natasha?" I blurted out. "I mean, you're workin at a women's health centre." I had not intended to be so blunt but all she did was hug me and murmur that she was tired and that we should sleep for a while. But all the guilt-drenched words and emotions coursing through me would not let me sleep. "Natasha," I whispered, "that night, when we came back from Coney Island, it's been on my mind every day."

Hugging me again, she said, "It's okay, baby, it's okay."

"No, it ain't, Natasha, it ain't." I paused momentarily, still deliberating if I should give vent to all the turmoil inside of me. I made up my mind and drew a breath. "See, you trusted me, you were sharin somethin very special . . . But you were sharin it with a guy who doesn't exist. Someone who's been livin a lie, someone who was lyin to you all the time."

Her arm around me relaxed and I felt her head move so she could see my face. "Lyin, Pete?"

"It's not Pete."

"What do you mean, not Pete?"

"My real name is Robbie Walker. I'm – I'm on the run from the authorities in England."

She pulled away from me and sat up. I remained where I was and stared at her back, trying to imagine the expression on her face. "Robbie?" she said vaguely, as if she were struggling with the notion that I had another identity. "Robbie. I'm not sure if I like that name . . .Why are you on the run?"

At that moment all that mattered to me was telling the truth – and in doing so I would somehow make amends for the way I had deceived her. I began by telling her about my mind-set as an angry young man; in an exercise of self-justification I told her that I had been sickened by the life I led back then, sickened by the way my destiny had been shaped by the bigotry of others. I told her about how, when two innocent black men had died during their arrests in separate incidents, something inside of me snapped. Although I did not know either of them, no man who has ever been called "black" can view as a total stranger someone who's been labelled in a similar way. With my friends Errol Morgan and Gilbert 'Hanimal' Peters, I had set out to avenge those two deaths by killing a cop.

"So," she said, "you're on the run because you killed a cop?"

It all seemed so terribly wrong now and it was some time before I could answer her. "No, we didn't kill a cop," I said quietly. "Me an' Errol ended up killin a Jamaican guy who was a crack dealer an' a police informer. Kinda ironic, I suppose, that we killed another black man. Then Errol an' Hanimal got killed in a car smash an' it kinda brought me back to my senses. But some years later my son Nathan was kidnapped after I punched the son of a guy who ran a gang of very bad men. A friend of mine, an Irish guy, was in England at the time, lookin for the men who had killed his father in Ireland. I asked him an' his friends to help me get Nathan back. A lotta people got killed, a lotta people, Natasha, includin a British MI5 man an' a twelve-year-old boy who got caught in the crossfire. I got my son Nathan back, only to lose him again because I had to leave him behind . . . That's how I ended up in America an' meetin you."

I stared at her shape in the darkness and listened to her soft breaths, waiting for her next question. I willed her to say something – anything – but after a time she simply lay down next to me again without uttering another word. Part of me wanted to explain my actions, excuse what I had done; another part was scared that I had already said too much. After taking my arm as a pillow, she turned onto her side with her back toward me. She sobbed quietly long into the dark hours and her tears dripped onto my forearm. I said nothing, and in a strange way I hoped that she spared a few tears for me.

When I woke Natasha was gone but I discovered that she had answered my question about her HIV status. On my table was a letter she had written just after our day in Coney Island but had never sent. She wrote that she had been infected when she was a much younger and impressionable woman and long before she had started working at the health centre. The man who had given her the virus was a tutor at an evening class she attended. He described himself as a nihilist and she, too young to understand what he meant, thought him sophisticated. She became infatuated and did not resist him. Natasha eventually broke off their relationship and it was some time later that she found out that she had become infected. The man rejected her assertion that she had caught the virus from him, and refused to submit himself to a test. My smarting eyes only skimmed the remainder of the letter, as much of it was too painful to read, but when it finished with expressions of love and regret I could not hold back the tears.

I put away her letter and thought that we had seen each other for the last time but I would meet Natasha again, and I would commit an act, the memory of which would never leave me.

14

I WOKE WITH THE thought that this was my day of reckoning, my day of decision, and the pressure was building until it was too much for me to stay in bed. An hour earlier than usual, I decided to make myself some coffee before I headed to Harry's Bar and Grill for breakfast.

I checked my watch – but it wasn't my watch, and I wished the way I'd come by it had been just a bad dream. The fleshy face and the words of the man called Mitch came back to me. It was more than a watch and a transmitter with a button: it represented temptation, betrayal and possibly death. My mom used to tell me that no one sets out to make the wrong decision, that they all seem to be the correct ones at the time and only hindsight informs us if we had made the right call. During my lifetime I had encountered people who had become so fearful of making the wrong choice, that they tried not to make any decision at all but attempted to leave it all up to fate, or the actions of others. Until now, I had held such indecisive people in contempt but now I thought differently as I prayed that something would happen so I would never have to see Danny Maguire again.

While I drank some coffee I wandered to the front room. The light was still on at Calvin's place; he must have had a bad night, too. I thought back to my first estimation of him and recalled sensing a certain vulnerability about him that I couldn't quite define. He had a man's body but had retained something of the orphan within him. Vonette was the much the stronger of the two, and she dominated him. Looking out at his house, I had the feeling that I was about to abandon Calvin. But I had done all I could for him and knew that he would have to come to terms with the killing of Little J Moses all alone – or else he would never be truly reconciled with what he had done.

My forty-eight hours of sensory bombardment and deprivation at the hands of Mitch meant that what I recalled of the experience only came to me randomly and sometimes out of sequence. "Have you any idea why Maguire brought you all the way down here?" he asked. "Didn't it ever cross your mind how come he didn't leave you in New York? Don't get any sentimental idea it was about loyalty, Walker. He was keeping you close so, if ever there was a hitch in his plans, he would have someone around who'd do what he asked without question."

"Plans? What plans?"

"From the intercepts we've put together, we know he's joined forces with a foreign terrorist group to commit an outrage in an American city."

"Bullshit! You're wrong, man, Danny might not be in love with the place but he's got no argument with America. An' what do you mean by 'outrage'?"

"A massive no-warning bomb in an, as yet, unidentified city. We managed to disrupt his plans and that's why he's disappeared – and that's how come we're confident he will have to turn to you to help him out. Cooperate, Walker, and you're not only helping yourself and your family, you're also saving hundreds of innocent lives. "

I did not believe Mitch then – and I probably did not believe him now – but the slim possibility that it might be true began to worm its way into my consciousness. I pushed the thought away, finished my coffee, and left the house.

My attitude had to change, my heart had to harden, if, later on, I were to make one of the most difficult decisions of my life. As I had done once before when I had travelled with my friend Errol to eradicate a crack-dealer, I had begun to steel myself, preparing my mind so that I would be able to deliver Danny Maguire to the FBI when the opportunity arose. Yet, on catching sight of my reflection in the windshield of my car, I could tell that the process was not yet complete – that there was still an element of reluctance within me.

As I sat in the car a voice said, "Don't look behind you. Start the car and drive on to town as normal."

The shock of hearing his voice jolted me out of my seat and almost had me hitting my head off the car's roof. I glanced in the rearview mirror and saw the top of a head peeking out from under a blanket I kept on the backseat. He smelled awful. Regaining my breath I asked, "Where the hell have you been, Danny?"

"Running for my fecking life, so I have. Just crack on a while, Robbie, head for the car park at the rear of Harry's as usual and I'll tell you all about it."

I looked at the watch, but I had been caught unprepared and my hand found the gearshift instead. Once we were heading down the road toward the highway he sat up. The car gathered speed, and the flickering pine trees became as blurred as my thoughts. I looked into the mirror again and wondered if I could push that button which would alert Mitch. Danny had three or four days' growth of beard and a body odour to match. He told me he had been staying in the woods and had made his way back to my place on two occasions but he did not bother to ask where I had been when he'd called.

"I suppose you heard about the shootin at the Fentons'," I said. "It happened just a few hours after the last time you were at my place."

Irritable, he said, "I've had too much on my plate to find time to tune into the news, Robbie."

"Well, I only mention it 'cause the guy Darlene shot was lookin for a Pete Foster. His partner disappeared an' left him to bleed. Would those guys have anythin to do with you playin boy scouts in the woods?"

He drew a breath and held it for a moment. "Christ, no. No, I wouldn't think so," he muttered. He scratched his bristled jaw. "Then, how come you're still here?"

"I'm waitin for you. You remember what Bubby used to say about panic when we were trainin?"

"It only makes a bad situation worse."

"Right. That guy's dead an' his partner's gone. Those guys weren't police or nothin – they weren't American, either. They came to do a number on me, an' I figure whoever sent them would reckon that here's the last place I'd be. Anybody with sense would've gone a long time ago."

It took him a few seconds to take all that in. Pensive, he said, "Dead on, Robbie, dead on. You're one in a million, mate, because most people would have fecked off and I'd bet you're right about what people would assume about where you are now." His brow creased, obviously calculating something else.

"Then you'd better tell me what the hell's been goin on with you," I said.

Danny seemed surprised by my question but gathered his thoughts in a moment. He leaned forward and, in a low, conspiratorial tone, told me about a meeting with José Ruiz. By the way he spoke I knew Mitch had told me the truth: Danny really had been plotting a terrorist operation. I glanced at the watch around my wrist again – but I needed to hear what he had to say before I made up my mind about pushing the button.

"See, Rob," he whispered, "there's stuff I've never told you about because I wanted to protect you. I dragged you into something once before, and you've been paying for it ever since, so this time I kept quiet and got on with it without telling you anything. I was only thinking of you, mate."

Angrily, I gripped the wheel and almost yelled at him that I knew what he was up to. I could have pushed the button at that instant but I made the mistake of glancing at the mirror again and seeing

Danny's eyes and knowing that they would follow me into my dreams. I looked back to the road and forced myself to breathe normally. "So what happened, Danny? What happened to José?"

"Him and me were having a meeting out somewhere quiet," he began shakily, "an' we walked straight into a setup. Six fellas jumped out at us with shooters. Christ, neither of us was tooled up. By pure luck I got away into the woods and I just kept running. The fella you knew as José was killed, and I guess they put him into the river to make it look like an accident." He met my accusing eyes in the mirror, and went on, "Yeah, I know what you're thinking; it's hardly original."

"You said *the fella I knew as José Ruiz*. Cut the shit, guy," I snapped, "an' tell me who he was an' what the hell you guys were plannin."

"It doesn't matter what his real name was, Robbie, but he was a top operator with the Farc. He came up from Colombia to take on something big, and I was asked by top people to move here and give him a hand. I can't say what's happening, Robbie, you know, everything's on a need-to-know basis."

"What's happenin? Does that mean that you're still goin ahead with whatever it is?"

After a long pause, he said, "That depends on a lot of stuff. Certain things might or might not happen now one of Farc's top men has been taken out. But that's all I can tell you, because I swear I'm not going to involve you in any of this, if I can help it. You got me, Robbie? It'll all be over in a few days, and then me and you will get the feck out of here. All right, mate?"

"Then why didn't you leave me in New York, eh?" I snarled, thinking of Mitch and his plans. "If you wanted to keep me out of it, why have me come down here with you? It sounds like shit, man, just shit you're givin me!"

His hand lightly touched my shoulder and then withdrew. Quietly, he said, "Because you and me are friends, Rob, because we're the closest thing to family either of us has left. You know, you went through a pretty bad spell during that last year in New York. I couldn't have left you like that."

We didn't say much else until we neared Harry's. I didn't want Danny to say any more about friendship, still less remind me of what he had done for me when I was tottering on the brink of insanity.

114

I told myself he had locked his mind onto doing something terrible and that he would do or say anything to achieve his objective. I had seen it happen before in him – and in myself. I thought then that I *could* push the button but this was not the right time.

"Park by that truck over there," he said, as I turned into the parking lot behind the diner. "I'll get out a few minutes after you, crawl underneath it and pop out on the other side."

Betrayal slithering into my mind, I said, "So, when are we meetin up again, Danny?"

"How about some time tonight? I've got to get myself a bit of a shave and shower. There's a powerful stench coming off me, I know." He laughed and his hand was on my shoulder again. "Every Sunday I like to put a wet flannel between my legs, whether I need it or not, and I badly needed it last Sunday, so I did."

I did not join in with his laughter. My heart began to beat a little faster. "Where do we meet?"

"I'll try and make it back here. Say, be here for eleven and wait in the car for me."

"Cool," I said.

"Before you head off," he said, "be careful, Robbie. Before he died, your old foreman thought there might be people around the factory keeping an eye on him. But, for all I know, it could have been bastards who he trusted most who set him up. Just watch yourself, okay? Trust no one."

While I was collecting my overalls, Colin the electrician approached me and said that if he were in my shoes, he would not be working here after what had happened to Jack Kirby. "I hear he's in hospital, with a pair of balls that swelled up overnight," he said. "Now, you know, Robbie, that I ain't got nothing against black folks myself, you understand, but there's people around here who won't take kindly to what you did."

"You mean shuttin up a loudmouth?"

He pushed out his bottom lip. "A white loudmouth quieted by a black man, that's viewed as something different. I tell you straight, if Billy Joe Watson hadn't laid down the law to Kirby, I doubt if you would have made it to work today. Robbie, you come across as a fairly level-headed fella, England being a civilized country and all, so, if you don't mind, I'm gonna give you a piece of free advice."

While I appreciated Colin's sentiments, I thought his tone of delivery could have been a little less patronizing. "Thanks, Colin," I said sarcastically.

"Make it two pieces, I'm feeling generous."

"I'm all ears."

"Vary your travel time and route to and from here. And watch out for Chuck Woodlow, because him and Jack Kirby are good buddies."

Stripped of their claws and feathers, the headless turkeys were conveyed to the waiting 'cut-up' workers. Dressed in chain-mail protective clothing, they looked like medieval foot soldiers. Large segments of the birds were carved away and tossed onto fast-moving conveyor belts to take the meat for further processing. Hoots of discontent went up from the workers as I made my way to the control panel which regulated the conveyor system.

Woodlow, on his first morning as foreman, hadn't issued any threats, nor said anything about his friend Jack Kirby, but he had let it be known just how he felt when he'd told me to increase the speed of the line. It was a move which was designed not to do anything for my popularity with my fellow workers.

At some other time the curses and derisive hooting could have affected me but it took only a glance at my watch to remind me that there much more important matters for me to consider. I thought about Danny's warning to trust no one, and, as I headed to the canteen for a midmorning coffee, I wondered if the glances from around the conveyor belt were about more than resentment at the increased workload.

The hoots abruptly changed into lecherous howls. I looked around and saw that the new quality-control worker, a young blonde woman, was nearby. She was also on her way to the canteen for the morning break. I was conscious of her walking close to me, but I felt too washed out to make conversation.

The lack of chinking cutlery and burbling chatter of mealtimes made the canteen eerily quiet. There was only a handful of people around, and Myrtle and Lilli were in the kitchen, preparing lunch. I poured myself a coffee and sat well away from anyone else. I was rubbing my sore eyes, thinking about what lay ahead, and what I might have to do before the day was through, when a voice roused

116

me. It took a few moments for my eyes, and mind, to refocus. "Sorry?" I said.

The blonde woman said again, "Is your name Robbie?"

Still not fully with her, I nodded.

She extended a hand and, as I took it, said, "Is it all right if I sit here? Lilli said you might be able to help me. By the way, my name's Kelly, I'm . . ."

"New in quality-control."

"Why, yes," she said. She sat down and gave me a well-practised smile, which I thought could mean anything the recipient wanted; in this case I took it to mean that she was flattered that I knew of her. "I'm going to England next month and Lilli said you might be able to recommend areas that would be worth visiting." She swept some of her hair behind an ear and let her fingers linger, while her eyelashes fluttered flirtatiously.

I was not in the mood for playing and said, "I'm afraid you've got the wrong man, Kelly. It's been a long time since I was in England. Anyway, from what I can remember, the part of England that I knew best is far from bein rollin meadows an' quaint villages. Definitely not the sort of place you'd want to hitchhike through."

"Oh," she said, clearly unsettled by my offhandedness and maybe puzzled by my reaction. "Would you know of any . . ."

"Get yourself a tour guide when you get there, it's much safer that way."

Her cheeks reddened slightly and she stood up. "Thank you for your help," she said through gritted teeth. I wasn't sure but I thought she muttered "asshole" as she walked away.

15

LIKE A VENOM RUNNING through my veins, mistrust had left me well and truly poisoned by the time I finished work. After my less than cordial chat with the woman called Kelly, the day had gone by even more slowly than usual, mostly because of my growing suspicions which interpreted every gesture and glance my way as possibly disguising underlying malevolent intentions. Even when Chuck Woodlow gave me an easier time than I expected, I took it that he was trying to lull me into a false sense of security. And when John Hunter came over and offered a congratulatory handshake for putting Jack Kirby in his place, I reacted by saying that he could stick his hand where the sun did not shine. I was not sure of his motives but it occurred to me that this unprecedented friendly gesture was, at the very least, an attempt at assuaging the hostility between us, which had come about with my discovery that he was in cahoots with Miguel, the contaminated meat thief. Danny's early morning appearance and his warning to trust no one had unsettled me and I wondered if I were slipping into the type of paranoia which had gripped me while in New York.

If I had been unsettled at work, I became a lot more so as I drove home. I was thinking about how it was exactly a week since I had been lured into Mitch's trap when a set of headlights flashed in my rearview mirror, just before a car overtook me. It passed and I caught a glimpse of Mitch's grim face. He raised an arm as he drew level and tapped his wristwatch with a forefinger. His car disappeared into the distance as I screamed obscenities at him, before I wondered if I had been under surveillance during the morning drive to work. I couldn't discount it, but I didn't think that I had been spotted in Danny's company. My mind then turned to thinking about how I could avoid being detected when I went to the parking lot behind Harry's later on. But I was reacting exactly in the manner Mitch wanted: his sudden appearance had been to sow doubt, to make me feel uncertain about when I was actually being watched. His tactics were working.

Once safely indoors, I put five of a six-pack into the fridge to cool. Before I opened a can, I turned to the sink and thrust my arm under the tap and applied most of a bottle of washing-up liquid in a futile attempt to slip the watch over my hand. It wasn't the first time I'd tried. My fingernails had never been so clean, but the watch stayed firmly around my wrist.

Frustrated, I sat at the table with a warm beer in my hand and a pool of sudsy water on the kitchen floor. I weighed up my chances of success if I were to make a run for Chicago to try and find Nathan . . .The first place Mitch would station his fellow agents . . . And Danny and countless other people might be dead by then. I snarled to myself that I would not allow any more arguments about going on the run: it would only make a very bad situation much worse. I would see Danny at eleven, but I still was not sure how I'd react when the time came to press that button.

I drank some more of the tepid beer, but it wasn't having the desired effect so I left the can on the table, collected the baseball bat, which I had begun to keep by my side while indoors, and went and lay down in the spare bedroom. I was mentally exhausted and soon nodded off, only to wake gradually, as if surfacing from dark depths, to the sound of someone knocking on my rear door. I heard Calvin call out but I could not bring myself to reply. After a few moments the noise stopped and I let out a relieved breath.

I must have dozed off once more and perhaps no more than a few seconds had elapsed before I was awoken again by the sound of the back door being forced open. In an instant my head was clear and I was out of the bed, clutching the baseball bat.

"Robbie!" hissed Calvin. "Where you at?"

I put the bat back against the wall and went out to him. "I was tryin to sleep," I said.

He furiously scratched the back of his head. "I was knockin at yo door a long time, man." There was urgency in his voice as he said, "You need to come with me now." I was about to tell him that I couldn't but he reached out and gripped my arm. "I'll explain in my car," he whispered impatiently. "It's yo white friend, Danny, he tol' me come git you."

This was not how I'd envisaged it. I had been building myself up for a meeting at Harry's, and imagined that while I drove there I would still be debating with myself over what to do. Calvin went to fetch his car while I went and put on some shoes. I waited by the back door, staring at the watch around my wrist. But rather than thinking about pushing the button, it occurred to me that Danny must be desperate to take such a chance by involving Calvin.

He pulled into my yard and wound down his window as the trunk flipped open. "He says you gots to travel in there for a while, jus a mile or two until there's no one else on the road."

I clambered in and pulled the lid to, but did not close it properly. We set off and I cursed every bump and pothole for what seemed a great deal more than two miles, until I felt the car swerve violently, then stop. I let the lid rise a little and saw that Calvin had turned onto a small side road. As I climbed out, I could not help recalling how the last journey of Little J Moses had been made in that same trunk.

I joined Calvin in the front of the car and asked where we were going. He was still agitated and didn't respond until we were on the main road and heading south. "A fuckin crossroads, man," he said bitterly, shifting gear, "between Tarry an' Cobbtown."

"Why?"

"How should I know? You's runnin out on me, Robbie, is that it?"

"Nah, guy," I lied, "I ain't goin no place."

"Then what's with this shit? You tell the white man what happened to Little J?"

His questions were like rapid fire and not making much sense to me. "I've said nothin about that to anyone, Calvin, so how about tellin me what Danny said."

"After work I got into my car, an' guess who was hidin in the back?" Calvin replied, his voice rising with every word. "Man, that mother frightened the shit outta me – I thought I was bein jacked by some crazy white boy fo sho. He had me drive him some place an' then he ax me to bring you to him. He said I wasn't to tell you where we was headin until you was in my car. He had a strange look in his eyes an' I can't figure out if he was scared outta his mind or jus fuckin crazy."

Empathizing with Calvin's shock at the manner of Danny's sudden appearance, I said, "He's probably crazy. But how long ago was this?"

"Man, jus now. I was doin some overtime to make up fo the time I missed. The last thing he tol' me was to drive straight to yo place an' said you had to come right away or he'd be gone."

Danny wasn't the sort of man to panic, and he wasn't easily scared but that he'd involved Calvin made me wonder what had happened since I had left him in the parking lot behind Harry's. Calvin was smarting and to break the fractious silence, I said, "Has Vonette been in contact?"

Almost petulant, he said, "I had a call from her today. She's comin down to see me soon but didn't say when exactly. The cops axed her 'bout the last time she saw Little J, an' they ain't been back to her since."

"Calvin, do you trust her?"

"Of course I do," he snapped. "You tryna make out she'd double-cross us or sumpin like that?"

"I'm not makin out anythin. I'm just wonderin how she's holdin up, that's all."

"Don't question her, man, Vonette's stronger than anyone I know. . . Look, I knows we owe you for wha you did, but don't diss the woman in my presence, man. I'm doin this for yo white-man friend 'cause of wha you did for us. An' jus like you ain't told a soul 'bout wha happened that night, you got my word that nuthin goin on now is gonna cross my lips to no one, not even Vonette."

I regretted having mentioned Vonette as her name was enough to make the atmosphere even more acrimonious. I had never seen Calvin like this. I understood his protective feelings toward his sister, but there was an extra edge to his anger. He obviously resented me for concealing the true extent of my friendship with Danny, and, as with so many things in this part of the USA, it was partly to do with race.

Strangely, it was our common skin colour which made our differing viewpoints more difficult for Calvin to come to terms with. In an attempt to further my argument about what makes up the essence of a human being, I had once asked Calvin whether he would rather be stranded on a desert island with a black man who held diametrically opposed views of how the world should be, or with a white man who shared most of his opinions. He looked at me blankly and then laughed as if I had asked a very stupid question. "The brother, of course," he replied. And that was where Calvin's difficulty in understanding me lay: in having a white man as a friend, whom I obviously trusted a great deal more than him, I was betraying not merely Calvin as an individual but a whole race. The insidious bigotry which had infected him – and many others I'd met – gave me yet another reason to leave the town of Petra without even a backward glance.

My mind was abruptly brought back to the watch: I should have pushed the button twice if I had intended to accept Mitch's offer but I convinced myself that I could put off my final decision for a little longer.

The car slowed. "There it is," said Calvin, pointing to a large, derelict house a little way ahead. The chain-link fence that had once surrounded it was mostly flattened or rusted away.

"I thought you said a crossroads."

"Well, this is the crossroads. You think the man gonna talk to you in the middle of the road?"

"How the hell did he find this place?"

"Why don't you ax him when you see him?" Calvin said. He turned into the long driveway, and the car began to lurch in and out of potholes.

From its size I guessed the house had once belonged to an 'old money' family like the Lavettes. The evening was still bright enough for me to see that its grandeur had long since faded and now it was probably home to racoons and all sorts of vermin. Calvin drove around to the rear of the building and stopped.

I told him to wait in the car. "I don't suppose he told you where he'd be?" I asked as I opened the door.

Calvin twisted his mouth. "Naw, he didn't," he answered with a shrug, "but there's a good chance he's on the other end of that flashlight." He gestured to one of the broken windows, through which I saw a beam of light moving.

I walked stiffly toward the ramshackle house. By the time I'd found a door the light had disappeared from my line of vision and I had to find my way inside in darkness. A sudden sound of a rodent scurrying along the floor had me catching my breath, which meant that I got a mouthful of acrid dust for my trouble. I coughed and spat until a beam of yellow light crept over the rubble and stopped at my feet.

"Danny?" I panted.

"'Bout ye, Robbie," he said, shining the flashlight into my face. Squinting against the glare, I saw that he held a .38 in his right hand. "I thought we were meetin at Harry's," I said.

"Change of plan."

"I gathered that much."

"The Calvin kid, can you trust him to keep his mouth shut?"

Danny did not have to tell me that if I answered in the negative that he would have no problem in going out and shooting Calvin right there and then. "He owes me somethin big. He ain't gonna say anythin."

"Good," Danny said evenly, putting the gun into a jacket pocket. "Did you take the batteries out of your phone?"

I said, "No need. The phone got broke. Now, do you intend to keep that torch in my face?" He grunted apologetically, and turned

122

it down toward the floor. "So," I said, "what's happened, man?"

It was hard to see the expression on his freshly shaven face, but as he pondered on his answer I heard angry air escaping from him like steam from a punctured boiler. While I waited, my pulse quickened and my guilt made me want to blurt out everything that had happened to me. I opened my mouth to confess but Danny spoke first. "Robbie," he said, "I told you that I don't want you involved in nothing I'm doing, so I'm having to tell you to leave Georgia right now, get away as far and as fast as you can. I mean go tonight. All I can tell you is that when me and José walked into that ambush it was part of a much bigger plan. I can't say what exactly. There must be a reason, that I haven't worked out yet, why they put him back into his car and made it look like an accident."

"Who's 'they'?"

"Not sure, mate, I'm not fecking sure. Maybe the CIA, the FBI, or maybe some agency I don't even know about."

"And what do they want?"

"Obviously to stop what José and his comrades are planning."

"Then come with me, an' we'll leave together."

"I can't do that, Rob. I've got to stay here and finish something. You go now before they link us and grab hold of you."

I put my hands to my face to wipe away what felt like cobwebs, and let my fingertips dig into my flesh. When I looked back into Danny's eyes I thought he knew what I was about to tell him. I held up my left arm and his gaze shifted to the watch. I said, "I'm to push a button twice when you've made contact to meet, one push for three seconds when I'm in your presence."

Flatly, without emotion, "When?"

"Last Friday night. They lured me to a motel outside Swainsboro. If I take it off they'll know. I suppose it's like a tag they put on guys doin probation or somethin."

He examined the watch briefly. "Bit too small for it to be a constant tracker," he said. He raised his eyebrows to signal his relief. "What are they offering?"

I was disconcerted, as I had expected him to ask who was making the offer. I looked away and said, "Nathan, he's in Chicago with his mom right now. A life with him an' my old lady. An' money, big money, an' a new identity. Your life an' the lives of all those you're gonna kill with that bomb."

I made myself face him again. His shoulders swayed for a moment and then he shone the flashlight straight into my eyes. "What are you talking about, Robbie? What bomb?"

"The bomb you're makin for the Farc . . ."

"Shite!"

". . .the bomb you're gonna put in some city without any warnin."

He lowered the torch and put his face so close to mine that I could taste his breath. "And you believe that shite? You know what I was like after the bomb in Omagh! I bawled my fecking eyes out for the best part of three days, so I did. Jesus Christ, I hope you know me better than that. Robbie, whoever's telling you this shite is lying, he's telling you that to turn you against me."

Feebly I said, "He calls himself Mitch. He's FBI, Homeland Security. He said if I didn't help bring you in there were others who'd see you dead, Danny. I didn't know what to think, I don't know what I'm thinkin now. He said you're teachin the Farc how to build bombs."

"That's bullshit, Robbie, I swear to God it is. And who's these other people who want me dead?"

"I suppose guys like the one Darlene Fenton shot, the one who was lookin for Pete Foster. I told you this mornin they were comin after me. Didn't you take me seriously, Danny, after all you've said about British Intelligence huntin us down?"

He plucked his lower lip for a while. Distracted, he said, "Yeah, I guess it could be the Brits, right enough, but it doesn't add up that they are down here figuring that you're still using 'Pete Foster'. . . You know that stuff about a bomb is only to convince you that turning me in will save a lot of innocent people from being blown to pieces, don't you? Did he say anything else?"

"He knew we were in New York. He knew everything about what happened to Paulie O'Sullivan."

"Everything?"

"Yeah, even the towel down his throat."

"Sh . . . How?"

"Obviously, someone's grassed. Maybe those other two got arrested an' decided to talk. So what are you gonna do now, Danny?"

He took my left hand and examined the watch. "You can't go anywhere with that thing on you. There's a man I know, a brilliant technician, a few hours' drive from here. I'll bring him to you. Are you working tomorrow?"

"Yeah an' for flat time. Where will we meet?"

"I can't say where. Keep to your routine and he'll find you. If he doesn't get to you before you clock in, don't lock your car and he'll wait for when you're finished, okay?"

"An' when it's off I'm supposed to just dig up an' go?"

"Aye, that's about the top and tail of it."

"What are you up to, Danny?"

He looked down at the floor to where his flashlight shone and shook his head. "I'm not involving you, Robbie. I'll get that thing off you and then I want you away from here."

"We've always stuck together, no matter what, no matter how dangerous, so what's so different about what's happenin now?"

When he raised his eyes I saw the answer. For the first time in all the years I had known him, Danny Maguire looked unsure of himself. Almost faltering, he said, "Stuff, stuff that makes no sense, stuff that I don't understand right now. . . Look, I'll try to see you tomorrow after work. I've got to go now."

"Hey," I said, pulling him back, "ain't you gonna ask me why I didn't tell you this mornin about this FBI guy an' his watch?"

"Well," he said, "I guess you were tempted. You were, weren't you?"

"Yeah, but . . ."

"And that's how come you're a virtuous man, Robbie. My da, God rest his soul, used to say that for virtue to exist there first has to be temptation."

"Yeah, but . . ."

"No temptation to take another course, no virtue. Makes sense to me. I'm going out another way. Tomorrow, Robbie."

I watched him clamber over the rubble. After all the wrestling with my conscience about leaving Danny, he was telling me to go without him. It should have made it easy for me – but it hadn't. "Tomorrow, Danny," I said, "I'll see you tomorrow."

16

CALVIN WAS MUCH CALMER on the journey home. "Robbie, I gots to apologize fo earlier on," he said regretfully. "I let things get to me, y'know. Yo friend snuck up on me when Moses was on my mind an' I was jus lettin off steam with you. There's stuff about that man Moses that I wanna say but can't. Y'know heavy-duty shit. But I guess there's stuff goin on that you can't tell me too, huh?"

"That's about it, Calvin. Some things are best kept to ourselves, like as in a trouble shared is sometimes a trouble doubled. But I do appreciate what you've done tonight an' accept your word that you'll say nothin to anyone about it."

"Sho thing, man. You gots my word on that."

After a mile or two he switched on the radio to fill the awkward silence which had wedged its way in between us. I was busy with thoughts of leaving Danny – and escaping Mitch – as reports of more deaths in Iraq drew a few angry words from Calvin. "Young guys, man," he said bitterly, more to himself than me, "young guys my age dyin an' fo wha? Fo rich men to gets mo rich. They's pourin billions into Iraq but wha did they give fo New Orleans, fo the black folks down there? Nuthin, man, they gets nuthin 'cause those billion-aires are too busy makin their money elsewhere. Robbie, fo black folks, the poor black folks, this still can be one unfair bitch of a country."

Vonette had accused me of not understanding what it was really like for black people like her brother in this part of the world but I easily appreciated Calvin's feelings of frustration, as they were not dissimilar to the those I'd had when I was his age. My frustration with my life back then had turned malignant and led me down a path of violence – which had led to life as a fugitive. Calvin was halfway there already and I hoped he could somehow turn around and go back the way he came.

As soon as he had pulled into his yard, I opened the door and was about to leave his car until he tugged at my arm. He drew breath but either the words were not there, or he had changed his mind about saying them. "You okay about things, Calvin?"

He released his grip. "About Little J? Yeah, I'm cool, Robbie. I'll let you know if I hear anythin from Vonette but don't worry 'bout me. It's gettin easier by the minute."

I crossed the road to my place wishing that I could believe him.

An hour later I was pacing the kitchen floor, thinking about Nathan and my mom and figuring that I would never speak with, nor see them again. Any future with them, as offered by Mitch, would never have provided me with peace of mind, as I would have bought it with the ultimate betrayal of a friend. Once the watch was off, I would leave Georgia, set up some place else and then ring Cristina and give her the option of joining with me in a new life.

A car driving into my backyard broke my thoughts. Instinctively, I went to the drawer and got the bread knife: if it were Mitch coming for me because he had discovered I had just met Danny, I would deal with him and then take my chances by cutting the strap and making a run for it. I heard the screen door creak open and then a forceful rapping. I swallowed hard and opened the door. My first reaction was one of relief and I was just about to say I had been thinking of her, when a smack across my mouth turned my face. "Bastard!" Cristina shrieked at me.

Her ring had cut the corner of my mouth. Anger ignited within me, but before I could either control or act upon it, she came at me again and drove me back into the kitchen with flailing fists. "Bastard! Bastard!"

The bread knife impeded me and I could only fend her off with my left arm. I yelled at her to stop but she was too enraged to hear me. I thought about slapping her to bring her to her senses, but as she threw another blow I rode it and turned her with a push on her shoulder. Once her back was toward me, my left forearm was instantly across her throat.

"You'd better tell me what the hell is goin on, Cristina!" I yelled, tightening my hold as she struggled.

I released my grip enough for her to say, "You had to do it, Robbie, didn't you?"

"Do what?"

She stopped struggling and quietly asked me to let her go. I let my arm drop as I reached over and put the knife on a high shelf. I waited for an explanation, but she looked down at her foot, which she was turning on her high heel. "May I go to your sitting room?" she asked. "I have something to show you."

I nodded and followed her out of the kitchen and when we reached the sitting room she turned on those high heels and began to unbutton her blouse.

Confused, I said, "Please, Cristina, I don't think this is the. . ."

Ignoring me, she let the white blouse slip from her shoulders and fall to the floor. Her skin was a mass of hideous bruises. "Are you happy now?" she asked.

It took a few moments to get my mouth working properly. "Jesus Christ! Who did that?"

"I think you know. What were you doing at his father's? . . . He flew all the way from Atlanta in his private jet to do this. Why did you go there? I said I'd leave him and go away with you. I said I didn't want you to try and retaliate, but you had to play at being a tough man, yes?"

Still transfixed by the marks, I told her I didn't know what she was talking about.

"Don't lie to me, Robbie! You were seen outside Charles Lavettes' estate, Henry showed me a photo of you trying one of the side gates. The whole place is alarmed and as you walked towards it, a sensor switched on a light and a camera took your photograph."

It was then I realized that she was talking about the estate where Calvin and I had buried the body of Little J Moses. Urgently, I asked, "Is that it? Was there just one photo?"

"How many do you need?"

For a while my mind was consumed by questions about the disposal of Little J's body, why Vonette had chosen that place, and if it were likely we had been seen burying him. My eyes travelled absent-mindedly to the cruel marks on Cristina's breasts. She said something, but her words didn't register. "Come again?" I said.

"I asked what did you think you were doing there, Robbie?"

My eyes were drawn back to hers. How I did desire her. For an instant my resentment of Goretti, because of her mother's uncon-ditional devotion to her, flared up within me. If it were not for the girl, I was certain Cristina would leave with me. "An' Henry, he did this to you because I called around to his father's place?"

"Yes. He was very angry, so angry that he beat me himself, and I can assure you he has to be really angry to get his own hands dirty. Anyway, what did you think you were going to do? Like his father, he's a powerful man and you have seen the sort of people he hires."

I took my time replying. Cristina put her blouse back on and I figured this was an opportunity to get answers to some questions. But first I had to satisfy my curiosity about Lavette and what linked him with Moses. "How does Henry make his money?"

"You know already, his family owns a lot of land around here; they own the factory you work in, and the lumber yard. They have a vast range of business interests."

"But what part of the business does Henry actually run? It's not the factory because Billy Joe Watson does that. I mean, what does he do on a day to day basis?"

"What does it matter?" She fastened the last button and glared at me reproachfully. "Okay, he makes money from diamonds. Is that good enough for you?" she sneered.

"How did you meet him? Was it after you came to Georgia?"

Cristina took in a sharp breath, as if considering whether to answer any more questions. She raised her chin and stroked her throat with a forefinger. I kept quiet and let my question hang in the air. "I met him in Colombia," she said, her voice cutting through the silence like a jagged blade. "He was doing some business with oil and diamonds there. You could say he rescued me from a difficult situation. We had a relationship and he said he would look after me if I ever came to America. I came, and he kept his word, if not in the manner I had imagined. His father had some difficulty with us getting married and insisted that Henry stay with a woman who was more of his social standing. I was not white, nor wealthy enough, you see."

"You mean this kinda shit is still goin on in the twenty-first century?"

"I'm surprised you haven't yet realized that this little part of America is still in the nineteenth century, Robbie. Perhaps you walk about with your eyes closed. Henry's father isn't ashamed to say he believes in segregation: to him you're either pure white or, as he says, some kind of nigger. One of my grandfathers was the son a black man and an Indian woman and for Charles that means I'm contaminated with inferior blood, and he was not prepared to have his son and heir marry me. And on top of that I had a child born out of wedlock."

"Is Goretti Henry's child?"

"Biologically, no, but in many other ways she is. That's why she's

129

staying with Henry now. I'm sure his wife's furious about it, but they can't have children of their own."

"You mean he still has a wife too?"

"Oh yes," Cristina said airily. "She knows about Henry and me. She lives in the grand house on the estate. When Charles would not allow me to live there Henry bought the house you were in for Goretti and I to share with him. He's proving something to his father. But whatever he does for me or my daughter is only a means of exercising control, as he controls his wife, as he controls his businesses, I know that much now. I thought he loved me but he only ever wanted to possess me. I came to America and he has reduced me to a *puta*."

"If it's not an indelicate question, who is Goretti's father?"

Her eyes turned to a far corner of the room. "When I was little more than Goretti's age now, I was captured and raped by a right-wing militia group; she was born nine months later. But that was not the end of our troubles. I went to live with an aunt in a little village called El Aro. Goretti was only a young child at the time, and I pray to God she does not remember what we saw there. I cannot forget when the government soldiers and a militia led by a devil called Pedroza surrounded the village. They made us watch as they tied a shopkeeper to a tree. They accused him of supplying provisions to resistance guerrillas and they cut out his tongue, castrated him and then gouged out his eyes. Eleven of the villagers, some with children in their arms, tried to run away. They were caught and brought back. The men were mutilated like the poor shopkeeper, the women had their breasts cut off. All eleven of them, including three children, were then beheaded."

She fell silent and I saw that she was trembling. I hoped that was the end of the story, but she took another quivering breath and went on, "After that they set the church on fire and took thirty of us away, back to the city. I cannot say what happened to the others – I think they were interrogated and then killed. But I was lucky. Henry saw me with Goretti in the back of a truck. He bribed a soldier and saved our lives." Her eyes flashed defiantly at me. "Now you finally know it all, how do you feel?"

Perhaps she knew the answer: I felt dirty. I felt no better than the men who had raped her, no better than the rich man who had brought her to Georgia to use her – as maybe I had used her.

Cristina said, "I have to go. I'm only here because Henry sent me. Before he flew back to Atlanta he told me to tell you that when he returns some time next week, he will personally tell you to leave Georgia. I think that's his way of telling you to get out before he gets back." She came close and put her hands on my shoulders. "Goretti will be with him until you are gone. I am sorry that we are not to be but you must leave alone."

My fanciful dreams of a future with Cristina instantly evaporated. Perhaps sensing the change within me, she came closer still, right up against my chest and then reached up and kissed me. I winced because of the cut on my mouth and she pulled away – recognizing the passion had gone the same way as my dreams for us. There was a strange look in her eyes, it was not sadness, it was more as if she were saying: "now it is over." The pain of that final kiss and her tale of her life in Colombia combined to make our final parting less traumatic than I had envisioned. It seemed in a few short hours two of the major reasons for my turmoil had met with me and told me that I would have to make my way without either of them. Cristina left without looking back and I did not linger at the door before I closed it behind her.

Resigned, or perhaps deflated, I went back to the sitting room and began cursing Henry Lavette. Part of me was regretting that he would not get the chance to personally tell me to leave town, as I would have been glad of the opportunity to pay him back for what he had done to Cristina. I switched on the TV and flicked my way through the channels at least four times before settling on the news. In a short few hours Danny's electronic expert would have the watch off my wrist and I could then make my escape. My lids were heavy but I did not want to sleep. I did not want to dream.

* * *

I saw the family resemblance as soon as she came into Beanie's. It turned out that she was Natasha's eldest sister Caroline. She must have been given my description because she headed straight for me to tell me that Natasha had left hospital and was in her apartment, waiting for the end. She told me that Natasha wanted to see me one last time.

We went to the second-floor apartment in Manhattan. On the

way she prepared me for the worst. "How long is it since you've seen her?" she asked. I guessed at a year. "Well," she said, "it's not goin to be easy, Pete, but please try an' be strong. So many people have burst into tears when they see her the way she is now."

My stomach did somersaults as I followed Caroline to the bedroom door on legs that were rapidly losing their strength. I took deep breaths but the air would not stay in me. She opened the door and looked in. She whispered to me, "She's dozing," then she called, "Nat? Nat, wake up. Pete's here to see you."

The sunken eyes flickered open and a smile spread across Natasha's cadaverous face when she saw me. I tried to smile back, but it was difficult when I compared the beautiful woman I had known to the skeletal form lying in front of me. The shock weighed down my tongue: I did not feel capable of making small talk, I did not dare ask how she was doing as she was obviously so desperately ill.

Natasha smiled at me again. Her voice weak and sleepy, she said to her sister, "I'll be all right. I told you he'd come. You can go to church now."

Caroline clasped a hand to her breast and shot a searching glance my way as she left.

As the door closed, Natasha patted the bed. "Come, Pete . . . Robbie, an' sit here."

I felt weak, and not just physically. I had seen photographs of people dying from AIDS, but not even the images of the most emaciated figures had prepared me for this. "How has this happened, Natasha?" I gasped. "This is America. I mean, there's drugs that should keep you alive for years. I just can't believe this has happened to you, I just can't."

She smiled at my insensitivity. "Well, they've kept me goin for a while now but there's always a small percentage who don't respond like the rest, an' you did tell me once that I was a special person. Would it trouble you if we held hands?"

Scared that, like the others, I might start bawling if I opened my mouth, I shook my head and took her hand. There was a small circular plaster on her forearm and I fixed my gaze upon it, in case I should lose all semblance of composure if I looked into her face.

"Been a long time since you took me dancin, Robbie. Somehow I don't think we'll be doin that again, huh? Not in this life, anyhow."

"Guess not," I managed to whisper.

"You know, I look forward to death. It ain't no end, it's a new beginnin. What do you think?"

I did not answer until she gave my fingers a feeble squeeze. Unable to raise my voice, I said, "Natasha, if you want the truth, I don't know."

"I remember that chat we once had," she said softly, "about particles existin in two places at once, at a quantum level, an' how everyone who's ever existed is still around the place, that they've just exchanged molecules an' been made up into somethin else. I think I might come back as a carrot. You know, there's nuthin wrong with bein a sweet, juicy carrot."

"We talked some weird stuff." The small chuckle quickly died in my throat. "It was easy to talk like that back then, Natasha. It ain't so easy for me now."

"It's not hard for me, Robbie. I've had plenty time to ready myself, to think, to say all the things I wanted to say to the people I care about. I suppose if there is any good thing about dyin like this, it's that you're put on notice, that you're given time to sort out your business. I've sorted out mine."

For a while she talked about the family and friends who had visited her, the money she had bequeathed and the funeral arrangements. I nodded and made approving murmurs but felt at a loss at what to say. The best I could come up with was: "You really have got everythin sorted out, haven't you?"

"Almost," she said, "but not quite. That's why I wanted to see you, Mr Walker from England." The change in her voice had me looking at her properly for the first time. She sounded stronger. Her once flawless skin was now mottled and had shrunken against her cheekbones. I thought of a time when my lips had brushed against her face and wished I had done things differently, I wished that I had been a better man. I glanced up to her eyes and saw they still had a spark within them.

She went on, "There's somethin I need you to do for me, somethin I couldn't ax no one else. I remember you tellin me 'bout the time when you went with your friend an' killed a gangster. It must've taken real strength to cross that line."

I thought I knew what was coming next. I, too, had lain awake at night thinking how I might avenge her, how I could track down the man who'd infected her and kill him for what he'd done. "Just tell me his name," I said, fighting the tremor in my voice, "an' where he lives or works, an' I promise you, Natasha, I'll make him suffer before he dies."

A laugh rattled around her frail body but emerged from her mouth as a choking cough. I took a glass of water from her bedside locker and held it to her lips. As I supported her head, the wig I did not realize she was wearing, slipped off and had her in convulsions again. With her head back on the pillow she laughed for an age, as if she were savouring every moment of it.

"Man, I could have . . . loved you if we'd had . . .the chance . . . We had some good times," she gasped. When the laughter finally faded she looked up at me with tearful eyes. "Oh, Robbie, my fugitive man, do you really think you could make him suffer more than I'm sufferin right now? This is what lies ahead for him. Every night I pray to God not to let me wake in the mornin, I ax Him to spare the people I love from seein me this way.

"In a hundred years' time we'll all be dead anyway, so what does it matter to anyone else if I live to see my thirtieth birthday or not? Surely it can only matter to me, an' what matters to me is the quality of my life, not longevity. If I was an animal they'd put me to sleep an' call it a kindness. But the doctors won't do nuthin for me an' that's why I came home, but my sisters can't, they just can't. So I have to ax you. I figured it wouldn't be so hard for you."

I did not understand her and asked, "What wouldn't?"

"It wouldn't be so hard, for you, Robbie, to end my life, right here, right now."

I sprang to my feet. "Natasha, Natasha, I couldn't do that, not to you . . ."

"Didn't you just offer to kill the man who infected me?"

"But he's not you. The stuff I told you about, things got outta hand an' a guy ended up dead, but that doesn't make me somebody who could just kill in cold blood."

"It's called euthanasia – Greek or somethin for 'a good death'. Won't you do this for me, Robbie? Won't you do me this one last kindness an' give me the death I want?"

I squeezed my eyes shut. "Sweet Jesus, Natasha. I swear on every-thin I hold dear that the guy I told you about deserved it. The guy who infected you would deserve it. But what you're askin me is somethin I could never do, not to you."

"Don't I deserve it?"

"No, no, you don't, Natasha! You don't deserve none-a this! I've lain awake many nights since I last saw you, cursin the person who gave you AIDS. I even cursed God for lettin me meet you in the first place. You know, we . . ."

"Clicked?"

"It's true, Natasha, an' I fell in love with you in a way that never happened to me before. An' I wish you never got AIDS, an' I wish you knew me for the person I really am, an' I just wish, *wish*, that me an' you could have had a chance. I realize now that I loved you, an' I'm not just sayin that 'cause you're here like this."

"Then take this pillow an' put it over my face before Caroline comes back."

"No! No! I can't, Natasha, don't ask me, 'cause I can't!"

"Be strong, Robbie. If you really loved me, you'll do this for me now."

"Natasha, please . . ."

"Robbie, if it's true that you loved me, really loved me, you'll do this me now. You gotta be strong for me – please. An' don't worry, there'll be no comeback on you, Caroline knows what I'm axin you. Let my sisters come back an' find their prayers have been answered. Robbie, please."

I looked out to the drizzly afternoon and heard the sound of the traffic below. I tried to rationalize, I even tried to moralize, but the only thought that would stay in my head was turning and running away, and calling out that I was sorry to have let her down yet again. I let my head turn toward the door.

"Don't think of runnin out on me, Robbie Walker," she whispered harshly, "don't think of it. Don't leave me like this! For God's sake, have pity on me an' my family." My gaze returned to the soft rain on her window; I caught the scent of the flowers on the windowsill and listened to the sounds of life outside as I tried to shut out her gentle sobs. I couldn't say how long I stood there; almost everything and everyone else outside Natasha's bedroom ceased to have any meaning.

"Peace, Robbie," she said, desperation taking the strength from her voice. "I want me an' my family to be at peace. Caroline tried to do it, but as soon as I started to struggle she stopped. She got it into her head that she was committin a sin. When she left here you didn't see any tears, did you? It's 'cause she's all cried out – this thing has sucked my sisters dry. So I'm beggin you. If you really loved me an' you walk out now, it'll stay with you for the rest of your life, Robbie, it'll put a stain on your soul."

I watched a bead of water makes its way haphazardly down the window and thought that, whatever I did, I would carry it for the rest of my life.

17

AWARE THAT DANNY'S ELECTRONICS specialist could make contact at any time, I took a seat at a small table in Harry's Bar and Grill and snagged a waitress as she wove her way to the counter. I was lucky to catch her attention. Harry usually employed four waitresses, but now he was down to just three because one young woman had reached her breaking point and had yelled out that she was no longer willing to take Harry's brusque commands without a 'please' or a 'thank you'. Only an hour into the breakfast shift, the white pinafores of the three who remained were less than pristine and their faces were already pinched with stress. After a longer than usual wait, one of them slid a plate onto my table. Instead of an omelette she had brought me bacon and scrambled eggs, and there was coffee instead of juice. When she inquired if everything was all right I told her it was: I was too busy trying to make some sense of what both Danny and Mitch had told me to give my breakfast much thought. Both men had made it clear that there were things they would not tell me. One, or perhaps both, had lied, but as in all effective deceptions there were strands of truth mixed into the falsehoods. But as my mother used to tell me: a half-truth is worth a whole lie. What Mitch had said about our time in New York, and about how Paulie O'Sullivan had died, was true. But he had also told me that Danny was building a bomb with members of the Farc and that they were about to commit an atrocity. Danny had admitted he was on a mission with the Colombian guerillas, but had vehemently denied planning to build a bomb. I believed my friend. He had the ability to kill, ruthlessly at times, but I could not believe that he would ever kill so indiscriminately. He had often told me that his actions, whatever they might be, were always informed by a belief that the ends did not always justify the means. He had said that he and the man I knew as José had been ambushed and I gave him the benefit of any doubt. My old foreman was dead – and that much was beyond dispute.

Mitch had claimed that in delivering Danny to him I would save both my friend's life and the lives of many others. I did not believe him. Nor, on reflection, did I think he would keep his promises to me. Another question arose in my mind: would I survive either man's plans?

I took a sip of coffee and when I looked up again, a man was poised to sit down opposite me. Even though the diner was nearly full, the fact that he had chosen my table made me regard him warily. He was of medium build, with dark hair and a squarish face, which was fresh enough to tell me he was no older than twenty-five. His blue eyes flitted my way before he raised his newspaper and made a screen between us. A waitress came and took his order and I discounted my initial idea that he had anything to do with Danny.

As I washed down the last mouthful of eggs and bacon, the young man folded his newspaper and stared out of the window, as if on the lookout for someone. "Don't get up yet," he murmured from the side of his mouth. He sounded American. "And don't look at me, just listen. Rest your arm on the table while you finish your coffee and leave it there while I take a look at the watch."

I realized then that this was Danny's electronics specialist. My pulse quickened and I turned my palm toward the ceiling so that he could inspect the fastening and I said a silent prayer that we were not being observed. The man turned his head slowly towards the frenetic activity at the counter and back again to the window.

"Right," he whispered, "while not impossible, I don't think it's likely that it has a constantly active tracking device inside. That's what the button's about. Pick up my newspaper when you leave. At the end of your shift go to the loading bay at the cold storage. A truck will be there, its licence plate number is written on page five. Once you have it memorized destroy it. The back doors of the truck will be left open after it's been loaded and you'll have two minutes to get yourself inside. The driver will expect you and he'll bring you to me and I will get this off you then."

The waitress came with his poached eggs and I went to the counter to pay my bill.

"Robbie," guffawed Harry, "how are you?"

Behind his genial expression I detected something else and guessed that he had something to tell me. "Cool," I said. "But what's happenin? You swap a waitress for all this flags an' bunting?"

He laughed, "It would've been a bargain if I did. I thought you knew that your bosses run a pro-am golf tournament every two years for the Charles Lavette Foundation. The old bastard has every local business putting in a contribution. That's the secret of the super rich, Robbie, they always use someone else's money."

"Then why don't you tell him, or whoever he sends around, to use his own money?"

Harry put my bills into his till. "You don't say anything like that to any Lavette, not if you want to stay in business. One man did as you suggested and was bankrupt in six months." He turned and put my change on the counter. "People stopped buying and more stopped supplying, so we make a little contribution to his game of golf for his fancy friends. It keeps life simple that way."

"Harry, you have me worried about the type of men I work for."

The smile slipped from Harry's face and his voice dropped to a whisper. "There's rumours that the INS is about and they are looking at the people the Lavettes have working for them, have you heard anything?"

"Can't say I have," I said, trying to appear calm.

"Do you remember that man who said he was a reporter, you know, the one who was asking about José Ruiz?"

I pretended I had difficulty recalling him, then said, "Oh, yeah, biggish guy in a bad suit."

Harry nodded and pulled a face as though he had tasted something unpleasant. "Got a bad feeling about him."

"Yeah? Like what?"

"Like he wasn't really a reporter. Like maybe he's from the Immigration Service. Probably Immigration – let's face it, we all know people around here whose papers may not be in order, if you get me. Just look around you. He didn't stay long after you left. It made me wonder if he'd been waiting for you all along. Maybe it's something, maybe it's nothing."

I gathered up my change and put it into the tip jar. "You know what, Harry, I think you're gettin to be a suspicious man," I said.

"A more aware man," he called after me as I left.

Out on the street, I wondered if Mitch was close by, watching me.

Henry Lavette certainly did mot mix his personal life with business. After what Cristina had told me about him seeing to it that I left town, once he'd returned from Atlanta, I turned up at the plant wondering if I still had a job. But my punch card was in its usual place. I guessed it was there because the maintenance department was still short-staffed and Ricardo had not turned in again – maybe he had heard the rumours about a possible investigation into illegal immigrants. Away from the clock I became aware that a sombre mood had settled over the factory. A member of the night shift had fallen down an elevator shaft used for sending the boxes of meat to the refrigeration rooms. I found out it was Miguel the 'dirty meat' thief. He had broken his neck and had died instantly.

"What was he doin in that area anyway?" I asked Colin the electrician.

"Beats me," he replied, "but you know how it goes, production doesn't stop. I heard they swept him up like he was one of those birds."

"Expendable, Colin," I said, "we're all expendable."

"Rumour has it, he opened the elevator's security gate and stepped out onto a floor that wasn't there."

"Ouch."

"The managers are pissed that production was temporally held up by the cops, but we all know they're only going through the motions. Health and Safety are pissed because of all the reports they'll have to write, and I'm pissed that it's you and me who's been ordered to go check the elevator for damage."

"What? The worksheet says I'm supposed to replace some reducer bearings."

"Yeah, well it's you and me who've to give it a once-over. I need a mechanical guy and Woodlow told me to get you. Must make you kinda pissed that a knee in Kirby's nuts is causing you so much trouble, huh?"

Ignoring his harmless needling, I picked up my tool box. "Who found the body?"

"Security. Funny thing is, they were scouring the area where he died for the best part of an hour, like they were looking for something important. The guys who moved the body reckon there was a powerful smell of drink and shit off him."

"Turkey shit is bad enough, Colin," I growled, "but I'm not cleanin up no dead man's shit."

He laughed and collected his tools while telling me that we had better get a move on.

John Hunter walked by and he responded to our greeting with only a small, reluctant nod. "What is that guy's problem?" I asked.

Colin shrugged and turned down the corners of his mouth. "He's always been the moody type. I think it's something to do with his military service. You know, some men carry around a lot of heavy baggage. Sometimes he seems okay, sometimes he's just downright hostile. But he's a man who has done his duty for his country and I respect him for that."

Colin won the toss and opted to stand by the switchgear to make sure no one interfered with the locked-out controls. He brought the top of the elevator, which only a short time before had been the final resting place of Miguel, to just below floor level. I lay on my stomach to make a closer examination. My narrowed eyes followed the beam from my flashlight to examine a small indentation in the flat metal panel.

As I searched for more serious damage, I said, "Hey, did you know this Miguel?"

"Not personally," replied Colin, "but I did know of him. He was a thief. I hate to talk ill of the dead, but he would steal from his own mother from what I heard."

"Sounds like the only one who didn't know what Miguel was up to was Billy Joe Watson."

"Heck, Robbie, you're talking like a real greenhorn. Billy Joe was taking a cut. He never really thought any of that meat should've been condemned by the USDA in the first place. He knew Miguel was selling that meat, to other Mexicans, of course. He wouldn't risk poisoning gringos, 'cause then there would've been real trouble."

"Just chasin the American dream," I murmured. More loudly, I said, "Everythin here looks okay to me. Why don't we send it up an' down a few times to be on the safe side?" Partially hidden by a pulley and bearing block, a glint of silver caught my eye. I stretched my arm as far as it would go until my fingers found a key which had become wedged under the block. I immediately wondered if this was what the security personnel had been looking for but I decided not to tell Colin about it when he asked me if I had found anything. Instinctively, I reckoned that this was the key which Miguel had used to gain access to the contaminated meat store. There were strict regulations about the security of meat which was deemed unfit for human consumption and I imagined that Billy Joe was now fretting over its whereabouts, in case it turned up somewhere which would lead to consequences with the USDA. In a short while, I would be waiting for a truck in that area and I supposed it would do me no harm to hang on to it. "It was nothin, Colin, my mistake. Probably just Miguel's duppy."

"Duppy?" Colin asked as I got to my feet. "What the hell is that?"

"Jamaican for ghost."

His eyes followed my hand as it slipped into a pocket of my overalls. He then looked up into my face. "Robbie, you must be careful," he warned me, with a hint of accusation. "I'm a Christian but I do believe that the ghosts of men like Miguel tend to hang around, and they're as bad in death as they were in life."

After we had tested the elevator several times and found nothing wrong with it, Colin and I went to find Chuck Woodlow. Unusually, workers were standing around and I guessed that production was down but Woodlow would not dare to repeat his order to speed up the conveyors.

My guess had been right, and to rectify the low level of productivity, Billy Joe Watson came to the canteen during the lunch break. With the aid of a translator, he told the assembled workforce that Miguel's family would receive funeral expenses and an undisclosed sum to compensate for their loss. The three shirt-sleeved men who had followed the plant manager into the canteen clapped loudly, as everyone else looked on in silence. When the four of them had beaten a retreat, most of us traipsed back to the factory floor, where we found security guards stationed all over the place, presumably to ensure production would not stop altogether because of vandalized machinery.

I turned to my original task of replacing the reducer bearings. Normally it would have taken no more than a couple of hours but I decided to draw it out for as long as I could because it gave me a vantage point from where I could see the trucks being loaded from the cold stores. Even though the truck I wanted would not appear until near the end of my shift, I was on constant lookout for its licence plate.

While peering out to the loading bay one more time, I heard someone call out to me. It was Woodlow. "What's going on, Barrett? A new set of bearings should've only taken an hour, two at most. Are you on a go-slow with the rest of them, or just jerking me around?"

I'd figured that Chuck would turn up at some point, so I had taken the precaution of committing a little bit of sabotage. I pointed to the bits of machinery arrayed around my feet. "When I stripped it down I found the drive shaft was totally shot. I've checked the stores an' we don't have a new one so I've had to get an old one from one of those reducers that are dumped out at the back."

He tried to look as though he knew what I was talking about. "So when are you going to get this finished?"

"How about if I stay on until it's done? You can fall in with me if you like, an' we'll get it done quicker."

On a technical level at least, Woodlow knew his limitations. He didn't take up my suggestion but, betraying some surprise, Woodlow said he appreciated my offer to stay late. When he'd gone, time moved slowly and my growing anxiety wasn't alleviated any when I checked my watch – Mitch's watch. I cursed and told myself once again that I had to place my future in Danny's hands.

Finally, another truck pulled in and interrupted my thoughts. My heart quickened as I caught sight of its plates. The new drive shaft was already in place, so I quickly closed up the gear box, hurried across the plant and punched my card. I decided to keep my overalls on so as not to attract too much attention as I made my way to the loading bay.

When I got there the truck had backed up to one of the cold storage units, and the driver, a wiry, mustachioed Latino, was talking to the forklift operator. They headed toward the dispatch office and I made my move. I tried to walk the fifty yards as nonchalantly as I could but I could feel my calves stiffen with every eager step. I was almost out of breath by the time I reached the rear of the vehicle. The doors were locked. I wondered whether the truck had been already loaded while I was punching my card, but quickly figured out it couldn't have been done in that short a time.

Voices warned me that there were people coming. Without

thinking, I stepped into the only available hiding place, the cold store, and edged my way around the stacks of cartons at the rear. There was no gap, no way of seeing through to the front, so I had to rely on my ears to figure out what was happening. Minutes passed, and the goose pimples on my skin were beginning to feel like golf balls, when I heard two people enter the unit. Their footfalls on the concrete floor came nearer, and I backed further into the maze of boxes. The footsteps came closer still, and words were exchanged, detailing the boxes to be loaded onto the truck. I held my breath and squeezed myself between the stacked cartons until I found a space amid them. I cursed my luck when I saw that the labels on the boxes around me showed that these were the very ones to be loaded. The voices grew more distant, as did the sound of the forklift truck. I knew I had to move now and hoped that my hunch had been correct about the key I had found. Crouching, I scuttled between the rows of cartons toward the front of the store, until I reached a small 'man-door' within a much larger side door.

The key was warm to the touch and slid smoothly into the lock. I stepped inside but kept the man-door open a fraction and stayed listening to every sound. Once there were no more loud scraping noises, as boxes on pallets were dragged along, I knew the loading was finished and I had to get into the back of the truck without being seen.

In my haste, my numb fingers fumbled and dropped the key, which slid across the floor and into a small gap between two pallets. Hissing all sorts of curses, I stooped to retrieve it, but the sight of a strange, plastic-wrapped package on the floor between some cartons stilled my tongue. The fluorescent light gave the translucent plastic a blueish tinge but I thought I could make out the shape of a hand. I was both drawn and repelled, but it was more than mere curiosity that enabled me to overcome my innate aversion. I looked more closely, and saw that the head was closest to me. Tentatively, I began to pull the plastic free. The body was wrapped tightly and I had to drag it toward me so I could uncover the face.

What I saw stiffened my spine and made me take in a sharp, cold, breath. I told myself it couldn't be him, but I recognized the small scar on his left cheek. Trembling, I put the body back where I had found it, and after quietly closing the man-door, I stumbled toward the truck on legs which had become almost lifeless. The driver was at the doors and greeted me with a look of startled bewilderment.

"I thought you were inside already," he hissed. "Quick, quick, get in now." Once I was inside, he added, "As soon as we're clear of the factory I'll let you into the cab."

He closed me in and left me to shiver in the dark.

18

BY THE TIME I HAD stumbled out of the back of the truck and into the cab I was frozen to my core. I was a little warmer by the time the truck drew up in a motel parking lot but the memory of the body I had discovered kept my blood running cold.

The man I'd met over breakfast at Harry's strode out to meet me. "By the way, the name's Joe," he said, as he guided me toward a stairway. I followed him up to a musty-smelling room. The blinds were drawn and a laptop computer and an attaché case full of gadgetry sat on the bed. He asked me to hold out my arm, looked at the watch and gently twisted my wrist. "Shouldn't be too much of a problem," he said. "Sit on the bed, please. It shouldn't take long."

I was too preoccupied to look closely at what he was doing. "Where's Danny?" I asked.

"Can't say I know."

"You've gotta make contact with him right away. I have to see him now." He looked up and I said, "I mean now, Joe, ring him right now. It's important."

He reached into a pocket and took out his cell phone. He pressed a few buttons and passed it to me. "Speak to him yourself," he said.

Danny answered on the third ring. "Joe?"

"No, it's me."

"Oh, right. Everything went okay?"

"He's takin care of it as I talk. There's somethin else."

Immediately picking up on my tone, Danny said, "Something important?"

"Life or death. I need to see you now."

"Right. . . Right, I won't be long."

As I handed Joe his phone he straightened up, the watch dangling from his fingertips. "I've neutralized the alarm in the strap," he explained. "The only thing that puzzles me is that this model's been superceded at least twice and its range is not the longest. Whoever is monitoring for a signal has to be mobile, say in a van, and can't be far away, less than a mile. I reckon they would have been parked up not too far from either your home or the factory."

"So will they know what you've done?" I asked.

Joe smiled and handed me the watch. "No, but you'd better put it back on before you leave here, because I guess you're under visual as well as electronic surveillance some of the time."

"But this thing does have a tracker in it, right?"

"The button or breaking the strap would activate it. In my experience, a device like this one means he wants you distracted so you don't think about other devices, in your car, or in your house. Danny says I might have to check them out too." Joe closed his case and shut off his laptop. "It's an honour," he said. I was too busy with the watch and trying to arrange events into some order in my mind to respond to him. Trying to concentrate, I screwed up my face and he said, "I was saying it's an honour to help you guys out. Danny's something of a legend, you know."

"Is that right?"

"Well, in some circles he is."

"Small circles."

"I guess."

"How old are you, Joe?"

"Twenty-three, going on twenty-four."

"Give it another while an' you'll find out that legends are usually built on bullshit. An' from what I know of Danny, he'd be pretty pissed to know that he's a little legend in some small circle. He's just an ordinary guy, Joe, with, more or less, the same vices an' virtues as everybody else. Don't build him up to somethin he's not."

Chastened, he went and sat on a wooden chair by the door, nervously slapping the tops of his thighs to break the uncomfortable silence my putdown had caused. I was not in the mood to make small talk and let the silence hang over the two of us. When the knock on the door came, Joe leapt to his feet.

"Give us a few minutes," Danny told him.

Though he did his best to hide it, he was obviously disappointed at not being taken into Danny's confidence. As he went to the door

Danny clasped one of his hunched shoulders and thanked him for what he had done. The appreciative words straightened up Joe a little and he went outside.

The smile slipped from Danny's face once the door was closed. "So, what is it?" he asked.

I stood up so I could look straight into his eyes. "Without the shit, Danny, tell me exactly what happened the night you say you an' José Ruiz were ambushed."

He frowned and scratched his nose. "And what shite are you talking about? I told you the truth, so I did."

"Try that bit again about José bein killed an' then bein driven into a river so it looked like an accident."

His frown deepened. "Well, you've lost me there, Rob, so you have. For fuck's sake, they pulled the poor fella out of the river, didn't they? . . . Are you making out that *I* killed him, or something?"

"No, but I am makin out that they didn't pull the man I knew as José Ruiz outta that river. I know that because he's wrapped in a plastic sheet in a cold store unit at the factory."

Danny's frown remained but his eyes began to dart from side to side, as if were searching the room for something. "Have you gone off your head? Didn't you see the TV pictures? The cops pulled him out of the river and identified him."

"As José Ruiz. In fact, it was Billy Joe Watson who identified the body."

"Well he had no family here, so the cops had to find someone to ID him."

"As José Ruiz."

"Of course."

"But you said that it wasn't his real name."

Exasperated, Danny sighed, "He could hardly use his real name, Robbie, not in the circumstances."

"So, however it happened, the body the cops pulled out of the river, and who Billy Joe identified as José Ruiz, wasn't the guy we both knew. I mean, no one exactly got a closeup of who they were draggin out."

"You're mistaken."

Annoyed, it was my turn to let out a harsh breath. "Danny, there's a dead guy in a cold store at the factory, scar on his left cheek, a guy I used to call José Ruiz. I saw him there less than an hour ago. And

146

the reason I was in there is because I found a key left by a Mexican guy who went down an elevator shaft. I reckon he was seen goin in an' out the cold store an' it was made sure he wasn't goin to tell anyone about what he had seen in there."

"It doesn't make sense, Robbie," Danny murmured. He paced the room, trying to come up with answers that might explain what I'd seen. Whatever answers he was finding resulted only in perplexed shakes of his head.

"Nothin about this place, includin why we came here makes sense," I said.

A tap on the door stalled his response. He opened it and said, "Joe, we're heading off to the factory. You check out Robbie's car while we go inside and take a look at something, okay?"

Joe went off to get his car, and Danny said, "It's not that I don't believe you, mate, but I have to go take a look for myself. I think we'll get in without too much trouble."

I nodded as images of nothing but trouble began to loom large in my mind.

Danny knew his way around from delivering turkeys over the last few months and made his own way. I went with Joe in his car and when we got to the factory's parking lot I gave him my keys and pointed out my car before heading for the gates. I had prepared an excuse about leaving my wallet behind but I wasn't challenged by the guard. Security was more about what was leaving the factory, rather than about who or what was entering.

As dusk approached powerful sodium lights on the factory's exterior started to glow, orange at first, then gradually turning into bright white light. Danny stepped out of the shadows and joined me at the door of the contaminated meat store. When we were inside, Danny said, "So, where is he?" I gestured to a spot behind him. He turned and I told him where to look. He straightened up again and gave me a shrug. "You'd better show me."

The body was not there. I pushed a few boxes aside, in case I had been mistaken about the exact spot where I'd seen it, but there was no sign of it. I was about to shift some more when Danny took my arm and said it was bitterly cold and that we had better leave. Outside the cold store we retreated back into the shadows so we would not be seen. I said, "He was there, Danny."

He rubbed some warmth back into his hands. "Everything all right, mate?"

"What do you mean by that, Danny? Are you implyin that I am off my head or somethin?"

He looked down to his feet and then slowly up into my face. "Pressure, Rob, we're all under pressure. I mean, pressure's affecting me, affecting my head. There's stuff going on but I can't figure out what, because of the pressure. Look, that thing around your wrist, and how it got there, is pressure. I do believe you saw something, right enough, but the mind can play tricks in these sorts of situations."

"Like it did before, you mean? Like it did in New York?"

"I didn't say that."

"You didn't have to, it's written all over your face! So I caved in once an' now you're makin out that I can't hold the pressure anymore. Listen to me, the body was there a couple of hours ago, wrapped up in a plastic sheet. There's another guy who's dead because he saw what I saw!"

"Think about it, Robbie. Why would José's – or anyone else's – body be there? It makes no sense. I mean, how could it be him?"

"I can't even guess why he was there, mostly 'cause you won't tell me what's goin on."

"That's to protect you. I thought I'd made myself clear on that one. Look, Joe's checking out your car and once he's done you're free to gather up your gear and get out of here. When this is all over we'll be in touch again." He handed me a folded piece of paper and said, "Memorize this and then get rid. It's the number of a new cell phone. Six days from now, Friday, I'll switch it on, at 6.00am. I'll keep it simple, you'll have six minutes to call and then I'll take the batteries out again. If you don't call then, I'll switch it on at the same time for six minutes for the following two days so you can let me know where you've landed. Remember, all the sixes. Now you take care, okay?"

"Danny, we've come this far together an' I'm not goin any place until you're goin too. Right, so I don't know what's goin on but I *know* José's body was in there just a while ago. I know you an' him were plannin somethin. I know that some guy from the FBI is on your trail, an' other people, too, maybe the men who turned up at the Fentons' and maybe people right here in this factory. I know you're goin to need someone to watch your back, man, to keep an eye on what is goin on around here. Just tell me one thing: when will this be over?"

The tip of his tongue ran over his teeth. "By the end of next week."

"So I'm here for another week."

Danny let out a heavy breath. "I didn't want you involved. Are you sure, mate?"

I sucked at my teeth. "I wouldn't say it if I didn't mean it."

He ran a hand over his cropped hair and scratched the back of his head. "Okay," he said, "I'll think about it but I'll do my best not involve you directly. Now, let's go see Joe."

We went to the parking lot. Joe had parked his car next to mine and Danny got inside and started it up. I could tell he was wary of sticking around for too long. Joe got out of my car and in a low voice, he said, "You've got a tracking device under the front passenger seat. Best leave it there, because if it's tampered with they'll know we're onto them. When you're ready to make a run for it pull it out at the same time you get rid of the watch."

I took my keys from him and Danny said, "I'll bring Joe so he can check out the house as soon as we can. I can't promise it'll be tonight. Until then, you get home and act as naturally as you can."

I laughed at the idea of his last remark – I wasn't sure what was "acting naturally" any more.

Miss Boo's lights were on. I hated myself for it, but I figured if I did not roll myself a joint before the night was through my stomach would stay in knots. I stopped my car in the road and walked around the side of her house to the kitchen door.

Miss Boo's husband Leroy was sitting on the back step with several empty beer cans at his feet. His slack jaw tightened as he saw me, and he turned his head away and stared out across his untidy yard. He took a long draw on his joint. "Wha you here fo, Jamaican man?"

"Some herbal medicine, man, just like what you're takin now."

"Ain't got none, not fo the likes of yous anyhow."

"An' why's that, Leroy?"

"Boo tol' me 'bout wha went on. You think my Stella ain't good enough fo you, muthafucka?"

"Hol' on, Leroy, before things get outta hand here. All I said . . ."

"You think I'm scared of yo boxin shit? I'll cut you into so many pieces they'll be able to send you back to yo momma in a iddy-biddy box." He began to sway a little. "Stella's a good girl – I treat her like she my own. Right purdy girl, a ripe girl, she buddin jus right, y'know wha I'm sayin? You gotta good fuckin job, man, you gots money, man, so what's wrong with sharin a little bit of it with Stella, eh, muthafucka? It ain't like she ain't gonna give you nuthin fo it."

Leroy's unfocused black eyes fixed onto me, and I knew that in his groggy mind there was bad intention. I heard the click of the switchblade – before he lunged at me, but that split second was enough warning. Whatever else drink did for him, it did nothing for his coordination. I stopped him with a right to the jaw. He fell so fast that my left punch skimmed the top of his wild, unbrushed hair. Now I knew how he had lost most of his teeth.

The back door flew open and Miss Boo hurtled out toward her prostrate husband at a speed which belied her massive girth. She dropped to her knees beside him and screamed hysterically at me until I pointed to the blade close to his hand. She fell silent.

I could tell what was running through her mind. "Pick it up, Miss Boo," I said, "an' you'll be sorry. Do you I make myself clear?"

Obviously, I hadn't. She made a grab for the blade but I was faster and stamped hard on her hand. She shrieked in pain and collapsed across Leroy. I picked up the switchblade: I thought it best to hang onto it. Leroy was beginning to gasp for air as his wife still lay across him, yelling that I had broken her hand.

Going back to my car, I caught sight of Stella by the back door. She was in that same small cotton dress, nervously chewing a finger. I could have been wrong but as she tucked her straightened hair behind an ear I thought I saw a hint of gratitude in her eyes. Well, I hoped it was gratitude.

I should have realized something was wrong when the light didn't come on.

"Just step inside, and don't worry about the light." Mitch stepped out from the shadows of my kitchen, his gun pointing at my head. He gestured with it to a chair by the table. The adrenalin was still charging through me after my tussle at Miss Boo's. I had left Leroy's switchblade in my car, and I scanned the darkness for the bread knife. Once I was seated and he'd replaced the bulb, I saw it was out of reach. "You're playing games, Walker, dangerous games."

While in Ireland I had received advice about surveillance – and counter surveillance – techniques. Mitch seemed to be tearing up the manual. His behaviour was contrary to everything I had been told to expect. "I don't know what you mean," I said.

"I've been trying to ring you but your phone is switched off. Switch it on again."

I knew that the signal from my cell phone was also a means of locating me and that's why he wanted it switched on but this was the opportunity to find out how extensive his surveillance really was. "I got jumped by three guys an' it got broke. I thought they had somethin to do with you."

"Walker, if I'd wanted you beaten, I wouldn't have waited until Tuesday. We couldn't intervene while they obviously roughed you up a bit, without blowing our cover. Do you know why these men would want to jump you?"

While he knew when it had happened, he had not contradicted the number of men who had attacked me. So while Mitch may have learned of the attack, neither he nor his men had actually witnessed it. "I haven't got a clue," I said, "maybe, as it was three white guys it was a racial thing."

"You keep on failing my little tests, Walker," he growled menacingly. "We know it was about a woman. You can mess around with your boss's little bitch-on-the-side but don't even think you can jerk me around. That would be so very, very dangerous." He studied me closely for a moment, while calculating what I was up to. "Show me the watch." My mouth dried as his eyes continued to drill into me. He took hold my hand roughly and pushed the button. I returned his stare, determined to give nothing away. A jolt went through me as his phone went off. He smirked and said, "Nervous?" He answered the call with his automatic still pointing at me. He grunted a couple of times and lowered the gun. "It's still working," he said, as he took a seat opposite me. "I've been wondering if there was something wrong with it since you haven't sent me a signal. I'm starting to wonder if you really love your mom and your son as much as you make out. So don't shit with me, Walker, and tell me when Maguire made contact with you."

What did he know? He knew about Cristina but had he found out about my journey with Calvin to the derelict house? Was he about when Joe had been sitting opposite me at Harry's? Had I been watched as I went into the back of the truck? He raised his gun again.

"I want an answer, Walker. You clocked out at your usual time but your car remained in the parking lot. Where were you?"

Mitch had just confirmed that I was under surveillance even at the factory and now, at least, I thought I knew what I could discount – as he had made no mention of Joe. "There was a note on my windshield," I said. "I thought it might be another one from you. It said to get in the back of a truck after I clocked out. When it stopped, I was told Danny would be there. It took me by surprise."

"Then why didn't you press the button?"

"'Cause he wasn't there when we arrived."

"You should have pushed it, Walker, that was the deal!"

"But you gave me a sequence to follow. I was taken by surprise an', anyway, he never turned up. Instead, a man I never saw before passed on a message for me to get outta Georgia. This plan of yours was only gonna work if Danny was considerate enough to give me notice. Your plan was flawed, man, an' now you wanna blame me. Now I'm thinkin if this is the best you can do I'm never gonna see Nathan or my mom again. Come up with a better plan an' I'll give you Danny."

Mitch compressed his lips and stayed silent – until he drew a long breath. I thought he was deciding whether or not to shoot me. "What else did this man say to you?" he asked.

"He just told me that in a couple of weeks Danny'll switch his phone back on an' I'm to ring to tell him where I am an' we might meet up. So do you want me to go, or do you want me to stay? I mean, I don't think he'll contact me again while I'm here, an' in two weeks or so you'll definitely have a lead on where he is."

The FBI man's jaw tightened angrily. "Two weeks is too late," he hissed. "You stay put. If we can't get hold of Maguire soon, a lot of people will die." A dangerous-looking smirk momentarily came to his lips. "But he's running scared, Walker, every hour that passes Maguire is getting closer to being cornered. He's getting desperate, so desperate that he will get back to you sooner rather than later. And you've just told me something that might prove useful, you may be seeing young Nathan yet. We'll find out which trucks left the factory shortly after you clocked out. We'll find that driver and, I assure you, he will tell us what he knows." He holstered his gun and told me to walk out to the yard with him. We were only outside a few moments when a sports utility vehicle pulled up. Mitch went to its rear and rummaged through more than a dozen cell phones, as I sucked in more exhaust fumes than were healthy for me, before he finally handed one to me. "I've put my number on it and you had better keep it with you. You're on notice, Walker. The next time, the next note, the next anything you'd better either call me or push that button, no matter what. We will get Maguire, and if we end up doing it without you, you can forget there was any deal between us. . . And without my deal, Walker, you have no future."

I watched the SUV with smoked windows whisk Mitch away. He knew I hadn't kept my side of the bargain and yet he had done nothing more than give me another phone. It was clear that, whatever else was going on, to Mitch, I was still useful as a piece of bait in one of his traps for Danny.

19

SUNDAY WAS A WELCOME day of rest. It was also a time to reflect. Once, as a much younger man, I had been under the delusion that I had been in control of my own life, that somehow my destiny was a matter of personal choice. Not that it had ever been true but the last week had shown me the stark reality: my fate would now be the result, or an unfortunate byproduct, of the contest between Danny Maguire and the FBI. Feeling listless as the sun rose to its highest point, I sat out in the shade of my porch. The sweat on my back glued me to the chair and by sunset I had figured that it was pointless for me to plan anything: I was a mere pawn on a chessboard and I had no say in where the players would move me.

With an immense effort, I finally peeled my back from the chair and went into the kitchen for another beer. I had only just pulled the tab when Vonette Norbury opened the screen door. "I can tell that you're not happy to see me, Robbie," she said, as she came in.

I took a swig and let the beer cool my throat. "Not happy, Vonette? You're a smart woman," I sneered at her. "I've got things on my mind right now, so how about if you get your ass outta here so I can finish my drink in peace an' I'll come over an' see you an' Calvin later on."

She pursed her lips. "Um, that won't be possible, I'm not staying with Calvin tonight. Let's just say there are issues he has to deal with and I'm not helping by being there."

I could not help but let out a bitter laugh: the woman was a mistress of understatement. Not only was she displaying a surprising lack of empathy for her brother, but she was too untroubled, too confident, and I thought I should tell her something which might give her pause for thought. "I know where we put Moses," I said. "So why did you want him all the way out in Lavette's place?"

Her face hardened instantly. "That's what worries me about Calvin . . ."

"Calvin didn't tell me an' it didn't take a lot of detective work. I'll ask you again, why there?"

She studied me for a few moments, no doubt trying to calculate how much I had found out. While I drank she began to tell me about Jerome Moses. "For all his preaching, all his political success, he was a flawed individual. But that's often an asset in a politician, look at our president, he's about as flawed as you can get. See, those flaws can give them extra drive, in the hope their achievements will camouflage all that's bad about them. But despite his faults, Little J helped many people, he did good for many black people in Georgia. But, unfortunately, once he was in Washington he started to think he could forget about the people who'd backed him. Other interest groups started to offer him money for his campaigns, make donations to his pet projects, and Little J forgot about his roots. He even took money from a bunch of red-neck oilmen shortly before he stood up and announced that he was backing the plans for war on Iraq."

The dispassionate way she talked of the congressman's life and career reminded me of the coldness I had seen in her the night he was killed. I drained the can of beer and asked, "So where do the Lavettes fit into this?"

Her voice quivered with scorn. "The Lavettes hated everything Jerome Moses stood for. The old man, Charles, he's still pissed over black people getting the vote, never mind getting elected to public office. Over the years he's backed nearly every ultra-conservative cause and think-tank that axed him for help. Anyone who organized against equality legislation, quotas, gun control, Palestine, the United Nations, or Bill Clinton got a share of Charles Lavette's money. Now a lot of them have influence in the White House and

I don't think people appreciate how dangerous a place this country has become."

"Believe me, Vonette, I think I can. But what about Henry Lavette?"

Vonette grimaced as if she had just taken poison. "His attitudes are pretty much like his father's. Originally, he made his money from oil in Colombia, but he's into cocaine now. Fire-water worked well against the native American, and he figures crack-cocaine will do the same job on African-Americans. For years black people have been talking about cocaine being a government conspiracy, but what they don't realize is that the politicians have become a sideshow. I've seen how they work close up, and democracy is a fraud!" She began to pace back and forth in front of me as she continued to recite the words which must have run through her mind hundreds of times. "It's people like the Lavettes who have the real power, it's the people with money who set the agenda. Just look at who have their snouts in the Iraqi trough and you'll see some of the people I'm talking about. The Lavette family has committed genocide in cities throughout this country but they'll never do time. They have too much power, too much money, and too many people between them and their crimes, for them ever to be brought to justice." She stopped in front of me and let out a rueful chuckle. "Like I said, Little J might do more damage to the Lavettes when dead than he could ever have done while alive."

"Like, an anonymous tip-off to the cops?"

"Maybe, when the time is more appropriate."

Everything about Vonette's demeanor signalled danger for me. I wanted to ask how she and Moses had ended up in my bedroom, but I doubted if I would get a truthful answer. Instead, I asked why she had come looking for me at this time. "Just to see how you're doing," she said, "to check out if you're the kind of man I thought you were."

I knew damn well that she was lying, but asked, "An' what sorta man would that be?"

"A man who can cope with stress, a man who might be able to help my little brother cope with his. A man who is not so easily ruffled. I mean, when I heard that Darlene Fenton shot that man the very night Little J died, I thought you might turn tail and run. Two killings in the same night, only yards from one another? Boy, on a psychological level, that must have put pressure on you but you stayed put. I think that's quite remarkable. There must be ice in those veins of yours, pure, cold ice."

Two of her fingers found their way inside her blouse either side of the top button. Now I wasn't sure if the woman was threatening or flirting with me. "You're not going to ax me if I would like to stay for coffee?" she giggled.

I gritted my teeth at her taunting tone and went and held open the screen door. "I suppose, whether I like it or not," I said, "I'll see you around, Vonette."

She brushed past me, paused and said, "Don't worry about that, Mr . . um . . . Barrett. We'll definitely see each other again soon."

The air had started to cool before I decided to work out some of my tension on the punch bag outside. I did not bother strapping my hands, I simply put on my bag mitts and started to imagine pummelling Mitch, Henry Lavette, Vonette Norbury and even Danny took a smack. It was starting to get dark and I was quite light-headed before I thought about stopping. I wanted to be so exhausted that there was nothing I could do but sleep when I finally lay down on my bed. Sweat was dripping into my eyes when a familiar shape appeared at the edge of my vision.

"Looks like you're doing good work," said Danny. The young electronics expert followed him into my yard from the direction of the river. Like Danny's, the bottoms of his pants were saturated. "We decided to take the river route and come by boat. I figure the road is being watched," Danny explained.

Joe looked tense and merely nodded in my direction as he walked toward the house. He crouched and fidgeted with something in his case before he went inside. Danny told me that Joe could be a while before he asked me to hold the punch bag. His left fist smacked against the leather and gave me a jolt. I adjusted my feet and braced myself. A lazy right thudded into the bag. "Like old times, eh, Rob?" he grunted.

While he pounded the bag I told him of Mitch's visit of the night before and the tissue of lies I had told him. Danny continued with his punching but when I said Mitch was going to check out the truck drivers he stopped and straightened up. He called for Joe to bring out his cell phone and made a brief call. When he had finished, I asked, "So who was it that arranged our new identities once we left New York?"

Danny resumed punching the bag. "I don't know," he said. "I dealt with Paulie O'Sullivan. He gave me a phone number after we first arrived. I never got to meet whoever was supplying the stuff for the false IDs. A pick up was arranged and that was it. It's all about security, mate, need-to-fecking-know basis."

"Then are you thinkin what I'm thinkin?"

"Depends what you're thinking."

"I'm thinkin what about if the person who arranged these identities also arranged for us to come here. An' if he did, I'm thinkin this whole thing since we left New York has been a setup."

"Hold on there, Robbie," Danny said dismissively. "It would be a bit of a convoluted way of getting us here. Before you lose the run of yourself, remember how many places we've been to before we got to this town. Anyway, I couldn't tell you before, but it was an order from Ireland that brought us here."

"An' it was people in Ireland who contacted you directly?"

"Ach, no, of course not."

"What about this place? Did the person who gave you the identities also send us to this address? Would this be the same person who told you about the orders from Ireland?"

"Well, yes, but . . ."

"An' what happens if Joe finds this place is bugged, what does it tell you? You were supposed to be stayin here with me, weren't you?"

". . . But . . ."

"But nothin, Danny! You don't see it? Whoever gave you these orders, gave you these identities, gave you this address, has to be behind everythin that's goin on around here. If Joe finds anythin in there it'll prove that this has all been a setup!"

Danny's mouth was moving but nothing audible came out. I wanted to make him see that someone had infiltrated the IRA and had manoeuvred us here. He found that hard to accept but, in some warped way, it made my own past mistakes easier to bear. But before he could speak, Joe came out of the house, shaking his head. He said, "I got so many lights flashing that it's like a goddamn fairground ride in there."

I felt not even a frisson of satisfaction as Danny and I exchanged glances. He immediately rallied and kept his inner turmoil hidden. "What do you reckon, Joe?"

"A very professional job," Joe whispered. "There is something in every room, including the john. It's not the sort of job that could be done in a day, or even a weekend, because they are embedded in wall cavities and the ceilings. They must have been built in and then the place was redecorated. That kind of stuff takes time and preparation."

His lips no more than a thin line, Danny said, "Cameras?"

"One in each bedroom and one in the sitting room. They're up by the light fittings. I can't say why they didn't bother to put them in other rooms. Maybe they were pushed for time, or are just relying on the audibles and the cameras came as an afterthought. Who can say?"

"So have you been seen checking the place out?" Danny asked.

"Hell, Danny," sighed Joe, "gimme a little credit, I disrupted the signal before I went in. It's back on now."

"Top man, Joe, top man. Get you back to the boat and I'll be there in a minute, so I will."

In silence, we watched Joe walk down to the riverbank. Eventually Danny said, "When we're gone, go back in there for a while. The disruption of the pictures might make them suspicious, so put them at ease and let them see you around the place. Act as natural as you can for an hour or two and then go. Give me a call on that number I gave you and when I'm done here we'll meet up, okay?"

"Act as natural as I can? Danny you keep tellin me that an' I'm not sure what you mean," I said. "I'm sick of tellin you, I'm not goin without you. How many times do you have to hear it?"

"You're going to have to."

"But, Danny, this whole thing is a setup, it's a trap! From New York, someone, somewhere, has been pullin our strings."

"There's more than me in the trap. There's some good people, who have a just cause, who are caught up too. I've got to see this through, Robbie, but there's no point you getting caught, right? While away an hour in there and then get in your motor and get away from here."

"I will if you come with me."

"I'm after telling you already, if it is a trap then there's others in it too, and I can't leave them. We have to see this thing through, because if we don't José and some others will have died for nothing."

"What have you gotta see through, Danny? What is so fuckin important?"

He bit his lip. "A few days from now, there's a fella, a state governor from Colombia, who'll be here as a guest of honour at the charity golf tournament in town. His name is Marco Pedroza and in the mid-nineties he set up a death squad which assassinated trade unionists, massacred villagers, killed homeless people and the like, while pursuing a policy he called 'social cleansing'. Back home he has a almost a whole army protecting him, so this is the first chance the Farc have had to get to him. I was asked to give them a hand. They're good soldiers, good jungle fighters, but they're not used to operating in this sort of terrain."

"But they're onto you, Danny! What do you think this thing around my wrist is all about, an' the bugs in the house? I mean, how do you know he's really comin this way, is it from the same source who got us here?"

"Pedroza is coming all right. He was in Washington yesterday, he's in Atlanta today, he'll be here next week, right enough, as a guest of the Lavettes. You say they're onto me. Well, they can't know everything if they think that we're using a bomb."

"Danny! This is America, man, this thing is gonna cause all sorta serious repercussions. The world changed on 9/11, don't you understand that? These people are nearly off their heads about terrorism in their own backyard as it is. If you go ahead with this then they'll hunt you down, no matter what. This isn't your fight, so why are you doin this, man?"

"It's what I have to do. My father was killed by a death squad, remember? "

"Maybe someone was pushin your buttons, Danny, have you thought of that?"

He said nothing as I imagined his mind was running through the chain of events which went from New York to a little town in Georgia, while I decided to retake some control of my destiny. "I'm not leavin here until it's done. That guy José Ruiz, he was in that cold store. There has to be a reason, Danny, there has to be a good reason why his body was bein kept there. Somethin weird is goin on, somethin that might come back on you guys an' it might just help if I find out what's goin on in the factory. Yeah?"

"I suppose," Danny said reluctantly. "Tomorrow, before work, go to Harry's as usual. Me or Joe will let you know the score." He slapped a hand onto my shoulder. "Thanks, Robbie. You don't have to do this, you know. You don't owe me anything."

"Owe you?" I said. "I owe you one bitch-lick when all this is done."

Danny was laughing quietly to himself as I watched him fade into the murk at the water's edge. I had made up my mind there and then that I would do my level best not think about the past, nor hope for the future, but I would deal with the present and do everything in my power to get the both of us out of this. I had a feeling it would take the fight of our lives for us to get out of Georgia.

20

I WENT INSIDE THE HOUSE. I had never felt at home in the place but the notion of being monitored made my skin crawl. It now occurred to me that Little J's death had been not only watched but also captured on tape. I would be on a tape, too, helping Calvin shift the body from my bed. That the watchers had obviously not passed on any information to the police filled me with foreboding: if they were prepared to remain silent about the killing of a congressman, they were also obviously prepared to go to any lengths to achieve their objective. Like the death of Little J Moses, my own, or anyone else's, would be not be allowed to get in their way.

Forcing myself not to look up to see if I could spot a hidden camera lens, I went to the sitting room to watch the news on TV. Even though I sensed a malevolent presence looking over my shoulder, I couldn't help a rueful smile when I saw the headline story was the disappearance of Jerome Moses. I had missed the start of the bulletin but I was in time to catch a reporter plotting the life of Little J from Atlanta to Washington: his works in an orphanage; as a preacher and community activist; and the "controversial" career after following his father into politics. In the archive footage Moses stood head and shoulders above all of those gathered around him as he roamed the orphanage. His large hands occasionally cupped the fresh young faces as the children lined up like troops for inspection.

At one point, I glimpsed Vonette, aged no more than fourteen or fifteen. Her small frame was soon obscured by larger figures.

Next to her, fleetingly, was a much younger Calvin. The footage then showed Moses singing with the 'Godfather of Soul' James Brown, as he celebrated his election to the House of Representatives before it moved on to the gloomy scenes of his defeat in the primaries. When the clip finished, the talk in the studio was of the search for Moses by the police and the rumours coming from Washington of a scandal that was about to break. The reporter said that he could not be specific – and while he was aware of how the congressman's family must be feeling – there was talk that Moses had been involved with a young male prostitute. I went to my window and looked at Calvin's house, his bare house, and I knew then that Little J Moses had not been killed in a moment of blind panic nor rage. Calvin's lights were on and I decided there and then to go across and make him tell me the truth about what had happened in my bedroom.

I found him sitting in his kitchen. Without looking at me, he got to his feet and took a bottle from his fridge. He sat down again, pushed it across the table, and signalled with his eyes that he wanted me to sit in the empty chair. I remained standing.

"I guess you saw what was on TV," I said. "We need to talk."

"I knew you'd come," Calvin said, "I got you a bottle of Guinness today, I thought you'd like it. I tried that stuff once, but I guess it's an acquired taste."

"Fuck the beer! We need to talk – now!" I felt like pulling him out of the chair and slapping him again. "I want the truth, Calvin. I want the whole truth of how come Moses ended up dead in my bedroom!"

"Vonette's back. She'll tell you."

"I saw her earlier. Do you two think I'm some kinda fuckin idiot? I just saw the TV, Calvin, an' heard what they're sayin about Moses an' a young male prostitute. I guess every newspaper an' TV news channel would like to track him down. How long do you think it will take before he gets found?"

His voice cracked: "Vonette tol' me today that we're gonna have to move soon."

I would not be denied. I leaned over and yelled into his face, "Right then, Calvin, *you* tell me how the three of you ended up in my bedroom."

"I wanted to tell to you but . . . I couldn't. I promised Vonette."

"I want to know why you involved me!" I shouted. I slammed my fist on the table and Calvin blinked before he looked directly at me. The fear in his eyes reminded me of his vulnerability and I made myself calm down before I took a seat. "I thought you were a friend, man," I said, "but there's a lotta shit goin on in my life right now an' I need *you* to tell me the truth, Calvin. Why don't you start by tellin me about yourself, an' this time leave out the lies."

"You wanna hear 'bout the orphanage?"

"That an' everythin else. About Vonette, Moses, I want you to tell me everythin."

Calvin took another drink and as he raised the bottle I saw his hand tremble. "I never knew my parents," he said quietly, more into his drink than to me. "I don't know if I got any brothers or sisters, 'cept for Vonette. All I ever heard was that I was a mistake. Some kinda whore slipped up an' got herself pregnant an' then tried to sell me for a fix. They shoulda left me to die but instead I ended up in the orphanage."

"An' that's where you met Moses?"

"Yeah."

"An' Vonette?"

"She mo than a sister to me, man, much mo. She was the first person who ever treated me with some dignity, the first who really cared. I was a skinny little kid, you know, an' I was always gettin picked on. When she came to the orphanage she looked out fo me." He dropped his head and began to sob. I saw his pain but I hardened my heart. I couldn't be deflected, I needed the information he'd kept from me. I was prepared to sit and watch him all night, if that's what it would take. Once I had the top off the Guinness bottle I reacquainted myself with the black stout's bitter taste. I'd drunk a good share of it before Calvin was back to me. "You must think I'm some sorta pussy bawlin like this," he said, wiping his face. "It's jus that it ain't easy to keep control when someone ax me 'bout my childhood, y'know?"

I tried to ease him gently back from his more painful recollections. "So, Vonette, she, um, became your sister?"

"Well, yeah, I suppose, an' when she tol' me that I had to get outta Atlanta an' come down here, she said to change my name to hers, so we would be like real family."

"So how did she end up in the orphanage?"

"She told me she came from a lovin family, immigrants from Trinidad, or somewhere. Her father was killed by a guy on drugs, a year after they landed. Her mother went outta her mind, an' that's how Vonette ended up in the same orphanage as me. Later on, she heard her ol' lady had died in some madhouse." Again emotion made him pause. It was becoming as painful for me as it was for him. "Nobody messed with V, man. We were all afraid of the people who ran the orphanage, but her? Naw, Vonette might've been small but she was as tough as any boy or man in the place. She was aware too, y'know, like black aware. Hell, man, she still won't watch MTV 'cause of the time when they wouldn't put on no black artists. She was the blackest an' the baddest when she took me under her wing, when she protected me from the older boys who used to beat me, once they found out."

I did not feel guilty about using some of the lessons I had picked up from Mitch about how to extract information: one was to ask a question to which the answer was already known so as to keep the person at the receiving end talking. "Found out what?"

He wetted his dry mouth with another swig of beer and turned his face away. I laid my hand on top of his and with a gentle squeeze encouraged him to continue. "Hell, you know why, Robbie, 'cause they found out I was different. . . ." He pulled his hand from under mine with such force that his arm knocked the bottle of Guinness to the floor. We both looked to the broken glass swimming in the brown liquid. "I'm gay, man. I'm a fuckin faggot." When I didn't respond, he added, "A faggot. Have you got that? Ain't that wha you wanted me to say, that I'm the guy who the press wanna talk to about Little J an' his affair with a young male prostitute?"

I needed him to tell me more and said, "I asked you for the truth, Calvin. An' as long as you tell me the truth, whatever it is, I'm cool with it." I wasn't sure if I was being honest. For a moment, I wanted to tell him that I passed no judgment; I wanted to tell him about Natasha and how she'd made me confront some things about myself, but this was not the time and I could not afford for him to be side-tracked. He bent down to pick up the pieces of the broken bottle but I took his arm and gently pulled him upright again. "Calvin," I said, "is that how Vonette got her job with Moses? She knew what the man had been doin with you when you were a kid?"

He nodded slowly. "He'd done the same sorta things with her. The man had . . . an appetite, y'know wha I'm sayin? But Vonette was smart, even as a kid. She hooked up a little cassette recorder

163

an' taped it, man, maybe thirty or forty times. She bided her time, waited until he was elected, an' then made her move. She got that job, an' later on, when things was gettin hot fo him, Little J arranged it so I could rent this place an' work at the lumber yard."

"So why did she bring him here that night, an' how come you ended up in my place? I've got a right to know, Calvin, so don't hold back on me now."

"Leave it, Robbie, please, just leave it. What's done is done."

"How can I leave it, Calvin? Man, my life's on the line if we're caught. You involved me an' I think I'm entitled to the truth about why you killed him."

"Shit, man, I didn't kill him. It was Vonette, she killed him. She was protectin me."

"Hold on, Calvin, so she killed him? Then how the hell did he end up in my place?"

"The first bit of what she said to you was true: I did go over to yo place to tell you 'bout yo white friend Danny. Me an' Little J hadn't seen each other fo a while an' I wasn't comfortable with the way he was lookin at me so when he went fo a leak Vonette tol' me to go stay in yo place until he fell asleep. But when he foun out I was gone he got mad an' made V tell him where I'd gots to. I got into yo place usin that trick with the back door an' after Danny left, I was tryna close it agin when Little J got to me. He started to do things. I wanted him to stop, I really did, but I knew he wouldn't until he'd got wha he wanted. When he came close an' I smelled his sweat, I was back to bein a little kid agin. I was cryin an' shit, an' he was pullin down my pants, an' then Vonette came to the door. He tol' her she could join in, an' she say, 'Sho, Little J, let's find a bedroom, I've got somethin special fo you.' I didn't see the knife in her hand – an' Little J sho didn't. She stuck it into him but he made a grab fo her. She did it agin but Little J was still goin fo her. I jumped on him an' took him down onto the bed an' Vonette kept stabbin an' stabbin. But her face, Robbie, it was kinda strange, like she was so calm. Blood was goin all over the place but it was like she was at peace while she was doin it. An' when she was finished she smiled at me an' say that he deserved to die, she say he was like the devil hisself an' she was sendin him back to hell."

I didn't need, nor want, him to say any more but he went on, "Little J first came to me when I was ten years old. Truth is, it's only when I look back that I see it was wrong. I mean, when you're a chil' you rely on grown-ups to show you what's right an' wrong. I said sumpin to a preacher, a white minister – it was befo Little J was one himself – 'bout some things that was happenin, but he jus said he'd pray fo me. Then I thought it was happenin 'cause Little J loved me, y'know? When I was older, like fifteen or sixteen, he started introducin me to other men. They gave me money an' I went along with it but I knew by then it was nuthin to do with love. One day he brought me to this man, an' it turned out to be the white preacher I first tol'. Now, that's when it started to fuck with my head."

Feeling my words were inadequate, I said, "Calvin, if it means anythin, I'm sorry for all the shit you've had to go through . . ."

"Wha you sorry for, Robbie? You had nuthin to do with my past."

Even if he didn't want pity from me, I still wanted information from him. "So when did you come to Petra?"

"I'd say, 'bout seven or eight months ago, maybe. Say, 'bout coupla months befo you got here."

"An' what did Vonette say when she was here today?"

"Jus that stuff was comin on the TV an' that I was to keep quiet, keep cool. That sorta thing. She say things will be happenin soon, an' then me an' her will be settin up home in Jacksonville."

"What things?"

"Shit, she don't tell me nuthin other than we's gettin outta this place real soon. She gotta a plan, man. From a kid she was always makin plans an' she was always tellin me, like when she was makin the cassette tapes, that timin is everthin. She jus say the time is close."

"Is she goin to blackmail someone about Moses?"

"Blackmail, she call it whitemail, but I don't know nuthin, Robbie, an' that's the kinda stuff I don't wanna know."

"But what she's got planned, has it somethin to do with Moses bein buried on that property?"

"If it do, she don't tell me, I swear she don't. Lately, she's been involved in sumpin, but I don't know wha it is. I mean, she's driven, really driven, like she comin to the end of a race an' she is jus puttin her head down an' runnin the final lap as hard as she can. When she put that knife into Little J I never seen that look befo. Sumpin 'bout her's changed."

I tried to make sense of what Calvin had told me and figured that Vonette had planned to kill Moses for a very long time. When the

165

opportunity arose she took it without hesitation, especially when that opportunity was in a place which would not be connected with her. How she thought she could use his corpse to extort money from the Lavettes was beyond me – but if there was a way I was in no doubt that she'd find it.

Calvin roused me from my thoughts. "Robbie, after wha I've tol' you, I understand if we ain't friends no mo."

I laughed quietly to myself. "We're still friends, okay?" I said. He searched my face for sincerity as I went on, "Calvin, believe me, you're not my only friend with secrets. I mean it when I say I hope you an' Vonette manage to set up that home in Jacksonville."

"I thought the gay thing might . . ."

"Might've been one time, it's no big thing to me now. You're still a friend, okay?"

He smiled weakly. "I glad 'bout that, Robbie, real glad that you ain't judgin me. I do enough of that myself. Y'know karma? Shit, I done bad, man, I done some real bad things. I still hear Little J screamin as I held him down, I hear him callin fo Vonette to stop. I don't deserve no happy home. I don't deserve no happiness, period."

I put a hand on his shoulder. My gesture took him by surprise and he looked at my hand and then into to my face more hopefully. I said, "Calvin, I once did somethin very bad an' guilt nearly took my mind. It took me a long time to learn that I had to leave the past be, to realize I couldn't change it, that all I could do was to accept the present as it is, an' stay hopeful for the future. Stay hopeful, Calvin, just stay hopeful an' you might just make it."

I could tell that he was regretful over telling me so much and he wanted me to go. I said goodnight and left him sitting there in his lonely kitchen and while stepping into his backyard, I imagined Natasha looking down on me approvingly from somewhere beyond the gathering clouds, and a small, reminiscing smile came to my lips. It faded abruptly when I heard someone hiss my name from the direction of the old chicken coop. I paused and Stella emerged from the gap between it and the gas tank.

"Robbie, don't go back to yo house!" she called in a whisper. "Men is in there – an' I think they's lookin to kill you!"

21

I MOVED CLOSER AND Stella continued, "Some men parked their truck not far from our place an' then they axed Leroy if he knew where you lived. He's still mad as hell that you punched him real good an' knocked out some mo of his teeth. They gave Leroy a bottle of Jack Daniels an' he showed them yo house. They's carryin baseball bats an' shit like that."

"How many of them are there?"

"Four an' they're all white."

"Does that make a difference?"

"I think they're Klan, Robbie. They reckon you put a friend of theirs in hospital. I heard them tell Leroy that 'cause you gone hurt their friend's manhood they's gonna hurt yaws."

They had to be friends of Jack Kirby and old Myrtle's warning about him and his family's connections with the KKK came back to me. I looked back at Calvin's kitchen door and thought about getting his rifle, but Stella gripped my arm. "I don't think it's safe to stay aroun here. I know a place where you can hide out 'til they's gone." I made to move but her hold tightened. "Please, jus come with me, it ain't far. I'll keep a lookout to see when they gone an' then I'll come git you."

I looked into her scared and pretty eyes and figured discretion would be the better part of valour – and there was enough trouble in my life without adding to it. "Where?" I said.

"Not far," she said. We went to the rear of Calvin's yard, clambered over the fence and went into the woods. In amongst the trees the bright moon was no help to us but luckily Stella had obviously taken this path many times before and after a few stumbles we reached an old shack in a clearing. She led me inside and lit a small oil lamp.

"Some of the kids still play in here," she said, "but most of them is too scared 'cause it's supposed to be haunted. There's some straw in the corner; you can lie down there. I brought it up for my little brother Joshua but he was too frightened to stay."

My eyes straining for signs of vermin, I tentatively sat down in the straw. To my surprise, Stella sat down beside me. "I thought you were goin to keep lookout," I said.

"Well," she said, "they ain't gonna be gone fo a while, so I might as well keep you company, huh?"

"Are you sure you're not makin all this up, Stella?"

The light from the lamp caught the hurt in her eyes. "On my little brother's life, Robbie, there's men in yo house lookin to hurt you. Why would I make it up?"

I did my best not to sound ungrateful for what she'd done. "Well, just stay a few minutes an' then head back, okay? I don't want to stay here all night if I don't need to."

The lamp made deep hollows of her dimples as she smiled. "So who's the friend of theirs that you hurt?" she asked.

"A guy at the factory."

"Why?"

"Personal reasons."

"Like woman personal?"

"An' what would a little girl like you know about those kinda things?"

"I'm not a little girl, Robbie. I'm a lot more experienced than you think."

"Well, for your information, a woman has nothin to do with it but that's all I'm sayin."

"I thought you might've got into a fight over that woman who called on you a couple-a nights ago. She sho looked purdy. . . Don't look so surprised. Nuthin much happens aroun these here parts without Momma knowin 'bout it."

"Hey, Stella," I snapped, still raw about Cristina, "watch it, now. Some things should stay personal, right?"

"I was jus axin," she said sulkily.

"Well, don't." Perhaps it was down to my dented male ego, but I'd figured that Cristina would have been more upset and I didn't like the way she had been so cool and controlled as she'd left me. I'd guessed wrongly that I was worth just a few tears. The light caught Stella's eyes again and I regretted being so sharp with her. Softer, I said, "Anyway, thanks for doin this for me, Stella. I really appreciate it."

"You do?"

"Sure."

"Then will you do sumpin to show me how much you appreciate it?"

Warily, I said, "Depends on the somethin."

"Jus a kiss." I groaned and she added, "Jus one kiss to say you appreciate wha I've done fo you an' then I'll know you mean it."

Reluctantly I said, "Well, okay, one kiss. An' then you go an' find out what's happenin in my place, right?"

I leaned over and pecked her on the cheek but she pulled away from me and made an angry frown. "One kiss on the lips, like you'd give to a woman, that's wha I want. I want you to show me how you'd kiss a woman you really love. See, I trust you, Robbie, an' I wanna know wha it feels like so when I git kissed agin I'll know if it's true when a man tells me that he loves me. You can close your eyes, if you want, an' think of the woman you've really loved while you do it." She put her face close to mine and added, "Jus pretend you are with her agin an' let me feel it too."

Those last words of hers caught me unawares. Perhaps it was all those dreams I'd had recently but as my mouth met Stella's, for a few magical moments, I was kissing Natasha again, kissing her how I wished I'd done all that time ago. I was lost in the memory of her beautiful lips until a hand found mine and held it against a warm, firm breast. I was jolted back into reality and pulled away.

"Why?" Stella asked, her voice trembling.

"'Cause the agreement was for one kiss, an' that's about all I can manage right now."

"We wouldn't be doin nuthin I ain't done befo. Robbie, I really like you, I kinda love you, especially after what you did to Leroy. He's always sayin I'm ripe an' things, an' when Momma ain't home he puts his hands where they don't belong. Come on, Robbie, let's jus lie back an' see wha happens. Let me show you how much I could love you."

"I said no! Look, Stella, I appreciate what you've done an' what you're offerin. You're a lovely girl, a beautiful young woman. An' one day you'll find out that sometimes when a man an' woman really think a lot of each other, a kiss is enough. A kiss says a lotta things, invites a lotta things, but some of the best kisses stay at kisses, understand?"

"I guess so," she said quietly. "Well maybe, in time, when I'm older, we might kiss agin an' you'll feel different."

"You never know, Stella, you never know." I cupped her face in my hands and gave her another quick kiss. This time I was kissing her and not Natasha. "That's to say thank you."

She smiled contentedly. "Will I head back now an' see if those men are still there?"

"I think that would be a good idea. Don't stay out too long, though, okay? If they're still there in an hour, go home an' come see me in the mornin."

"Like early?"

"If you don't mind. I still gotta go to work."

She stole another brief kiss. "I don't mind doin anythin fo you,"she said. "If I'm not back in an hour, I'll see you in the mornin."

Once I was alone, I lay down and watched the flickering flame of the lamp. I was about to set the alarm clock on the cell phone Mitch had given me but while searching my pockets I remembered that I had left it in the house. I wondered if he were watching the men via the cameras embedded in the house and if he might have rung me to say that I was in danger. Probably not. Eventually, when it became obvious that Stella wouldn't be returning for me until morning, I closed my eyes. Listening to the wind blowing through the branches, I wondered about what was ahead of me: what would come of my search for the body I had seen in the cold store and my next encounter with Mitch? But my last thoughts, as I drifted off to sleep, were ones of preparing myself to do anything it would take to survive.

I woke to find the lamp was out. The sun was up and I decided not to wait for Stella to come and get me. The hut's surroundings looked disturbingly unfamiliar in the morning's first light. I could see nothing but trees in every direction, but I had a rough idea of the way I should head, and I found a narrow path made by the trampling of countless feet over the years. Rain had left the air fresh and full of the sharp scent of pine and I savoured the fresh, clean taste.

After a short distance the path divided. I hesitated over which way to go, and then took the left fork. It turned out not to be the path we'd taken the night before, and I ended up on the road just down from Miss Boo's house, rather than in Calvin's back yard. But my choice had been a fortunate one. From here I could see that my bleary-eyed Mexican neighbours were getting ready for work, and that there was no sign of the truck belonging to Jack Kirby's friends. I breathed a little more easily and crept around to the back of my house. The screen door was hanging off its hinges and the sight of the damage put a knot in my chest as I entered the kitchen.

I edged my way through broken cups and plates and found similar scenes of destruction in the sitting room and bedrooms. The sight of the phone Mitch had given me also lying smashed on the floor brought a smile of grim satisfaction to my lips. There wasn't a lot left intact: they'd even slashed my punch bag and left its innards strewn beside it as though it was a butchered beast. I had a small stash of money hidden but I decided not to take it for the time being as I was aware that Mitch and his colleagues were watching and I did not want to signal that I was preparing to make a run for it. My clothes were thrown around the place but otherwise intact. Following a few minutes of futile cussing, I took some consolation from the fact that my years of experience as a fugitive meant that I kept a packed bag in the trunk of my car in case I needed to make a quick exit. I hurried for a wash and put on clean, if crumpled, pants and a shirt and headed to Harry's.

The aroma of coffee was fresh and still pleasant at this hour. "Robbie," said Harry, "you're early. How are you this morning?"

"Cool," I said. "The usual breakfast, H. If it's not wastin my breath, no grits, please."

He smiled as though I had just wasted my breath, and pushed an envelope across the counter. "A man came in just as we opened," he said. "He asked me to give you this. Normally I wouldn't."

I smiled back, but didn't open the envelope until I was seated at a table. Inside was a small sheet of paper with "RAW" written on it – Danny's code for "ring after work". It wasn't quite what I had expected but as I heard the door opening and someone coming in, I automatically put the note into my pocket. My head jerked back when I saw it was Mitch in the disguise he had used before. He came and sat down opposite me, smiling at my discomfiture. I waited for him to ask me about the note, but he couldn't have seen me reading it because he said, "Rough night, Walker?"

I knew his surveillance equipment enabled him to see the damage to my rented house. "You could say that. A few uninvited guests."

He turned down the corners of his grim mouth. "I called in but you were already gone, and I figured you'd be here. So who were they, these guests who made such a mess of your place?"

His deceit was as well hidden as his cameras. It occurred to me then just how much of my recent life he'd witnessed. I said to him, "Guys who are gonna stop me an' you doin business. I guess they came to tell me that my time was up an' that I was to leave town. A few days ago I had a disagreement with a man called Jack Kirby, he's head of security at the factory. Apparently, some friends of his wanna fight his battles for him."

"And where were you while they were rearranging your interior design?"

"I spent the night in the woods. Mitch, this is the second time I've had a bunch of guys attack me or my property an' you've done nothin to help, so I want out, 'cause your deal means nothin if I'm dead. You've already said that I've committed no crime in this country, so let me go an' carry on an' find Danny by yourself. I mean, those guys were serious, Or maybe you think I'm makin this up an' I smashed up my own place."

His eyes bore into me as he took in that last remark. I silently cussed myself for trying to be too clever and that he might now figure that I had found out about the bugs in the house. "Jack Kirby, you say?" he grunted. "You have my guarantee that neither he nor his friends will bother you again." The thick lips pursed and colour came into his cheeks. "Walker, I need Maguire soon if we are to avoid hundreds of innocent people becoming casualties. From what we know, we've got no more than a couple of days. I hope we understand each other and you're not thinking of goofing me around." He paused as my breakfast arrived and then he dipped a sausage into my egg. "If I think you're not keeping your side of the bargain, Walker, not only won't you get to see your mom and son, you might just end up as an accessory to mass murder."

Mitch stood up and he squashed the sausage onto my plate. "Maguire *will* contact you again and you do exactly what I've told you. It could be a fatal mistake if you don't."

I didn't eat much after he left, and I went to the counter to pay my bill.

"That was the so-called reporter who was in here before, wasn't it?" Harry asked.

"Yeah, that's the guy."

Suspicious, Harry said, "So how's his story about José Ruiz going?"

I put the coins he gave me into the tip jar and stuffed the bills into a back pocket. "He reckons he's workin to a deadline. He's only got two days or somethin an' he wants me to help him out."

"You reckon he really is a reporter?"

"I guess so."

"And are you going to help him?"

I turned for the door and said, "I'm not sure if I have much of a choice, Harry."

22

THERE WAS TURMOIL AT the factory gates. I didn't know what it was about but I knew that something highly unusual was going on when Darren Clayton and another dozen security guards shoved through the crowd and cleared a path for me and a few other guys.

"What's goin on?" I asked, as we pushed our way toward the factory.

"Fuckin lock-out, man," snarled Darren. "These fuckin spics have messed with the machines once too often. They're gone – orders from Watson. The man says he'll close the factory down before he has those fuckin wetbacks in here agin."

While I was putting on my overalls, I'd heard that the management had refused permission for workers to take time out to attend a memorial service for Miguel in the parking lot. Not that most of them had any great love for the man who had fallen down the elevator shaft, but their attendance at the service was to be not only about the loss of a colleague but also a message to the management that, whatever the person's status or nationality, every life in the factory should count for something. To the management the service smacked of a walkout, and they'd threatened to fire anyone who passed through the gates without permission. The ultimatum turned out to be a serious error of judgment, for despite all the security guards on the factory floor, several very expensive machines had been damaged during the night shift and production in key areas had ground to a halt.

When I went to collect my worksheet, Chuck Woodlow's response was unexpectedly cordial. "Good to see you've come early, Barrett," he said. "Every machine's got to be stripped and checked; maintenance schedules are being brought forward one month. Couple of the night crew won't be back and, if he goes along with the rest of the spics, it looks as if Ricardo won't be in again today, so that also means we're on double shifts. You have a problem with that?"

As far as I was concerned, the more excuses I had to stay out of my house, the better it was for me. "Is that double shifts all the way through?" I asked. "I mean, what sorta breaks are we havin?"

"You'll finish your normal shift an hour early. Then be back here for eight and work until around two, but you'll get a full night-shift payment."

"Okay, I think I can handle that."

"Right, I want you to start on Sector Three. And by the way, Jack Kirby's back. I'll put it to you straight, the man's a friend of mine but Billy Joe has told me to make it clear to you both that he won't tolerate either of you causing any problems. Jack's agreed and says that, if you're man enough, he'll sort out outstanding business with you, on a one-to-one basis, once this plant's up and running again."

"Man," I said, "I definitely think I can handle that. An' how are his balls?"

"Don't push your luck, Barrett," growled Woodlow.

In the now eerily quiet Sector Three, I saw Jack Kirby in the distance. When he caught sight of me he did his best to look menacing, but the white gown and hairnet he had to wear in the production areas made him look more comical than threatening. I decided to keep away from him as much as possible. I didn't need another fight.

The morning flew by with so much work to do. My thoughts regularly turned to the body I had discovered in the cold store. I figured that either the corpse of my foreman had been stolen from the local morgue, or it had never arrived there in the first place and someone else was on a slab, under the same false identity that he had used when working here. However, the motive for doing such a thing was something I could not work out. The body couldn't have vanished into thin air and I had a hunch it was still somewhere within the factory compound. I hadn't yet had an opportunity to try and find it – but I would, first chance I got, while mindful of what had happened to Miguel.

After lunch I was put to work with John Hunter in the 'Further Processing' department, where, it was suspected, that someone had placed a metal bolt on the conveyor which fed a large deboning machine. I had been hard at it for over twenty minutes when I noticed that Hunter had wandered off in the direction of the elevator shaft where Miguel had been found. He had a preoccupied look about him and it was obvious to me that he was searching for something. "Hey," I called, "I could do with a hand here with this screw auger. The damn thing's welded itself to the perforated screen. These guys knew where to sabotage."

"Give me a minute, Barrett." He had the elevator doors open and was looking down the shaft.

"What's the problem?" I asked him. "Did you lose somethin?"

He wandered back to me. "When you an' Colin were checkin out the elevator did you come across anythin unusual?"

I immediately thought about the key I'd found. "No," I replied, "we found nothin wrong with either the gear or the electrics."

I went back to the machine. Hunter finally joined me and ducked behind the safety screen I'd erected to shield us from the sparks generated by the disc cutter. He put his head close to mine and said, "The night-shift boys sure did a good job stoppin these machines. It's gonna cost a small fortune to get this one goin again."

"Yeah," I said sarcastically, "they must really miss their buddy Miguel."

He shot me an uncertain glance. "How well did you know him?"

"I didn't, not personally, an' not as well as you. I heard that he was a thief."

Hunter frowned and said, "Barrett, I didn't know him like how you're implyin."

"So what was it with you gettin all defensive an' tellin me that I hadn't seen you an' him talkin down by the cold storage that time?"

Hunter took hold of the disc cutter and muttered it was about time that he did his share. The sparks began to fly and I backed off and went to his rear to give myself a little more protection. It was then that I saw the angular bulge beneath his overalls at the centre of his back: Hunter was armed – and, by the shape, I guessed armed with a semi-automatic. It felt as if I had been belted in the stomach. Now everything about his demeanor made sense: he had been looking down the elevator shaft because he somehow knew that Miguel's death had been no accident; and his attitude toward me had changed since I had been picked up and interrogated. Hunter had to be working with Mitch.

I was so busy cussing myself for not figuring out Hunter before now, that it barely registered with me that he had stopped cutting. His brow was glistening with sweat. "I reckon we've earned ourselves a coffee," he said.

It took me a couple of moments to respond. "Sure, why not. Let's go wash our hands."

I led the way to the washroom, now feeling Hunter's eyes were on me and scrutinizing my every move. There was only the two of us by the basins when his voice dropped to a whisper: "I'm gonna level with you, Barrett, Miguel had somethin belongin to me." He stared at me intently. "That's what I was talkin to him about when you saw us that time. But that somethin has gone missin an' Colin has told me you were the one who inspected the elevator. Be straight with me, Barrett, did you find anythin like a purse, or a money clip? You can keep the damn money, it's somethin else I want."

"Shit, Hunter, I'm no thief, an' I don't steal off the dead," I retorted, while angrily squashing a paper towel into a ball. I thrust it into his hands, convinced he was looking for the key – but I was just as determined that neither he, nor the people he was working with, would get hold of it before I made another search for the body of the man I had called José Ruiz.

Maybe Hunter's questions had hastened it, but the coffee break seemed to me to be the best time to take another look in the contaminated meat store, as there would be even less people about. I took my box of tools with me for appearances' sake and headed for the refrigeration units. As I unlocked the door there was a slight tremor in my hand but this time it had nothing to do with the cold. It was a large area to explore, with many boxes and large plastic bags of condemned meat stacked in high rows and I figured that Danny and I could not have made anything like a thorough search. I left my toolbox by the door and ventured inside. The hum of the lights and throbbing of the refrigeration system added to the creepy atmosphere generated by the colossal mounds of dead flesh. I realized then that if José's body was still in here, he was probably under any of a vast amount of bags of meat. I guessed if he were anywhere, he would have been put towards the rear of the unit. The fog of my breath came thick and fast as I pulled and pushed a few bags. Sweat was instantly turning cold and adding to the chill down my back. My numb fingers had just taken hold of another bag at shoulder height when a noise stilled me. I listened more intently but when I heard nothing other than the normal hum, I guessed it was the sound of gas moving through the pipes. The bag slipped from my grasp and slapped the smooth concrete floor the moment before I glimpsed a movement at the edge of my vision.

"What the hell you doin in here, Barrett?"

I saw the clouds of agitated cold breath escaping from the mouth of John Hunter before I saw his gun. Miguel's death had obviously made him edgy. "There's no need for that," I said, "we're workin for the same side."

Hunter let out a disdainful snort. "We don't work for the same side, Barrett, an' you've just proved that you've been holdin out on me. Give me that key now, slowly, an' without any sudden movements."

I reached into a pocket and eased out the key. I saw a look in Hunter's narrowed eyes that told me that he was ready to shoot without hesitation. Once I followed his instruction to place it on the floor and step back I told him that I was also working for Mitch. "Mitch? I don't know any Mitch, Barrett, or whatever your real name is. I work for the INS, an' Miguel was gatherin information for me about the people who are bringin in illegal immigrants into this part of Georgia. I did some checkin on you durin the weekend an' all I've come up with is a blank. In my experience that usually means you're illegal yourself an' now you're in serious shit."

He stepped forward and picked up the key. I thought then that he did not know of its significance and decided to gamble. "I'm not in as much shit as you, Hunter." I slowly raised my arm and turned it so he could see the wristwatch. "If I push the button on this watch, in a matter of minutes this place will be crawlin with FBI an' then that's two operations fucked. It's a personal protection device given to me by an agent who calls himself Mitch. Now, how about if I lower my arm an' you lower that gun before we go find ourselves somewhere warmer to talk."

Hunter had been taken by surprise and spent a moment or two calculating before he slowly nodded and put away his gun. On my suggestion we went back to the machine we were repairing, as the two of us talking together there would not attract any undue attention.

The walk calmed Hunter and his nervous energy had seemingly dissipated. "Before we go any further," he began, "you have to level with me. Did you mention to anyone at all that you saw me talkin to Miguel that time?"

"No one."

He searched my face, in a manner which was similar to Mitch's, then said, "Too much of a damn coincidence that they cleared the place of so much illegal labour only forty-eight hours before we were due to hit this place."

"Well, I hate to break up your conspiracy theory, Hunter, but last week down at Harry's I heard that the INS was about. So someone's been leakin information."

The muscles on Hunter's face visibly tightened again and he hissed several profanities from between his clenched teeth. "So you found that key down the elevator shaft?" he asked.

"Yeah, an' I've a feelin Miguel told you that he'd found somethin big, but wouldn't tell you what, until you gave him somethin big in return. Problem is, someone else found out that Miguel was in the meat store an' threw him down the elevator shaft before he could tell you what he'd found."

"Sounds like a whole lotta guessin on your part."

"Well, you can tell me if I'm right about the first part, an' if I am, we both know I'm right about the second."

Hunter sighed heavily. "So, as I figured, Miguel's death was no accident." He looked to my watch. "An' you say you've got somethin goin down with the Feds, so what's got them so interested about here?"

I figured that I had to bargain with him from a position of strength. "That's only 'need-to-know' an' you don't need to right now. But I am willin to tell you what got Miguel killed if you can cut me a deal."

My attitude was needling Hunter. "Fuck you, Barrett, or whatever your real name is. Why should I cut a deal with you, if you're workin with the FBI, an' why would you wanna try an' cut a deal with me?"

"Because the deal is for me alone. An' you're right, I am in this country illegally, like a friend of mine who I arrived with. If you give me an' my friend a deal, I'll give you somethin that could turn out to be way bigger than illegal labour."

He looked over his shoulder and then back to me. I could tell that he was at least taking me seriously and had made some calculations. "I'm a small cog in a big machine," he said. "The best I can do is go back to my boss with what you've got to offer an' see if he's interested."

"How do I know that's not just bullshit?"

"You don't. But I'm down a man an' I'm not tryin to make out it's a great deal. I'm just tellin you what I can offer right now. We don't want you, or any of poor bastards who works here. We want the big fish like the Lavettes an' bad guys like Kirby who's usin his time with Border Patrol to bring illegals into Georgia. An' it's because you probably damaged his balls enough to prevent that son-bitch breedin that I'll talk to my boss for you, but that's providin there is somethin you can tell that's worth a deal."

He was nibbling at, but had yet to jump on my hook. "What I know, got Miguel killed. It's worth more than what you're offerin. Hell, man, I might as well stick with the FBI, so no deal Hunter."

"Hey, listen, asshole, you'll have to give me more than that, if you want somethin better."

I decided that this was the time to load the bait. "I was in the cold store shortly after Miguel went down the elevator shaft, an' that's when I found the body of José Ruiz."

A puzzled frown creased his forehead. "José Ruiz? I thought they recovered his body from the river."

I said, "A body, Hunter. But I'm tellin you, our ol' foreman was lyin there with all the contaminated meat. An' before you ask, I don't have a clue about who's the guy who's lyin in the morgue that they're callin José Ruiz – but he's not the guy we knew."

He was quiet for a while. "Why take a body an' keep it in the freezer at a meat plant?"

"I don't know but I've got a friend, a guy who knows a lot more about how José was killed. He wasn't involved, but he kinda saw somethin. I could bring him to you but you're gonna have to come up with some sorta arrangement for him too."

"Hey! You're in no position to be demandin deals."

"You're the guy who's talkin about bigger fish like the Lavettes, I'm just sayin it could be an even bigger fish than you thought."

"I could just arrest you."

"An' have the FBI lookin for a piece of your ass?"

Hunter's professional scepticism resurfaced. "So how come that you're workin for the Feds an' not your friend?"

"They approached me first, last weekend, to be precise. Now, I got a deal but their attitude stinks. I'd prefer to do business with you, if you can help my friend, but can you do business with me?

"What are the Feds offerin?"

"Immunity an' witness-protection programme."

"An what are you offerin in return?"

"Information, but I can't tell you more than that."

"You tell them about the body?"

"Not yet."

Pensively, Hunter stroked his cheek. His fingers slid along his chin and pinched the flesh at the base of his throat. "Immunity an' witness protection, that's axin some. What do you have that's worth that?"

"My friend knows stuff about who José Ruiz really was. I can't say what that is, exactly, but it's somethin about the type of people comin illegally to this country from Colombia an' places. The FBI reckon it's worth a deal. What about you?"

Hunter looked at the ground. He was an ambitious man who was trying not to let it show that he was getting out of his depth and I hoped he would not take the chance of damaging his career by bringing down an FBI operation. I figured he was debating whether to run with what he had, or trust me and wait for information which could enhance his job prospects. "Listen," he said, "I need to talk to people at my office before I can make a deal like that. You're doin the late shift too, right?" I told him I was and he went on, "Okay. I'll meet you here tonight, after the first break. Don't go lettin me down, now."

"Hunter, you're the one with nothin to lose. I'm riskin everythin."

We went back to work and I put myself under one of the machines again. The job was made all the more difficult when I imagined how I would tell Danny that I was about to save the two of us by playing the INS off against the FBI. Only then did the magnitude of what I was trying to do dawn on me. My hands just would not stop shaking.

As it got close to clocking out time, I headed for the payphone in the canteen to ring Danny as he had requested in his note. I took the long way around and strolled past the loading bay watching out for Hunter, or anyone else, carrying anything unusual in or out of the cold store. But I saw nothing out of the ordinary except for a truck by the units with a wheel missing and its axle resting on large blocks.

I dialled the new number he'd given me and Danny answered on the fourth ring. "Drive to Creektown for nine o'clock."

"Can't make it for then. We've got a double shift tonight. Say, seven?"

"Okay, seven then. Drive slowly, someone will come to you."

He disconnected and I returned to fretting over the implications of Hunter's discovery that I was using a false name. Now he had a measure of power over me but I hoped my mention of the FBI would negate it. I completed my shift without seeing him again. Heading for the punch clock, a succession of thoughts tumbled through my mind about what was really happening all around me. A lot of my previous assumptions had turned out to be very wrong, and a lot of the people I'd come into contact with were not what they had seemed. Hunter was really an INS agent; and it was safe to assume that there were Farc guerrillas amongst the workers as well as people working with Mitch. And there was another group which involved Jack Kirby – and probably his buddy Chuck Woodlow – that brought in illegal immigrants. I had an hour to persuade Danny that we had become entangled in something far more complex than we could have imagined and that a deal with John Hunter might be our only chance to get out of this place alive.

23

THE LIGHTS HAD TURNED RED. I listened to the engine idle and started to wonder what would happen when I met Danny and whether he would at least hear me out. I'd got to Creektown at ten to seven and had driven slowly around the neighbourhood for almost fifteen minutes. The first stirring of nocturnal life was gradually emerging onto street corners. There had been no sign of Danny but I guessed he'd watched me at some point to check that I wasn't being tailed.

A tap on the passenger window almost had me jumping out of my seat. However, the face that looked through the glass at me did not belong to Danny Maguire. It was a young and pretty Hispanic woman in a red polka-dot dress who was peering in at me. She looked like a hooker and I shook my head and waved her away, but she merely nodded, as if acknowledging a question I hadn't asked. The lights were changing. A car behind blew its horn, and the woman opened the door and slid onto the seat beside me. "Hey," I snapped, hastily making a right turn, "don't you understand? I'm not lookin for business so get your . . ."

"Drive, Robbie," she said. The mention of my name was enough to tell me that she'd been on the lookout for me. She inhaled on a cigarette and said, "I will show you where you have to go."

We drove for another five minutes, in silence except for a few curt instructions to turn left or right. We had almost completed a circle of a couple of blocks when she flicked the butt out of the window. Blowing the last of her smoke from the corner of her mouth, she said, "Okay, just making sure we were not followed. Take this next turn to the left and stop. We will walk to the building with the old man playing a guitar outside. When I've shown you to the door, I'll come back and drive your car around for a little while."

The tuneless strumming of the guitar faded as I followed her up the stairs of a three-storey apartment building; my eyes were drawn like magnets to her honey-coloured legs. She paused at the top of the stairs and my face almost collided with the back of her thighs. She turned her head and smiled down knowingly, before leading me to a grubby and blistered door. As she put a key in the lock, a man, unshaven and with his zipper still open, came out from another door, with a much younger woman close behind. I guessed that the old guy with the guitar was probably on the lookout for cops and would strike up a proper tune if they turned up.

With a nod, my pretty guide signalled that I was to enter first. I opened the door and saw no one. The air in the apartment was sticky and smelled of greasy, damp cardboard. The ceiling sagged and there was a large brown stain on the wall ahead.

"Come on in, Robbie," called Danny from the doorway of another room, which I figured was a bedroom. He was wearing a fluorescent-green short-sleeved shirt which was pinched at the armpits. I entered and saw a familiar face over his shoulder. It was young Ricardo, dressed in a similar shirt of shocking-lemon, though his was two sizes too big for him. While I tried to hide my surprise at seeing him, the young woman closed the apartment door behind me and I heard her clip-clop down the stairs. Danny smiled, "Don't be fooled by the way she looks, mate, she is one tough cookie."

"Besides findin a crate full of crappy shirts," I said, "what's goin on, Danny?"

He smoothed the front of his shirt with one hand. "Don't you like them? I'm after picking up a load very cheap, so I am." I didn't return his smile. He gestured to the moth-eaten sofa. "Sit you down a wee while, Robbie. We need to talk."

"You're damn right," I said, glancing at the shocking-lemon shirt. "It seems everyone's in on this fuckin thing 'cept me."

Ricardo gave me one of his cocky smiles and he took a seat at a rickety table. "Listen to your friend," he said. "You need to hear what we have to say."

"Shut the fuck up, Ric, I don't need to hear anythin from you." I strolled over to Danny and stared into his face. That he'd kept me in the dark for so long was beginning to cut deep. For a moment I came very close to punching him – and he knew it when he saw the look in my eyes.

Apologetically, he said, "Ach, look, mate, like I told you before, I didn't want you to be a part of any of this, but you keep saying that you'll not leave until I do. So this is your last chance, Robbie. Do I tell you what's the plan, or do you turn and walk out the door with no hard feelings? It's up to you now. You know the score if I start explaining."

I knew the score: once I'd been told, once I was in the loop, there could be no backing out. But, even without Danny explaining to me what he had planned, I already knew that we were both involved with something neither of us fully understood. There were things I wanted to tell Danny, about how a deal with Hunter could save the two of us but it couldn't be mentioned with Ricardo present.

I'd asked Danny while he was at my place about why he was doing this, about why he would not, or could not, leave with me, and he'd given me bullshit about a 'just cause'. But I reckoned that what Joe the electronics expert had told me about Danny being hailed as a legend was nearer to the truth. The notion of becoming part of Irish republican, or Colombian Marxist, folklore had seduced him. He'd backed himself into a corner because he supposedly had a reputation to uphold.

His gaze pressed me for an answer, as if every moment of my silence was a growing embarrassment for him. Barely raising my voice above a mumble, I said, "I meant what I said. I'm stayin until we leave together."

His eyes, instantly full of pride, darted in Ricardo's direction, while I shifted a plate encrusted with the stale remains of a meal and sat down on the sofa. Danny said, "Right, Robbie, I've already told you about Pedroza's visit and what a bad bastard that man is. I also said he's coming here as a guest of the Lavettes. What I didn't say is that he will be carrying over twenty million dollars' worth of diamonds. Henry Lavette made his fortune dealing in diamonds but a lot of it was from some very shady dealings. Let's say you're a member of the Russian mafia, or even of al-Qa'ida, and you want to do an arms deal, or launder some money without it being traced, especially by the US government, then you go and buy yourself West African diamonds. From Africa they go to Colombia, where some are exchanged for weapons or equipment, and the rest goes to Europe for polishing and cash. So we're going to bring Pedroza to account and put those diamonds to good use, or, at least stop him putting them to bad use."

Ricardo wriggled impatiently on his chair. "We don't have time for all this. Are you going to tell him or am I?"

"Tell me what?" I asked Danny.

He grimaced and said, "Everything's in place to go ahead, but after what you told me about being picked up and that thing on your wrist, we did a risk assessment and decided it's too big a gamble to carry on without trying to nullify it."

"Nullify? Cut the bullshit, man, an' tell me straight."

"Tomorrow, just before the operation gets underway, we will have to take out the man who put that thing on you."

"Shit, Danny! This is an FBI agent you're talkin about. You kill him an' you can forget about your operation, about Pedroza, about diamonds, 'cause this place will be flooded with guys lookin to find who killed that man! It's a crazy idea, man, pure fuckin crazy!"

"You're right," said Ricardo. Laughing, he continued, "Yes, I said it would be easier all round to get rid of you."

Danny's eyes flashed a warning at me. He had obviously told members of the Farc assassination squad that Mitch had picked me up in order to capture him, and they had responded that the most logical solution was to dispose of me. Danny then must have offered them the elimination of Mitch as an alternative. "He claims he's an FBI man," said Danny, "but Joe said that gadget you're wearing is out of date, and, from what I know, the FBI don't use anything but the most up-to-date gear. And let's face it, Robbie, this isn't some big sprawling place like New York, it's a small town, so why does he need the likes of you to help track me down?"

"Because you're good at what you do, man. You know how to keep yourself scarce."

A vanity that I had never seen before put a thin, satisfied grin on his lips. "Well, okay," Danny said, "but there's another thing: to respond in the time he's talking about, once you've pushed that button, he'd have to have choppers on standby, SWAT teams and the like around the place. He's playing mind-games, Rob. Joe's been monitoring radio traffic. FBI and government stuff is encrypted, so he can't tell what's what, or who's talking to who, but he can tell if anyone is talking. From what he's hearing, there's no more than the usual amount of communication going on around here."

"Then what about the bugs an' stuff in my house? What about the tracker in the car? How come he knows what went on with Paulie O'Sullivan in New York, an' knows Nathan's an' my mom's phone numbers? He knows who I am, Danny, an', whoever he is, the man's workin for the American government. Get real, guy."

Danny's cheeks reddened, and I immediately realized that I shouldn't have spoken like that in front of Ricardo. "Ach, I'm not saying he's not a government agent," Danny explained, "I'm just saying that he's not any part of a big operation. Maybe he is FBI, but he could be a fella in a local office who thinks he's stumbled onto something and is trying to make a name for hisself. He's bluffing, Robbie, using that thing around your wrist to throw you. A bit like a conjurer's trick: he's distracting your attention from what he's really doing. We'll take care of this fella and it might even give us the bonus of distracting his comrades for when Pedroza comes to town."

I could have challenged Danny but I reckoned that he must have played down Mitch's importance to the Farc in order for them to go along with his plan to take him out. "Then what do you reckon he's up to?" I asked.

"We might find out before we deal with him, then again we mightn't. The important thing is that we deal with him as soon as we can."

"So how are we gonna do that?" I asked.

"To keep it brief, me and you will travel somewhere tomorrow. You'll push that button like the man told you to and I'm prepared to gamble that there'll be no choppers or SWAT teams turning up. I'd say your man will, right enough, and a support team cutting off the exits. But we've got a better plan, and we have the advantage of choosing the time and the place. Joe will meet you in the factory's parking lot tonight with another car and instructions where you're to go. He'll take your car back to your place so not to arouse suspicion."

"But what'll happen when they don't see me in the house?"

"They'll think you're over at Calvin's while we get things ready for this fella Mitch."

I figured I had the best plan of all: just get the hell out of Georgia. Before I left the dingy apartment, I told Danny that I'd already had a case packed in the trunk and that Joe wasn't to turn up at the factory until I had finished my shift at two. Ricardo asked why I was bothering to go back to the factory but Danny saved me the trouble of telling another lie when he interrupted and said it was for the best if I returned and saved sending out an alert that something was about to happen. I nodded in agreement while silently hoping that my next meeting with John Hunter would be one which would provide a means of escape for Danny and me.

Still distracted by Danny's plans for Mitch, I ambled down the stairs and didn't notice the couple coming up until I was almost on top of them. The woman was young, Hispanic and a stranger; the man I knew all too well. She carried on up, and Chuck Woodlow and I faced each other. I could see how uncomfortable he was. He said, "Um, hi, Barrett, I didn't know you came here, too."

"My first time."

"Yeah? Which one?"

"How the fuck would I know?" I said, "The one who took my money."

"They all do that, one way or another. This is just taking the more direct route," he said, with a mirthless grin. "You'll be back at the factory for eight, right?"

"I'm headin there now."

His fist smacked into the cup of his other hand, as he searched for the words. "So, um, right, I'll, um, see you there later on."

"Take your time," I said, "foreman's prerogative."

Once he was on the landing he disappeared from my line of sight. I waited until I heard the closing of a door before I bounded back up the stairs. There had been something more than embarrassment about Woodlow's expression.

I rapped on the door of Danny's apartment. Ricardo, in Spanish, asked who it was. Not too loud, I answered, "Robbie. Quick, open up."

Two automatic pistols were pointing my way when the door opened. Danny lowered his first. "What is it, Rob?"

I could tell he was worried that I had returned to tell him that I'd changed my mind. "I was just goin downstairs when I ran into the foreman from work called Woodlow. Ric knows him."

"Woodlow?" said Ricardo. "Did he say anything to you?"

"He asked about which woman I'd been with, an' said he'd see me later."

"Was there a woman with him?"

"Yeah, she had on a blue top an' yellow skirt." I did not have to add it was a short skirt; they were all short in Creektown.

"That'll be Ana," said Ricardo. He turned to Danny. "Your friend Robbie just seems to cause us problems, man. Woodlow's one of the bad guys for sure. I reckon they've tracked Robbie's car here, Woodlow must've seen the girl driving around and made out he wants business as a way of coming in here to check things out. And now he's seen Robbie in here," he hissed, while producing a switch-blade from his pocket, "I say we have to take care of him straight away. For all we know, he might be calling someone right now."

Danny ran a hand over his head, and stole a glance my way. "You're right, we'll have to deal with him. What about the girl?"

"Ana?" said Ricardo. "She'll be okay with it. I think we can let her live." A chill passed through me as I understood they were talking about killing Woodlow right away. "I'll go with Robbie," he went on. "He can knock Ana's door and call for Woodlow. I'll do the rest."

"Right," said Danny, "then you'd better hurry on and do it."

Ricardo smirked at me. "Do you think you can manage it, Robbie?"

Not bothering to even look at Danny, I opened the door and gestured for Ricardo to lead the way. Ana's door was at the end of the landing, next to a stinking communal bathroom. I thumped on the door and called, "Chuck? Chuck, can I have a quick word?"

"Barrett? Is that you?" he asked.

"Yeah. Can you give me a minute?"

"You're fucking joking, right? I'm busy here."

"It won't take a minute. I gotta ask you somethin."

"Goddamn! Leave it 'til later, huh?"

I glanced at Ricardo, who had his back to the wall and his blade at the ready. He urged me on with a bad-tempered jerk of his head. "It's kinda urgent, Chuck. It's about José Ruiz. I found his body in the cold store."

Ricardo had said Woodlow was one of the bad guys, which reinforced my view that he was also one of the people most likely to be involved in hiding José's body within the factory complex. It was just a hunch but I thought I was on the right path when he didn't respond by questioning my sanity. In fact, he didn't say anything else before I heard him unlock the door. He opened it only a few inches at first. I could see his bare chest. "Did you just say that you saw Ruiz's body?"

"In the contaminated meat store," I said, "an' I don't know who I should tell."

He looked at me, suspiciously I thought, and then stepped back. "You'd better come in for a minute," he said.

Like a blur, Ricardo was in ahead of me. Woodlow froze, his mouth and eyes wide open; it took a couple of seconds for me to realize that the knife was already in the side of his neck. Woodlow gasped and then gurgled as his shaking fingers sought to pull Ricardo's arm away. Ricardo reacted by pushing the knife deeper and once he had forced Woodlow down onto the floor, he twisted the blade and brought it out through the front of Woodlow's throat. Blood gushed over the wooden boards like a fountain, a ghastly crimson fountain.

"You'll keep those hands to yourself now, eh, you bastard," Ricardo sneered, surveying his handiwork. He wasn't even out of breath. He wiped the knife on Woodlow's pants, closed it and put it into his pocket. "Tip for you, Robbie. Bring the blade out through the windpipe and you'll take out the voice box, too. They don't get to scream that way."

There was a gleam in Ricardo's dark eyes. The young woman named Ana sat up naked in the bed and made no attempt to cover herself. Ricardo shouted at her in Spanish. Whatever he said, she seemed unable take in a word, and he had to repeat himself. Danny came in with a couple of blankets and closed the door behind him. Ricardo's face broke with a wide smile. He said, "Ana says he was going to call someone as soon as he came in here, and she thinks it was about Robbie. She persuaded him to do the business first, she told him three minutes wasn't going to make much difference. Looks as though we got to him just in time. By the way, Danny," he laughed, "I want another one of these shirts. This one's got blood all over it."

Seemingly untroubled by the appalling sight, Danny nodded and began wrapping Woodlow's half-naked corpse in the blankets. There seemed to be gallons of blood about the place, and the blankets were soon soaked in it. "Fuck," he growled, looking at his bloodstained hands. He said to Ricardo, "Tell the girl she uses our apartment from now on, and the rent's paid for the next month." To me he said, "It's interesting that he opened up when you told him about José's body – there maybe something in it, right enough. We'll tidy up here. You'd better get to the factory and I'll see you later on, mate."

Rendered numb by the swiftness of it all, I went downstairs and back onto the street. My car went past but I didn't see it until the woman in the red polka-dot dress tooted the horn. She stopped a little way up the street. She waited for me on the sidewalk and when I got to her she said, "I didn't say before, but I've seen you in Duke's. Give me a call the next time and I might even give you a discount."

The shapely figure in the short dress walked away. She looked over her shoulder but I merely forced my lips into a reluctant smile before getting into my car and heading for the factory.

Ricardo had fooled me completely at first, but while in the apartment, even before he cut Woodlow's throat, I'd begun to see a very different side to the brash young man. Now I was aware that not only could he kill ruthlessly, he could also kill with relish. I had also picked up on a certain friction between him and Danny. There was a goading lilt about Ricardo's voice when he had spoken to us, and Danny had constantly needed to assert his authority over him. I knew my friend a lot better than the young Colombian did – and thought he was playing a very dangerous game.

But more than anything, it was the blind determination to proceed with assassination of the Colombian governor that troubled me. The notion that the FBI had even a hint of their plan should have had them call it off but, to me, this had all the makings of a suicide mission as they seemed determined to go ahead with their attempt to kill Pedroza no matter what. Danny's view of the world had led him to become involved with a bunch of fanatics – and now I was even more convinced that I was right to try to make a deal with John Hunter, and I could only hope that it wasn't too late for my friend to also make his escape.

24

THE EVENING WAS HOT and sticky, and now that the machines were shut down there was no chilled air inside the factory to cool me. But it was more than the clammy air that made me feel uncomfortable: the look in Ricardo's eyes stayed with me as much as the sight of Chuck Woodlow's blood and what I saw in the young Colombian put a hot and sickly feeling within my stomach. I cursed Danny – again – for getting involved with an organization like the Farc. He had saved my life a number of times but I had to start facing up to a side of him that I had been too ready to overlook. Although he rarely mentioned it, the death of Danny's father at the hands of men working for the British government was the fuel for his involvement with several killings. But vengeance had provided only fleeting satisfaction and I wondered just what it would take for Danny to be reconciled to the fact that no amount of death could compensate for the loss of his father, who was, ironically, a gentle man who opposed to all forms violence. Then again, I could be giving Danny too much credit, maybe he had been simply seduced and then intoxicated by power. Now here he was, a man with little formal education, shaping the destiny of whole nations, aware that he was already being feted as some sort of heroic freedom fighter. Whatever Danny's motivation, with each passing minute, I was becoming more convinced that he was travelling the wrong path and I was the only one in a position to turn him around.

I searched in the hope of seeing Hunter, but saw only Jack Kirby talking to a sanitation crew; perhaps he was asking about his friend Woodlow. I went and checked the maintenance rota and found out that Hunter was working in the eviscerating area. Part of me wanted to go find him right there and then, but it was quite a distance and I still hadn't worked out just how much more I should tell him.

At around eleven the call went out that there would be a fifteen-minute break for coffee. I certainly did not need a shot of caffeine to keep me awake, as I reckoned it was time to go looking for Hunter. He wasn't in the eviscerating area, nor the canteen, and I immediately became anxious that he had not turned in at all. I went out to the cold-storage units, in the hope of finding him snooping about, but he wasn't out there, either. Fretting, I ventured over to an isolated spot behind the 'machinery graveyard' to figure out what I should do if I did not meet up with John Hunter before clocking out. My legs ached and so I found a place to sit on a grass embankment while I gathered my thoughts. Consumed by the consequences of what Danny and the Farc were planning, and the growing thought that Hunter might prove to be our only way out, I looked up at the stars, just hoping there was someone up there prepared to watch over me.

I would have missed Billy Joe Watson if I had not been roused from my thoughts by a painful insect bite. Normally, the factory manger would be tucked up in bed at this time of night and his presence at the plant immediately sparked my interest. My curiosity about what he was up to grew when I saw him sneaking around the perimeter fence, toward an area near where the builders kept their materials. From behind the rusted remains of an old picker, I watched Billy Joe open the metal rear doors of a truck and then clamber inside with a package in his hands. He reappeared for a moment and looked out furtively before he pulled the doors shut behind him.

The minutes stretched and the incessant noise of insects seemed to grow louder as I waited for Watson to reappear. I checked my watch as the suspense stiffened my every sinew. Then, just as cramp was making me move to relieve the pain, he emerged from the back of the truck. He scanned the surrounding gloom and I hastily slid back behind the picker. I counted to five and chanced peering out again: Billy Joe was empty-handed and scurrying off toward his office. My pulse quickened, as within my brain, the answers, like round pegs, began to find the round holes made by my questions about what was really going on. It now loomed large in my mind that despite all the grounds I had given him to fire me, Billy Joe Watson had not only ignored them, he had even promoted me.

Whatever he was up to, he had done his upmost to keep me here at the factory.

As I made my way back inside, I had a gut feeling that I might have discovered where the body of José Ruiz was now. Even though there was no foreman to check up on me, I knew there were others in the factory who might be watching. I made up my mind that my next course of action should be to get my work done so as to keep up the pretense that I thought Woodlow was about. Once I was finished I'd go and find out what was in the back of that truck.

I detoured past the eviscerating area and saw Hunter. There was a moment of relief as I watched him gazing at an array of flexible hoses, giving the impression he was hard at work. But when I got closer I saw that he was deep in conversation on his cell phone. I coughed. Startled, he spun around and scowled at me. "I hope you ain't listenin to my conversations," he grumbled, shoving the phone into his pocket. His eyes searched the space behind me. "Okay," he said, "what do you have for me?"

"I thought you were seein your boss an' comin back with somethin for me an' my friend."

He chewed his lip, then, "I ain't sure if I have anythin to offer you."

This was the reaction I'd feared the most. "What the hell are you talkin about, man?" I hissed. "I thought me an' you had reached some understandin."

"My hands are tied. I passed on what you told me but it's been kicked upstairs. My bosses are goin to the top to see if they can find out what the FBI is up to, mostly to make sure that our operation doesn't get fucked up. I might get an answer tomorrow but the bottom line is to achieve mission objective, and that doesn't include bodies in cold stores or anywhere else. I have no choice but to continue with what I'm doin."

"That's shit, man, an' you know it! You can't just ignore the fact that our foreman was dumped in with the contaminated meat."

"Barrett, or whatever your name is, you're a non-person an' you've told me a story that, without any evidence, is a non-story. You haven't given me any proof whatsoever that I can show my superiors. Personally, I'd give you the benefit of the doubt 'cause I can't figure why you would make it up. But the same doesn't go for my bosses."

"So what about the FBI? You think I'm bullshittin about that, too?"

"There's no way of checkin," he said flatly. "But I have to tell you that the story you told me has a few holes in it. Put it this way, can you give me a contact number, or some proof of an FBI operation so I can run a check on it? Or can you tell me how you're supposed to communicate with this agent you call Mitch?"

The mobile phone which Mitch had given me was my only link but it had been destroyed by Jack Kirby's buddies. I briefly thought of mentioning the Homeland Security's 'Sleeping Dogs' operation but quickly discounted it, in case it gave Hunter grounds to immediately arrest me. Stung by his sceptical tone, I said, "Earlier on, were you givin me bullshit about catchin 'big fish'? Come on, Hunter, what's changed since then?"

"Stuff outta my control. Red flags have gone up all over the place about us trying to access certain files."

"Well, doesn't that prove FBI involvement?"

"Circumstantial, but not hard proof. Somethin's goin on, an' maybe it's to do with stuff you've talked about, but it's way over my head, an' I have no way of confirmin any damn thing you've told me."

Aware that the plan to kill Mitch and then Pedroza would be enacted within a few short hours, I tried not to sound too desperate. "Hunter . . . Look, man, this could benefit us both. You have no idea how big this thing is."

"Big thing? What the hell is this big thing? Tell me what you know an' maybe we can do somethin for you guys. But you're holdin out on me."

"Hunter, you're offerin me nothin!"

"That's 'cause you're givin me nuthin, nuthin I can go back an' show my superiors. An' in a way, though it's stopped my guys tellin me to bring you in, you kinda shot yourself in the foot by tellin me about the FBI. It's not that our agency is adverse to gettin one over the Feds when we can, but we have to be on solid ground or else our sorry asses are out to dry."

I reckoned that John Hunter was in full retreat and covering his ample behind while doing so, or maybe he was a way better operator than I'd thought, because now I was considering that I'd have to feed him more information if I were to persuade him to give Danny and me a way out. "What about usin your own initiative?" I said.

"You still don't understand," he said. "I need proof!"

"Hunter, don't take this the wrong way, but, fuck, man, with all this buck-passin I now understand how those guys got on the planes on 9/11 an' killed nearly three thousand people. What if I told you the assassination of a foreign dignitary is gonna happen any day now, an' this factory has somethin to do with it?"

"Go on."

My thoughts went back to Billy Joe Watson sneaking into the truck. "You want proof an' there's stuff I wanna check out, but I know for certain that things are bein planned that will have repercussions for national security. Hunter, you can come outta this smellin sweet like roses, or like a pile-a horseshit. It all depends if me an' you can come up with a deal."

Dismissive, he shook his head and said, "Then why bother with me? Why don't you just give it to the FBI?"

"Because their deal is just for me an' not my friend too."

His tongue dabbed the corner of his mouth and I tried to hide my relief that I'd regained his interest. He took a scrap of paper from his pocket and scribbled a number on it. "That's a very special phone number. The minute, make that the second, you got somethin I can give my boss, you ring me straightaway 'cause time is runnin out. Come back to me with proof, an' I'll see what I can do. Give me somethin concrete an' I'll give somethin back, you have my word on that, Robbie. Even if time is too short to get some sorta deal outta my bosses, you give me somethin an' I'll see to it that you an' your friend get a twenty-four hour start before the shit starts flyin. That's the best I can do off my own bat."

It wasn't what I'd wanted to hear from him. I wanted to go back to Danny with a deal but the cards I hoped to play were still in the deck. I could only wait and see if they were shuffled in my favour and if I would find something in the truck that I could bargain with.

My productivity dropped dramatically over the following two and a half hours, because I couldn't concentrate. Mostly, I was distracted by the notion that I'd told Hunter either too much or not enough. Maybe the only way left for Danny and me was to carry out his plan to kill Mitch. But before I resigned myself to doing that, I was going to find out what was in that truck.

With fifteen minutes to go before clocking out I wiped my oily hands with a rag, tucked a flashlight into a pocket of my overalls, and headed for the truck. There was a large *Abloy* padlock on the rear doors and I cussed myself a little bit for not having realized they'd be locked. I hadn't much time, so I decided to go to Billy Joe's office and see if the key was kept there: I could get in by the trapdoor under the washroom, as I'd done when I dumped the rat in his toilet. I hurried over, and was about to get down and slide underneath, when a security guard appeared.

"Hi," I said, trying my best to sound unflustered. "Would you know where Billy Joe is?"

He eyed me suspiciously. "Watson? You must be joking, man. He's never at the plant this time of night. That's for suckers like us."

"Oh, I, um, thought I'd seen him at around eleven."

"These hours," he said, grinning, "they mess with a man's head, they make you think you've seen all sortsa things. Put it this way, if he was here, he didn't come through the main gate but I'd say old Watson was in bed with that new young wife of his by eleven."

"I guess you're right, I must've misheard what someone told me." We hovered awkwardly, each expecting the other to come up with a punch line. "Okay, I might as well get cleaned up. We finish at two," I offered weakly.

"That makes you the lucky one outta the two of us."

"Not as lucky as Billy Joe."

We both forced a laugh my remark didn't merit, and headed in opposite directions. I resisted the urge to glance over my shoulder and waited until I got to the nearest corner before I looked back to see where he had got to. Now I was down to ten minutes. I walked back the way I'd come; my legs were stiff and burning by the time I'd reached the cabin again. I lay on my back and slid along to underneath the trapdoor, using the waste pipe as my guide in the darkness. A rat scuttled past, and had me bouncing my head off a support beam – payback for the brother or sister that had gone into Billy Joe's toilet.

The trapdoor moved with the first shove and I squeezed up through it. Enough light came in from the halogen lamps outside for me to examine the keys hanging by the door without using my flashlight. Not one of them was an *Abloy*, and I feared that Billy Joe might have taken the key with him. The only other place it might be was in his desk. When I opened the top drawer I immediately saw the glint of metal. Even before I turned it to the light, I knew it was what I was looking for.

Getting out through the trapdoor was a lot harder than getting in but I did it without either bumping my head or encountering any more rats. After a brief pause by the old picker to ensure that no one else was around, I darted to the rear of the truck. The key slid into the lock and I took in a gulp of air before I climbed inside. With the doors closed, the smell of diesel was almost overpowering. I shone my flashlight back and forth, but there was no sign of José's body. Unsure of how I should feel about that, I moved further into the truck. There was nothing but large plastic bags of white granules from top to bottom, with a narrow gap down the middle. The smell was too strong to come from the truck's fuel tank and I thought I'd better get out before I threw up. I shuffled backwards and almost fell over when my heel snagged on something. At first I thought it was a rope, or it was a wire, but my blood instantly turned cold as I recognized it was Cordtex.

The explosive cord was looped around the bags: I was in the middle of a two-thousand-pound bomb, the bomb Mitch was looking for. I pierced one of the bags with the key and let a little of the contents trickle into my hand. I'd seen powder like it once before, in an outhouse in Donegal: ammonium nitrate which had been milled, mixed with diesel and then dried. Danny had given me a tour while we waited for our false documents. He had actually told me the exact amount of diesel which was required for every hundred-weight of ammonium nitrate. "It's a formula that adds up to a hell of a bang," he'd said.

I stumbled out of the truck and locked the doors, aware that I had to rapidly make a decision: should I run and get Hunter, or should I return the key to Watson's office first? I didn't have long, but I thought I'd better return the key as Hunter was going to need reinforcements to secure it and in the meantime if it were discovered that the key was missing, it might impel someone to move the truck away.

Inhaling dirt, I crawled underneath the cabin. I got through the trapdoor easily enough. Four strides and the key was back into the drawer. Four steps back and I slid feet first down the hole. The lid slipped from my damp hand and thudded back into place; as it turned out, so loudly that it attracted the attention of a security guard. His feet only inches from my face, I willed him to move on but he seemed to take an age. I inched back on my stomach as he came down the steps, muttering something into his walkie-talkie.

Hunter would be clocking out at any time now. If I sprinted, I could get to the gate in less than a minute and catch him there. But the guard stayed where he was, and vital seconds were ticking away. I glanced at my watch: half a minute had gone by. If he didn't move soon I'd have to crawl out and try to bluff him with an excuse about a leaky waste pipe or something. But, at last, he finally moved. I counted a very quick ten and dragged myself out.

I wanted to run, but I could not afford to draw attention to myself, as there was an unknown number of dangerous people in and around the factory complex, one of them being the man who ran the whole place. Once I got to the production area I began to jog but when I reached the punch clock my stomach turned: Hunter wasn't in the queue. Despite the glowers from the people in the line, I went straight to the front and asked Colin the electrician if he'd seen him.

"Yeah, Robbie," he said, "he headed for the gate only a minute ago."

Ignoring Colin's shout that, as I hadn't punched my card, he would do it for me, I ran to catch Hunter before he got to his car. My eyes were fixed on the dim figures at the other side of the parking lot, and I didn't see Jack Kirby until the very last moment.

"Hey, Barrett, where you going now, boy?" he said.

My lungs felt as though they were on fire. I tried to gulp in air. "Not now, Kirby," I panted. "I haven't got time. Woodlow told me that we'll sort this out once the factory is back up an' runnin.'" When he didn't move, I craned my neck, hoping for a sign of Hunter and said, "He isn't gonna appreciate you breakin your word."

"What makes you think I'm gonna do anything that will bother Chuck?" Kirby snorted. "This is strictly business between you and me, nigger."

Most of the cars were moving out, and I spotted Joe sitting in one beside my own. Kirby was still talking but I wasn't listening to any of it. "We'll sort this out some other time," I said.

I went to pass him but he grabbed my shoulder and pulled me towards him. Using the momentum, I smacked my forehead into his nose. There was a crack and he staggered back, blood pouring from between his fingers. I was thinking about a kick to his already damaged nuts when something thudded across the base of my skull. I pitched forward but stayed on my feet. A blurred shape came at me but I sidestepped in time to throw an uppercut under the ribs. The shape groaned and fell from my line of vision. An engine roared and a car pulled up right behind me. I thought it was Joe and made to turn, but a heel smashed into the back of my legs, and a punch to my stomach made my guts heave. Shapes and light melded into one another as I fell to my knees. The engine roared again and I got a mouthful of exhaust fumes. I tried to get up but the bones in my legs had dissolved. Someone hooked an arm under mine and hauled me upright. I shook my head and gathered my senses – just as Kirby's fist hammered onto my jaw. I fell backwards, into the trunk of a car. The stars in the sky began to spin and then there was nothing but blackness as the lid slammed down.

25

IT DID NOT TAKE LONG for the buffeting about in the trunk to bring me back to consciousness. As I came to, I imagined the noise from the exhaust as the roars of a crowd and that I was a fighter once again heading to my final bout. Slowly, I began to gather every experience and memory that might help me to survive.

I tried to figure out what had happened. I must have been seen going in and out of Billy Joe's office, or getting in and out of the truck. Mitch had warned me of its existence and about what Danny was really up to with the Colombians, but Danny had given me his word that he knew nothing about it. He had the expertise to create a bomb and at least one of the truck drivers, the man who'd driven me to the motel to get the watchstrap disabled, was a member of the Farc. Maybe I'd let friendship cloud my judgment yet again and Mitch was the only one who could save me now. My finger found the button and pushed it twice, the signal for standby. I'd push it again and hold it in for three seconds once the car had stopped. Then I'd have to pray that I could stall my captors until the FBI arrived. I timed the journey: forty-six minutes later, the car came to a halt on what sounded like gravel. The last two minutes had been the bumpiest, and I reckoned we'd been on a dirt track. I pressed the button and counted to three. I could hear men's voices and the wind in the trees. I tried to create a barricade in my mind to keep out the fear. I'd sent the signal to Mitch, but had it been received? "This is when the fight begins," I whispered to myself. "Stay strong."

Part of staying strong was figuring out what I'd tell Mitch when he arrived: I may not have delivered Danny to him but I found the truck bomb; and discovered that Billy Joe Watson was one of the conspirators, as was Jack Kirby. Thinking more clearly, whatever they were up to, neither Danny Maguire nor the Farc would be their kind of people. Also, there were the deaths of José Ruiz and Miguel and I could safely assume that Billy Joe and Kirby had played some part in them, too.

But doubt was gnawing at the edges of my mind: if Mitch didn't show up, how would I get out of this? "Stay strong, stay strong," I repeated, as the wind picked up and the branches creaked.

A fist thumped against the lid of the trunk and had my heart trying to beat its way out of my chest. "Can you hear me in there?" called a muffled voice. "I said, can you hear me?"

"Yeah," I called back.

"I want you on your side, facing the front of the car. We're gonna open the lid just a little bit, and you put your two hands back so we can tie them. Anything stupid and that trunk is gonna be your coffin. Do you understand?"

I said I did, and rolled onto my side and put my hands behind me. "Ready," I said. The lid lifted and I pushed my hands out for someone to expertly tie my wrists together. Seconds later I was hauled out. Blinded by a flashlight shining into my eyes, I tumbled forward and my knees thudded onto the dirt.

Squinting, I saw that we were in a clearing in a wood. Standing before me was Jack Kirby. He had a gun pointing at my head.

"Ain't you gonna blindfold him, Jack?" asked a voice from behind me.

"What's the point?" said Kirby. "He's already seen me, and he saw you coming out of the truck, Billy Joe. He saw my fist, too. Pretty good punch, eh, Barrett? Kinda shows that you'd have taken a helluva beating if I'd had the chance."

"You've got your chance right now, if you untie my hands, Kirby.

Why not let someone else hold the gun? We can sort this it out now, if you really want."

He smiled down at me, as if tempted to take me up on my challenge, or as if he had read my thoughts about looking for a chance to escape.

"If you're not going to blindfold him, I say kill him now," said Billy Joe Watson.

I turned my head but, from where I knelt, I still couldn't see him. "Hey, Billy Joe," I said, "if he was gonna shoot me he would've done it by now. The man has to wait on orders."

Kirby's smirk became a scowl as Watson came around and stood beside him. Billy Joe smoothed his hair with a palm and measured me with wild eyes. "Christ, you're one uppity nigger," he snarled, "I've been waiting for months to do this!" He roared with anger and brought his fist around in a wide arc. I tucked my chin into my chest and let my forehead take the blow. It hurt me but, I reckoned, by Bill Joe's howl of pain, it had hurt him a lot more.

Mitch should have been on his way by now, but I'd have to stall, buy more time – but how long would be it until he arrived? I sneered at Kirby and goaded him: "It seems like none-a you guys can punch properly." He was the calmer of the pair and chose not to respond. Turning my attention to the nervous-looking Billy Joe, I said, "You'd better get your scrawny ass outta here, Billy Joe, unless you wanna end up like that guy McVeigh. Word is already out that I saw you in that truck."

Clutching his sore fist, Billy Joe looked to Kirby. "He's lying," Kirby said. "We were watching him every step of the way. Neat trick with the trap door, Barrett, but we know you didn't communicate with anyone after you got out of the truck, unless you're referring to that brief exchange at the punch clock."

I shrugged and just hoped that I'd sown some doubt – it was the only weapon I had available. Billy Joe strode away to the fringe of the clearing and paced aimlessly in circles, while Jack Kirby continued to stare down at me, rubbing his bloodied nose and obviously planning revenge for the head-butt.

In the distance, amongst the tall pines, I heard a car engine. It grew louder, and my heart began to pump furiously. Mitch was coming and I could only hope that Kirby wouldn't panic and shoot me before I was rescued. But when I glanced quickly up at him there was no alarm on his face: he was expecting someone and, right then, it felt like I had been hit with a blow far harder than the punch he had thrown at me.

Moments later, the bouncing headlights caught Billy Joe in their beams. He froze and clamped a hand over his mouth as he watched darkened figures emerge from a car. The lights were dazzling me and I could not make out much as I heard doors being slammed and footsteps approaching. As they came closer, someone said shakily, "B-Billy Joe, Billy Joe, what's this all about?" It was Colin the electrician. He stood in front of Kirby, quivering and with tears trickling down his plump cheeks. "Billy Joe," he whimpered, "m-my wife will be awful worried if I don't get home real soon."

"Your wife should be asleep at this hour, Colin," said Kirby.

His trembling voice barely intelligible, Colin said, "S-she's a light sleeper. She n-never really settles until I'm home."

Kirby nodded toward me and said, "We won't keep you long. This man talked to you as you were punching your card. What exactly did he say?"

It was only then that Colin saw me. "W-What are you doing with Robbie? T-This isn't right, Billy Joe. We shouldn't be t-treated like this."

Billy Joe came closer. "Just answer the fucking question, Colin, and you might get outta this alive."

"A-alive?" he blubbered, "W-What do you mean? My wife, she won't s-settle . . ."

Kirby put his gun to Colin's head. "Shut the fuck up about your damn wife, you quivering pile of shit! I'll blow your fucking brains out if you don't tell me exactly what Barrett said."

Colin's crumpled face turned toward me. It was a plea for help: he was so frightened that I doubted if he could remember his own name. There was a large wet patch on his trousers where he'd already pissed himself. He shook his head helplessly. "P-Please," he begged me, "please tell them what you said. I don't remember a-and my wife will be waiting . . ." Wet wind started to escape from him, his humiliation was complete. ". . . Please, Robbie."

I knew it then, even if Colin didn't, that he was as good as dead, and nothing I could say would save him. "I asked you to punch my card, Colin. I told you I was in a hurry, remember?"

"Yes, yes, that's right," he said. "I-I know it's against the rules but I promise I won't do it again. H-He was in a hurry and he asked me to punch his card. I-I'll never do it again. Can I go now? Only my wife . . ."

"Did he say anything about a truck to you?" Kirby demanded.

"T-Truck?"

"Yeah, a fucking truck. Did he mention a truck, or ask you to pass on a message about a truck?"

"A truck? M-Message? . . .M-My wife will be waiting and getting upset if I d-don't . . ."

"Shut the fuck up about your fucking wife! Did Barrett mention a truck to you, yes or no?"

His mouth wide open, Colin blinked slowly, as if he'd just remembered that I had asked him about John Hunter. "You sons-of-bitches," he said, calmly, almost dreamily. "He asked me to punch his card, just like he said."

Perhaps he realized what was coming and found a measure of courage at the last. Perhaps he hoped he could save John Hunter from the same outcome. Colin glanced my way, as if he were asking me if he had done the right thing. I compressed my lips and made a small reassuring smile to communicate with him that he had. I heard no sound but I saw Colin's hair fly up, as if caught by a gust of wind, I saw the back of his head explode, I saw him fall. The impact as he hit the ground threw his arms back over his head, as if he had surrendered to his fate.

Kirby lowered his gun. "Well, that settles that, Barrett. You should-n't have talked to anyone. I mean, now look what you've gone and done." I moved to straighten my knees but strong hands immedi-ately gripped my arms. I was hauled upright and two men frog-marched me toward the trees. I glanced over my shoulder and saw Colin's corpse being dragged in the opposite direction. I wished that Mitch could have arrived in time to save him, too. I was still looking back at him when my feet clattered against some wooden steps, making me stumble. A door creaked open and the musty scent of damp wood greeted me. Kirby and the other guy threw me face down onto the floor. I raised my chin but couldn't see higher than his knees.

He ordered the other man to tie my ankles. "Don't worry, Barrett," he sneered, "you'll be soon wishing you could have it as quick as Colin. But you sure as hell won't if I have anything to do with it."

I put my face to the floor and took his kick on the top of my head. I stayed still until I heard them leave and close the door behind them. Maybe all wooden buildings smell and sound the same, but when I raised my head again, and my eyes adjusted to the dark, I got the feeling I'd been here before.

26

THE FEELING THAT I'D BEEN here before grew stronger, and I rolled onto my back so I could get a better look at my surroundings. As the dark shapes around me gradually came into sharper focus, my head fell back against the boards and I cursed out loud. This was to where I'd been brought after being lured to the Old Glory motel. This was where Mitch had interrogated me. I guessed he'd be arriving soon – but whose side would he be on? I thought I knew the answer but I hoped I was wrong.

A new light now shone on the events and the motives of people around me. When Danny escaped the ambush in which José Ruiz was killed, Billy Joe Watson had falsely identified another body as José to the police. It was decided that I had to be kept at the factory, no matter what, as a route to Danny. But had Mitch known all along that the truck bomb was at the factory? The fact that I'd been brought back to this cabin might mean that he and Billy Joe were in cahoots, unless – I hoped – this was a convoluted FBI undercover operation to entrap Billy Joe and Jack Kirby – and anyone else involved in the conspiracy.

Noise on the steps outside put an end to my deliberations. I thought about rolling back onto my stomach but before I could move, the door opened and three men came in. Jack Kirby switched on the light. The redness of his damaged nose glowed angrily. He had changed his clothes and now wore a black zip-up jacket and pants. In a show of bravado I smiled up at him. He nodded in my direction and the two muscular men who'd followed him in hoisted me roughly onto a chair. One of them pulled my arms over the backrest and expertly fastened them to it, while the other loosened the ties around my ankles before binding them to the front legs of the chair.

Kirby grinned and said, "Nasty lump on your head there, Barrett."

"Yeah," I said, "an' there's a nasty red lump on your face where your nose used to be. An' how is ol' Billy Joe's hand?"

His lips twisted spitefully. "He isn't worrying about his hand anymore."

I knew in an instant what he meant. Billy Joe's panic-stricken reaction to my capture had sealed his fate. I guessed he was now lying with Colin in the sandy soil somewhere amongst the trees. Kirby and the rest would have learned from the Oklahoma bombers' experience that no one who looked likely to break under pressure could be left alive to talk. Kirby gestured to the other men to leave.

I said, "How are you goin to explain it when Billy Joe doesn't turn up at the factory again?"

"Billy Joe Watson is on the run from the INS for employing illegal immigrants and the USDA for selling contaminated meat. Billy Joe will not be missed."

"It's a big white truck, Kirby. Too many people will have seen it around."

"Is that right? There's a lot of white trucks around and the way I see it, the factory's closed and from now on nobody gets near that truck but my most trusted men. In fact, you're the only one to have paid it much attention, Barrett. Curiosity, it kills a lot more than cats."

The door slammed behind him but at least he'd left the light on. I wondered why I hadn't been killed like Colin and Billy Joe. Thoughts about torture and a slow death were gathering at the edges of my mind, lining up like an enemy horde, waiting to overwhelm my defences, if I dropped my guard even for a moment. I knew the danger of imagining what might happen, if I didn't fix my mind on the reality of the present, no matter how precarious it seemed. I'd let fearful thoughts overpower me once before, on the day of Natasha's funeral.

I could not bring myself to enter the church, I'd simply watched from the other side of the street as they took her coffin from the hearse. After the service, I joined the congregation and went to the cemetery and let every sob cut into me while imagining that I deserved to be punished for what I'd done to her. Somehow, though

I have no memory of it, I got back to my apartment and over the next week I drank myself into a stupor.

When I awoke, the stench of stale beer and urine filled my nostrils. Danny Maguire and my landlord were standing over me. After a brief and feeble struggle, Danny picked me up and hoisted me over his shoulder. I told him to leave me be but he carried on downstairs and threw me into the back of a car, and then returned to the apartment with the landlord and packed my gear. I continued with my descent into some dark and awful place. I was never quite sure how high I had climbed since then, but I always had the feeling that I remained a long way off the point from where I had fallen.

I dragged myself back to present reality and with the thought that I'd given the signal and Mitch would come. Whether he would come to save me, or something else, I'd have to wait and see.

Footfalls on the steps outside disturbed the make-believe conversation with my mother about how I'd got myself into this fix. Unless Mitch was following the FBI tradition of cross-dressing started by J Edgar Hoover, the person coming to the door was a woman in high heels. My stomach knotted as I anticipated who it might be.

I did my best not to look surprised when Vonette Norbury came in and closed the door. She was wearing a brown trouser suit with the collar of her white blouse opened over its lapels. In a low voice she said, "I'm here to help you, Robbie."

Confused about how, or why, she was rescuing me, but mightily relieved, I told her to go to the kitchen and see if she could find a knife to cut the ropes that bound me to the chair. My relief was short-lived. She halted in front of me. "I'm here to help," she said again.

Anger and suspicion stirred. I growled, "I heard you the first time. Go fetch a knife."

She crouched down and stroked my cheek. "I want to help you, Robbie," she said in a soft, seductive tone, "but you're gonna have to help me first." I dragged the tip of my tongue over my dry lips as she continued, "We need to find Danny Maguire. You must tell me where and when you last saw him. Was it when you were in Creektown?"

"'We'? Who the fuck is 'we'?"

She straightened up and stepped languidly behind me, letting her fingertips run under my chin. "We need Maguire today. If you help us get him today, I can help you. Otherwise . . ."

I wondered if the 'we' included Mitch, and decided I had to find out right away. "I wish I could help you, Vonette, but I'm already helpin the FBI with that one. They should be here any minute. If you don't believe me, take a look at my watch. It's got a device inside that sent them a signal a few minutes ago."

Seemingly unmoved, she began to stroke my chin again. She said, "If I were you I wouldn't put my faith in technology, or the Feds. I'd take my offer." Her other hand began to run over my chest. "I like you, Robbie, I've liked you since the first time I saw you. You're a fine-looking man, and I like the way you handle yourself. I really wanna help you but you have to help us find Maguire first."

"You're gonna have to tell me who I'd be helpin besides you. I mean, are you talkin about the likes of Kirby? Shit, Vonette, his buddies are in the Klan! Is that what you've sunk to, bein used by guys like him?"

Vonette's hands stopped moving. She moved back to where I could see her and she took the chair Mitch had used when he'd questioned me. As she smiled at me, I reminded myself that this was the woman who had stabbed Little J Moses to death. Ignoring my question, in a distant voice, she said, "Perhaps there are important issues, about what's happening in this country, issues that you aren't aware of."

"Perhaps I'm aware of more than you think."

She leaned back in the chair and crossed her ankles. "I wonder, Robbie, but I doubt if you really are. The threat's so great, that I'm even prepared to *use* the likes of Kirby. They're a means to an end, nothing more. We're about to start a war with a cabal who back in '99 staged a coup d'etat, we're about to strike back at the people who've been working for the last twenty-five years, or more, to subjugate the African-American once again. It started while Reagan was president, continued with Daddy Bush, but unfortunately for them Clinton came along."

It sounded off the wall to me but I was happy to keep her talking. "An' so?"

"Hillary wasn't wrong that time when she talked of a vast right-wing conspiracy to get her husband outta the White House, she just didn't realize how vast. There were several schemes funded by billionaires like Charles Lavette, to get rid of Clinton. When they failed, they vowed that, come hell or high water, they weren't going to let another election stop them finishing what they'd started. Crackers like Kirby reckon the conspiracy's run by a liberal Jewish clique, who are masquerading as conservatives so as to push a Zionist agenda. But those Jew-boys are only being set up as fall guys by the people who fund them."

"Then, according to you, who is really behind it all?"

"Same people it always was: vested interests. They don't mind the Jews taking the heat with this neo-con bullshit, or Osama bin Laden with his al-Qa'ida, or anyone else who is *out there*. The names and faces may change, but the agenda never does and it really doesn't matter who gets elected president next time. See, I know from my time with Little J that democracy is an illusion and the enemy's right on our doorstep, eating away at the foundations of the new society the civil rights movement helped create. I know, from what Calvin's told me, that you think the same way about a lotta things, and that's why I'll help you if I can."

"Yeah, Vonette, but what I don't know is why I'm tied up in a place like this an' talkin to you."

"You're here because of your links with the biggest cocaine dealers in the world, because you chose to fraternize with people who are willing to destroy the lives of hundreds of thousands of poor African-Americans."

I thought a while before replying. I reckoned she might be trying to trick me into saying more than was healthy for me, or Danny. "That's bullshit, Vonette, I'm not dealin with any coke dealers, unless Miss Boo has started sellin it. Look, I thought me an' you had reached an understandin, you know, like cleanin up your mess after *you* stabbed Moses to death. So how about you takin a knife an' cuttin me loose? That way we're even."

"Hm, I wondered how long it would take before you got around to that. Sorry, but the only deal is the one I just offered. Help us get Maguire right now, an' you're free."

I let out a bitter breath through my tight, dry lips. "I don't know where Danny is," I said, "but I do know there's two guys, killed less than an hour ago, lyin out there in the woods, Vonette. One of them was the manager at the factory. The other poor bastard knew nothin at all about what's goin on, but I'd had a quick chat with him an' just that small thing was enough to get him killed. You're lookin at a dead man talkin, unless the FBI gets here soon."

Again there wasn't a flicker of a reaction when I mentioned the

FBI: either she didn't believe me, or she knew no one was coming. I figured then that Mitch was probably a part, if not the person at the centre, of the conspiracy but my mind was clear and I was already working on another way out. "Yeah, Vonette, the guys who have planned this are not gonna leave anyone around, not even the people who's helped them, so if I were you I'd be lookin for a way out. I mean, why are you here, anyway?"

She tried to look as though she was unruffled and laughed quietly, but I thought the news about Colin and Billy Joe had troubled her. Then it hit me: if Mitch was in fact the chief conspirator, rather than the investigator, I reckoned I knew how Vonette, Calvin and Moses had ended up in my bedroom. If my hunch was right, this might well be my last chance of survival. "About Moses," I said. "Calvin told me everythin. He told me how you killed him." Her jaw tightened but before she could react I continued with my bluff, "See, Vonette, there are things I know. I know that there was a plan for Moses to be blackmailed by the people you think are on your side. I figure that plan went wrong when he lost the nomination an' when news of the scandal broke, they got worried that he might start talkin about what he knew as part of a deal to get him off the hook. So he had to go, an' this is where a bit of guesswork comes in. If I'm right, that's why you were told to come here now, to talk to me, an' why you don't have too long to live."

Although she shifted on her chair, her eyes never left mine as she abstractedly reached for the cross hanging around her neck. I had managed to turn the tables. "Go on," she said.

"I'm guessin that a man approached you a while ago an' he told you how to find Calvin, who wasn't doin too well in Atlanta. Months ago he warned you that a scandal was about to break over Moses' relationship with Calvin an' he might've said that Calvin would be better off leaving the city and goin somewhere quiet, outta harm's way until the nomination campaign was over. He told you he knew a place Calvin could have an' that he could get him a job in a lumber yard. Of course, you didn't tell Calvin this, you made out that Moses had made the arrangements an' that he'd agreed to get you two a place in Jacksonville later on. Calvin, scared an' vulnerable Calvin, trusted you an' did exactly what he was told. An' when I turned up, he was told to keep an eye on me an' tell you what he saw. So far you'd just been a conduit, passin information to this man but when

Moses loses the nomination, the man tells you that he has to die because he's goin to cut a deal with someone so he doesn't get prosecuted for child abuse. He says Moses has to be taken out, otherwise all the work that's been done over the years is gonna to be wasted. . . Stop me if this is nonsense."

"It is nonsense but you might as well carry on to the end. I was always a sucker for stories."

"The man says you have to get Moses outta Atlanta. 'Say, how about takin him down by Calvin,' he says. Then he gives you the bit about how the guy's an animal, how he never really suffered for what he did to you an' the other kids. He says it's time you paid him back, Vonette." There were tears behind her eyes, and I knew I was on the right track. "Take him to Calvin, he says, an' watch how he'll start slobberin like a darg when he sees him. An' it all came back as you watched him oglin Calvin, didn't it?"

"I warned Calvin not to tell you."

"Now, Vonette, if what I'm gonna say next is anythin like the truth, I reckon you an' Calvin will be dead very soon."

"So you say." There was anger as her tears fell but she made no attempt to staunch them.

I said, "He told you that I'm a bad guy an' that my name isn't really Barrett. Then he says to try an' get Moses over to my house an' kill him there. That way, if anythin goes wrong, all the evidence will be in my place an' it will keep you in the clear. When Calvin went to check if I'd got home, you knew already I wasn't there an' you seized the chance. Moses didn't chase you to my place, you led him by the hand! Maybe it was your idea to involve me by movin the body, but if I'm right about the rest, I'm right about you two not livin much longer, because I know the real reason you were told to kill Moses in my house."

"And if any of this chicken-shit is right, what do you reckon that reason is?"

"So it would all be on camera. My mom always says that when you're cookin you should clean up as you go, an' that's what he's doin now, Vonette, he's cleanin up as he goes. Moses gets it first 'cause he's the most unstable, then it's Billy Joe Watson's turn, an' then it's gonna be anyone who can link him to Moses. I figure that's you. You an' Calvin will die in an accident, or may be a suicide pact, an' some time later the tapes will appear to explain why Moses disappeared: a revenge killing by kids he'd abused. Case closed, nothin else to look for."

Vonette wiped the tears from her long lashes. When her eyes opened again they were ablaze.

"You pathetic, lying, piece-a shit!" she spat, her voice rising with every syllable. "Do you think you can undermine me so easily? You think this *poor, little woman* is gonna run scared because of your dumb-ass story? You have a choice about telling us about Maguire: you can tell us the easy way, or the much longer and much more unpleasant way." She went for the door.

"Wait!" I called.

She looked at me over her shoulder, a triumphant glint in her eye.

"Ring Calvin now, right now. Ask him to go to my place an' look in the ceilin of the room where you killed Moses. Tell him to tear it down if he has to. I'm not shittin you, Vonette. I only recently learned about it myself. Danny Maguire had an electronics expert check out the place, an there's a camera in each bedroom. We don't have much time. Ring Calvin now an' tell him to call you right away when he finds it. Give me ten minutes before you walk outta that door. If you don't call him, Vonette, none of us is long for this world. Think about it, think about why you, of all the people involved, was asked to come here now an' ask me questions anyone could ask me. Ask yourself why are you wanted here!"

She stood still for an excruciating time as she considered what I'd told her. I held my breath and willed her fingers to fall from the door handle. Slowly, she turned, and as she faced me her hand at last left the door. I allowed myself a shallow, soundless sigh of relief but said nothing. She reached into her pocket for her cell phone and dialled. Her eyes fixed on mine, she put it to her ear as the number rang. I looked down at the floor, silently begging Calvin to wake up and answer.

The silence lengthened until it seemed never ending. I looked up and saw alarm on Vonette's face. Finally, she lowered her phone. Her voice subdued, she said, "He's not answering."

"No, he won't be," called a voice. As soon as I heard it my heart began to thump. When I turned my head, I saw Mitch standing in the doorway to the kitchen.

27

HIS GUN MOVING TO AND FRO, Mitch stepped into the room. "No," he said to Vonette, "Calvin isn't taking any calls." He called to someone behind him to come in. There was a rumble of footsteps and the two men who'd tied me to the chair came through the kitchen doorway sideways. They were dragging Calvin's limp body between them.

"Get back to Jack," Mitch ordered them. "I'll take care of business in here."

I expected Vonette to run to Calvin but she was frozen with fear. "I-I was just coming to tell you," she said, "he told me that . . ."

"You don't have to tell me, Vonette, I heard it all." He gestured with his pistol. "Take a seat."

She had just sat down when Calvin moaned softly and rolled onto his side. Now I could see that his face was streaked with tears and dirt, and that the lower half of his tee-shirt was saturated with blood. Vonette saw it too and made to move towards him but Mitch halted her in mid-stride. "Leave him be," he said in a voice brittle with excitement. "There's nothing you can do for him now."

Her lips twitched, as if she were mouthing words of regret. When she was seated again, Mitch said to me, "Good story, Walker, but you're wrong about a suicide pact – too messy. What would you say if I told you this miserable faggot was selling you out and telling me all about how he drove you out to see Maguire? I always figured you would never keep your end of the deal."

"That's because you never fooled me into thinkin there was really a deal!"

Mitch's chuckle was thick and menacing.

Vonette sobbed, "You bastard, you promised me you'd leave him out of this!"

Mitch went on chuckling as he looked down at the blood seeping onto the floorboards. I thought the man was losing his sanity.

"Why are you laughing? You sick, lying son-of-a-bitch!" Vonette shouted.

Ignoring her, he said, "You see, I have a way more interesting story than yours, Walker. It begins some years ago in New York. I selected Maguire as a man who would perfectly fit in with my plans and bit by bit I manoeuvred him until he was exactly where I required him to be. There is no one he, or you, knows who I haven't touched. Everything you've done, leaving New York, coming to Georgia, finding work, finding a house, I planned it all. And I know everything there is worth knowing about you, Walker. Your boy, Nathan, it's his birthday in a weeks' time, and your mother has an appointment to see a cardiologist in three and a half months. Jeez, what kinda health service is that? I know you're a moral deviant, I know about the drugs you've bought and your trips to Creektown. I pride myself on knowing these things."

I was still transfixed by the sight of Calvin. "So what?" I shouted. "So fuckin what?"

"Call it hubris, but I'm showing you how completely I've controlled your life, you pathetic son-of-a-bitch. Remember Brian Hanlon?"

"Can't say I do, an' I couldn't give a fuck about him, either."

"No? Really? Well, you were still recovering from your breakdown when you met him. He was the man who drove you to the warehouse in New Jersey. He was the one who convinced Maguire that Paulie O'Sullivan was informing on you. It wasn't true, of course, but Maguire was only too ready to believe it. Everything they did to O'Sullivan, even down to the towel down his throat, was following my instructions. See, Hanlon was mine, Billy Joe Watson was mine, and these two sorry specimens here, and plenty of others were all mine to control. In a way, Maguire was mine. I was the one who told him there were orders from Ireland, I was the one who fed him the line about the negotiations for amnesty, but I could only control him through others, especially you. For a while I thought you two were like Calvin here and were queer for one another. I put pressure on Maguire in New York, but I couldn't budge him until you were getting better."

Calvin moaned and turned his dull eyes towards me, as if he understood what was being said.

"Why are you doing this?" Vonette asked. "We did everything. Everything you axed for, we did. We were loyal, we got rid of Moses, so why are you doing this to us?"

Mitch said, "I like how Walker's mother puts it, 'you should clean up as you go.' She sounds a sensible woman, makes me wonder how her only child turned out like he did. I've heard enough of your bullshit, Vonette, your belly-aching about what's happening to the niggers who haven't got the sense nor the moral strength to do anything but live in shit and squalor. It's always someone else's fault. 'De devil made me do it, massa.' You and your kind make me puke."

Wearying of his games, I said, "Why don't you just do what you came here for?"

Mitch frowned and pointed his gun at my head, but I was reconciled to my fate and a strange calm had come over me. "Get on with it," I said. "Come on, an' shoot me first."

"I'm not going to kill you yet, not before you hear why I planned all this."

"Don't you understand, you crazy bastard?" I sneered. "I don't fuckin care!" Calvin's eyes widened and I was instantly consumed by rage because of what had been done to him. I strained against the ropes, rocking the chair until it toppled sideways. Calvin blinked as my shoulder thudded hard against the floor and his eyes met mine. Looking into them, I could see that life was draining from him.

Curiously, Mitch seemed provoked by what I'd said; it seemed important to him that I cared. I was transfixed by the young man slipping away before me and I didn't pay much heed to Mitch at first. He said, "I did three tours in Colombia. That's a war that's been going on for more than fifty years; first as a dirty little war on communism, and then as a war on cocaine and the cartels. Now it's become one of the most important wars we've forgotten to fight, way more important than Korea or 'Nam, because what's coming out of there is a slow poison that will eventually destroy this country. If it just killed the niggers and the spics no one would give a damn, but it contaminates everything and everyone, from the old lady whose bag gets snatched to the cop on the take. History, Walker, tells us that every empire starts to collapse from within. Fuck Afghanistan, and fuck Iraq, yeah, and fuck Israel and the rest. To protect America, the war has to be first fought in the Americas."

"Yeah, yeah, yeah," I said, "so what does that make you besides a racist nutcase?"

"It makes me a patriot, Walker. And I don't see how what I've said is racist. I mean, Vonette here, and Moses, were always harping on about what cocaine was doing to their community, but I never heard either of them talk about the damage it was doing to other ethnic groups. Does that make them racist?"

"Could be, or maybe just blinkered. Maybe as blinkered as a man who thinks that plantin a bomb that could kill hundreds of innocent Americans is doin somethin patriotic."

"Collateral damage, Walker, a justifiable sacrifice for a much bigger cause. . ."

"Please!" Vonette yelled. "Please let me get Calvin to a hospital. He's still breathing, we can still save him!"

Two flashes of flame erupted from the muzzle of Mitch's gun. Calvin's body arched and contorted as black-red blood began to trickle from his lips. The eyes that rested on me were wide and empty now.

Leaping up, Vonette gasped, "Jesus! No, Calvin, no!" A moment later she was sitting down again, this time against a wall, her legs splayed and a dark stain on her jacket. Her eyes were turned up in her head and she breathed in short gasps which communicated her shock and pain.

My ears ringing, I looked up at Mitch as he studied Vonette with the fascination of a child who had just plucked the wings off an insect. He laughed again. "Right, perhaps now I can finish without her interrupting. Where was I? Oh yes, the bigger picture. Democracy, if it ever existed, it's a bit like Vonette over there, barely breathing, but in reality this country has become a plutocracy. I guess an educated man like you knows that a plutocracy's only concern is to protect the interests of the rich, like the Lavettes. People like old Charles Lavette gave money to the Jews who've set up the pseudo-conservative clique which now controls America's foreign policy, and that's why people like me have had to stage what you might call a 'counter-counter-revolution'. The plutocrats have used the Jews in Washington to focus foreign policy on the Middle East so as to get access to oil . . ."

"Shit, man, I think what's happened in Iraq kills that particular conspiracy theory."

". . . It's a win-win for them, Walker, even if it didn't work out as they'd planned, look at the stocks and shares: the Lavettes and their buddies have still made trillions. And while they've been doing that our rear flank's been left exposed and all the sacrifices made by people, who were friends of mine, now count for nothing. 9/11 was exploited to turn foreign policy around. Well, what's gonna happen in the next few hours will turn it around again – this time so it's facing in the right direction."

I had started off not caring but now I was curious. I said, "So you lured the Farc here so they would take the blame?"

"Sure," he said. "I said it before, you're a smart one for a black man. When I found out that the INS were about I made sure a rumour got around so to get them out from the factory. I need them, you see, so when the bomb goes off everyone will see what a threat to this country these people can pose if they've a mind to."

"But they haven't got a mind to, not in that way. An' I suppose it was you who fed them the line about Pedroza bein here."

"Marco Pedroza is in Atlanta right now but when he wakes up in a few hours, his security people will learn of an anonymous call which has made a threat to his life and then they will put him on the first plane home."

"You drawin the Farc here, I can understand, but why do you want Danny?"

"For the life of a friend, and because I don't like the Irish very much. My friend was in the wrong place at the wrong time. He was killed when the Farc launched an attack on a village on the Venezuelan border, using mortar technology given to them by the IRA. I wanted Maguire here to highlight how the double-standards of these mealy-mouthed politicians have come back on us. *Now* they talk about a war on terror because it suits their own ends, but for years they let the IRA, a bunch of commie terrorists, do their fundraising in this country because they thought it wouldn't impact on Americans. I'm showing them how wrong they were."

"But Danny's too smart for you."

"Smart, or just lucky. But I've made sure that, one way or another, he's going to pay for his crimes. If I don't get him this time I have a Plan B, and if that fails there's a Plan C. I'm very, very good at that sort of thing. And he really isn't that smart; those two men who turned up at the Fentons' place weren't British agents, they were hit-men from an IRA splinter group. Paulie O'Sullivan was in the process of defecting to their organisation, and they're pretty pissed that Maguire killed him. They got word Maguire was down this way because he's been making contact with people he trusts, but now they think that he's working for British Intelligence. He's slowly finding out that I've cut off all his escape routes. Whatever happens now, Maguire doesn't have long to live."

Mitch let out a heavy sigh, as if he were rapidly tiring of my questions and his own boasting. He examined Vonette with disinterested eyes before he came back to me. "And now I've got you, my Plan D; it looks as though you've won yourself a ride in a truck. I really wanted Maguire in it as the bomb went off, but I've had to bring matters forward. Shame, because I had also planned for the Farc to take out the Lavettes for me. I let it be known that Henry Lavette is a big-time coke dealer and that a big transaction between him and Pedroza was about to go down. Never mind, I have another plan for the Lavettes, too."

"Henry Lavette doesn't need shit like cocaine, so who the hell would believe that?"

Mitch's eyes became dull again, as if his mind had travelled to someplace else and some other time. He said, in a distant voice, "You *are* a smart guy, Walker, smarter than I thought, smarter than Vonette. Must be something to do with an English education, huh?" His tone changing abruptly, he went on, "You're right, oil and diamonds are his thing but I fed Vonette's prejudice about the big cocaine conspiracy so she'd do what I wanted. I also put out that he was doing business with Pedroza so the Farc would take action against Henry. It is more like personal between me and him."

"An' that's why you told her to put Moses' body on the Lavettes' estate?" He nodded absentmindedly, and I tried another question: "Why did you bring Moses into this?"

He looked at his watch and frowned before he turned to me. "Why Moses?" he murmured. "Is it you think all these dots have got to join up? That's not real life, and that's not smart, because if they all joined up they would eventually make a line back to me. Jerome Moses was going to be used for a future project but he went running to a friend of mine in the FBI and told him that someone was trying to blackmail him. Of course my friend let me know immediately . . . And Vonette had wanted to kill him for years, so, I thought, why not let her fulfill her ambition before she dies. None of them, Moses, Calvin or Vonette, were going to be of any use to me, so I applied my flexible thinking to the situation. It could be that documents will be found in the future that links the Lavettes with a plan to murder the good congressman."

"You certainly have a thing about the Lavettes. Did you know Henry from your time in Colombia?"

The instant I asked that question I knew I had hit the bullseye.

He came and stood over me, his gun only inches from my head. "Did you enjoy her?" His voice was now shrill and angry.

"Who?" I said.

"Who, you black son-of-a-bitch, *who*? Your friend Maguire, he told her to go find you. When he found out you were getting drunk, visiting whores in Creektown, and buying hash, he knew you might compromise his operation so he had her prostitute herself for you."

"I really don't know who the fuck you're talkin about."

"Cristina, my wife, that's who!"

As I tried to take in what he had just told me, the gun in his hand began to shake and I heard him take in a deep breath. Without warning, a vicious kick to my stomach sent my whole body into spasms and I rolled onto my knees, the chair over my back like a shell. My forehead on the floor, I desperately sucked in air around the edges of my gritted teeth. "She's a phenomenon," he said, above the rasp of my laboured breathing. "I wouldn't put it past her to have messed with the air conditioning so as to meet you. If you hadn't turned up then, I'm sure she would have taken the chance and ventured into Creektown. . . Bitch! . . She wasn't much more than a kid when I first met her. There had been an incident in a place called El Aro and I was in charge of the debriefs. She'd been brainwashed by the Farc and I made it my business to bring her back. One day I found out that Henry Lavette had bribed a guard and several officials so he could keep her in his apartment and make her his whore. When he abandoned her and returned to the States, I met her again. A year later we were married, and I was in the process of adopting Goretti when Lavette came back to Colombia. I couldn't face up to it then, but he'd turned Cristina's head with all his money and empty promises. Later on, she moved up here and he made her a whore all over again. Then it turned out that I hadn't reprogrammed her as thoroughly as I thought, and she was still working with the Farc. But she made her choice a long time ago and now she'll have to face the consequences."

My forehead was still pressed to the boards but I could now breathe easily again. I snarled, "You're full-a shit! Patriotic? You're a joke, man, a sick joke. You talk bullshit about the rich, or the Jews, or 9/11, but this is all to do with Cristina, isn't it? She dumped you for a rich guy, an' then, ironies of ironies, according to you, the Irish guy you're tryin to kill goes an' sets her up with me. Christ, you must be burnin up inside. Kill me now, man, while I'm laughin at you. Do it now, you sick bastard!"

He kicked me again. It didn't hurt like the first one, but I gave a loud groan as if it had.

"You're going to die all right, you black son-of-a-bitch! I'm going to put a needle in you to paralyse you so you'll still be conscious before you're blown to pieces. And after they sweep you up I'm going to make sure that they find out your identity and where your son is so they can make a DNA match. You'll be the link to Maguire, who's the link to the IRA. It's not quite what I wanted but I assure you, after your death there'll be enough evidence of your journey from Ireland and what you got up to in England with Maguire to convince the investigators who you were working for. See, I plan for all eventualities, Walker."

I turned my head slightly, so he could see that I was not scared but Mitch had disappeared from my line of vision.

The ceiling exploded. Powdery fragments showered onto me, as automatic fire poured into the room. A door crashed open. At first, I saw only feet. A hand touched my shoulder and I peered through the choking dust and saw Ricardo. There were more bursts from assault rifles outside, and the single cracks of smaller arms, which echoed and grew more distant and then faded away.

Someone else came in. It was Danny. He crouched down and began pulling at the ropes around my arms as Ricardo ran to the kitchen door. I was sitting up as Ricardo came back. "He's gone," he said.

28

THE ROPES FELL AWAY. Every muscle in my body had cramped and I found it difficult to get myself upright. Danny, who like Ricardo, was dressed in army-surplus camouflage gear, hooked a hand under my arm and lifted me. Once I was on my feet, he rested his other hand on my shoulder. "Christ, Rob," he said, "I thought I'd lost you."

It wasn't like the guy to get all emotional on me but there was something about him that had changed since we'd last met in that dingy apartment in Creektown. We had both watched Ricardo kill Chuck Woodlow, and as Danny looked down at Calvin's body, perhaps he now realized that we were caught in between two sets of ruthless people who would kill anyone who got in their way.

"How did you find me?" I asked.

"Joe was waiting for you in the parking lot, remember? He followed you most of the way, and calculated where they had taken you with one of his fancy GPS devices. Then he called me and told me where you were. It took almost as long to get up from the road without being seen, as it did to drive from Petra."

"We should make that guy Joe into a legend some day."

Danny gave me a knowing smile. "But we know legends are built on shite, don't we, mate?"

My own smile faded as Cristina appeared. She, too, was dressed camouflage fatigues. Unsure of how to greet her, I simply said, "Cristina."

Without warmth she replied, "Robbie." To Danny she said, "He got away in a van with two others. There's one man dead on the track, he either fell, or was pushed out of the back." She looked around at the damage and pulled a face as though she was unimpressed. "So many bullets and he didn't take one hit?"

Ricardo scoffed and said, "Danny said to shoot high so we didn't hit his friend."

Cristina pursed her lips, making it plain where she would have aimed. Only days before, she'd said she wanted to go away with me. It looked as though what I'd thought was love, or at least desire, had turned to contempt, and I knew why: it ran along the lines Danny had described when the mother of his child had witnessed his weakness. Even before I'd arrived in Georgia, I'd become a self-indulgent and weak man, who'd put at risk my closest friend and everyone linked with his operation because of my behaviour. Cristina had tolerated me only as she'd tolerated Henry Lavette and now I doubted if her display of feelings for either of us had been any more than doing what was necessary for the sake of the Farc's mission. Shifting my eyes away from her, I said, "I think I have somethin you guys need to hear. The guy who got away, I don't know his real name, . ." I couldn't help glancing at her, " . . . but he called himself Mitch."

Flatly, she said, "His name is Tom Keeler, and he was with the DEA."

"Well, whatever," I said, matching her tone. I noted that Danny didn't seem surprised that she knew his name. "He says Pedroza isn't comin. It's all been a trick to get the Farc here. Before they dumped me in the trunk I found a truck bomb at the factory." I looked over at Ricardo to gauge his reaction, and continued, "He wants you here so you can take the blame for this bomb he's gonna set off. An', Danny, he wants you here so the IRA get turned over, too. He's been playin us like a pair of banjos ever since New York. Brian Hanlon was his man, which is how come he knew everythin about what happened to Paulie O'Sullivan. This is serious shit, Danny. The guy was goin on about turnin around American foreign policy. He told me that he's had to bring his plans forward, it could be that he'll detonate the bomb in a few hours, an' I reckon they're on their way to the factory right now. If we don't make a move, that bomb will be goin off in some city."

"So?" said Ricardo. "Let them do it. We'll head for Mexico right now. Let the Americans experience some of the pain we have suffered because of the crimes they have committed in our country. You say we'll get the blame, Robbie, but I say it'll be the glory."

"Ric," I said, "why do you think your leadership has never done somethin like this in America? It's because they know what would follow. Man, America would take their biggest bombers an' flatten every inch of territory they think the Farc might be in. All those daisy-cutters would shred every plant, animal an' human in there."

"So you say," he retorted.

Cristina said, "We need to contact home and see what we should do."

I said, "That'll be too late. While they're makin their minds up, the bomb will have gone off. Danny, what do you think?"

Before he could answer, a faint moan drew our attention. "Please," Vonette whispered, "help me."

Danny glanced at the other two, then meaningfully at me. I went quickly over to Vonette and squatted down beside her. Dust had settled on her face and gave her a macabre, corpse-like appearance. I reached under her jacket and felt a faint, uneven heartbeat. She had a cell phone, and perhaps the only way of stopping that bomb was to call John Hunter. My hand slid into her pocket, and her head lolled as she questioned me with a frown. The phone was small enough for me to palm easily. As I stood up I looked at Danny and shook my head. "If she doesn't get help right away . . ."

A blast of gunfire erupted behind me. I looked over my shoulder and saw thin wisps of smoke coming from Ricardo's M-16. He'd put a burst into Vonette that had torn her apart. Her blood smeared the splintered wall behind her as she slid sideways to the floor. Her whitened, dusty face was distorted and fixed in a last moment of agony.

"We don't help the enemy where I come from," said Ricardo. "We kill them. That's war, Robbie."

Danny's disapproval showed in his face. "Ach, one in the nut would have done her. You'd better save your ammo, Ric, if you're coming with us."

"Coming with you? Where?" asked Cristina.

"The factory. I'm going to stop this bomb with or without youse. Make up your mind right now because me and Robbie are away any second."

The muscles in my neck tightened as my eyes drifted to Danny's finger, which had found the trigger of his Armalite.

"He's right," Cristina told Ricardo. "For the sake of our movement we cannot allow that bomb to go off."

He replied to her in Spanish and then nodded. Danny's finger uncurled and returned to the trigger guard. I let out a quivering breath as quietly as I could, and, while they were all watching one another, slipped Vonette's cell phone into my pants pocket.

"Right, Cristina," said Danny, "you and Ric take the van and go with Jorge, and me and Robbie will head to the factory with Joe. You'd better keep up because we don't have time to fuck about in the parking lot waiting for youse. As soon as we're there we'll get into the factory – Robbie will show us the way to the truck – and then we hit them quick and hard. Whatever else happens, the first thing we do is disable the truck. Keeler told Robbie that his plans have been brought forward, so I doubt if it's primed right now and that might give us some time. But they've got a head start, so we won't have long."

Danny took out his cell phone, called Joe, and told him to start driving up the dirt track and that we'd meet him halfway.

I thought this would be my only chance to telephone Hunter. "Hey, man," I said, "all this excitement has got me burstin for a piss. I'm just gonna take a leak, yeah? I won't be a minute."

Danny grunted that I had better make it quick and I hurried to the same bathroom where I had been sick the previous weekend, after agreeing to betray Danny to the man I would always think of as 'Mitch'. This time I didn't feel like a betrayer. I knew that Danny didn't fully trust either Cristina or Ricardo, and, as he'd said, stopping that bomb was our first priority. On the fifth ring the phone was answered. "Hunter," he said gruffly.

"It's Robbie."

"Man, I just got my head down. Why the hell are you ringin me at this time of the mornin?"

"I tried to reach you before you left the factory. You wanted somethin concrete an' I've got it. I found a truck bomb . . ."

"A what?"

"A massive bomb in a truck at the factory. Just listen, because I haven't got time to say this again. Billy Joe's dead. He was one of the people involved with the bomb. Kirby is too, one of the bombers, I mean. He killed Billy Joe an' Colin the electrician. The brains behind it all is a man called Tom Keeler. He lured the Farc here, an' my Irish friend, too, to take the blame. He's the guy who was makin out to me that he was FBI, but I think he's DEA – check it out. We're goin to the factory now to try an' stop them. We think they're gonna try to detonate the bomb within a few hours."

"Where?"

"A city, but we don't know which one. That's why we have to stop it before it leaves the factory. It'll take us forty minutes, or so, to get there. Rustle up who you can an' get down there, Hunter. Do you need me to repeat any of this?"

"No, I have it taped. I'll see you down there, Barrett, as soon as I can."

"Hunter, one more thing . . ."

"Yeah?"

"I want you to know that me an' my friend have already talked about headin for Mexico right now rather than goin after the bomb. So if we survive this I want that deal for me an' my friend Danny. Nothin fancy, I just want you to let us walk an' let us take our chances. No ifs or maybes. Do we have a deal?"

A long exhalation followed a deep breath. "You have a deal. You got my word on that."

I disconnected and then debated whether or not I should leave the phone in the bathroom. It took two seconds to figure its job was done and I left it on the cistern.

I joined the others at the front door and we made our way down the dirt track. The three of them had their rifles to their shoulders and trained on the trees. In the still air I heard the distant strains of Vonette's phone ringing. Part of me was relieved that I'd left it in the bathroom, another part thought it might be Hunter calling me back and I wondered what he wanted. If anyone else heard it they didn't say.

The oscillating whine of an engine grew louder and then headlights appeared around a bend in the track. The beams of light illuminated a body lying on the ground ahead of us. By the time we got to it, the car was stopped only three or four yards further on. I hoped it was either Jack Kirby or Keeler, but it was one of the guys who'd tied me to the chair.

"Never ceases to amaze me," said Danny as he stared down at the dead man. "Doesn't matter how much muscle you put on, it only takes a wee piece of lead to make all that effort worth fuck all, so it does."

Joe turned the car with a seven-point turn and we headed for the road, with Danny sitting with him up front. After a rocky couple of minutes on the rutted track I was grateful for the pitted tarmac. A little way along the road we came upon a parked Dodge van. Joe pulled up behind it and everyone except him got out. Danny went to the van's rear doors and pulled out another M-16 and a jacket like his. He thrust both at me.

"I'm not into uniforms, Danny," I said.

"Put it this way," he said impatiently, "anyone I see who's not wearing one of these is a target. There won't be time for friend-or-foe shite, so just for me, eh, Rob?"

Cristina watched me put on the jacket. "Suits you," she said, before she went around to the front of the van. I wasn't sure if she had meant it as a compliment. Danny reached into the van again and brought out a handful of magazines. "Put a couple of those into your pockets," he said to me. I went and sat in the back of the car and watched him giving a few last instructions to Jorge, the driver, before jogging back and sliding in beside me. "Right, Joe," he said, "we're heading to the factory."

"Back to the factory?" Joe's surprise and fear were obvious.

"Yeah, but get a move on. We have a few bad bastards and a truck bomb to be taking care of before breakfast."

"Are you serious?"

"Do I look as though I'm joking? Now hurry on, because we don't have much time. But make sure you don't lose the van, okay?"

At first, we sped along a road which was hemmed in by towering pines. In the distance ahead of us the dark sky was beginning to draw up the first rays of pink light above more tall trees. Behind us were the headlights of the Dodge van.

"Danny," I said, "that guy Mitch, I mean Keeler, he really was playin with us in New York. The guy's a complete an' utter control freak. He spends his whole time plannin, an' makin back-up plans in case the first ones don't work."

Danny's mouth tightened. I guessed he was regretting killing Paulie O'Sullivan. "Yeah, well, even the best laid plans go astray, mate."

"He told me it wasn't a Brit agent Darlene Fenton shot, he was a comrade of Paulie's an' he was a member of a dissident IRA organisation. I don't know how the hell they knew we were here . . ." I let my words hang reprovingly " . . . but Keeler reckons he's made sure you can't go an' hide in any Irish community in this country. . . . I thought I'd better warn you."

His tight lips made a painful smile, before he turned his head and stared out of the window.

I thought it best not to tell him that Mitch had put it about that he was working for British Intelligence, but Danny had probably figured out that much for himself. We travelled a few miles in silence and I wondered about the three Colombians in the van. I said to Danny, "What do you think those three behind us are talkin about?"

"Whatever it is, it's in a language I don't understand."

I knew then that he'd read my suspicions and he too had considered that they might make a sudden turn before we reached the factory. I imagined Ricardo arguing that there was no good reason to put themselves at more risk and Cristina countering with the repercussions for their people if they didn't. Jorge, the man with his hands on the steering wheel, would have the casting vote.

Our driver, Joe, kept silent, though, even from the rear, I could see the tension in him. I thought about how scared he was and wondered why I wasn't. I'd never thought of myself as brave but I'd seen bravery in the face of death, or perhaps it was only resignation.

I thought of Colin and how he'd shown true courage. It wasn't what I'd expected from him. He'd been an ordinary guy, nothing special to look at, leading a pretty normal, humdrum life. And yet, when his moment of truth arrived, he'd been brave and sought to save John Hunter's life by not telling Kirby that I'd asked of his whereabouts. That last act defined the sort of man he had been at his core but there would be no posthumous medals nor citations for him. I hoped that when my time came I would handle it as courageously as the ordinary-looking man named Colin.

Joe slowed as we reached the highway and let the van get closer before treading on the gas again. "Don't you be worrying yourself about any Highway Patrol," Danny said. Poor Joe was so rigid that he couldn't even turn his head to see that Danny was joking. In his most serious voice Danny said, "Robbie, I was just thinking."

"Yeah?"

"I was just thinking, why would this man draw us all the way down here? I mean, why not just put the bomb in New York, or Dallas, or Atlanta, instead of going to the trouble of getting us to come to Petra, of all the godforsaken places he could have chosen?"

"Personal reasons."

"What do you mean, personal?"

"Weren't you surprised that Cristina knew his name?"

"Well, she is the Farc's best intelligence officer."

I stared at him. "An' he told me that you set her up with me, Danny. What gave you the fuckin right?"

He dropped his head and a forefinger smoothed an eyebrow. "Christ, mate, you were sliding down the shitter, so you were. It was though you'd lost all your self-respect, and you'd become a stranger to me. I mean, you were drinking like you never did before, buying women, doing dope. I tried talking to you, but you weren't listening. Now, I didn't, or couldn't, tell Cristina to go sleep with you. Remember when we'd had that row? Well, that was after Cristina and her crowd reckoned you were a security risk. What she did was her choice. All I asked her to do was talk to you. When I couldn't get through, I thought you needed a woman to talk to . . ."

"I wish you hadn't, Danny!"

"There was stuff you needed to get off your chest, didn't you talk about it with Cristina?" I recalled the times when she had mentioned my secrets and thought about how dishonest I must have seemed to her. "Didn't you?" persisted Danny.

"I never got around to it. She shouldn't have got involved with me in the first place."

"Well, Creektown's a rough enough place, and her lot didn't want you drawing the law on yourself." Regret cast a gloomy silence over me. I looked out at the flickering landscape, which was smudged with shadows as the light grew.

"You didn't answer my question," Danny said, after a few miles. "What did you mean, there were personal reasons for Keeler to bring us all the way down here?"

"Cristina was married to him in Colombia an' then Henry Lavette took her away from him."

Danny let out a quiet whistle. It was a few moments before he spoke again. "That woman," he said, "she's some operator. No wonder they rate her as the best. Christ, I was told she was even tapping the DEA for info, but they didn't tell me she'd married one of their agents. So she, Lavette and this fella had something of a love triangle going on?"

"A love quadrangle if you count me in."

"Quadrangle is right," he laughed. Then, serious again, "The Keeler fella wants to kill as many birds as possible with this one big stone. He must have been working at this for years. Makes you think about the workings of the human mind, eh?"

"Makes me think that the guy's a dangerous maniac. But at the same time I think I understand why he's doin this, why he's plantin a bomb to turn things around again more to his likin. He sees it worked with 9/11, but he knows the power an' the resources that will be used to hunt the bombers down, so he has to cover his every track. In some ways what he's doin has a logic to it an' he can justify it all to himself. The guy thinks he's savin America, so what does it matter if a few hundred, or even a few thousand, people die for the greater good?"

Danny shifted uncomfortably in his seat. "And fucking up his ex-wife," he murmured. Over the years, on the rare occasions when we'd talked of such things, we had always justified our own violence with phrases like "the lesser evil" and "the greater good". Perhaps such conversations were merely exercises in reinforcing the self-deception that helped us to carry on with our lives. There was only one action with which I had never been fully reconciled, and my inability to justify it to myself had brought me to the brink of self-destruction. We returned our own thoughts and I said nothing until I saw the religious billboard and told Joe to take the next turn. I glanced over my shoulder and saw the van following us. There was only a mile to go. My mouth dried and a warm tingling ran over the tops of my legs. Danny stared straight ahead. I didn't have to ask: I knew what was on his mind.

With only a few minutes until we reached the factory, questions about the mentality of the man who had planned all this loomed large in my mind. Keeler had boasted that he had controlled most of the people I knew, and the only way he could have managed that was by identifying and then exploiting their weak points. The Farc's collective weak point was their lust for revenge on Marco Pedroza; Danny's was his adherence to the Irish Republican movement and his inability to refuse what it asked of him. Moses' depraved appetites had made him an easy target; as had Vonette's lack of belief in the USA's political system. As for the likes of Billy Joe Watson, Chuck Woodlow and Jack Kirby, it had probably been their conviction that the Federal Government, whatever its policies, was the enemy of the American people. And me? I had so many weaknesses that I must have given Keeler a headache over which one he would use against me. He obviously considered himself intellectually and morally superior to everyone he had drawn into his elaborate plan, but I wondered if, for all his intelligence and guile, he had ever recognized how much of what he had done was centred on his relationship with Cristina. Because I, too, had desired and lost her, it was obvious to me that his feelings for her were his main motivation. He deluded himself that he was driven by patriotism, but in reality losing her had provided the fuel for his appalling scheming.

My tongue dabbed at the corners of my mouth as I thought of what he might have in store for us at the factory.

29

I FIGURED THAT BEHIND Danny's impenetrable façade he was turning over what I'd told him about how he'd been duped into killing Paulie O'Sullivan, and that the hit squad who had arrived in Petra had been made up of fellow Irishmen, rather than British agents. After all he had done, becoming a pariah within the Irish communities throughout the USA would hurt him the most. But I knew that all other considerations, even of his own death, would be swept aside so, when the time came, his mind would be clear and set only on capturing the bomb.

I told Joe to take the road that skirted the factory's parking lot. Further on was a small wooded area which would give us some cover while we figured out our next move. I looked around, making out that I was checking that the van was still behind us but in fact I was searching for a sign of John Hunter. I began to think that I might have acted too hastily in calling him: while I might be able to prevent Danny killing him, if he showed up now, I doubted if there was any way I could stop the three Colombians. On the other hand, if Hunter arrived with plenty of reinforcements, we might be the ones who ended up dead. We parked amongst the trees, and the van drew up alongside.

"What is this shit?" growled Ricardo as he clambered out. "I thought we were going to hit them hard and fast and use the element of surprise."

Danny rolled his tongue over his teeth but said nothing until Cristina and Jorge were out of the van, too. Looking straight into Ricardo's face he said, "There's two ways out of the factory that the truck could use. I want Joe at the front, with his car parked across the road. Jorge will go with him. If the truck heads out that way, shoot at the tyres. But I think they'll probably go out by the loading bay, and I want you and Cristina there with the van to stop it getting out that way, if me and Robbie don't get to it first. We'll head for the truck once the four of youse people start shooting and creating a diversion."

"I-I don't think I can do this," said young Joe. "Hell, man, I'm just a technician."

Danny's cheeks rippled as they reddened with anger. "By fuck, boy, you'll get yourself a shooter from the back of the van and stand with Jorge."

"Shit," complained Ricardo, "you're spreading us too thin, man. We don't have the firepower, especially if one of your men is already messing his pants. I say we drive both vehicles through the gates at the same time, get to the lorry and kill anyone who gets in the way."

"And what about their shooters?" snapped Danny. "We don't know how many of them there are but I'll bet they'll have plenty of fellas on the lookout by the gates with shooters that will put a lot of holes in your van before you get anywhere near that truck."

Ricardo edged closer to him. "I have fought the Yankee since I was twelve years old, and without air support they are nothing. The Americans have grown soft, they love their comfortable lives too much to fight to the death. I say we rush them and they will scatter like sheep."

Cristina said something in Spanish to Ricardo, and he gave a little ground. She said, "Danny's plan may not be perfect but we do not have time to stand here arguing. I say we go along with it."

"Okay, Cristina," Ricardo replied, "then I will go with Danny and Robbie can go with you."

"No way, Ric. I want Robbie with me," said Danny.

"You need somebody like me who's experienced enough to give you cover."

"Robbie's with me, and there'll be no more talk about it. I want youse to get to the gates. As soon as I hear shooting, me and Robbie are going over the fence. Right, now we check our watches." We did so and Danny said, "I want you to open up in three minutes. We don't have much more time."

Joe looked pale and drawn as an M-16 was thrust into his hands. Danny wrapped an arm around his defeated shoulders and guided him swiftly back to the car, whispering words which seemed to be of little comfort. I felt for the young guy: this wasn't his fight and I didn't want him wasted like Calvin. The contrast between his faltering gait and Ricardo's swagger was stark. Their outlooks, shaped by their experiences, was so different and so apparent.

The doors slammed and wheels sprayed the loose earth as the two vehicles headed back to the road. The engines' roars faded into the distance and I felt a charge of resolve go through me that put a tingle on my skin. Like as it was when I used to step into a ring, there was nothing for me to do but concentrate on the fight ahead and visualize myself emerging intact.

Danny produced a 9mm pistol from under his coat. "Put that in your waistband, mate," he said. "And watch out for Ricardo, don't you be turning your back on that wee bastard."

I tucked the gun into my waistband at the small of my back. "He shouldn't get in our way, should he?"

"I have a feeling him and Cristina might want to act the heroes and fight their way in. You know, like give us a bit more cover by the truck."

"Well, that can't be a bad thing, can it?"

Danny snorted before he said, "That all depends. Come on, we'd better get moving."

We crossed the road and, stooping, skirted the chain-link fence, looking for the best spot to scale it. The pale sun was already making the air hot and humid and Danny's forehead was glistening with sweat as he led the way, the barrel of his M-16 resting in the crook of his arm. As we manoeuvred around by the old machine grave-yard, the truck came into view. I could see no one about. We lowered ourselves onto our haunches.

Danny checked his watch. "Another twenty seconds and we go over. You okay, mate?"

"Yeah," I whispered, "I'm all right. But what are we gonna do once we've finished here?"

"I haven't really thought about it."

I wanted to tell him about my call to Hunter. "Danny, I think I might have a way out for both of us to . . ." The crackle of distant gunfire cut me short. They were a few seconds early.

I got to my feet and made a stirrup with my hands. Once he'd thrown his M-16 over the fence, Danny put his foot on them and I gave him a heave up. The fence rattled and he landed on the other side with a thud. I threw him my rifle, put my fingers through the mesh and started to climb. It wasn't easy. At the top, the chain-link swayed and my descent was a lot more rapid than planned. Winded, I joined Danny behind the rusting hulk of a machine. He checked my M-16 and pushed a lever at the top of the hand grip before handing it over.

We heard shouting and voices drawing nearer. Someone was

running to the truck. Single shots punctuated the rattle of automatic fire. I recognized one of the voices as Kirby's. He was ordering his men to take up defensive positions as they fell back from the front and rear gates.

"Right, mate," said Danny, "we'd better get to that truck. I'll let you lead the way."

We at least had the advantage of being undetected. Bending low, sometimes crawling, we made our move, hoping to get on the blind side of Kirby and his men. The gunfire got louder, and I guessed our guys were advancing.

In the distance, a scream of agony went up: "Oh, fuck! Oh, fuck! I'm hit. Jesus, help me!"

I peered around the edge of the machine to try and see where the wounded man was.

"'Sake," hissed Danny, "that's Joe. He doesn't sound too good." I bristled at such cold sarcasm. Danny went on, "If he doesn't shut up now, those bastards will zero in on him."

Helplessly, I listened to sustained bursts of automatic fire, the muffled thuds of bullets as they hit the dirt and then sharp whines as others ricocheted off the metal pipes that surrounded Joe. Amid another burst, his howls of pain abruptly ceased.

Why hadn't we opened up, I wondered, and at least drawn some of the fire pouring at Joe? I challenged Danny with a look but he showed not even a flicker of emotion. In his mind Joe was just another casualty of war who could not be afforded the luxury of a moment of regret. A feeling of nausea came and went as I thought of the wasted life. "Come on, we've got work to do," Danny said, tugging at my jacket. "I want you to put yourself behind that oil drum. When I give the signal, fire as many rounds as you can at those bastards. I've set your shooter to three-round bursts. You got thirty rounds in the mag, so I want you counting out your ten and then putting another one in, okay? And don't be shooting blind like you're a Yank. Keep your eyes open, and there's a chance I might survive your friendly fire, right, Robbie?" He smiled and slapped my shoulder, before he headed for the grassy verge while I crawled in the opposite direction and duly put myself behind the oil drum. My trigger finger trembled as I looked along the barrel of the M-16. Men were moving around the truck. I looked over at Danny, alert for his signal. He was lying on the grass, on his side, craning his neck for a better view. He seemed so relaxed that I could imagine him reaching over and picking one of the wild flowers.

A volley of shots came from my right but it wasn't Danny who was firing. It sounded like Cristina and Ricardo were closing in on the truck. Danny gave me a thumbs-up, and in an instant I turned back and began to fire. The stock hammered into my shoulder. I tightened my grip and fired again. The men by the truck looked frantically around, trying to figure out where my shots were coming from. One of them had fallen with my second burst. By the time I let off the third the men had moved out of my line of vision. Adrenaline had heightened my senses: I could smell the cordite and taste the sulphur on my tongue; I heard the groans and curses of my targets; even in my peripheral vision, I could clearly see Danny moving toward the rear of the truck as I fired another burst.

Fragments stung my face as bullets hit the ground around me. I returned the fire, not really sure where my shots were going. Instinctively, I dived out from behind the oil drum, a moment before it was punctured by a barrage of heavy-duty rounds. From my new position I could see one of my attackers lying flat on the ground. I had him kissing the dirt with my next burst. Shit, how many bursts was that? Danny was now in full view. There was a terrible grace about his movements, which looked supremely confident and without fear. Almost serenely, he aimed and fired with deadly accuracy. Men howled and fell to the ground. I knew they wouldn't be getting up again.

In no more than a few seconds it was over. The silence was eerie after all the noise. Dizzy, I got to my feet. Cristina and Ricardo began turning over the fallen men and putting a bullet into any who showed a sign of life. Danny looked on impassively and then beckoned me to him. By the time I reached him Jorge was there, too. He told Danny that Joe was dead and that he had chased two men into the factory after opening up on their car as they tried to escape. "I think one of them was hit for sure," Jorge said. "There's a trail of blood."

"Did you see who they were?" I asked.

"The head security guy and a stocky man."

Danny called over Cristina and Ricardo. "It looks as though Kirby and the Keeler fella have gone into the factory. Hunt them down now. It could be that the bomb's to be set off by a cell phone, so the four of youse had better get a move on."

I began to follow them, but the thought of Danny's vulnerability halted me. Cristina looked back and I shouted to her that I was returning to the truck to give him cover. He was examining the truck's rear doors. "What are you doing here, mate? We're in serious shite if those two fellas get away."

"Yeah, an' they might just circle around an' come back here for the bomb. Come on, man, let's get this thing defused before I crap myself."

A couple of shots from Danny's M-16 took the padlock off the doors. He climbed inside while I watched for Kirby and Keeler. The quiet unsettled me. I was hoping to hear gunfire erupting from within the factory, to signal that the three Colombians had found their quarry.

"Robbie," called Danny, "look at this."

With my gun trained on the factory, I stepped back a couple of paces and looked over my shoulder. I saw the soles of a pair of shoes first. Danny didn't have to tell me that it was the body of José Ruiz. Keeler had explained that his and Danny's fragmented bodies were to be found in the wreckage. Danny came out, puffing heavily. "Christ, it could have been made at home, it's that good."

"What about the detonation?"

"Well, if they're keeping it like a perfect copy, the power and timer unit will be in the cab somewhere."

Danny moved swiftly and I edged toward the front of the truck. I heard him grunt as he reached under the driver's seat. Within seconds he had a plastic box and a bunch of wires in his hand. "That was quick," I said.

"Ach, the sweaty fingers bit is for the movies. If you know what you're doing it's simple enough, as long as there's no anti-handling device."

I had learned that nothing was simple about the man who had planned all this. A chill went through me. "Danny," I said, "this guy was talkin about havin a Plan B an' a Plan C. There's another way of settin this thing off, believe me."

Danny bit his lip, as if the painful realization that defusing the truck bomb had been *too* easy and had just come as a stinging slap across his face. He tossed the power and timer unit away and put his hands to his face as he tried to guess where a second detonation unit might be hidden. "Right," he muttered, and he threw himself to the ground. He put his head under the truck for a few seconds and then pulled back and looked up at me. "Dead on, Rob. Your man's got another unit under here, waiting for a phone call, by the look of it. He was leaving nothing to chance, right enough."

The echo of gunfire drew my eyes back to the factory. "Can you tackle it, Danny?"

"Well," he snorted, "I do have a knife. I mean, that's one better than using my teeth."

There were more shots. "Man, if you can't do nothin with it, let's get the hell away from here before that guy makes a call."

"Ach, I reckon he won't let it off unless he's convinced he won't be getting his bomb back. So just keep a lookout, eh, Robbie, in case they head this way again."

The gunfire was increasing in frequency and loudness. I cursed every shot as it meant that either Kirby or Keeler was still alive and maybe closer to escape. For the first time since the shooting had started, I thought about Hunter and wondered why he wasn't here. Another burst of shots put him out of my mind and made me put the stock of the M-16 to my shoulder. They were getting nearer.

"Hey, Danny," I called down, "the way it's soundin, I think we might have bad guys headin our way. How much longer, man?"

"I don't know. The man who rigged this up was one devious bastard. I'm trying one more thing. If doesn't work, we'd better be able to do a quarter mile in twenty seconds."

My heart was thumping again. A movement caught my eye. I swung the rifle around and saw Cristina and Ricardo in my sights.

"I got Kirby," panted Ricardo. "Cristina and Jorge chased Keeler, but he got away."

My eyes flashed at Cristina: could she have softened at the last moment and allowed him to escape? "Well, where is he?" I snarled.

"He was up in the roof heading back this way," she said. "Jorge went up a ladder to corner him. We heard shots, but it was Jorge's body we found on the floor. We thought it best if we came back here and secured the truck."

Perhaps the bomb was our first priority but I wasn't about to let Keeler just disappear. He knew too much about me, too much about my mother and my son. None of us would be safe if he remained alive. "Stay here," I said to Cristina. "If he's still in there me an' Ric will know where to look. Danny's still tryin to defuse this thing, so keep a good lookout."

Ricardo said, "It will be better if only one of us goes inside, if you drive him out I will be ready for him."

It was not what I had expected from the battle-hardened Ricardo. I squatted down and called to Danny what was about to happen. He had his back to me, as he reached up to a box fastened to a section of the chassis. "Do your best, mate," he said, "and don't let him get away if you can help it." He rolled over onto his back so that he could see me. "And by the way," he added, "if there's a big bang don't waste your time coming back here, Robbie. There won't be much of us left to see."

30

RICARDO PUSHED HIS BACK against a set of metal shutters and gestured with his head that he would circle around to another exit. If Keeler had tried to escape via the roof space, there were only two ways he could come down. Pointing the M-16 at the pipes and suspended walkways, I pressed my back against a wall and scuttled around the edges of the factory, listening for any sound of Keeler overhead. I tried to think as he would. He'd follow the pipes and look for ones he could climb down, but I knew that there weren't any and fairly quickly he would realize that the only way down was by means of one of two metal ladders.

Water dripped, gas hissed from a fractured pipe, but there was no other sound from above. I could only cover one ladder at a time and briefly regretted my decision to not insist that Ricardo came in with me. But I knew it was something I had to do by myself: Danny had told me not to trust Ricardo and I also had a nagging doubt about whether Cristina could kill her ex-husband without a split-second's hesitation which might cost me my life. It had just crossed my mind that Keeler had got away when I heard metallic footfalls: he was going for the second ladder. I sprinted between the machines, trying to glimpse him as he ran along the suspended walkway.

Suddenly, I was flying through the air and the M-16 was sliding along the smooth concrete in front of me. I landed so hard it felt as though I'd split my kneecap in two. I grabbed the gun and, rubbing my knee, I looked to what had tripped me. Jack Kirby had got a little more revenge: it was his corpse that had sent me flying.

The clunking sound of Keeler coming down the ladder made me forget Kirby and the pain. In another moment he was at ground level. I edged my way to the door nearest the ladder and entered the Further Processing areas. I strained to pick up any noise in the sterile air, which still had the tang of death about it. Footsteps echoed down the corridor, heading towards the eviscerating rooms. I followed warily; there were so many hiding places in there that I might be hurrying towards a bullet. Taking care to avoid contact with the hanging shackles, I made my way down the aisle.

I felt Keeler watching me, as he'd done ever since I'd arrived in Georgia, and I knew he was lying in wait. My only chance was to make him move. I eased myself back to the electrical distribution box which supplied power to this section. Keeping my gun at the ready, I switched all the breakers on, and within seconds the air was filled with the sounds of the machines coming to life.

Crouching below the level of the moving shackles, I watched for a movement other than that of grey stainless steel. There was a flash of black shoes. I pulled the trigger and sparks flew as the three rounds struck the moving metal. The shoes were gone but I knew he was heading to the fire exit. Once he was outside and past the new office buildings, it was only a short distance to the fence and the cover of the small wood.

My pursuit stopped almost as it began – a bullet fizzed past my face and clattered against the machines behind me. Angrily, I wondered where the hell Ricardo was and I held the rifle above my head and fired. Danny's caution about firing blindly came back to me, but I figured Keeler was already out and running.

With mucus rattling in my airways and legs like jelly, I sprinted to the exit in time to see Keeler already at a gate in the fence. I briefly cursed his good condition, and fired three shots which were well wide of their target. The gun was hot, my skin was warm, the sweltering air burnt my throat as I gasped for breath. Sweat clung to my clothes and my head was filled with the sound of my own breathing as I skidded through the gateway. I didn't want to follow him into the woods, and I hastily let off another short burst. He stumbled and I thought he was going down, but within an instant he was up and running again, and disappeared amongst the trees.

Blowing hard, I paused at the edge of the wood. Jesus, I was scared. But the thought of what might happen if Keeler got away had me moving again. The trees were young, thin and well-spaced. I could see his flickering image ahead of me, growing more solid as he slowed with every step. He had reached the riverbank and there was nowhere for him to go. He turned, not even looking at me, and his hands fell to his knees as his back arched in his desperate attempts to take in air.

There wasn't anything more that I wanted to hear from him, I just wanted him out of this world. I put the M-16 to my shoulder and pulled the trigger.

When he heard the click and the sound of the rifle hitting the soft ground, Keeler lifted his red face and began to laugh, quietly at first, and then progressively louder and more manically. "Shit, Walker, you get this far and run outta bullets? You were good but here's a lesson; *I* saved a bullet."

"Then do the world a favour an' use it on yourself."

"It did cross my mind," he wheezed, "but there's always a Plan B, I told you that. Where are the others?"

"Where do you think?"

"The truck, I guess." He raised his gun. "Stay right there and I'll let you live long enough to hear the fireworks."

As it had been since I'd tossed the empty rifle away, my hand was by the small of my back and on the pistol in my waistband. By the time Keeler had reached for his cell phone my 9mm was out and pointing at him. He bared his teeth and his lips moved but I could hear nothing other than my blood pumping through my veins. I saw a flash of flame erupt from the muzzle of his gun but I was already looking to go to ground. His eyes were wide, and fleetingly regretful, when his one shot missed and I took aim. My first shot went wide, but the second slammed into him and spun him around. He fell backwards into the water.

I lay there, frozen, waiting for the explosion but five seconds passed, ten, twenty . . . There was nothing but the sound of birds singing in the warm sunshine. I walked to the water's edge on lifeless legs and saw that Keeler's body had been carried downstream by the fast-flowing water. I picked up his cell phone, wondering what numbers would have brought about the carnage. The best place for it was the river and I sent it there, along with my gun.

I trudged back to the factory, too drained to be elated, or even satisfied with what I'd one. When Natasha had once asked me what it was like to kill someone, I'd told her it was unlike anything else and that I'd been left feeling diminished in every way possible. Physically and mentally I was drawing on my last reserves. When I came out of the trees, I realized there was activity all around but I'd been too preoccupied with getting air into my lungs for it to register that about ten men in helmets and dark uniforms were pointing their guns at me. I didn't wait to be told and I raised my hands above my head as I sank to my knees.

Two burly guys cuffed me and ran me back to the truck. I stumbled more than once but they didn't let me fall. Danny was kneeling by the front of the truck, as a blonde woman aimed a gun at him. Beside him were the crumpled bodies of Cristina and Ricardo. Each of them had a single hole in their foreheads; it appeared that they had been summarily executed. I looked to Danny for a clue about what had gone on, but he was staring defiantly at the woman.

From the corner of my eye I caught a sudden movement. I turned my head and, with relief, saw John Hunter pushing his way through the crowd that surrounded us. But something about his expression said to me that he was ready to kill. He put his gun to Danny's head and I felt certain he was about to fire.

"Hunter!" I yelled. "Hunter, that's my friend! I thought we had a deal!"

Danny stared over at me, as if he couldn't believe his ears.

Hunter swung around and pressed his gun barrel against my forehead. "Fuck you," I hissed. "We've just saved God knows how many hundreds of American lives. We coulda gone, man, but we came back an' stopped it!"

I watched a bead of sweat zigzag down his cheek and did my best not to blink. I had the feeling that the instant I took my eyes off him it would be all over for us. Hunter lowered his gun. "Put these two in a car," he said.

The sun's rays were divided by the bars on the high window. The smell of chlorine hung in the air and dust particles danced in the shafts of light. I sat on the slatted bench fixed to the pale-green wall and waited. I waited for Danny. He had been at the far end of the corridor in another cage until two cops had come to escort him away in the direction of the offices. Time passed. The sun rose higher in the blue sky and its beams fell onto my arms, warming me. When Danny didn't return, I wondered about John Hunter. There had been no sign of him since our arrival in Atlanta and I asked myself if he had gone back on our deal.

At first, I'd felt numb, remote from what was going on around me. The excited barks into radio handsets, the high-speed journey in the back of a car, the clank of the cell door behind me: it all seemed so unreal.

Shortly after arrival, I'd pushed my face between the cell bars and assured Danny in a loud whisper that everything would be all right. He'd laughed bitterly. There was no further response before they came for him and so I retreated to the bench and sat down. Slowly the numbness faded and images of the firefight at the factory came back to me. Cristina was dead and I recalled the tender moments between us and wondered if everything we'd shared had been a deception. Probably: something vital at her very core had died a long time ago. I remembered that last kiss, how she'd trembled while describing the torture and killing at El Aro, and I also acknowledged that she'd been true to her beliefs. But in the end, as I pictured her body lying beside Ricardo's, she seemed to me now more fanatical than steadfast. Such is the fickleness of desire.

The sun crept along my arms and shone on my face. There was no sound but the vague hum of electricity. My thoughts turned to Vonette and Calvin. Like Cristina, they'd been hurt and damaged when young, and that had irrevocably shaped their lives and justi-fied their violence. Rather than dwell on their deaths, I grieved over the way their lives had turned out.

A cop came down the carbolic-clean corridor and, without looking at me, slid a plastic tray through a slot in the bars. "Has John Hunter been in contact?" I asked. There wasn't even a pause in his stride. I took the top off the cup of tepid coffee and added the whitener and sugar but it still tasted awful. The burger was barely edible but I wolfed it down in three bites.

I puzzled over what, if anything, Danny was saying to his inter-rogators. The truth seemed so incredible that I doubted if anyone, except for Hunter, would believe that an agent with the DEA had not only plotted to detonate a truck bomb in the heart of an American city but had also concocted an elaborate scheme to frame the Farc and the IRA.

Footsteps echoed on the smooth concrete floor and a pair of cops came to my cell door. One of them had a wide brown leather belt and a set of manacles in his hands. Before they opened the door, the other cop told me to stand and face the wall with my hands on top of my head. I obeyed and within moments the belt was around my waist, my hands were then brought down and my wrists put into the cuffs attached to the front of it by a short chain. "This way, please," said the cop, as if I had a choice.

They led me through several pairs of double doors and I sensed the air within the building was moving with frenetic activity but I saw no one as I was escorted down a flight of concrete stairs and into a windowless room. A fluorescent ceiling light buzzed above a small wooden table. "Take a chair, please, sir," said the polite cop.

I sat there quietly, not knowing who I was waiting for but hoping it was for Hunter. The drone of the light almost put me into a trance, but I snapped awake when I heard the door opening. Two guys and a woman came in. She was the woman who'd pointed a gun at Danny and now I realized that I'd met her once before in the factory's canteen: she'd told me her name was Kelly and she'd asked me about England. "Where's Hunter?" I asked her.

She smoothed her hair and looked for guidance to the shorter of the two men and in doing so, she gave away who was really in charge. "He's indisposed," she said. "I am Suzanne Janowitz, a colleague of his with the INS. This . . ." nodding to her right and then her left ". . . is Dexter Rankin of the DEA, and this is Special Agent Gus Rosenberg, FBI." She sat down opposite me, and the two men stood behind her. "We want you to tell us everything about your involvement with the bomb that was discovered in Petra this morning."

"Involvement?" I said furiously. "Find Hunter, let him tell you how I rang an' alerted him to what was goin on. Me an' Danny saved countless American lives, an' you put me in a cell an' cuff me like I'm a fuckin criminal. What the shit is goin on? I mean, why are we banged up? We had an agreement with Hunter that we were goin to be let go. So fuck your questions until I see him."

"Please, Mr Walker," said Rankin. "I can understand your frustration, but surely you must understand we have to ascertain what has taken place."

Rankin was tall, with fine fair hair and thin lips which betrayed his nervousness. Next to him, Gus Rosenberg looked squat and surly. He was around fifty and had a mottled face with spiteful little eyes. He said, "Answer Ms Janowitz's questions, and less of your profanity."

Her lips twitched briefly with an embarrassed smile. "We already know that you are one Robert Walker," she said. "For the record, we do need to hear from you how you came to be in the USA and what you know of the bomb plot."

"An' then are we free to go?"

"Providing what you tell us is the truth."

I looked away and tried to figure out what Danny might have said and how much I should tell them. They knew my real name, so I decided to begin with my crossing from Ireland to New York, and then the journey to Georgia. I said nothing of Paulie O'Sullivan, but I told them about meeting Cristina Méndez and the man who had called himself Mitch. "He told me he was FBI but I've since found out that his real name was Tom Keeler and that he was an agent with the DEA. He knew everythin about Danny an' me. He knew of Danny's involvement in the Irish republican movement an' later on he told me that he wanted him in Petra with members of the Farc so they'd get the blame for the bomb. Keeler had already killed a Colombian usin the alias José Ruiz, an' it's his body that's in the back of the truck. His real identity, as a member of the Farc, was to come out after his remains were sifted from the bomb damage. When I asked Keeler what about the innocent victims, he said they'd be collateral damage, a justifiable sacrifice for a bigger cause."

As I went on to tell of my discovery of the bomb and of subsequent events, the reactions of the three people in front of me were very different. The face of Dexter Rankin, the DEA man, became visibly taut, while Gus Rosenberg of the FBI continually shook his sceptical head. Suzanne Janowitz, on the other hand, looked as if she were having trouble containing her excitement. She, after all, was part of the organisation which could claim most success from this operation. "Mitch, I mean Keeler," I continued, "was workin with the factory manager, Watson, an' the head of security, Jack Kirby. Kirby killed Watson last night. He also shot an' killed the maintenance electrician, Colin. Now that guy was a hero. He could've mentioned Hunter an' maybe got him killed, but he didn't, he backed up my story, an' that was one-a the bravest actions I've ever seen. I was kept tied up in some sorta hunting lodge, an' after Danny rescued me I telephoned Hunter an' warned him about the bomb." I finished with a sanitized version of the gun battle at the factory. I made no mention of how Danny found me at the lodge, or of Vonette and Calvin's presence there; I figured I would deal with questions about all that as they arose.

Rosenberg remained unimpressed. He leaned right across the table and put his raddled face close to mine. "Bull . . .shit!" he said scornfully. "Do you really expect us to believe any of that? What proof do you have that you and the mick aren't just a pair of killers trying to avoid death row by concocting a wacko conspiracy involving one of the DEA's best agents? What proof do you have that Tom Keeler was involved in any of this, rather than trying his damnedest to stop it?"

"Ask Hunter about my call. An' ask the DEA man next to you what he knew of Keeler's operation to stop the bomb. I mean, Keeler would've told his superiors about somethin this big, right? Why don't you go an' find the watch they took off me when I came in here an' look at the trackin device in it? Go to my house an' find all the bugs Keeler put in there. Go to my car an' look at the tracker under the seat."

Dexter Rankin looked most uncomfortable. His body language was in sharp contrast to Rosenberg's: he was not about to lean across the table and ask questions. He'd been a colleague of Keeler's, maybe even his superior, and his agency had the most to lose from this affair. Rankin would have known of what had happened in Colombia and the marriage of a DEA agent to a woman who turned out to be the Farc's top intelligence officer.

In contrast to Suzanne Janowitz's look of serenity, Rosenberg was visibly furious. I figured that was because the FBI had failed to find out anything about the bomb until it had been discovered and disarmed by men he regarded as foreign terrorists.

I thought I was in a strong position. "Right," I said, "so Danny an' I entered this country illegally, like a few million others, but we haven't committed no big crime here an' we've just saved American lives. An INS agent, I know as John Hunter, promised us that we would go free. So I suggest you guys get your heads together an' decide if you're goin to let him keep his side of the bargain. If not, I wanna speak to a lawyer an' we'll let a judge sort it out." The last bit was pure bluff but I hoped the risk of the very bad publicity would be enough for them to let us go.

Rosenberg said, "I think Mr Walker has had enough questions for now, Ms Janowitz." And then, clearly remembering that she was supposed to be the chief inquisitor, he added, "That's unless you have any further questions."

She went through with the pretense of being in charge and told me that I would be returned to the cells for a short time while they made contact with Hunter. She finished by apologizing for the handcuffs, her voice trailing off under my glare as she mumbled something about procedure.

I was taken back upstairs and through all the double doors again. I felt confident in my strategy. I had those bastards by the short and curlies, without even mentioning what had happened to Moses. I figured that they would prefer to see Danny and me gone, rather than risk us telling all that we knew in open court and highlighting the failures of another 'Homeland Security' initiative.

Striding past the cell in which I'd been kept, the cops took me to the one at the end of the corridor. Danny was sitting on the bench with his feet and arms crossed, and only gave me the briefest of sideways glances as the cops took the belt and cuffs off me. When we were left alone I sat beside him. Staring at the wall opposite, he said, "I hope you said fuck all, Robbie."

"What did you tell them?"

"Nothing."

"An' how exactly is that gonna get us outta here?"

He was silent for a while, then whispered, "Walls have ears. Why do you think they've stuck us in together, eh?"

There was a hint of a smile on his face, which made me boil over with frustration. "Then fuck you, Danny," I said, raising my voice, "because I told them about our deal with Hunter. I told them we just saved countless American lives, an' either we walk or they'd better get us lawyers."

His smile vanished and he swung around toward me. "What are you at?" he hissed.

"Gettin us outta here, as your plans tend to end up with us in serious shit, all right?"

"No it's not all right. Christ, what did you say?"

"About how we got to America, how this guy was tryin to frame you an' the Colombians with the bomb. The trackers an' bugs he put in my house an' car. Man, they don't want any of this comin out in court, so they're gonna let us go, like Hunter agreed, right?"

"Wrong, Robbie, by Jesus, you've never been more wrong!" he said, fighting to keep his voice down. "What kind of country do you think we're in? Are you after losing your memory as well as your senses? You heard of Guantánamo Bay? Because, if we're lucky, we'll end up there in an orange jumpsuit giving praise to Allah and no one outside of here will know anything about it."

"An' if we're not lucky?"

"Think about it. We don't exist here in the legal sense." He turned back and crossed his arms again. "Ach, get yourself some rest."

Within minutes Danny was snoring. I marvelled that he could sleep, but it wasn't long before my own lids started to close. I woke with a start, unsure of how long I had been asleep. The sun no longer shone through the windows, and the cells and corridor were bathed in blue fluorescent light. I woke Danny with a sharp dig to his ribs.

"Christ," he yawned, "my mouth tastes like a wrestler's jockstrap, so it does."

I rubbed my eyes. "I didn't think I could sleep in a place like this."

He got up unsteadily and stretched. "Tell me, did you get a cup of coffee and a burger that tasted like shite not long before they questioned you?"

"I can still taste them."

"Then," he yawned again, "I'd say they were laced with something, right enough, maybe sodium amytal."

"What's that?"

"It's to make us less inhibited, it's like a truth drug. Maybe that's why you said a bit more than you should have."

I got to my feet and stretched my stiff legs. "Well, it hasn't affected your memory."

"As long as it hasn't affected my testicles," he huffed.

We paced the small cell for a while, Danny did a bit of shadow boxing and playfully aimed a few punches in my direction. "It's a wee bit quiet, isn't it?"

"It was quiet before," I said.

"Not this quiet, Robbie, not this kind of quiet."

Once he said that, the silence began to press in on me and became threatening. I listened hard, straining for any sounds at all. There were none. I went to the cell door, intending to call out, but as I grasped the bars the door swung open. Astounded, I looked back at Danny.

He said, "We're supposed to be either stupid or drugged up enough to think they forgot to lock it."

If there were any drugs in my system, fear had instantly flushed them out. I looked at Danny again, hoping that he could say something that offered us a chance of surviving the night. He read my thoughts and said, "Looks like our only chance is the Hunter fella."

We both knew that to step out of the cell in full view of the closed-circuit cameras at either end of the corridor might well be a death sentence. We paced around again, fighting off the fearful images which tried to invade our minds. But no matter what else I thought about, what Danny had said earlier kept repeating over and over in my head: in a legal sense we did not exist. If we died, no one would have to know.

The sound of a door closing at the end of the corridor stopped us both. Footsteps echoed.

Danny smiled ruefully and held out his hand. "It's been a pleasure, Robbie. Let's do our best to stay strong, eh?"

The sound grew louder and I guessed it was death that we heard approaching.

I was shaking Danny's hand, my back to the cell door, when I heard it squeak open. Danny nodded and I turned around. It was John Hunter.

"Don't ax no questions. Come with me."

Danny and I exchanged a silent question: would it be to a place of execution?

When we didn't move immediately, Hunter said, "Look, whoever left this door open wasn't doin it for the good of your health. I've come to keep my side of the deal, Robbie. Either you guys come with me now or I doubt you'll be here in the mornin to regret that you didn't."

Danny nodded and twisted that grim mouth of his.

We followed Hunter out of the cell. He was our only chance.

245

31

TENSION KNOTTED MY EVERY MUSCLE. Every movement took a conscious effort as Danny and I followed Hunter down several flights of stairs to an underground parking lot. Our footfalls echoed and at one point they convinced me that we were being followed. I stopped for a second, until I realized that the sounds of rapid feet slapping the cold concrete were coming only from the two men in front of me. I caught them up as they left the stairwell, in time to see Danny stiffen slightly as we walked between the rows of vehicles. It was as though he, too, was anticipating that someone might emerge with a gun. 'Shot while trying to escape' would seem plausible. We exchanged glances over the roof of Hunter's car before we got in, Danny in the back, me beside Hunter in the front.

It wasn't until we were through the barrier at the top of the ramp, and out onto the road, that I felt able to ask where we were going. Hunter said, "I'm takin you guys back to Petra, back to the factory an' your car. All you have to do then is drive an' get outta this country within twenty-four hours."

"Is this official or unofficial?" I asked.

"This is me keepin my part of the deal, okay?"

"Not quite, Hunter. I mean, do I take it we're gettin safe passage? If we get stopped by the cops or someone, do I give them your name or number?"

"Shit, the last thing you do is give anyone my number, or even mention my name. I'll tell you straight, I've had my ass grilled for the last eight hours. I thought I was gonna have me a promotion, or at least a little award, for this shit. Hell, the way they were goin on, it was though they thought I was in on it with Keeler. I had tried to access a particular data base to find out what I could about one 'Robert Barrett' and it stirred up all sortsa shit. I wanted to find out how your false identity was created an' by who. Well, I'm only guessin, but it looks as though Keeler had someone workin for him within the INS as well as the DEA, an' maybe in the FBI, too. In his day, Keeler was some hotshot an' had all sortsa contacts, which he'd obviously used, so a bomb of that size was able to get under everyone's radar."

246

"So this thing involved a lotta people who work for different government agencies? Man, Oliver Stone would have a field day."

"Not many," he snapped at me, "an' that's the problem. It only takes a few well-placed an' determined people to put their heads together to bring a society like this to its knees. This thing Keeler had planned probably involved no more than a dozen, or so, people – an' most of them, includin him, were killed by you an' your friend in the back. In fact, from what I can work out, the only ones, outside of government agents, who know anythin about this are you two."

I took that last remark as a warning about our dire predicament and glanced back at Danny, hoping to see he'd at last understood that what he'd got us involved with was far too big for us to handle on our own. There had been times recently when I had let both of us down but now I felt a small measure of redemption.

Once we were on the highway heading south, I asked Hunter about how our cell door had been left unlocked. He let out a snort and said, "How? When you were asleep. Why? I think you know it wasn't left open for the good of your health."

"I thought this was a democracy, Hunter, rule of law an' all that shit."

He stared ahead in silence for a moment, as if mesmerized by the streams of headlights coming towards us. Then, ponderously, he said, "I fought for this country, lost blood an' a few friends for this country. But the more you see, the more you question. From what I heard, Tom Keeler was a helluva operator, a patriot, an' I kinda understand what motivated him."

"To kill a heap of innocent Americans?"

He kept his eyes fixed on the road and chuckled bitterly. "Fuck it, man, it's mostly innocent people who get killed anyhow, wherever they are in this fucked-up world. Ain't you the guy who used to try an' rile me over what happened in Panama City, Mogadishu, or even on the road to Basra? Too many innocent people have died right in front of my eyes, Walker, more than I can ever count in my dreams. A guy like Keeler . . . he was only actin like he was trained to do, 'actin for the greater good' it's called. What's a few thousand, you're told, or a few hundred, or even two guys in a cell who know too much, when you're protectin the lives of millions? There's even mothafuckas about who reckon they're just sendin you to God, a little early, for Him to sort it out."

"So they were gonna kill us right there in the cell?"

"Give them a little credit, they would have at least dragged your sorry asses out into the corridor."

"An' I suppose you're just doin this outta the kindness of your heart, right?"

Angry, he said, "I've killed people, Walker, more than I like to think about. But when I heard that you guys might not be around to corroborate what I was telling them I decided that, whatever else I was, I wasn't a murderer. That don't mean I like either of you guys, or what you represent, but I figure you didn't have to go after that bomb, you coulda just hightailed it out. In my book you two are bad guys, but soldiers too. An' fuck it, man, no way am I havin anythin to do with killin prisoners. I'm gettin your asses out, period. The rest is up to you, but if you're still in this country come tomorrow I doubt if you'll be alive for much longer than that."

Over my shoulder I saw Danny, dismissive as ever, crinkle his lips and shake his head. Irritated, I turned my attention back to Hunter and told him about Colin, how he'd got caught up in the affair, and how bravely he'd died. For the first time, Hunter's eyes met mine. He said, "I would never have guessed it." He looked back to the rear-view mirror. "Kinda makes me think that they ain't all bad."

We were entering Petra and it wouldn't be long before we reached the factory. Danny was sitting up straight now and straining his eyes at the surrounding darkness.

"What's the time?" I asked.

"Six minutes past midnight," replied Hunter.

It struck me then just how much had happened in the last twenty-four hours and how many people had died in that short time. The images of all those recent deaths came back to me but faded just as quickly as Hunter stopped the car at the edge of the factory's parking lot. "What are you gonna tell them about how we escaped?" I asked.

"Let me worry about that, Walker. You just worry about stayin alive."

Danny was shifting on his seat and looking all around him. "Come on, Robbie, we'd better be heading off." He got out of the car without expressing a word of gratitude.

"Your friend," Hunter said, "he's the suspicious kind. He's thinkin I must be in on some sorta plan to have you guys bumped off back at where all the action was happenin."

"An' are you?"

"Why would I drive you all this way? Walker, I promised I'd give you as much of a head start as I could. It might only be a few hours, I can't say, but what I'm doin has nuthin to do with anyone but me. As far as I'm concerned you're a big-mouthed Jamaican, but you did save a lot of people today."

"Technically, it was yesterday."

"Yeah, well, that there's the kinda stuff that used to get me pissed about you. Anyhow, I hope you . . ."

"Survive?"

"Somethin like that. But here's a free piece of advice. Ditch the Irish guy, it'll improve your chances." He looked out at Danny, who was heading for my car. "Can either of you hot-wire?"

"There's a spare key under the carpet."

"Then you'd better go. Head west an' then south an' get outta this country."

"Thanks, John," I said. "I appreciate that you've put yourself at risk for us."

Hunter compressed his lips. "There's one more thing," he said gravely. "Keeler was probably workin for an organization we call 'The Seventeenth'. An' because I mentioned that possibility to the people who want to know what's gone on, it probably means my days with the INS are numbered, too. An' that's one of the reasons that made my mind up to get you two out."

"What's 'The Seventeenth'?" I asked.

Hunter put his car into reverse as he mulled over his answer. Finally, he said, "There are sixteen known government security agencies but it was rumoured in the months following 9/11 another, top secret, agency was formed, so secret we don't even know its proper name, so we nicknamed it 'The Seventeenth'. Again, most of this stuff is rumour, because nobody knows for sure, but it's said that some of the very best personnel from every agency were secretly inducted, an' some were even brought outta retirement to create it. That's why I was given such a hard time by my superiors, just in case I was in it alongside Keeler, mostly 'cause they thought it was too much of a coincidence that the bomb was in the very place I was runnin an operation – an' that I had failed to spot it. Truth is, if 'The Seventeenth' does exist, I can't tell you if it's workin in parallel, or for, or against us. An' Tom Keeler covered his tracks,

Walker, nuthin he used, down to that watch he put on you, or any of the bomb equipment in the truck, or any-damn-thing at all can be traced. But that in itself is an indicator that we're dealin with a very powerful force here. You axed me about where's democracy an' law an' order. . . It's an illusion, Walker, projected to stop us seein the real scary stuff that is really goin on. . . Now you had better go."

I briefly thought about what Vonette Norbury had said to me about her perception of the American model of democracy shortly before she was killed. "You take care," I said, as I began to leave the car. Hunter nodded, I thought resignedly, like a man facing a hangman's noose, and drove away without looking my way again.

When I got to my car, Danny, cursing the darkness, was underneath it. He heaved himself out and told me to flip the hood. After studying the engine compartment for a few minutes, he said to open the trunk. "Well?" I asked.

He tossed away something I guessed was the tracker which was planted under the seat, and said, "Go you and stand well back. A clever bastard could have wired something to it so it'll go off when it's moved." I stayed put and watched him slide his head and shoulders into the foot well. He looked up and scowled at me. "I'm not fucking joking you! Get yourself far away for a wee while."

Conflicting feelings came to me as I complied. I felt as if I were deserting Danny, yet thought he was also wasting precious time. Once he'd checked underneath the car, as well as the trunk and under the hood, we should have got going.

"Do you still keep a spare key under the carpet?" he called out. I shouted back that I did. The door was open and I watched him put the key into the ignition. He looked over at me and said, "Keep well back now!"

Like my stomach, the engine churned slowly. When it died I wanted to call out that he should leave it, but he'd already turned the key again. My heart raced as the engine whinnied and picked up speed. A loud roar echoed, black smoke belched from the exhaust, and the muscles in my neck went into spasms. Danny was grinning as he slammed the door and took off. Tyres screeching, he drove around the parking lot at high speed, then, after one circuit, pulled up level with me. "Just checking for a tilt switch," he said. "Hop in then, mate, we don't have time to waste."

"You crazy, crazy bastard," I puffed as I sat in. "Where are we headin? Hunter reckons west an' then south, to Mexico, I suppose."

"Well, I have to go back to my trailer first. Will we stop by your place as it's on the way?"

"Will it be safe?"

"I figure whoever was involved with what's gone on are either dead, or running. I think we'll have a couple of hours. I mean, when they find out that we've escaped, I don't think they will figure that we'd come back here."

I had lost a lot of faith in Danny's judgment but I reckoned that John Hunter had been genuine in his wish to see us make a successful escape and had used a similar logic in bringing us back to Petra. It really should have been the last place we would go to. "Might as well," I said.

It wasn't until we'd left the highway and neared the lumber yard did we speak again. I had been content with the silence. Every passing minute of quiet distanced us a little more from the horror of the recent events. I supposed that this was yet another episode in our lives which wouldn't be talked about once we'd left Georgia. I wondered how many more chapters there would be, how much more of my life I'd have to pretend that I couldn't remember, or had never happened.

"You were right, Rob," Danny muttered.

"About what?"

More strongly, he said, "About how many of my plans end up with us in the shite. You were right about that, mate, and you were right to deal with the Hunter fella." He paused but I thought it better not to interrupt him. "We would've never have got out, otherwise. I was wrong to kill Paulie, so I was, and I was wrong to get involved with the Farc crowd. That fella Keeler, the fucker used me, but I was there to be used. You know, I'm sick of this life, Robbie. A few weeks ago I couldn't have brought myself to admit it, but I'm tired, tired of all this hiding, tired of being at war with most of the world. But, you know, Rob, I've been a lot more scared of peace than I've been of war, scared about what I'll find out about myself once the fighting has stopped. Now I'm thinking about taking a chance and going home again."

"Back to Belfast?"

251

"Well, maybe not Belfast, but somewhere closer than here. I'm after thinking that, if you want me to, I could give you a hand to find Nathan and then we could head to Canada. There's a contact in Toronto who could give us passports. That's if you want me involved, mate; I'd understand if you didn't. But maybe you could go back to England and live in another town and be close to your ma."

I wasn't far from emotional exhaustion and thought we should both collect our belongings before I gave him an answer. Hunter had said I should ditch Danny: I didn't like to think of it in that way, but I did reckon we stood a better chance if we went our separate ways.

Danny swung the car into my back yard; the place seemed to have aged and become ramshackle since I had last seen it. He kept the engine running while I went inside the house. The kitchen door was open and creaking and there was more evidence of visitors: it was obvious because of the damage to the walls and ceilings that the house had been stripped of all surveillance devices. I had some clothes already packed and in the trunk, but there was a package to collect, a tin box containing my stash of two thousand dollars, which I'd hidden in my bedroom the week I arrived here. I'd kept my word to Danny and left the money untouched so it could be used in an emergency. A little surprised that it had been left by whoever had used – and removed – the surveillance equipment, I prised away the skirting board with a bread knife and once I had stuffed the bills into my pockets I ditched the small metal box.

Every minute counted but there was something I felt I ought to do. I scribbled a note and put it into an envelope. On the way out, I placed it on the kitchen table. I had a feeling she would come looking for me sooner rather than later. I salvaged the few bits of food and cans from my fridge and put them onto the back seat of the car. I was about to get in when I saw Stella standing there. She looked frightened.

"You leavin, Robbie?"

"I guess so. What are you doin out at this time, pretty girl?"

"I was listenin out fo any kinda noise, in case those men came back here. An' I was kinda hopin I'd hear yo car. There's been bad things happenin around here, Robbie, men come here an' smashed up yo place. Then they went an' pull Calvin outta his house. Momma reckons that's the last we's ever gonna see-a him."

"Anyone ring the cops about it?"

"I don't think so. Was you leavin without sayin goodbye, Robbie?"

"It's the wrong time of night to go knockin on your door but I left a note on my kitchen table for you. Go check, if you don't believe me."

She ran inside and I responded to Danny's impatient frown by getting into the car. Stella dashed out again, her face almost lighting up the yard. "Those 'x's, they're kisses, right?"

"Sure they are."

"My readin ain't so good. The money's really to jus buy myself a dress?"

"That's what the note says – an' make sure it's a real pretty one."

Her bottom lip started to tremble. "Befo you go, can I have one of those kisses, Robbie?"

Danny let out an exasperated sigh when I told her just one. Stella leaned into the car and started to slobber all over my face. "Goodbye, Robbie. I'll never fo'get you."

As we drove away, I turned and waved at the forlorn figure until she was out of sight.

"What in Christ's name was that all about?" asked Danny.

I said, "Hopefully just a makin a happy memory in case she needs to grab hold of somethin' if her life turns out to be as shitty as I think it will."

On the way to the trailer park I told Danny how Stella had guided me to a place of safety while Jack Kirby's thugs smashed up the house. Then, I asked, almost wincing, "Cristina, what was her thing with Henry Lavette? I mean, was it all business with her?"

"I reckon so. She despised everything people like the Lavettes stood for. She tapped Henry for information, but the fella was so infatuated that he never cottoned on to just how many of his business associates in Colombia were kidnapped by the Farc over the years. I suppose, when she was with you she was checking how watertight I was. I mean, if you'd even hinted that you knew what I was up to, the plug would have been pulled on the whole affair."

"Pity I didn't."

"Perhaps. . . Perhaps, you're right, mate."

I let another mile pass before I put to Danny the question I'd wanted to ask him from the moment I saw the bodies of Cristina and Ricardo. "Did you kill her, Danny?"

He grimaced and said nothing for what seemed an age. "Yeah, mate, I did. I didn't want to say, because I knew how you felt about her, despite everything."

I felt my throat tighten. "Is it too much to ask why?"

"Remember in that lodge, when I said we were going back for the bomb and Ricardo said something to her in Spanish? Unfortunately for them I understood most of it. I'd never let on I could speak their lingo, although they'd tested me a few times. So, the young cocky bastard says to her that they should go with us, get the truck, deal with us and leave it in Dallas on their way to Mexico. While you were out chasing Keeler, I felt outnumbered, so I did. Ricardo comes up and says in Spanish that the key's in the ignition and they should plug us as soon as you get back. But she says to kill me there and then, pick up the detonation unit I'd left on the ground, and leave right away. You should have seen their faces when they realized I understood their every fucking word."

I retreated again into the sanctuary of silence. Perhaps Danny had tried to offer me some consolation by saying that Cristina had wanted to leave before I returned, but right then I felt only sorrow.

Lights from the trailers helped us to avoid some of the potholes in the dirt track. Danny pulled up by the place that had been his home. "I was thinking," he said, "if you do want me to go with you to get Nathan, maybe it would be better if I followed you and drove my pick-up. You know, if we travel separately there's less chance of us drawing attention."

It hit me then that, without me, Danny had no one. I had someone, someone who was my flesh and blood, even if it were only in my yearning and in my dreams. The mere notion of seeing Nathan again had given me hope when all goodness had seemed to have vanished from my life. The idea that one day we'd be reunited was an aspiration – a buried treasure – and during the times when I wondered if it was worth carrying on, it had provided me with the will to see another day.

I was all Danny had. Keeler had told me that there had been no way he could get him to leave New York without me. Suddenly I was back to pondering about that strange bond between us and I knew I couldn't leave him now. "That's a good idea," I said. "You go get your stuff an' I'll turn the car around."

The anxious look on his face immediately gave way to a broad grin. "Right. I'll only be a couple of minutes."

I watched him skip into his trailer with the exuberance I thought he must have had as a child when getting ready for Christmas Day. It wasn't long before he was throwing his gear into the back of his pick-up and tying down the canvas sheet to make sure nothing got wet. He jogged over to me with a biscuit tin in his hand. "It would be better if you kept this in . . ."

His expression, that lazy smile, will always remain etched on my mind. There was a loud crack and then a distant thud. He grunted and fell down. It was only then that I recognized the loud noise as gunfire. I threw myself down across the seat as more high-velocity rounds peppered my windshield. I heard the bullets sing as they cut through the metal panels, I felt the pulse of air as they passed above my head. I reached out and opened the passenger door, as glass showered in on me. The padding in the backrests was reduced to fibrous dust in the moments it took to slide out and put myself under the car. I kept still, my heart beating the ground, until I heard screams and commotion above me. Cautiously, I looked out and saw more lights come on and people stream from their trailers. I heaved myself clear and, using the hood for support, staggered around to the other side of the car. Danny was on his side with his feet crossed at the ankles and his head resting on an arm.

Just by the way he lay there, I knew my friend was dead.

Epilogue

One week later

THIS WAS NOT HOW I'D PICTURED IT. I had left the trailer park in Georgia thinking I knew where I would head for, even though my mind had been numbed by shock and grief. But unlike John Hunter had suggested, I didn't head west and I didn't head south: I went in the opposite directions and had ended up in New York again on a beautiful summer's day. The surroundings were tranquil and the air smelled not of gasoline, as I had recollected, but of freshly cut grass. I sat with my back pressed against cool marble and let the sun warm me, and I again remembered the death of Danny Maguire.

As his neighbours in the trailer park milled around, the instinct for self-preservation overcame my initial dismay at what had just taken place. People were standing over Danny's body making signs of the cross and muttering prayers, while I began to put my bags and the tin he'd given me into his pick-up. Conchita, the young girl I'd met once in Danny's trailer, came to me with a man she introduced as her father. He spoke in Spanish and she translated. Through her, I told him that it was too dangerous for me to stay and talk to the police. He nodded knowingly and talked softly to his daughter. She said, "My father says we will look after Danny and give him a burial. I don't know why, but he is asking you what name we should put on his stone."

It was hard for me to take in that I was discussing the funeral arrangements for my friend. "Major John Riley," I suggested.

The man nodded mournfully, as though he understood to what I was alluding. I reached into a pocket and pulled out some money. "For the coffin."

He waved a finger at me and frowned indignantly. Conchita said, "My father says it will be our honour."

After one last look at Danny, as four men lifted him, I drove away in his pickup. The image of his head flopping back as he was raised, and his blind stare, stayed with me as I headed north. It wasn't just that my friend was dead, it the way death had arrived, not even allowing him to finish that final sentence, that affected me most. But it had not been so difficult to accept: we had faced death so often that subconsciously, at least, I had prepared myself for the day it would finally take him. From a distance, Danny may have cut an admirable, and even noble, figure but closer up there was a poignancy about him – and always a sense of danger, too. I just hoped that he had finally found peace in those final few minutes before that bullet ended his life. For the next few days, rather than grief, the emotion which threatened to overpower me was one of total isolation.

As I drove, I listened avidly to the radio news stories about the truck bomb, and I stopped periodically at roadside diners to eat and get the TV versions. On the third day I stayed in a cheap motel in North Carolina, so that I could wash and spend more time watching the bulletins.

So far, the media had been given little information except that a bomb had been discovered. This had led to wild speculation about another attack by al-Qa'ida, until Suzanne Janowitz had been pushed in front of the cameras to spin the story that the bomb had been found during a joint INS and FBI undercover operation. When a Colombian connection was revealed, it provided an excuse to run old footage of choppers flying over jungles and talk of "narco-terrorists." Pretty, blonde and blue-eyed, Janowitz was instantly a 'media babe' of heroic proportions. I wondered about the fate of John Hunter and if he were skulking in the wings and cursing the underlying prejudices that made her a more viewer-friendly face, or if something far more dire had befallen him. It then crossed my mind if I should take the chance to call him again on the number he had given me.

But I remained unsure whether he'd been in on the plan to kill Danny and me. I thought there was only a slim chance that he had, because Keeler had informed me that the man Darlene Fenton had shot was one of two dissident IRA hit-men who were looking for Danny. Perhaps the survivor had eventually tracked him down and taken revenge for Paulie O'Sullivan. In a way I hoped so, because if that were the case I could take some cold comfort in that there might be now, at least, a chance that I didn't have government assassins on my trail.

Flicking from channel to channel, I became acutely aware of how many opinions – and how very few facts – the public were being offered. The news was managed and massaged for the masses: four unidentified aliens had been shot dead at the scene by government agents. There was no mention of Tom Keeler, and I guessed that his body had yet to be pulled from the river and, when it was recovered, no doubt we'd be told that he'd died valiantly thwarting the bombers. I figured that much when it was implied that Jack Kirby and the other factory security men had been aiding government forces when they died. On hearing that I switched off the TV.

The following morning the pick-up's engine blew as I reached a little town just south of Petersburg, Virginia. Before abandoning it in a field, I rummaged through Danny's gear, looking for a keepsake. He'd only packed clothing and the solitary item worth taking was a pair of boots which looked new and unworn. I muttered to myself regretfully that there was so little to show for his life. There wasn't even a tombstone with his name upon it to record that he had once existed. Perhaps he had done many wrong things – and many bad things – but I had known him as a man who had been full of good intentions, which had unerringly taken him along a path of violence after his father had been gunned down. But whatever else he was, Danny Maguire had been a good friend to me.

Another vehicle would have made a big hole in my finances, even though I'd found over sixteen thousand dollars in the tin he had handed to me. I bought a money belt and decided to take a bus to New York, the city with which I was most familiar, while I made up my mind about where I should go to next.

My son had celebrated another birthday without me while I made that bus journey. I had intended to begin my search for him as soon as I had got out of Georgia but now I was full of doubt about what was the right thing to do. Part of my hesitation was anchored in reservations about the person I had become and if it were right for me to intervene in Nathan's life again. All I had to go on was Keeler's comment that Sharon's husband was not the right sort of person to bring up my son – but how much was that really worth? Keeler had been a master of mind games, an accomplished liar and puppeteer, who had controlled the lives of many people in his vain bid to dominate just one woman. How it must have crushed his ego when he discovered that Cristina had been using him all along. But that hurt had made him even more dangerous and the fact that I'd killed him did not trouble me at all.

The sun was high and I turned my face toward it. The burble of distant traffic and far-off voices became like a stream trickling over a bed of pebbles as I drifted into sleep. I resurfaced with someone casting a shadow over me. "Pete?" she called. "Pete!"

The voice was familiar and I thought I must be still dreaming. I blinked slowly and did my best to focus, but the sun was behind her and all I could make out was a silhouette. "You're the last person I expected to see," she said.

Using my hands to shield my eyes, I was still trying to make her out. "Caroline?"

"Yeah. How long have you been sittin there?"

I got to my feet. "A while. I need guidance, so I spent some time chattin to Natasha, well, her headstone, anyway."

Close up her eyes were melancholic. "I do the same sorta thing on my way to church," she said. "I come to talk over a few things with her, an' leave some flowers." She was carrying some now, wrapped in newspaper. "I always feel better for it. So what have you been doin with yourself, Pete?"

"This an' that. I went down south for a while."

"But you got stuff on your mind, right?"

"A big decision to make. I'm not sure which direction to take so I came here, I don't know why. A little peace, maybe. Me an' Natasha used to talk a lot an' I was just rememberin some of the weird stuff she used to talk about. She had this fascination with . . ."

"Atoms, molecules an' stuff like that, right?" I smiled, but couldn't help feeling a pang of resentment that what Natasha and I had talked about, had been shared with someone else. Caroline continued, "She was like that from when she was small. Of course, not all she read, like about how this world was created, sat easily with our faith. I remember once she came across an article about how every cell in our bodies is replaced several times . . ."

"The one that says, if every cell we started off with is replaced several times during our lives, how do we retain memories an' a sense of self?"

"Yeah," she laughed. "That's the one."

"It used to cause a few arguments between us, about consciousness an' all that. Natasha used to say that, even though our bodies change, we retain a sense of self 'cause we constantly tell stories to ourselves about who we are. So I said that sounded like a recipe for self-delusion . . ."

"An' she said everyone has an element of self-delusion about them. Sounds like we had the same kinda conversations." She smiled sadly and paused to compose herself. "I felt lost when Natasha died, so very, very alone," Caroline went on. "That presence, even when she was very sick, it was still precious to me. But that was me bein selfish. When I cried at her funeral I was deludin myself that I was cryin for her; really I was cryin for me, cryin for what I was losin. They were selfish tears, an' in a believer they should've been tears of joy. Pete, I gotta tell you, my faith was sorely tested when I saw how she was sufferin right at the end. She was too beautiful a person to deserve that. But she's not sufferin now, an' if I learned anythin it's that there are some things worse than death. I believe she's in a better place now an' I'm grateful for that."

We lapsed into an awkward silence. Not only did I not share her faith but in some ways I resented it. Caroline's actions, or lack of them because of her beliefs, had once shifted a terrible burden onto me. Or perhaps it was down to Natasha: she had known that I was already a grievous sinner and that final request of hers would have only sullied Caroline's immaculate soul. Caroline avoided the look of bitterness growing in my eyes by squatting down and unwrapping the flowers. She removed the withered ones from a vase at the foot of the headstone and replaced them with the fresh ones. As she traced Natasha's name with her fingertips, a gust of wind snatched up the sheets of newspaper and scattered them across the graves.

"I'll get them," I said. I felt as though she'd interrupted a private conversation and I didn't want her hanging around any longer than necessary.

"Thank you," Caroline said, as she stood up. "I really should get goin to church." She walked a little distance, her steps deliberate and heavy, then stopped to face me again. "An' thank you, Pete," she added hesitantly, "thank you for what you did for our little sister. . . We all pray for you."

When I didn't answer, she hurried on her way and I watched her disappear into the distance. Our conversation had brought back memories of how Natasha talked about the stories we tell ourselves and the element of self-delusion they contain. In Georgia I had seen and heard so many people deceiving both themselves and others with the stories they told. I thought about my own self-delusion when I saw Natasha as she lay waiting for the end.

* * *

Natasha watched me as I stared at a bead of rainwater as it made its way haphazardly down the window. She told me that she longed for peace, for herself and her family, and the only way she could find it was in death. She had asked them to let her die, even to help her die. Caroline had tried, she had told me, but had stopped as soon as Natasha had started to spontaneously go into spasms.

"So I'm beggin you, Robbie. If you've really loved me an' you walk out now, it'll stay with you for the rest of your life. It'll put a stain on your soul."

The bead of water came to rest at the bottom of the pane and I made up my mind. I turned and fixed my eyes on the door. I strode out with my hands over my ears so that I couldn't hear Natasha's anguished cries. Before I ran away down the stairs, I paused and listened at the apartment's front door. I could no longer hear her crying and I thought then that I had shut her off from me.

That night – and the six that followed – I lay tormented every time I went to my bed. My eyes were raw and my bones ached with tiredness as I calculated the days, hours, even minutes that Natasha had lain in her bed, suffering since I had run away from her. Yet again I had failed her, yet again she had made me despise myself. For a while, I even turned to that same God her sisters prayed to and asked for Natasha to die quickly.

The following Sunday, I went to Beanie's, as usual, but I couldn't eat and just fiddled with my food while I deliberated. I concluded that I had never communicated very well with God and divine intervention was unlikely. I had delayed for long enough, probably for too long, and I pushed my plate aside. I had to go back to Manhattan.

Caroline opened the door.

"Is she . . .?"

"Alive?" Her voice was hard and contemptuous. "If you call it livin."

I went into the bedroom. Natasha's eyes were closed. "Natasha," I said, "are you awake?"

262

Her head rolled to one side and her eyes slowly opened. "Why have you come?" She sounded pitifully weak.

I turned to Caroline. "Shouldn't you be goin to church?"

"I don't think that's any of your business."

We both looked at Natasha and silently asked her what she wanted. "Go say a prayer, Caroline," she said, her voice strengthened by hope. "Say a prayer of thanks that mine have been answered."

Caroline made to speak but couldn't summon the words. Tears came to her eyes as she looked to me and then down to the bed. She pressed her quivering lips together and gave Natasha a kiss. A solitary tear had reached her chin by the time she left the room. A minute later the front door slammed and a thin curl appeared on Natasha's lips.

I sat down on the bed. "You keep findin me out, Natasha," I said. "You keep makin me see me for what I really am. An' I don't like what I see."

"I see a man who really, truly, thinks somethin of me, someone who must love me," she said softly. "It's a beautiful sight for me to see right now." She took my hand and raised it to her mouth. "Thank you for comin back, Robbie Walker, thank you for findin the strength."

I asked her if she were really sure.

She kissed my hand. "I have never been more sure."

"Oh, Natasha, Natasha, I'm so sorry that I've let you suffer."

"Don't be sorry, baby. You're here now an' that's all that matters."

My heart began to quicken as I got to my feet. I kissed her on her forehead and her lips.

Her eyes locked onto mine. "I'm ready," she said.

Already half-blinded by tears, I place one hand over her mouth and the other compressed her nose. I pressed a little harder but I could not feel her breath on my palm, so I had to keep looking into her eyes in order to see the moment when life finally left her.

Her body arched briefly, a hand came up a few inches and then fell back. My hands remained in place until the muscles in my arms started to burn. I did not think I could go through with it if she had continued to breathe once I had removed them. I blinked away the tears and looked into her eyes again. It is the stillness of her glassy stare that I remember most, I will always remember the stillness.

I looked at her corpse for only a moment before I fled to the bathroom and vomited. It took a while before I could return to Natasha and close her eyes. And as I did, I recalled that very first time I had seen her beautiful face. I had taken life before and had done so since, but no killing had ever troubled me like that one. A yawning black abyss swallowed me and, for a long while, I lost all bearings: time; place; morality; and the code I lived by, all had vanished into the darkness.

* * *

Now, as I stood beside her grave, some of what I had been, some of the stories I used to tell myself, returned. I thought of her, and of Danny, and of the parts they had played in my life. In different ways, both of them had made me act more bravely than I would have done if left to my own devices.

A sheet of newspaper was picked up by a gust of wind and stuck to a headstone three graves down. I'd said that I'd collect Caroline's newspapers, so I thought I might as well collect this one, too. I checked my – new – wristwatch, I had an appointment to keep and I heaved my bag onto my shoulder and headed for the cemetery gates once I had said a last goodbye to Natasha.

I had come to a decision about my son Nathan. My tears over him had been like Caroline's at Natasha's funeral: I had really been crying for me, for my own loss rather than for his. Maybe it would be for the best if I let things as they were. A man with a baseball cap pulled down over his face approached me. "Who was that woman?" John Hunter asked.

"Just the sister of someone I used to know."

He continued to scan the surroundings with eyes that could not keep still. "You took a chance ringin me again, Walker. Look, you had better tell me this information you have an' get the hell away from here, 'cause I can't guarantee you jack shit. They've put me on leave so I don't know what I can give you. Damn you, man, I told you head for Mexico!"

We had already talked of Danny's death over the phone and his initial stunned silence had been enough to convince me that he had played no part in it. He figured Danny was killed by a member of 'The Seventeenth', while I still reckoned – but kept it to myself –

that it was an IRA man who had been responsible. We started to walk and Hunter asked if I had seen the news. I told him that I hadn't read a newspaper for a couple of days, as I'd been suffering from media overload and had decided to give my brain a rest from all the half-truths and downright lies. He said, "It looks as though Keeler partly got what he wanted. The agenda's already changin and there's now way more support for puttin up that seven-hundred-mile fence on the Mexican border. It won't keep people or drugs out but it's one way to draw people's attention to the 'threat' from the south." Hunter steered me toward a *Starbucks* and once we were at a table he continued, "There's also a small article in today's newspaper about the head of the Colombian army visitin the Pentagon tomorrow to discuss the latest installment of US military aid. A spokesman said the meetin' had been scheduled months before an' it was not connected to the truck bomb in Georgia. Now, heck, after all that bullshit about Farc involvement, who is gonna believe that?"

I shrugged and told him too many would.

Hunter went and bought two coffees. "One thing Keeler got right," he said upon his return, "was his estimation of the reaction to the bomb. God knows what would be happenin now, if it had gone off."

"But it didn't," I said quickly, "thanks to Danny an' me."

He nodded. "I give you that, Walker."

"But with all this reaction," I said, "does this mean Keeler still succeeded?"

"Walker, one thing I've learned is that things only succeed in this country, if the powers-that-be want it to. Iraq is a quagmire an' the tide is turnin. America wants out but, as they say, we're an industrial military complex, man, and we, as a country, require perpetual war, or at least the threat of war. When we get out of that hell hole called the Middle East, our military an' economy will require another enemy waitin in the wings. Keeler, an' whoever is behind his organization, were busy plantin the seeds for the next campaign. I guess the next enemy will be Latin, south from here, an' what we will see as threatenin an' communist."

It left an empty feeling in me that despite all the deaths, including Keeler's own, he had still partially succeeded in his objective. "I may not be a hero, Hunter, but why am I a fugitive?"

"You know the answer. I'll tell you straight – you're an enemy of

265

the state, period, an' whatever information you've got, I'm still not sure it's gonna be enough to help you. I gave you just about all you're gonna get – a head start."

John Hunter blew at the white froth and started to drink his coffee. I said, "All I want is safe passage back to England with a passport an' new identity. I need to see my mom again."

"Nice sentiment, Walker," he chuckled dismissively. "Even if my bosses agreed to that, which I doubt, what is this thing you say you have that's worth it? Walker, it took me two days drivin an' twelve years of trainin for me to get here without bein followed by a bunch of guys who will definitely kill you, an', probably me an' you both, if we're caught together."

"This is somethin big, but I need guarantees."

"Shit, Walker, I can't guarantee either of us seein tomorrow the way things have worked out. Look, you had better at least give me a clue about what you've got."

I took a sip of my own drink while I figured out how much I could tell him. Hesitant, I said, "What I've got is information about Jerome Moses. I can tell you where his body is."

Hunter's response was not what I'd expected: he leaned back into his chair and began to laugh. It took a while before he could find the breath to speak. "You're serious, right, I mean, you dragged me all the way up here an' risked both our lives for that?"

In case he had misunderstood me, I said, "I'm talkin about Little J Moses, the missin congressman. I can tell you where his body is."

Hunter's expression became serious. "Give me a minute, Walker," he said.

He went to the counter and engaged a young male employee who gave a slightly puzzled nod before he disappeared into a room at the rear. Within seconds he was back and handing something over to Hunter.

"So," said Hunter, as he retook his seat, "you want me to go to my superiors an' ax them to fix you up with a new identity an' a flight to England because you know where the body of Jerome Moses is." He laid out a newspaper in front of me. "Too late, Walker, you're a day too late."

I looked down to the front page of the previous day's *New York Times*. The main headline read: "*Police Seeking Missing Congressman,*

266

Raid Billionaire's Estate." It reported that the police were searching the estate of Charles Lavette, 'the philanthropist and reclusive billionaire', after receiving a tipoff that the body of Congressman Jerome Moses had been buried there. The story continued on page five but it was missing. I frantically turned the pages back and forth searching for it before a terrible realization came and hit me with the impact of a high velocity bullet. Apart from myself, Calvin and Vonette, only one other person knew where Little J was buried: the man with the blue scar on his forehead, the man who had first introduced himself as an FBI agent called Mitch. I realized then that he'd survived the bullet I'd put into him. I realized, too, that the tipoff to the cops was Keeler's revenge on the Lavettes.

Revenge had been the driving force behind everything Tom Keeler had planned: whatever else about his political motivation, the timing and the location of the bomb were contrived so he could also punish his former wife and the man who had stolen her away. Revenge had been the catalyst in his warped mind as he concocted his terrible scheme but in that instant I also knew that his plans had not finished there. Hunter was talking to me but nothing sank in until he asked, "There's somethin more than surprise on your face, what is it, Walker?"

"There are only two people left alive who know where Moses was buried," I murmured. "There's me . . . an' there's Tom Keeler."

Hunter let out a silent profanity as I got to my feet. "Where are you goin now?" he asked.

"Revenge," I said, "it's Keeler's fuel. He knows where my son is."

I left the coffee shop – with John Hunter calling after me – and began to run along the sidewalk.

Now I had my destination: I had to find my son before a psychopathic killer named Tom Keeler did.

If you have enjoyed this novel, the author recommends

Love, Lies and Bleeding

By

J. S . Noon

Former cop Justine Manley is now a private investigator on the trail of a people-trafficker known as the 'Falcon'. Her search takes her from Toronto to London, where she enlists the help of two eccentric debt-collectors Patrick 'Pinkie' Pinkowski and the huge Roy 'Monster' Houghton. But Justine soon realizes that she is not the only one looking for the Falcon and his lover. A group of professional killers seem to be one step ahead of her and hell-bent on eradicating anyone connected with the 'Falcon Operation'.

And there is Roy's psychopathic brother Glen, who makes his money robbing 'high-class' massage parlours and is now planning to take a cool five million from the notorious armed robber Dave Bent. Glen does not know it, but he is sleeping with the Falcon's lover – the enigmatic and beautiful Sonia.

'Packed with action, plot and wonderfully observed
characters, this is a truly impressive
and very enjoyable novel.'
Sylvester Young